THREAT AXIS

DAVID BRUNS

J.R. OLSON

SEVERN RIVER PUBLISHING

Severn River Publishing
www.SevernRiverBooks.com

This is a work of fiction. Names, characters, businesses, places, events and incidents are either the products of the author's imagination or used in a fictitious manner. Any resemblance to actual persons, living or dead, or actual events is purely coincidental.

ISBN: 978-1-64875-411-1 (Paperback)

ALSO BY BRUNS AND OLSON

The Command and Control Series

Command and Control

Counter Strike

Order of Battle

Threat Axis

Covert Action

Never miss a new release! Sign up to receive exclusive updates from authors Bruns and Olson.

severnriverbooks.com/series/command-and-control

To Kent and Christine

1

Marbella, Spain

Although the calendar read mid-November, to Manson Skelly the weather on Spain's famous Costa del Sol felt more like June. The scenery on the ride from the Málaga airport into the sere, rocky hills above the coastal town of Marbella reminded him of Southern California. When he left the air-conditioned comfort of the Mercedes sedan, the sunshine and the dry heat only reinforced the feeling.

Skelly was irritated that the man he'd come to see had not deigned to meet at the front door. In fact, Skelly had not even seen the front of the villa. The car entered the compound via a small back gate used for kitchen deliveries and stopped at a side entrance to the main house. A young man in a polo shirt and khakis opened the car door.

"Mr. Skelly," he said. "Come with me, please. The general is occupied at the moment, but he will be with you in due course, sir."

The whole chain of events left Skelly with the distinct impression that even though he had been invited, he was not a guest. He was the help. The young man, who did not introduce himself, deposited his charge in what appeared to be the general's study and departed without a word.

The room was done in what Skelly supposed was a Spanish style. High ceilings, tall bookshelves with a rolling ladder that ran along a brass rail, and a thick area rug covering the tile floor. At one end of the room, a massive dark wood desk faced a pair of armchairs. A flat-screen television the size of a dining room table took up the whole wall between the chairs. Behind the desk, a tall window offered a panoramic view of the Mediterranean Sea. A distant freighter the size of a child's toy chugged across the horizon.

Skelly dropped his computer bag on an armchair and went to admire the view. When he arrived at the edge of the window, a new sight greeted him.

In the courtyard below, a pool party was in full swing. Skelly grunted a note of satisfaction. Whoever the general used to recruit female talent was a true professional. Not only that, but the general was also an equal opportunity employer. Ebony-skinned beauties rubbed shoulders with platinum-blond Scandinavian ice queens. A broad-shouldered woman with skin the color of milk and a cascade of dark hair to her waist sat with her back to Skelly, bare feet dangling in the water.

The women all had two things in common: they were all stunningly beautiful and all wore next to nothing in the way of clothing. On the far side of the pool, in a close grouping of chaise lounges angled to catch the afternoon sun, lay half a dozen Arab men clad only in wraparound sunglasses and Speedos. Skelly was a hairy guy, but these men had pelts. Most of them were pear-shaped, and the hair on their domed bellies glistened with sweat and sunscreen. White teeth flashed in dark beards as the men joked with whatever woman happened to be perched on the edge of his lounger. One of the blondes threw her head back in silent laughter. Skelly observed the curve of her elegant neck.

He took a quick head count of the male-to-female ratio. Maybe if this meeting went well, the general would invite him to join the party.

You need a vacation, he told himself as he spun away from the window. He stalked back into the room, feeling a flush of irritation. He'd come all this way, where the hell was the general?

The TV behind the desk was tuned to the Al Jazeera network with the sound muted. Skelly's lip curled when he saw President Rick Serrano's face flash across the screen. The United States presidential election was now two weeks old, and everyone was still talking about it, even here in Europe.

Still, he had to hand it to Serrano. That bastard had beaten the odds on this one. Somehow, despite taking the planet to the brink of World War Three—not once, not twice, but *three* times—that asshole had managed to win a second term. Skelly knew nothing about politics, but he knew a master when he saw one. The President was a clutch player.

He ran his fingers idly along a ruler-straight row of books. Maybe I should buy a place like this, Skelly mused. Hang up my spurs and enjoy the good life. God knows he had more than enough money and an unlimited capacity to earn more. Sentinel Holdings, of which he was now the sole owner, was bigger than his next four competitors combined. And that was before he counted the absorption of the Wagner Group after the Ukraine debacle. He'd split off the Wagner assets into a separate, off-the-books entity for special covert operations that were prohibited under his contracts with the United States.

Jobs like the one he was here to pitch to the Saudi general.

Managing the separate Wagner entity was a drain on his time and energy, but it was necessary. Pavel Kozlov, his number two at Wagner, was a good operator in the field, but the man didn't have a strategic bone in his body. Skelly huffed out a breath of frustration. Good help was hard to find.

On the wall opposite the door where Skelly had entered, one of the bookcases swung open, and a man who'd been poolside only moments before entered. General Ahmed bin Syed was a head shorter than Skelly with a moon face and a wispy beard. He was dressed in a fluffy white bathrobe and sandals.

"Mr. Skelly." He held out a limp hand. It was like shaking hands with a dishrag.

"Our appointment was for tomorrow," the general continued in a voice as soft as his doughy exterior.

"You said you wanted a live demonstration of my field capabilities," Skelly replied. "I have a target, but it's time sensitive."

The general turned up the collar of his bathrobe as if he'd felt a chill and walked to the desk with a rolling gait. He pulled out the high-backed leather armchair and plopped down without ceremony. He waved his hand with a weariness that seemed to say, *Get on with it, man.*

Skelly worked to tamp down his growing annoyance. He was bringing Grade-A actionable intel to the First Officer in the Saudi National Security Center, and he was getting the blow-off?

Skelly tried a new tack. "It's a beautiful day." He adopted a light tone and a wide smile. "Perhaps we could do this down by the pool. It will take a few minutes to set up, and the view is much better down there."

The general pursed his lips. In a deadpan voice, he said, "I don't mix business and pleasure, Mr. Skelly."

What is it with these rich assholes? Skelly thought with a fresh rush of irritation. They always wanted him to do their dirty work, but when it came time for a little public recognition, he was yesterday's garbage.

Just like Serrano. How many times had he called the President's Chief of Staff for a simple invitation to dinner at the White House? Was that too much to ask after he'd saved Serrano's political ass in Ukraine?

No, Wilkerson told him again and again. The President could not risk being seen with the CEO of a private military contractor before the election. Certainly not while there were congressional hearings going on. President Serrano needed to reinforce his role as a peacetime leader, Wilkerson said. It was all about optics.

After the election, Skelly called him back. "I want an invitation to the Inaugural Ball," he'd said. "Not one of those side parties, either. The main event, the one with the big donors."

"You have to stop calling me, Skelly," Wilkerson replied.

"I want an invitation," Skelly insisted.

"I'll see what I can do," Wilkerson said.

"Mr. Skelly," the general interrupted his thoughts. "Can we get on with it, please? I have things to do this afternoon." He cast his eye toward the window.

Skelly wondered how long he'd been standing there like a fool. His face grew warm, and he twinged with anger at the man's tone.

He extracted his laptop from his bag on the armchair and snapped it open. The device automatically searched for and connected to the waiting proprietary satellite uplink. He could see that Kozlov and his team were already on the battle network.

There was a discreet knock at the door, and the general raised his chin. "Come," he called out.

The dark-haired girl who entered was dressed in a white polo shirt and a very short matching miniskirt. She might have been sixteen, but Skelly guessed younger, much younger. She carried a tray with a steel dome and glass of wine the color of pale straw. As he watched a bead of condensation roll down the side of the chilled glass, Skelly realized two things: there was only one glass on the tray, and he was very thirsty.

The general's moon face broke into a wide smile. "Rana, what a pleasant surprise. Put it here." He patted the desk in front of him.

The girl placed the tray on the desk and lifted the steel dome to reveal chunks of lobster and a cup of drawn butter. As the smell of the food wafted across the desk, Skelly's stomach rumbled. The general casually slipped his arm around the girl's waist. She stiffened at his touch.

"Rana," Skelly said loudly, causing the general's arm to drop. The girl stepped away from the desk.

"Yes, sir."

"May I have something to drink, please?"

Rana looked at the general, who nodded. "Bring a glass of water for my guest, please, Rana." He smiled again. "I'll be finished soon, my dear."

As Rana fled the room, the general selected a silver fork, speared a chunk of lobster, and dunked it into the drawn butter. "Will you be much longer, Mr. Skelly? I'm very busy today."

Skelly pointed to the television. "Can I cast on your screen?"

The other man shrugged. "I don't know how to do that."

Skelly did not bother to reply. He tapped a button on his laptop, and the image of the Al Jazeera host was replaced by the view on his own screen.

"Fortunately," Skelly said, "I do." He plucked a pen from the decorative holder on the general's desk and strode over to the television. "What you're looking at is an aerial view of Am Bourougne in eastern Chad." He slipped a controller from his pocket and used it to zoom in. "The reason why I am here today is this village."

"Mr. Skelly," the general said, his eyes bright. "I want you to proceed with the operation."

Skelly gave an inward sigh of satisfaction. He'd been pursuing the Saudi account for months, and this action would seal the deal once and for all. From his bag, he pulled out a slim headset and slipped it over his right ear.

"All units, this is team leader," he said into the microphone. "How do you read?"

"Your transmission quality is excellent, Manson," replied Mama, the Sentinel AI system.

"I can hear you," came Kozlov's voice. The general's ears perked up at the Russian accent. "The team is in place."

"Very well," Skelly replied. "Mama, what's our surveillance picture?"

"You have a twenty-two-minute window until the next satellite pass, including oblique imagery collection opportunities," Mama replied. "All other ground-based surveillance sources are out of visual range."

"Excellent, Mama. Bring up the targeting program for Operation Barnburner. You are weapons free. Fire at will."

Skelly stripped off the headset. "We use the AI for all targeting and firing sequences." He nodded at the wall screen. "This is my favorite part. Watch."

The targeting display for the Raptor attack drones, four of them, reappeared on the screen. The landscape under the black reticles shifted and zoomed in as the drones lined up for an attack run.

"Commencing firing sequence," said the AI in her calm voice.

The area inside the reticle blinked red three times, then a series of flashes obscured the view. Skelly counted three pulses of light.

"Weapons away," Mama announced.

Skelly shifted the display back to the Condor overwatch video feed just as the barrage of Hellfire missiles impacted the village. The screen blossomed with fiery light. Red, orange, and yellow. He pumped a fist. "That's what I'm talking about."

The general's mouth gaped.

"Well?" Skelly said.

Before the general could answer, Mama interrupted. "Preliminary bomb damage assessment indicates possible survivors. Recommend a second bombing run."

Skelly held the microphone to his mouth. "Negative, Mama. We'll take it from here. Kozlov, execute a search-and-destroy action on the ground."

"Boss," Kozlov replied, "why not just do a second drone run?"

Skelly seethed. This idiot knew nothing about sales. You needed to put on a show for the customers. "You have your orders, Pavel. Clean up any leakers. Now."

The general had not moved, which Skelly interpreted as indecision. He shifted the video feed on the wall screen to a ground-level image of a burning building.

"We use Gremlin aerial drones for close-in reconnaissance and jamming. These are deployed and controlled by ground forces."

He took control of the drone's camera and shifted it to show a three-man fire team advancing from the brush toward the building. The helmeted men were outfitted in full combat gear and moved at a deliberate pace, weapons up.

"Give me my drone back, Skelly," Kozlov's voice said. "We're entering the village."

"Keep your pants on, Pavel. I'm just demonstrating—"

On the edge of the screen, a figure lurched out of the burning building, running for the surrounding brush. The fire team reacted instantly.

Pop-pop-pop.

The sound of small arms fire sounded almost innocuous over the audio feed. The running figure collapsed.

"Cover me." Kozlov stepped away from the fire team to identify the victim. Skelly followed with the drone.

"I think we got one of your terrorists, General," Skelly said, letting the excitement he felt shine through. He truly loved these moments.

Kozlov poked the facedown body with the muzzle of his rifle and got no reaction. He used the toe of his boot to roll the corpse faceup.

It was a young man—or rather, a boy—probably no older than Rana. The bullets that had killed the young man had entered from the side. The exit wounds had blown apart the right side of his chest, revealing shredded internal organs. Skelly admired the high-definition, larger-than-life image on the massive wall screen.

"Terrorist, my ass, Skelly. It's just a kid," Kozlov said in disgust. "Moving on."

Skelly heard what sounded like a croak and turned to his sales prospect.

The general's face was gray and covered with a sheen of slimy sweat. He gagged again.

"Turn it off," the general managed to say as he gulped in great breaths of air.

Skelly tapped on his laptop, returning the screen to the Al Jazeera channel. A smiling President Serrano filled the entire screen.

"Mr. Skelly." The general had his palms flat on his desk, and he breathed heavily. When he finally straightened up, his hands left sweaty imprints on the dark wood. The front of his robe was open to his navel, and sweat ran down his flabby chest.

"Send me the contract," he said.

Skelly broke into a wide grin. "You got it, General." He held out his hand.

The other man looked at the outstretched palm, then looked up at Skelly. He made no move to return the gesture. "I have one condition," he said.

"Name it." Skelly pulled back his hand.

"Don't ever show me anything like that again."

The general's sandals slapped against his heels as he made for the door, leaving Skelly alone in the room.

2

Santa Lúcia, Brazil

Diego Montalban squinted into the setting sun. He'd forgotten his sunglasses again. He adjusted the sun shade on the visor of his Fiat Strada just in time to read the road sign that flashed by:

Santa Lúcia 10 KM.

Diego had been driving through pancake-flat agricultural land for the last two hours. His throat was dry, and he hadn't had anything to eat since breakfast. His gaze dropped to the fuel gauge. Just below a quarter tank. With that much fuel, he could make it to the border with Paraguay.

A car straddling the center line came at him out of the sun, and Diego swerved to the side of the road.

"*Pendejo*," he muttered to himself as he readjusted the eye shade.

Route SP-257 was one lane of traffic in either direction with no barrier. He was tired, his attention wandering, and Brasileños drove like maniacs.

On impulse, he took the next exit. He was hungry, and he wanted a beer. No, he *deserved* a beer.

It was a risk, he knew. The smart play was to keep going another ninety minutes or so to the safety of the Paraguayan border. In the Tri-Border Region, where the countries of Paraguay, Brazil, and Argentina fit together like the pieces of a jigsaw puzzle, he was safe. Well, relatively safe. Law enforcement was minimal, and borders were porous. The TBR was a place where people didn't ask uncomfortable questions like why a man of obvious Chinese descent had a Spanish name like Diego Montalban.

In the TBR, everyone had a past, and no one cared. His kind of place.

One beer and a quick plate of food, he told himself. Thirty minutes and he'd be back on the highway, headed to safety.

He selected the bar for all the right reasons: small, locally owned, close to the highway exit, and most of all, no CCTV surveillance. Diego pulled his car into the half-full lot and backed into a parking space.

Bar Matos was a low-slung brick structure with cracked stucco and a sloped red tile roof. It was located on a corner in a quiet residential area of less-than-modest homes of a similar construction to the bar. The interior did not disappoint. Open ceilings, where strings of lights looped between the rafters did little to dispel the gloom. There were a half-dozen square tables with mismatched chairs in the central floor area and a few high-tops with stools along the walls. A group of eight people, a mix of men and women of varied ages, had pushed the smaller tables together, and they ringed the makeshift gathering spot talking in animated tones. Their table was crowded with empty beer mugs and glasses.

Diego ignored them and took a seat at the corner of the bar with his back to the solid brick wall and a clear view of the door. The windows in the building were barred, but he'd glimpsed a rear exit in the kitchen behind the bar. It's only for a half hour, he told himself. Food, one beer, then hit the road.

He nodded at the beer tap, and the bartender brought him an Itaipava pilsner in a mug. Diego took a long pull of the cold drink and shivered with delight.

"Food?" the bartender asked in Portuguese.

Diego ordered beans and rice in the same language. His Portuguese wasn't as good as his Spanish, but in this part of South America, where the two languages merged, he could get by.

He scanned the room. The group at the cluster of tables seemed to be having some kind of meeting, led by the woman seated at the head of the table. She was in her early thirties with a fall of long dark hair that flowed over her shoulders like silk. Full lips and a generous mouth that seemed inclined to smile. Her white teeth flashed as she laughed, and Diego caught himself staring at her.

A pair of men entered, crossing the room to occupy a high-top table against the wall. Odd, Diego thought, they seemed to take care not to look at the gathering in the center of the room. The group was loud, and the woman was someone most men would automatically notice. As he surveyed the new arrivals, the woman got up and made her way to the bar. She had an easy stride. Probably a dancer, he decided.

"Another round for the table," she said to the bartender.

Diego found himself watching her. She wore formfitting blue jeans with a macramé belt and matching sandals. She had on a man's dress shirt, but she rolled up the sleeves like cuffs, left several top buttons undone, and knotted the material across a well-muscled abdomen.

"I'll bring your drinks to the table, señora," the bartender said.

"I'll wait," she said. Her eyes slid over to meet Diego's. He looked away, but it was too late.

"*Olá*," she said in a friendly tone.

Diego nodded, lifted his beer, said nothing.

"Are you from the area?" she asked.

Diego shook his head. Now that she was closer, Diego could see he'd misjudged her age. She was late thirties, maybe early forties. Her deep brown eyes studied him intently, her friendly smile never wavering.

"Do you speak?" she asked with a chuckle.

"As little as possible," Diego replied.

Her laugh was like music. How long since he'd made a woman laugh? Years, he realized. Not since Isabel.

"I've cracked the wall of silence." She moved down the bar and slid onto the stool next to him. "Gisela." She held out her hand.

"Diego." Her grip was firm, the nails a sensible length and covered with clear nail polish. He wondered why she was here, in a bar like this, in a town like this one. Based on her dress and manner, she was a woman with means, yet she was in a dive bar with a mixed group of people mostly younger than her.

A college professor slumming for the evening? He didn't think so. For all her signs of class, Diego could detect not even the slightest hint of condescension about her. She had another reason to be here.

Mind your own business, he told himself. Drink your beer, eat your food, and get the hell out of here.

A fresh beer appeared in front of him. The bartender jerked his chin at Gisela. Diego felt the heat of her smile.

"*Obrigada*," Diego said. So much for his one-beer plan.

"Diego seems an odd name for a man who is clearly Chinese," she replied.

His defenses went up automatically. The blunt statement from someone else might have been interpreted as an insult, but her tone and manner signaled genuine curiosity.

"It's the only name I have." That was a lie. In his past life, Diego had changed names like he changed underwear. One passport for a trip into a country, a new identity for the trip out. With all of his covers backstopped by the Ministry of State Security's technical team, even a deep dive into the backgrounds of those identities would yield previous travel, business contacts and residential addresses, credit histories...all the details needed for an operative to stay hidden in the digital age.

But those days were long gone. Now, his remaining identities were precious entities.

Stopping here was a mistake, Diego thought. A huge mistake.

"Are you familiar with Santa Lúcia?" she asked.

Where is my food? Diego wondered. Were they growing the goddamn beans back there? He shook his head and drained his first beer.

"Can I tell you about the nickel mine on the Rio São Salvador? It's only a few miles from here." The woman was talking faster now, in an urgent tone. "If it opens, it will destroy this community. I've seen it happen before. I'm with Mundo Verde."

Green World. She was an activist, probably a lawyer or some other professional. That explained the gathering in the bar and her clothes and everything else. Diego relaxed.

"Thank you for the beer," he said, "but I'm just passing through."

"There's a protest tomorrow," she continued. "The company is flying their board of directors here for a site visit. We want the best possible showing of local opposition to the mine." She put her hand on his arm. "Please."

As pleasant as it was to talk to a beautiful woman, there was no way Diego was attending a public gathering. A public protest meant cameras.

He smiled at her. "Like I said, I'm just passing through."

Gisela squeezed his arm. "I hope you change your mind." She picked up the tray of drinks and turned back to her table.

If Diego had not been following her with his eyes, he might not have noticed the two men who entered the bar at that moment.

Despite their casual clothes, they carried themselves like professionals. Ex-military, he guessed. They both wore their shirts untucked, and Diego spotted a bulge at the small of one man's back as he and his companion took a high-top table on the wall. The armed man made eye contact with the pair of men against the opposite wall who had come in earlier.

Diego's stomach twisted. Somehow, some way, they had found him. He eyed the entrance to the kitchen. Could he make it out before these guys were on him? Did he have a choice?

As if on cue, the bartender emerged from the kitchen and slid a heaping plate of rice and beans onto the bar. Diego picked up the fork nestled against the pile of food. It was better than nothing.

Two more men entered. The lead man was burly with a blond crew cut, and he walked with a loose, confident stride. His eyes swept the room, clocking his two teams on either side of the bar. His gaze passed over Diego and kept going.

They're not here for me, Diego realized.

The blond man crossed the room, stood next to Diego, resting his midsection on the bar. He jerked a thumb over his shoulder at Gisela's gathering. "A round of drinks for my friends at the tables," he said.

The bartender was a perceptive man. He filled a tray with beers and gin tonics in short order. The blond man pulled a bankroll from his pocket, peeled off two US twenty-dollar bills, and dropped them on the bar. "Keep the change."

Tray in hand, the blond man strode over to Gisela's table. His arrival stilled the animated conversation. He placed the tray on the table in front of Gisela.

"What's this?" she asked. He was standing close to her, and Diego could see it made her nervous. The boisterous conversation around the table died.

"A peace offering from the boys at Sentinel," the blond man said. "And a suggestion: get really drunk tonight. So drunk that y'all miss your little protest tomorrow."

Gisela stood. "Get out of here. You can't come in here and threaten people." She bared her teeth and got in his face.

"No threats." The man's grin widened. He pulled the wad of cash from his pocket and tossed it on the table. "Drinks are on me."

Gisela's hand lashed out. In the quiet room, the slap sounded like a rifle shot. The meat of her hand against his jaw landed hard enough to make the man take a step back. He looked at her with surprise.

"I was hoping you'd do something stupid." He balled a fist and drove it into her stomach.

Her mouth flew open, and she doubled over. The two-man teams on either side of the room closed in on the table. The bar erupted in a chaos of thrown beer mugs, screams, chairs scraping against the floor.

Run, Diego thought. This is your chance.

The blond man gripped Gisela's arm, signaling to his partner to take her other side. They started to drag her toward the door. As they passed Diego's chair, he hooked his foot in the blond man's instep, causing him to stumble.

When he looked up, Diego smashed his beer mug into the man's temple. The blond man crumpled to the floor next to Gisela.

His partner was slow to realize what had happened, so Diego punched him in the throat. The man dropped to his knees, gagging.

Diego hauled Gisela to her feet. Her face was white, and she gasped for air. He pushed her toward the door. "Get out," he shouted.

The blond man gripped Diego's ankle and tried to punch him in the crotch. Diego deflected the punch with his thigh, then slammed the barstool down on his attacker's face. With all the noise, he couldn't hear the man's nose break, but he felt a satisfying crunch shimmy up the leg of the stool. The grip on his ankle relaxed, and he spun toward the exit.

Get out of here, he told himself. Now. Run.

But Gisela had not run from the fight. When Diego turned, she was trying to hit one of the attackers with a chair. The man caught the chair leg in midair and wrenched it out of her grasp.

Diego still had the fork in his hand. He drove across the room, slamming into Gisela's attacker at chest height while his leg swept the man's feet. The man hit the ground flat on his back with all of Diego's body weight on him. Diego felt the guy's ribs crack under his knees.

He rolled, sweeping his leg to take out another attacker while stabbing out with his weapon. The fork sunk into the Achilles tendon of a third man, and Diego twisted until the handle broke off in his hand. He heard a bellow of pain. When the man turned on him, he drove his heel into the man's groin.

Diego popped to his feet. There were still two attackers, and they both now came to the realization that the landscape of the fight had changed. Diego saw one of them reach behind his back.

The gun, he thought. One of them had a gun.

Diego threw the useless fork handle. He had no expectation that the projectile would cause any real injury, but it made the man hesitate for an instant, and that was enough. He launched across the table, spinning his body into a powerful roundhouse kick that caught the man on the side of the head.

His face snapped around, his body following. But the table Diego used as a platform tipped over, and he ended up on the floor in front of the last remaining attacker.

The man's heavy boot crashed down on Diego's head. Pain sparked in his brain like fireworks. He tried to roll away, but the man stamped a foot on his arm and slammed a chair down on his chest. Diego felt the breath leave his body in a blast.

Then the man was on top of him, his knees pinning Diego's arms to the floor, his fists pounding Diego's face.

A gunshot rang out. Everything went still.

Diego blinked the blood away from his eyes. Gisela held a pistol against the man's temple.

"Get off of him," she said.

Diego's attacker held up his hands, then got to his feet.

"Lie down on your stomach," Gisela said. "Lace your hands behind your head."

Diego rolled over, then got to his hands and knees. He gripped the edge of the table and pulled himself upright. He tested his arms and legs. Nothing broken. That was good.

"You need to get to a hospital," Gisela said. She was still holding the gun. "I called the police."

Police. The word rang in Diego's head like a clarion.

"Need to...go." Diego's lips felt like fat pillows.

He took a step, and the room seemed to tilt. He felt his head bounce off the floor again, but it didn't hurt this time. The tile was cool, and a smashed beer mug a few inches from his face gleamed in and out of focus.

Then Diego passed out.

* * *

"He's awake."

The volume level of the male voice made Diego wince. Why was the man shouting at him?

Someone lifted his hand, but he couldn't feel anything.

"It's okay, Diego." A female voice, familiar. "You're safe."

Why did he know that voice?

Then it all came back in a rush. The bar, the girl—Gisela, that was her name—the fight.

He opened his eyes to incandescent brightness and immediately closed them again.

"You're safe," Gisela said. "You're in the hospital."

He forced his eyes back open. The hospital room was airy and painfully white. Bright sunshine streamed in through an open window.

Morning, he realized. It was morning.

Fear surged in his chest. He needed to be out of here, back across the border.

He tried to sit up, but Gisela put a hand on his chest.

"You're safe here," she said.

No, I'm not, he thought.

An older woman in a white lab coat appeared in the doorway.

"He lives," she said. "You had us worried." She moved to his bedside and lifted his hand, which Diego could see was bandaged. Her fingers felt cool against his wrist. The doctor took out a penlight and shone it into his eyes, one at a time. The light stabbed into his brain, but Diego said nothing. He needed to get out of here.

"You've got a concussion," she said. "Some very serious contusions, but no broken bones. You live a charmed life, Señor Montalban. I thought we were going to have to operate to relieve pressure on your brain that first night."

First night? Diego froze.

"How long have I been here?" he asked. His voice sounded like he'd swallowed broken glass, and he realized the swollen lips he remembered from the bar were now normal size.

The doctor paused, looked at Gisela. "Um, two days?"

"Three," Gisela said.

Three days. Diego felt his heart start to race. "I need to go."

The doctor shook her head. "Maybe the end of the week," she said. "If you're lucky."

"You don't have to worry about those guys from the bar," Gisela said. "The police arrested them, and the mining company fired Sentinel. The protest was a success." She smiled, white teeth in a generous mouth. "Besides, you're a hero. The internet is calling you the Spanish ninja."

Diego's racing heart stilled. "What are you talking about?"

"Someone took a video on their phone and posted it on the internet," Gisela said. "It's got like a million views, and Mundo Verde has gotten thousands of donations. You're a hero, Diego."

The doctor made a note on his chart. "I'll leave you two alone. Take it easy, Diego. You've earned it."

After the doctor left, Gisela held his hand. "I want to thank you," she began. "If you hadn't stepped in, I don't know what they would have done to me."

Diego forced a smile. "I know a way you can repay me."

"That's a little forward," she said, but her voice was mocking and she tightened her grip on his fingers. "We barely know each other."

"I was hoping maybe you could get me some chocolate," Diego said. "I'm really hungry for chocolate."

Gisela blushed. "Of course. There's a shop downstairs. I'll go get some."

"You're an angel."

As soon as she left, Diego pulled the IV out of his arm and swung his legs over the side of the bed. The room swayed crazily, forcing him to shut his eyes. He took two deep breaths and reopened his eyes.

Everything stayed level. He got to his feet and carefully made his way across the room to a cabinet along the wall. Inside the drawer, he found his clothes.

Diego winced as he dressed. He hadn't been this sore since...

His thoughts wandered to another woman and another fight. He forced his attention back to the present, and he finished buttoning his shirt.

Then he stepped into the busy hallway and walked away.

3

***

Scorpions Ascent, Israel

Rachel leaned on the windowsill, staring through the rain-streaked glass at the darkened desert. A blaze of lightning whitened the landscape, and she caught a glimpse of the Scorpion Trail highway that wound up the nearby slope in a series of hairpin turns.

Moisture was a rare commodity in this part of the world—the average annual rainfall in the Negev Desert was only two hundred millimeters—and it seemed that they might get an entire season's worth of rain in one night.

In the morning, when the buses came from Tel Aviv and Jerusalem, the tourists would marvel at how the ancient wadis that covered the landscape would be carved anew. She imagined how they would exclaim about the starkness of the desert, the harshness of life, as their buses rolled along the highway. If they stayed for sunset, they'd be amazed by the colors that showed up in the light of the setting sun. Reds and ochres defined by deep purple shadows. If they were atop the highest peak after dark, they might catch sight of lights in the desert and wonder who lived here.

The lights belonged to a secret Mossad training facility, Rachel's home.

She turned away from the window. The thought of a changed landscape did nothing to ease her anxiety. Most nights about this time she walked in the desert, alone with her thoughts—and her ghosts.

She scooped up the remote for the television set and flipped through the channels at a furious pace to confirm what she already knew: there was nothing worth watching. She turned off the device and dropped the remote back on the couch.

Rachel paced back to the window, but it was raining as hard as before. Even if the rain stopped now, there was always the risk of flash floods. Face it, she told herself, no walk tonight.

As an instructor at Scorpions Ascent, Rachel rated a small apartment. Consisting of a bedroom and bathroom en suite, a tiny kitchenette, and a small sitting room, it wasn't much, but it was enough for her. She took her meals in the cafeteria and taught whatever classes were assigned to her. Apart from those two mandatory interactions, Rachel kept to herself. She didn't have friends here, nor did she want any. She'd given up her apartment in Tel Aviv years ago, after the death of her husband, Levi. Most of the other instructors went into the city for the weekend to see family or to party, but Rachel had given all of that up long ago.

If anyone asked, and they rarely did anymore, she would have described herself as a monk. A monk who killed people for a living.

She smiled wryly. A monk who *used* to kill people. Her last assignment had been a takedown of a secret bioweapons lab in Sudan. She had posed as personal security for the CEO of a genetics research company. The smile deepened. The personal part of the job took on a whole new meaning when she became the man's lover.

She'd crossed lines, she knew it then, she knew it now, and she did not care. Her hand pressed against the puckered bullet-wound scar on her abdomen. She'd paid her price in flesh and in places where there were no scars—not visible ones, at least.

The nostalgic smile clicked off like a light. Don Riley's team from the CIA had saved her life, but the injury ended her field career. She'd been given two options: retirement or a position as an instructor at Scorpions Ascent.

Rachel looked around her apartment, devoid of even a single personal photograph. The thought of retirement scared the hell out of her, so she'd chosen the purgatory of Scorpions Ascent.

That was five years ago. Five years of routine classes and solitary meals followed by nightly walks in the desert.

She checked her watch. Nine p.m. Too early to go to sleep, and she wasn't tired, anyway. She thought about going swimming, but she'd already been in the pool today. She'd go to the gym and do some light stretching. Maybe a quick workout would tire out her body enough to quiet her mind.

She quickly changed into workout gear. Yoga pants, sports bra under a loose-fitting T-shirt, and trainers. She pulled her kinky hair into a tight ponytail and headed out the door.

The gymnasium was the size of two basketball courts ringed by an indoor track. The center of the ring was filled with matted areas set aside for sparring and hand-to-hand combat training. This part of the gym was empty, which was not unusual for this time of night. From the adjoining weight room, she could hear clanking noises where a few diehard gym rats were still pumping iron. She unrolled a yoga mat in a shadowed corner and began to stretch.

After a few minutes, the door to the gym opened and a man and a woman entered. They did not notice Rachel, and she stayed still as they walked to the sparring mat farthest from her.

Good, she thought, glad that she didn't have to engage in small talk.

She studied them as she bent into a hurdler's stretch. The man was a guest instructor from the United States, a CIA guy. Chet? Biff? Something like that. She'd only met him once but had immediately disliked the man. Most of the Americans in the intelligence service were reserved and professional. Chet—or whatever his name was—seemed to believe he was special and was unashamed to share his wonderfulness with the world.

She recognized the woman, too, and remembered her name. Miriam had red hair and a fair complexion. She was slight of frame, and as Rachel recalled from the hand-to-hand combat class, Miriam was not the most capable fighter.

Chet was talking loud enough for Rachel to hear, and Miriam nodded along. Was it possible this was a date? Rachel wondered. Oh, Miriam, you could do so much better than Chet.

The young man stripped off his shirt to reveal a toned chest and an impressive six-pack. He jogged in place and swung his arms. "Let's spar a little," Rachel heard him say.

Miriam laughed nervously as she stretched. "You have to go easy on me," she said.

Rachel could see his grin all the way across the gym. "Never," he replied.

She went back to her own stretching but kept an eye on the romantic encounter. The two were clearly outmatched, and she was curious to see how Chet handled himself.

The two squared off. Chet moved fast, taking her down in one sweep. Miriam did not fall like Rachel had taught her, and when she got up, Rachel could see the landing had been hard.

"Ow," Miriam said, rubbing her shoulder. "That's not funny."

Chet jogged in place, stretched his arms over his head. "Sorry, don't know my own strength. I'll be more careful this time."

They squared off again, and Miriam fended off a first attack. Then she dropped her right arm and caught a blow to the side of the head.

"Keep your guard up," Rachel called out. "I taught you better than that, Miriam."

The couple looked up in surprise. They either hadn't realized Rachel was watching them or hadn't cared.

"You're dropping your right arm," Rachel said. "Keep your guard up."

She got to her feet and walked over to the mat. Rachel took a stance with her fists up, then let her right forearm droop.

"If you drop your guard, he's gonna take advantage of you. He's much bigger than you and faster. As a matter of fact, I think he's a bit of a bully."

Chet flushed red. "Who asked you?"

"Just helping out a former student," Rachel replied.

She stepped back and crossed her arms. The pair faced each other again, and Miriam nodded that she was ready. Chet's swift attack blew through Miriam's weaker defenses and took her down with a leg sweep that knocked the wind out of the young woman.

Rachel realized that by challenging Chet, she'd made the situation worse for Miriam. A little spark of anger lodged in her chest.

"That's a little rough for friendly sparring, don't you think?" she asked. "You're out of line."

Chet wiped sweat off his forehead. Ignoring Rachel, he held out a hand to Miriam. The young woman got to her feet slowly. "I'm done," she said.

"Too bad." Chet bounced on the balls of his feet. "I'm just getting warmed up." His head swiveled over to Rachel. "You want to have a go?"

Rachel knew she should say no, but this guy was *such* an asshole.

"Sure." She stripped off her T-shirt and heard Miriam suck in a breath. The bullet had entered the right side of her abdomen and exited out her back, narrowly missing her kidney. Between the bullet and the subsequent operations, the right side of her belly was a mass of twisted scar tissue.

Chet stopped bouncing. "You okay to spar?" He pointed at her injury.

Rachel stepped onto the mat. "Why don't you come find out?"

His attack was fast and fierce. Rachel found out the hard way that he had actually been holding back with Miriam. She held off his first attack—barely. When he came at her again, she parried twice, then shot out her left for a jab. He seized her wrist, twisted, and threw her.

He grinned down at her. "You all right?" he taunted.

Rachel rolled to her feet. The little spark of anger fanned into a flame. He was faster than her, younger than her, and stronger than her. The smart play was to end this thing right now.

Walk away, Rachel, she told herself.

If only it hadn't rained tonight, she thought as she jogged back to the center of the mat.

"Best two out of three," she replied, "and don't take it so easy on me this time."

Chet was warmed up and aggressive, anxious to show off for his girl-friend. Rachel withstood two attacks from Chet. On the third time, she gave him an opening by dropping her left guard. He swallowed the bait whole. When he overreached, she got him off-balance. She swept his leg, put him flat on his back, and touched his Adam's apple with a simulated throat strike.

"I think that's one to one," she said with a grin.

He surged to his feet, his face flushed. From the way he watched Miriam out of the corner of his eye, Rachel could tell she'd gotten under his skin. The young woman tried to hide her smile, but didn't try too hard.

You made your point, Rachel told herself. Walk away now.

Chet bounced his way to the center of the mat. "Let's go, grandma."

Then again, Rachel thought, maybe the point needs to be reinforced.

On the third round, Chet hung back, letting her press the attack. Rachel realized he was a smarter fighter than she'd given him credit for. They tangled three times with neither fighter gaining an advantage. Chet blocked a flipper kick and nearly captured her ankle, but Rachel managed to evade his grasp.

As the minutes passed, she was getting tired. Chet's new strategy seemed to be one where he wore her out, then attacked. He was both younger and stronger than her, so it was a good plan.

On yet another rotation around the mat, Rachel saw Miriam texting on her phone, then holding up her phone to record them. Rachel cursed to herself. This had gotten out of hand. She heard the gym door open, and Rachel made the mistake of allowing her focus to shift away for a split second.

That was all the opening Chet needed. He rushed her low, going for a brute-force takedown. She sidestepped and whirled her body, latching onto his wrist as he hurtled past her. Using his own momentum, she drove him into the mat face first. He tried to twist away, but Rachel secured a solid wrist lock and extended his arm straight into the air. She slammed her knee between his shoulder blades and pushed against his extended arm like a lever, one hand on his wrist, the other on his elbow.

Chet was pinned, but Rachel wanted more. She leaned down. "Tap out," she whispered.

"Fuck you," he said through gritted teeth.

The flame of anger she'd felt all evening flared, and Rachel increased the pressure on Chet's extended arm.

"Tap—"

She felt the sound before she heard it. The bone in Chet's arm shifted under her fingers, and his arm suddenly bent all the way forward.

Then she heard *snap* as the bone broke.

Chet screamed in pain.

She released him, and his arm flopped to the floor at a right angle to his torso. Chet's body contracted into a fetal position, and he screamed again. Rachel fell on her backside, then pushed away from the man.

She looked up, realizing for the first time that there was an audience. At least ten people stood around the mat, and two of them had their phones out.

Miriam dropped to her knees next to Chet. "Call a medic," she shouted.

Rachel got to her feet. Everyone was looking at her like she'd just kicked a puppy. The doors of the gymnasium burst open, and the duty EMTs rushed in carrying medkits.

"What happened?" one of them said.

Miriam pointed at Rachel. "She broke his arm." The young woman was crying.

"Shit," Rachel said.

4

Emerging Threats Group
Tysons Corner, VA

Don Riley studied the photograph on his computer. A man, late thirties, Chinese descent. Long hair, thin mustache, wispy beard. On the Metro this morning, Don had probably seen ten men like him. It was the kind of face your gaze would capture and then discard. Unassuming, harmless, forgettable.

The perfect face for a spy.

It was the eyes, he decided. Even in the picture, the eyes seemed unfocused. Not dazed, just distant, as if to say, *I'm nobody. Nothing to see here.*

"You're sure it's him?" Don looked across the desk where Michael Goodwin and Dre Ramirez watched him expectantly.

Michael took the lead, which was unusual for him. "We're sure, Don."

Dre nodded, said nothing.

Was she coaching him on this? Don wondered. Maybe not the best time for a training session. To make a call about something this big, you couldn't just be sure, you needed to be 100 percent, no-possibility-of-a-false-positive certain.

This kind of call would invite scrutiny from all sides. If they were right, this information would kick off an international manhunt the likes of which the world had not seen since the hunt for Rafiq Roshed.

Don still had a bullet-wound scar on his thigh that ached whenever it rained from that ordeal. And the nightmares. He thought of the lives lost in that campaign. Good people, friends, who'd died in the pursuit of an international terrorist.

No, if he ran this piece of intel up the flagpole, he was going to be dead certain in every possible way.

Don threw himself back in his chair and spun to face his wall monitor. "Convince me," he said.

Michael stood. He was a tall man with dark skin, broad shoulders, and a quiet smile. When Don had recruited Michael to attend the Naval Academy, he'd wondered if the skinny kid from Southern California would cut it as a plebe, Navy-speak for a freshman at the United States Naval Academy. The kid was brilliant, that was never in doubt, but Don had no idea if he possessed the emotional intelligence to navigate his first year at the Academy.

Don knew from experience how the system was designed to test the mental, physical, and emotional limits of each individual. That kind of pressure over a sustained period of time had consequences.

Most candidates made it through the process. A few people flourished. Some cracked.

Like Don. He'd washed out in his first year. Although the reason for his departure from the Academy was medical, he'd never really fit in. In his darker moments, he wondered if he could have made it all four years or if the sudden illness was a blessing in disguise.

Still, the experience changed him for the better. After the Academy, he found a new path that led him to where he was today: running the CIA's Emerging Threats Group, a team of professionals whose sole mission was to find and eliminate national security threats to the United States. Hopefully, before they blew up into international crises. To do his job, Don had to navigate budget battles, CIA turf wars, political backbiting, as well as actual national security threats.

With a swipe of his finger, Michael broadcast the contents of his tablet to the wall screen in Don's office. The first image was a grainy nighttime video of a car going through a gate.

"Three years ago, we tracked a foreign agent via a mobile phone signal to a public storage location in Singapore. By reviewing CCTV footage, we were able to identify the car he was driving. There were no clear images of the man driving the vehicle. The guy was a pro. He knew where the cameras were and how to avoid them. He left no usable forensic evidence at the scene."

Don watched the video. He knew from the original analysis that the car was a Toyota Corolla Altis, the most popular car in Singapore. It was tan, the most common color of the most common vehicle. The license plate number did not yield the identity of the agent either. However, it had given them one clue.

The next day, they were able to confirm that the same car had passed over the Johor-Singapore Causeway, the highway bridge that connected the island of Singapore and the Malaysian peninsula across the Straits of Johor. The Toyota Altis had stopped to pay the Malaysian toll.

Michael continued. "By time we were able to get the video footage of the tollbooth from the Malaysian authorities, another day had passed. The agent demonstrated his skill again. He wore sunglasses and a hygienic mask over his face. But we did get one clue."

The black-and-white image might as well have been a Rorschach test. A single frame pulled from a crappy CCTV video.

"Enhancement gave us this." Michael split the screen. The left side was a fuzzy blob. On the right, a clear image of a human ear.

At the time, the clue had given Don hope they might be able to capture their target, but over time, his enthusiasm faded. Although ears were unique to each individual, almost all of the data sources they had ready access to did not have ear images. Passport photos, ID cards, driver's licenses all had full face shots. Unless the target had been arrested and had a mug shot taken, they were out of luck.

When they had exhausted all the available databases—Don had suffered through thousands of ear jokes and bad puns from his colleagues —they gave up on the project.

At least Don thought they had.

"You're going over old ground, Michael," he snapped. "What's changed? How do you know that this guy"—he pointed to the photograph on his laptop screen—"is the guy from Singapore?"

"We kept at it, Don," Dre said quietly. Dre Ramirez was a trim woman with dark hair that she usually wore pulled back, contained by a hair clip. For casual Friday, she wore blue jeans and a polo shirt with the Naval Academy crest. She was also one of the best coders Don had ever seen in any company or government agency.

Dre was an extrovert with a capital E. To see her acting so restrained told Don a lot about the gravity of the situation.

"We didn't do anything illegal," Dre said in response to Don's frown. "We set up a data-scraping program to capture images and video from public internet sites." She grinned. "We called it the Ear-igator? Get it?"

"I get it." Don's reply was a little sharper than he'd intended, and Dre wiped the smile off her face. "So, you wrote a completely legal program and searched publicly available sites for a match to the magic ear?"

"No hacking," Dre said. "Cross my heart and hope to die."

"I'm serious," Don said.

"So am I," Dre replied. "I set it up and let it run. It's been running in the background for the last two years with no results."

"Until this morning," Michael added.

"Until this morning," Dre repeated. "Show him, Michael."

"This is from a YouTube video that was posted two days ago." Michael touched a button on his tablet, and a video began to play.

The picture was shaky, clearly taken from a mobile phone. Don could make out a dim room, which, based on the number of beer bottles and glasses, was a bar. There was lots of shouting in a foreign language.

"Is that Spanish?" Don asked.

"Portuguese," Michael replied. "Brazil."

A woman wearing a white shirt tied off at her navel was being helped to her feet by a man with dark hair. Behind the pair, a bar fight raged in the center of the room. The dark-haired man pushed the woman toward the door. He shouted something at her.

"That's him," Dre said, pointing.

The man lifted a barstool and slammed it down. He spun, took a step toward the door. The woman was not there. His head turned, looking for her.

She'd gone back to the fight.

The dark-haired man leaped after her. He slammed into one of the attackers, swept the man's legs, then appeared to drop all his weight on the man he'd taken down. While he was out of sight, a second man went down hard, then a third. He popped back into the frame.

"He's a one-man wrecking crew," Don said.

"Watch this part," Dre said.

Two men on the other side of the table turned, seeming to realize at the same time that their friends were on the floor. One of the men reached behind his back.

"He's going for a gun," Dre said. She'd hitched her body all the way to the edge of her seat. "Our guy reacts."

Don watched in amazement as the defender drove his body into the air. Somehow, with his hand on the table as a pivot point, he managed to get his entire body parallel to the ground. He launched a powerful kick that caught the gunman on the side of the head. The gunman's head snapped back, and he toppled over.

"Holy shit," Don said. The move was like something out of an action movie.

Then the illusion failed. The table he was using as a pivot point proved unstable. The table tipped, and he fell. The last remaining attacker used the advantage. He moved in, and Don saw him stamp his foot down. He kicked again and again, then dropped down.

The person holding the mobile phone moved in closer, angled his shot at the floor. Don watched the man who had taken down multiple attackers suffer a brutal beating.

A gunshot rang out.

When their target's head flopped to the side, Michael stopped the video. The picture showed a clear image of the unconscious man's ear.

"That's the money shot," Michael said. He cleared the screen, then displayed pictures of two ears side by side. "The one on the left is our template. The one on the right is from the video."

Don's mouth was dry. "How good is the match?" he asked.

"One hundred percent," Michael replied.

"There's no such thing in our business as a hundred percent, Michael."

"The earlobe, Don," Michael said gently. "It's him."

Don fell back in his chair. Of course, he'd forgotten about the earlobe. The agent had been missing the tip of his earlobe. That was why they'd had such high hopes of finding him three years ago.

"The earlobes match, Don," Dre said. "*Exactly.*"

Don turned back to his laptop screen. He studied the face anew.

"Where was the video taken?" Don asked.

"Three days ago in Santa Lúcia, Brazil," Michael said. "Hospital intake records list him as Diego Montalban, citizen of Argentina. He checked himself out yesterday."

"Dammit," Don said.

"There's more, Don," Dre said in that same uncharacteristically quiet voice.

Don turned away from the screen. "More?"

Michael put a new photo on the wall screen. It might've been the same man, but it was hard to tell. From the information at the bottom of the screen, Don could see the man's name was listed as Ian Thomas. This version of Diego Montalban was clean-shaven with a stylish haircut.

"This was taken at JFK airport immigration three years ago," Michael said. He split the screen again and put up a photo of Ian Thomas taken through a car windshield.

"This is from the tollbooth on the Claiborne Pell Bridge in Newport, Rhode Island." He paused. "One day before the Naval War College bombing."

Don came out of his chair like he'd been launched from a catapult.

Over a hundred men and women, most of them high-ranking officers from navies all over the world, had perished in that terrorist attack. The perpetrator remained at large. Although the United States held China responsible for the attack, there was no actual proof, and China denied the accusation.

He looked Michael in the eye. "You're *sure*?" he demanded. "Absolutely sure?"

Michael met his gaze without flinching. "Ian Thomas never left the country. He used a different passport to exit the US. It's him, Don. I'm sure." He looked at Dre. "We're sure."

Don stalked to the wall screen, studying the images. After all this time, this was hard proof that not only was the Naval War College bomber alive, but that they knew where he was—or at least where he'd been.

This was big, beyond big. His mind spun out the possibilities. If they could catch him, they could bring him to justice and expose the Chinese government at the same time.

"Get this presentation together," he said, without turning around. "We're going to see the Director. Right now."

5

Beijing, People's Republic of China

The windows of Senior Colonel Yichen Gao's apartment were still dark when the mobile phone on his bedside table vibrated with an incoming call.

Next to him, Mei Lin stirred but did not wake. He slid his legs out from underneath the covers, his feet automatically seeking out the slippers on the floor next to his bed. He stood, the chill air of the bedroom prickling the flesh of his bare chest.

The phone buzzed again.

He slipped on a pair of reading glasses and looked at the caller ID.

The number was blocked. He took a deep breath and accepted the call.

"*Wéi*," he said, his voice clogged with sleep.

"Senior Colonel Gao," said a male voice. The man spoke clearly, no traces of sleep, and his tone had a slight nasal edge. Gao recognized the voice, but his sleepy brain could not place it. He walked to the window. From his eighteenth-floor apartment, he could see the dark horizon against the glow of the city. There was not even a trace of dawn yet.

"Senior Colonel Gao?" the voice repeated. "Are you there?"

"Speaking," Gao said, then added, "sir."

"A car will pick you up outside your apartment building at 0500," the voice continued. "Be in uniform."

The line went dead. Gao let his hand drop to his side and blinked at his reflection in the darkened window. He wore only boxer shorts. The fingers of his free hand traced the scars on his chest and the side of his face. Reminders of his part in the invasion of Taiwan. Even though the invasion had failed, Gao had succeeded. Promoted twice in the course of only two months. Decorated with two Medals of Loyalty and Integrity for his battle wounds and exposing a traitor—at least that was the story.

Medals were one thing. Scars were entirely different. They were a calling card that he wore in and out of uniform. Wherever he went, people asked him about the scars and were treated to the story of his bravery in battle. It was even better when Mei Lin was there and she told the story. He could bask in the glow of her admiration behind a veil of false modesty.

The voice... The sudden recognition of who had just called jolted him back to reality, and he nearly dropped his phone to the floor.

Gao whirled, strode to the bedside table, and snapped on a lamp.

"Mei Lin, wake up. I need your help."

Minister of State Security Yan Tao was not a man to be trifled with. The MSS had tentacles everywhere. Every CCTV camera, every digital app, every military unit and police station throughout the People's Republic was a data stream for Minister Yan. Information was the source of his power. Since the death of Minister Fei in the last hours of the failed invasion of Taiwan, Yan did not hesitate to wield his power in very real, and often deadly, ways.

And he had just called Gao in the middle of the night, demanding a meeting. Had this man found out the truth about what had happened in Taiwan?

Despite the time constraints, Gao forced himself to stop and analyze the situation. If the Minister wanted him dead or arrested, he would have sent armed men through Gao's door.

So, what did he want? The car indicated a face-to-face encounter was necessary.

Gao pushed it all aside. All this speculation would have to wait. For a meeting with the Minister of State Security, he needed to look professional, competent. Not guilty of anything but an overwhelming love for the Party.

"Mei Lin," he roared. "Get up!"

The young woman bolted upright in bed, her long black hair shielding her face. "What?"

Gao strode to the en suite bathroom. "I need your help. Get out a freshly pressed dress uniform and put on my medals. Quickly!"

He caught a glimpse of red silk as she scrambled out of bed and ran to the closet. She was obedient, a good partner.

He checked his watch as he turned on the shower. He had fifteen minutes to be downstairs. With Mei Lin's help, that was plenty of time. He dabbed toothpaste on a brush and rammed it into his mouth. The water in the shower was still cold. Sometimes he needed to run the water for five minutes before it got hot. That was time he did not have. Still scrubbing his teeth, he stepped under the icy spray. He gasped, feeling his muscles contract in the cold. He spit out the toothpaste and held his face up to rinse his mouth. When he stepped onto the tile floor, shivering, his head was clear.

Mei Lin appeared in the doorway. "Your uniform is ready, Yichen. What's going on? Should I get dressed?" Mei Lin hugged herself in the chilly air.

"It has nothing to do with work, my love," Gao answered. "Go back to bed."

She studied his face. "Is something wrong?"

Gao considered the question. Was something wrong? Getting a call from the Minister of State Security this early in the morning was probably not a good thing, but Gao clung to the hope that if Minister Yan wished him harm, it would have already happened. You didn't get warnings in the People's Republic of China.

He took Mei Lin's face in his hands and kissed her deeply. "Everything's fine. It's just an early meeting." He turned her around toward the bedroom. "Go back to bed."

A few minutes later, Gao paced the sidewalk in front of his apartment building. The November air held a bite of frost, and his breath steamed before him as he walked. The street was deserted, quiet. He'd chosen an apartment in the trendy Shuguang residential district because Mei Lin wanted to be close to the nightlife around the universities in the Wudaokou section of Beijing.

Few military officers lived here, which suited Gao just fine. The relationship between him and Mei Lin was technically against PLA regulations. Using some of the influence he'd gained after the invasion of Taiwan, he'd managed to get her into an officer training program. Still, even after she was commissioned, a junior captain living with a senior colonel was still an issue. Gao told himself their living arrangement was an exception to the regulations because he'd advanced so quickly in his career, but that was a rationalization, and he knew it. There was an age difference, too. There were times—not often—when he and Mei Lin on a date were mistaken for father and daughter.

He pushed these uncomfortable thoughts away. If he wanted, all these issues could be solved by marrying the girl.

At the end of the block, in the park across from the apartment building, headlights illuminated the trunks of trees. A car appeared at the intersection and turned toward Gao. His heart beat faster as he identified the vehicle as a long black Hongqi limousine, the model favored by high-ranking Party officials. As the car drew closer, Gao could see the rear windows were tinted.

Before the car had stopped at the curb in front of Gao, the passenger door opened and a burly man in a dark suit stepped out. He opened the rear door.

"Good morning, Colonel," he said.

Gao nodded. Private security for the Minister of State Security was to be expected, he told himself. All the same, he gripped the doorframe with extra intensity to disguise the trembling in his hand.

The dome light in the rear of the car did not illuminate. In the dim light of the streetlamp outside, Gao was able to make out the shapes of two men facing him. Then the car door closed behind him, and the passenger compartment was plunged into darkness.

Gao's body pressed back against the seat as the car accelerated. After a few seconds, accent lighting along the floor and ceiling came on. In the soft illumination, Gao recognized the angular figure of Minister Yan. The second man was heavier, blocky in shape with a doughy, placid face.

Gao swallowed. He saw that face every day when he reported to work at the Defense Ministry in his role as Executive Assistant to the Minister of Defense. Gao often attended the Central Military Commission, which was chaired by the man sitting across from him.

"Good morning, Your Excellency." Gao thought his voice sounded hoarse.

Yi Qin-lao, President of the People's Republic of China and General Secretary of the Chinese Communist Party, looked out the window as if he had not heard Gao's greeting.

Minister Yan thrust a tablet at him. "Do you know this man?" he snapped.

Gao studied the face. A Chinese man in his thirties, long hair, scraggly beard, Gao thought he looked like a bum.

"No, sir," he replied. "I've never seen him before."

"You're sure?" Yan pressed.

Gao shook his head. "Who is he?"

"One of Fei's men," Yan said, a sharp edge of disgust in his voice. "A covert agent who could bring great embarrassment to the country."

"What has he done?" Gao asked. "If I may ask, I mean."

"He was the agent behind all of my predecessor's plans. The uprising in India, mining the Panama Canal, misleading the North Koreans."

"And the Naval War College bombing in the United States," the General Secretary added. "This man was behind that, too." His thick lips compressed into a grimace. "And he's supposed to be dead."

Yan's thin face contracted in anger, giving him a skeletal look in the dim light. "Your Excellency," he said, "I only reported the best information I had at the time. Even after his death, Fei still has his loyalists in the Ministry. I need more time to root them out."

Gao watched the exchange, saying nothing. Fei had been gone for more than two years, and Minister Yan was still battling his ghost? That was surprising to Gao, but he hid his emotions.

"As you can see, I need someone I can trust, Senior Colonel Gao," the

General Secretary continued in an acid tone. "Someone who has a proven track record of handling difficult assignments, discreetly."

Minister Yan picked up the conversation. "The General Secretary feels —and I agree, of course—that we need someone outside my organization to take care of this problem."

"I'm not certain I understand the problem, Minister," Gao answered.

Yan held out the tablet with the picture of the long-haired Chinese man. "Fei's agent was spotted in Brazil three days ago. He's disappeared again—"

Yan broke off as the General Secretary made a hiss of disapproval.

"We have a team searching for him," Yan continued. "When they find him—and they will find him—I want you to personally make sure this man is dead."

"I understand, sir," Gao said.

"Additionally, I want you to do a full investigation of Minister Fei's treachery. There can be no more surprises, no more dead men surfacing after all this time. We must put this treasonous incident behind us once and for all. Is that clear?"

"Of course, sir." Gao watched the General Secretary out of the corner of his eye. Despite the placid exterior, the leader of China was clearly agitated.

"You will have full authority to access whatever resources you need to complete the mission," Yan continued, "including all of Fei's personal effects. Lastly, you will report to me, and only me." The special emphasis on the last phrase spoke volumes to Gao. He might as well have added, *That includes the General Secretary.*

Gao looked the Minister in the eye. "I understand, sir."

"Fei was a traitor," the General Secretary intoned. "A traitor to his country, to his Party, and to me." The leader of China reached out and placed a fleshy palm on Gao's knee. He felt a tingle of excitement run down his leg.

"Your country needs you, Colonel," he continued. "If the Americans find hard evidence that China was behind the Naval War College bombing, it would be a major embarrassment to the Party."

And a major embarrassment to you, Gao thought. Possibly a fatal embarrassment. Could the leader of the Party survive such a disclosure?

The Americans would exact harsh revenge. They would demand a sacrifice. The Party would be forced to respond.

Gao felt a lightness in his chest. His good fortune knew no bounds. He was being courted by the most powerful men in all of China, maybe the entire world. If he succeeded, there were no limits to the favors he could extract from these two men.

And if you fail, he reminded himself, they will end you.

He put his hand over the General Secretary's hand. "I will not fail you, sir." He flicked a glance at Minister Yan. "Either of you."

The car slowed, and Gao realized they had pulled up in front of his apartment building. The security man in the passenger seat opened the door for him.

"Speed, Colonel," the Minister said as Gao stepped out of the vehicle, "and thoroughness. I need them both."

The door closed before Gao could reply. The car pulled away in a haze of sweet-smelling exhaust, and he was alone on the sidewalk. As his breath steamed in the air, he allowed the quiet of the predawn to settle around him. In less than an hour, these streets would be packed with pedestrians, clogged with cars. But for the moment, they were all his.

It would be easy to believe that the past thirty minutes were a waking dream, but he pushed aside the feeling. Now was the time for cold analysis and careful investigation. This assignment had the potential for great reward, but Gao was clear-eyed about the real reason they had chosen him for this task.

Gao was expendable.

He slid his mobile from his pocket and dialed Mei Lin.

"Get dressed, my love," said Gao. "We have work to do."

6

In the last four years, Don believed he had witnessed President Rick Serrano exhibit every possible emotion. Grief, anger, denial, rage, triumph, even joy. But nothing compared to the air of euphoria in the Oval Office when Don arrived with CIA Director Samuel Blank.

Serrano rose from behind the Resolute desk and crossed the room, hand outstretched. "Sam," he said, engulfing Blank's hand in both of his own. "Come in, please." He turned to Don next. "How have you been, Riley?"

Don felt the expressive brown eyes draw him in. There was a reason why it was called the Serrano Stare.

"Fine, sir," Don said.

The room was abuzz with activity. A man stood on a stepladder behind the President's desk, laser measurement device in hand. An older woman, dressed in a business suit and armed with a tablet, was conferring with a young man about a painting hanging over the fireplace.

"We were thinking about the JFK portrait by Shikler," Don heard her say. "The one where his head is bowed."

"Margie," Serrano said. "I need the room." He pointed to a pile of paint samples and fabric swatches on the coffee table between the sofas. "Clear this stuff out and bring some coffee, please."

"Right away, Mr. President." The older woman emptied the room with the efficiency of a drill sergeant.

Serrano grinned. "Since I'm going to be using this office for another four years, I figured I'd do a little redecorating." His laugh had the pure joy of a child.

Not that Don blamed him. If you believed the polls, only a few weeks ago Serrano was a dead man walking. The incumbent was behind by three points, and nothing the President tried in the last days of the campaign moved the needle.

But the pollsters seemed to ignore the fact that presidential elections are a binary choice. People didn't vote for the best candidate; they voted for the best choice of what they were offered.

While Serrano soldiered on, emphasizing his national security credentials and all the unfinished business on his domestic agenda, his opponent attacked relentlessly. Serrano offered a vision of the future, while the other guy couldn't stop talking about the past. Against all odds, Serrano booked more than eight million popular votes than his competitor and took the electoral college.

The day after the election, newspapers of both political flavors called it a "Truman moment," referring to Truman's win after his predicted defeat in 1948.

In his victory speech, Serrano claimed he had won a mandate for his second term. From the look of things in the Oval Office, Don could see Serrano wasn't going to waste one minute making the most of his new lease on life.

Ever the gracious host, the President ushered the Director and Don to one of the sofas. He took the armchair and said with a chuckle, "Since you rarely show up in my office with good news, Sam, I've asked Irv to join us. He'll be along shortly."

Chief of Staff Irving Wilkerson arrived in the Oval Office with the coffee service. Known as Serrano's Obi-Wan in Washington circles, Wilkerson hid a keen, ruthless political mind behind a grandfatherly façade. He was on the shorter side and rotund, with carefully barbered gray hair and a trim mustache.

As they shook hands, Don felt the Chief of Staff's eyes size him up from behind large wire-rimmed glasses. There was no love lost between them— not that Don blamed the man. More than once, he'd convinced Serrano to go against the advice of his own Chief of Staff. While Don's advice paid off, Wilkerson seemed to hold a grudge for reasons Don could not fathom.

Serrano poured coffee for everyone and offered cream and sugar. He settled back in his chair and crossed his legs, sipping his drink as if it was the best thing he'd ever tasted.

"I just need you to know," the President announced, "that even Riley does not have the power to break my good humor today."

It was a joke, but Don felt the barb of truth in the words. His cheeks warmed. On the opposite sofa, Wilkerson's lips traced a ghostly smile.

Serrano sighed. "All right, Sam, enough of the cloak-and-dagger stuff. Let's hear what you've got."

Director Blank chose a frontal assault. He powered up his tablet, opened it to the picture of Diego Montalban, and passed it across the table to the President of the United States.

"That's the Naval War College bomber, sir," he said. "Riley's team found him in South America."

The President held the tablet as if it might explode. For several moments, he studied the picture, then handed the tablet to Wilkerson.

"I suppose you better start at the beginning, Mr. Riley," Serrano said.

Don had briefed the President many times over the last four years. He knew exactly what the man needed to understand the situation. With an efficiency born of long practice, Don laid out the facts of Diego Montalban and the sighting in Santa Lúcia, Brazil. Serrano steepled his fingers, index fingers pressed against his closed lips as he listened. When Don finished, he looked up.

"You identified him by his ear?" he asked.

"Ears are as unique as fingerprints, sir, and the missing chunk out of his earlobe makes that a very distinctive trait."

Serrano nodded. The ends of his fingertips had gone white with pressure. "Why is he in South America?"

Don hesitated. "It's possible he's on the run, sir."

"On the run from what?" Wilkerson asked.

"Presumably from the Chinese," the Director replied. "We know that Minister Fei was taken out of action in the aftermath of the Taiwan situation. If the Chinese follow their normal practice, anyone associated with Fei would be eliminated, especially anyone directly associated with or taking orders from Fei."

"And you think this guy," Wilkerson asked, "not only got away but managed to avoid the Chinese for three years?"

The Director shrugged. "It's possible. It's not unusual for deep cover agents to create their own escape plans, and they generally have the resources."

Serrano ignored the last exchange. Don saw the man's teeth worrying at his lower lip, a sure sign that he was thinking hard.

"Do the Chinese have the same information?" he asked.

Don shook his head. "There's no way to know, sir, but they have facial rec that's every bit as good as ours, and the source material is an internet video. We have to assume they do."

Serrano stood, began to pace his office. The tension had left his body. He had a bounce in his step, and the wide smile was back. "This is fantastic work, Don. Just amazing."

Don had gone from "Riley" to "Don" and received two compliments in a row. Something was up.

"If we launch a full-scale effort, do you think we could catch this guy by, let's say, middle of January?" The President's eyes lasered in on Don.

Don looked at the Director, then at Wilkerson, but neither of them seemed to be willing to throw him a lifeline.

"The FBI has been after the Naval War College bomber for some time, sir," Don said. "If we got them this information ASAP, they might—"

Serrano held up his hand. "You said it yourself, Don. The FBI have been after this guy for the last three years, and they've got nothing. The last briefing I got from the FBI was that they believe the Naval War College bomber is dead. Yet, today, you walk in here with evidence to the contrary."

Serrano strode back to the table, picked up the tablet, and shook it in the air. "Not dead. Obviously." He dropped back into his chair, leaning forward. "What we need is new leadership, Don, a change in perspective. You were the one who hunted down Rafiq Roshed, right?"

Don forced himself to nod. "Along with many other good people, sir."

They'd killed Roshed—in fact, Don had pulled the trigger—but that operation had cost the lives of two men that he considered friends. He had no desire to go through anything like that again.

Serrano continued. "This picture proves that the guy is no longer on US soil, so he's fair game for the CIA, right, Director?"

Blank nodded, but it seemed to Don he showed an equal level of reluctance. "That's technically true, sir."

"So?" Serrano ignored the Director's careful qualification. "Why can't we center the manhunt out of the Emerging Threats Group? You found him once. Surely you can catch this guy before Inauguration Day, Don."

And there it was, Don thought. The President wanted to make this a political win.

Serrano was on his feet again, pacing. "Think about it, Irv. If we announce the capture of the Naval War College bomber during my inauguration speech." He pumped a fist in the air. "What a way to kick off a second term! We'd be unstoppable."

Don saw the Director shoot a glance at Wilkerson, who just shrugged. This was getting out of control. Don tried a new tack.

"Sir, the resources needed—"

"Resources?" Serrano paused his manic pacing. "Whatever you need, Don, just ask. Irv will get it for you."

"We'll need the help of some allies, Mr. President," Don said. "Our network in South America has some holes in it." Don ignored the Director's glare. If he was going to get railroaded into this plan, he was damn well going to get what he needed to succeed.

"Who?" Serrano asked.

"The Israelis have the best counterterrorist network in that part of the world," Don said. "They use it to keep tabs on Hezbollah operatives in the Tri-Border Region. The British are always watching the Argentines because of the Falklands situation."

"Those are both okay," the President said. "Anybody else, you clear it with Irv."

"There is one other resource, sir," Don said. "I'd like to use Sentinel Holdings—"

"Out of the question," Wilkerson interrupted suddenly. "We do not want to use a private military contractor." He turned to the President. "Sir, this needs to be handled exclusively by government agencies. Even a whiff of a PMC in this operation would give your critics something to latch on to."

"Their AI is the best in the world, sir," Don countered. "It would give me an edge over the Chinese."

It was true. Over the last three years, Sentinel had used the financial windfall gained from their privateering operation during the Battle for Taiwan to upgrade Mama, the company's in-house artificial intelligence. Don knew the Sentinel computer system was the first true exascale machine in the world.

"Mr. President—" began Wilkerson, but Serrano waved him into silence.

"Explain," he said to Don.

"Our target is in the wind, sir," Don said. "The only way we find him is if we get a hit on facial recognition. A security camera at a gas station, a tollbooth, an ATM camera—anything connected to the internet. Even if we limit the geography, that's billions of images to process every day. It's all about speed. If we use Sentinel's system, we're an order of magnitude faster than the Chinese. We'll find him first."

Serrano clocked a glance at his Chief of Staff. "The man makes a good argument, Irv."

Wilkerson set his jaw. "It's too risky, sir. If word got out, you'd be putting everything you've worked for in jeopardy."

"They're a contractor, sir," Don said. "They have everything to lose if they break confidence. I've used their AI before and been able to conceal my searches." Don leaned forward. "I need this, sir. If you want me to find this guy before the inauguration, this is the best possible path."

Serrano stopped another argument from Wilkerson. He looked at the Director. "What do you think, Sam?"

The Director cleared his throat as he shot a look across the coffee table where Wilkerson was glaring daggers at him. "If Don says he needs it and we can maintain security, then I say go for it, sir."

Serrano chewed on his lip with a ferocious vigor.

"Fine, Riley," he said finally. "But I need you to keep this quiet. I don't want some disgruntled FBI agent leaking word to the *Washington Post* or some rando podcaster announcing that the Serrano administration is hunting for the Naval War College bomber in South America. When I give that speech on January twentieth, I want every jaw in Washington—and in Beijing—to hit the floor at the same time, got it?"

Don noticed that the President had shifted back to calling him Riley. He ignored the Chief of Staff's heated glare.

"Got it, sir."

7

Sterling, Virginia

Over the rim of his coffee cup, Manson Skelly looked past his visitor, his mind wandering.

The vibe in this office was pure Abby Cromwell, and he hated every square inch of the place. Black leather furniture with blond wood accents formed a sitting area around a gleaming glass coffee table on the far end of the room. The desk he sat behind was huge, made of heavy, dark wood, probably passed down through Abby's family from the freaking *Mayflower*. The bar next to the sitting area was stocked with only the finest whiskeys. Even the little white coffee cup he held in his hand sucked. The handle was too small for even one of his thick fingers.

Pretentious bullshit, he thought. All of it.

And yet, this was the office of the CEO of Sentinel Holdings. His office.

Of course, Abby had been dead for over two years, he could have redecorated the place in his own style, but he'd never bothered. Besides, did he even have a style? Maybe a Western theme, he mused. He could have saddles instead of chairs to encourage people not to sit down—

Too late, he realized his guest had stopped talking.

"Do I have your attention, Manson?" the man said.

Will Clarke, CEO of Falchion Limited, was tall and lithe with caramel-colored skin and eyes that always seemed to be probing for something. Right now, Clarke's intense brown eyes were probing him.

"Skelly," he said. "Just call me Skelly."

"Skelly," Clarke repeated, then gestured at the tablet in front of his audience. "As you can see from this map, we have a solid base of assets all over Southeast Asia. We use a mix of locals and ex–US military to make sure we have good coverage for all contingencies."

Skelly tried to concentrate on the tablet, but the borders of the countries all ran together as his attention waned. It didn't matter, anyway. Landie had already done his due diligence on the company, and this was what they needed.

He ran his gaze across the screen. Vietnam, Cambodia, Laos, Thailand, down the Malaysian peninsula to Singapore and up into Myanmar. All places where Sentinel needed additional coverage. Falchion and Will Clarke were the answer to that coverage gap.

The map disappeared as Clarke advanced the slide on the tablet.

"We're proposing a ninety-day trial period," Clarke said. "You can see we have a regional base rate, then a sliding scale based on specific needs in each country."

Landie had already reviewed the package and advised Skelly that the Falchion prices were more than fair. Will Clarke wanted to do business with Sentinel.

"How much?" Skelly asked.

Clarke's brow furrowed, but the smile remained. "That's the pricing schedule right there. That's our offer."

Skelly put down the stupid white coffee cup, leaned back in his chair, and laced his fingers behind his head.

"I don't want to rent your company, Will," he said. "I want to buy it."

Clarke's smile faded. He sat back in his own chair. "It's not for sale, Skelly," he said quietly.

"C'mon, Will," Skelly said. "Everything's for sale. You built something great, and now I want to buy it. This is your payday, man."

Clarke's gaze turned hard. "Like I said, not for sale."

"Just for kicks," Skelly countered. "How about you give me a number. Aim high. Make me say no."

Will Clarke had gone very still in his chair, his lips pressed together in a thin, straight line.

Skelly widened his smile, turned on the charm. "I don't like to negotiate, Will. I'm even willing to overpay. Just name a number."

"There is no number, Skelly." Clarke reached across the desk to retrieve the tablet.

"C'mon, you don't have to play hard to get," Skelly pressed. "I'm practically begging you to rape me here."

"They were right about you," Clarke said.

"What does that mean?" Skelly came forward in his chair.

"When I prepped for this meeting, everyone I talked to told me the same thing: he's gonna want to buy your company. If you don't want to sell, don't take the meeting."

"And that's a bad thing?" Skelly asked. "Most people want to get rich, Will."

"You know?" Clark stuffed the tablet into a leather bag. "I knew Abby. We served together on a tour in the Sandbox. Long time ago, before she met Joe. Solid lady, good operator, smart as a whip. When she started Sentinel, I said to myself, that's a woman who wants to make a positive difference in the world. I assumed a lady that smart would pick good partners. I see now that I was wrong."

Skelly felt his pulse tick up, and he licked his lips. "Get out of my office."

"Trust me," Clarke said. "The door will not be hitting me in the ass."

As the door closed behind the Falchion CEO, Skelly pushed his body out of the desk chair and paced the room. He tried to breathe through the anger and gave up.

What an asshole, he thought. I try to make a guy rich, and he insults me. Well, fuck him and the horse he rode in on. He'd take the money he was going to spend on buying Clarke's company and use it to put that prick out of business.

His mobile phone buzzed. The caller ID said Landersmann.

"Landie," Skelly answered.

"Boss, you'll never believe who just showed up on our security perimeter," Landersmann said. He could hear the sneer in the man's voice. Skelly closed his eyes. Landersmann was loyal, but he talked too much.

"I'm not in the mood, Landie. What do you want?"

The implied rebuke did not register with Landersmann. "Don Riley just rolled into the parking lot. He wants to see you."

Skelly looked at his watch. Half past seven in the evening and Riley shows up unannounced?

"Give me ten minutes," Skelly ordered, "then send him in."

Skelly crossed to the bar, selected a bottle at random, and poured some into a crystal tumbler. He took a swig, enjoying the burn of the alcohol on his tongue.

He lifted the bottle. Benromach 35. Joe's favorite drink. Abby didn't drink scotch, Skelly thought, so why had she kept it? There was a scant inch left in the bottle, and Skelly felt a little guilty for drinking his best friend's special booze. He had no interest in fine liquors. Alcohol was a tool used to get drunk—the quicker, the better.

"To you, buddy," Skelly muttered, raising his glass. He took another long pull.

The comment from Will Clarke bothered him, he realized. Who was talking trash about him behind his back? Jealous, petty assholes, that's who. The Sentinel reputation was golden. They were the best in the business, even if they did do some shady deals with the Wagner element, like the Saudi job in Chad.

Abby would never have taken that job. Joe probably wouldn't have either, Skelly admitted to himself. But the world was different now. If you wanted to be the biggest, you had to take on the good and the bad deals. He wasn't here to play God and judge his customers. He was here to get rich. Abby never understood that. She came from money. For her, Sentinel was a hobby.

There was a knock at the door, and Don Riley stepped into the room. Skelly hoisted his glass.

"Join me, Don," he said. "For old time's sake."

Don hesitated.

"Just one, Boy Scout," Skelly prodded. "What'll you have?"

"I think Abby's drink was bourbon, right? I'll have a bourbon, no ice."

Skelly looked at him sharply.

But Don wasn't paying attention anymore. He'd taken a seat in one of the black leather armchairs that Skelly hated.

"Bourbon it is," Skelly said. He picked up a bottle of Bowman single-barrel and poured a measure into a matching tumbler.

Don accepted the proffered drink. "Cheers," he said. They touched glasses, and Skelly sat down.

"It's been a while, Riley," Skelly began.

He watched Don shift in his seat, his eyes casting about Abby's office. Skelly never understood what Abby saw in this guy. Pushing fifty, soft around the middle, his red hair was shot with gray and he had bags under his eyes. He knew Don was supposed to be some kind of computer genius intel analyst, but all that was for the birds. He let Landersmann handle all of that stuff. He was a man of action.

His only real connection to Don Riley was during his time as CIA liaison officer to Sentinel for the Taiwan job. Even then, the CIA officer had worked mostly with Abby.

That felt like a long time ago. All Skelly really remembered from that experience was that Don was always asking questions and always, always taking Abby's side of the argument when there was a major operational decision on the table. Neither of them ever wanted to take chances, but what they didn't understand—what he saw so clearly—was that big risks meant big rewards.

"I ran into Will Clarke in the parking lot," Don said. "Good man."

Skelly wondered if that was a crack at him, but Don was smiling.

"Really?" Skelly said. "I thought he was kind of a prick."

Don's grin faded. "You're probably wondering why I'm here."

"I thought maybe you missed me," Skelly replied.

"I want to use Mama to run some search routines."

That was...odd. Even Skelly knew the CIA had their own computers. Why did they need Mama? "What kind of searches?" he asked.

Don's expression hardened. "The confidential kind, Manson." He passed an envelope across the table. Skelly scanned the document, a directive on White House letterhead, ordering Sentinel to permit Don Riley to use Mama for confidential searches, referencing a section of their contract. Skelly stared at the signature at the bottom of page: Ricardo T. Serrano.

He tossed the letter onto the table. "I think I'm entitled to know what my equipment is being used for, Riley."

Don smiled thinly. "These are simple search routines, nothing special. Mama can chew through internet databases faster than anything out there. Speed is crucial."

Skelly took a drink of the scotch to give himself time to think. None of this made sense. Riley shows up out of the blue with a letter signed by the President to execute a "simple search" on the company's AI. The CIA had access to plenty of computing power. What was Riley after, and why wouldn't he share?

"Are we good, Manson?" Don pressed.

Skelly narrowed his eyes at Don. "You're really not going to tell me anything?"

"I'd like to get started as soon as possible," Don replied.

"Tonight?"

"Right now."

"Whatever you say." Skelly pulled out his phone. "I'll get Landie in here right away."

Don cleared his throat. "I need your assurance that this will be confidential, Manson."

Skelly shrugged. "Uncle Sam pays the bills around here, Don. I do what my master tells me."

There was a sharp rap on the door, and David Landersmann entered. He was a short man with sloping shoulders and a paunch. He had patchy brown hair and a three-day growth of beard. His dress shirt showed a food stain on the third button. As usual, he wore a lopsided smile. "You rang, boss?"

Skelly summarized the task, emphasizing the confidential nature of Don's work.

Landersmann gave a mock salute. "You got it, bossman."

After the two men left, Skelly rattled the ice in his drink. What could be so important that Don Riley himself came all the way out to Sterling to personally set up searches? And to come armed with a letter from the White House?

Only one way to find out, he thought. He pulled out his mobile phone and dialed.

A man answered in clipped tones. "I told you not to call me again."

"Good to hear from you too, Irv," Skelly replied. "You must be very proud of your guy's big win."

"I'm working on an invitation to an inaugural ball, but I can't promise anything," Wilkerson said.

"Not *an* inaugural ball, Irv," Skelly said. "*The* Inaugural Ball. The big one, and face time with the Big Man. Anyway, that's not why I'm calling."

The line was silent, so Skelly continued. "I just had a visit from Don Riley."

More silence.

"He wants to use my supercomputer and flashed a letter that says I have to let him do it. Why all the hush-hush, Irv?"

"Stay out of it, Manson," Wilkerson said. "That's all I can tell you."

"I thought we were friends," Skelly replied, letting an edge into his tone. "We have history, Irv. We need to stick together. You know, all for one and one for all."

"Don't call me again, Skelly. It is inappropriate for a defense contractor to contact the White House directly. From now on, you work through your designated official channels." Wilkerson hung up.

Skelly's grip tightened on the phone. He cracked the empty glass down on the coffee table. Irving Wilkerson should treat him with more respect. After all the things Skelly had done for him...

He brought his phone screen to life and sent a text to Landersmann.

I want to know what Riley is doing.

8

Scorpions Ascent, Israel

Rachel woke up late. She listened to people passing in the hallway outside her door. After the rush of the morning meal, the traffic dwindled until it was only the occasional passerby. Still, she stayed in bed. She'd been given word the previous night that her classes would be handled by another instructor until further notice.

For most of the morning, she stared out her window at the desert. She watched the sun creep above the peak of Scorpions Ascent and illuminate the sandy landscape. The light became harsh as the morning wore on. Dawn shadows melted away as the sun rose in the sky and disappeared above the top of her window.

Rachel stayed in bed.

There was another burst of hall traffic around the midday meal, then that faded as well. She tried to watch TV and gave up. Tried to read a book and found her mind wandering away from the words.

In the mid-afternoon, she made coffee and sat by her window.

She should feel regret about her actions, she knew, but instead she felt...nothing. It was an accident, she told herself. Or maybe, a darker part of her mind suggested, it was another attempt at self-sabotage.

By evening meal, hunger forced her to take action. She showered, dressed, and made her way to the mess hall, timing her arrival for the tail end of the dinner hour when there would be fewer people in the cafeteria. She walked through the line, made up a tray, and carried it back to her room. That was another privilege granted to instructors.

For now, she thought, you're still an instructor. But tomorrow? Who knows? You've really done it to yourself this time.

In the quiet of her quarters, she ate without tasting the food, her attention on the desert outside her window. The sun was setting, creating long shadows across the landscape. Colors that had been hidden in the harshness of direct sunlight emerged. Reds, ochres, velvety deep oranges all painted the world outside the glass.

If they send me away, she thought, this is what I'll miss. The beauty of the landscape blurred as she blinked back tears.

This is your fault, she thought. You did this. You broke the guy's arm... was it really an accident, or did you mean to do it?

When the desert grew dark, Rachel decided to take her evening walk. Although she'd spent the day out of sight, she had not been officially confined to her quarters. No one said she *couldn't* leave the base to walk in the desert night.

Why not? she thought. It is better to beg forgiveness than to ask for permission.

Her phone rang. Not her mobile, but the land line.

"Jaeger," she answered.

"Report to the base commander's office," said a voice. "Immediately."

Click. They hung up.

Rachel gripped the phone.

So, this is it, she thought. You gave Old Man Cohn the perfect excuse to fire you. He probably spent the entire day arranging the dismissal with Tel Aviv.

She didn't blame the base commander. Although she continually pushed the boundaries of base regulations, Rachel was useful. An instructor who was qualified to teach most of the classes on base and welcomed a flexible schedule was a valued asset—even if she was a pain in the ass. But when assets go around breaking the arms of visitors, especially from the CIA, then they become less valuable.

Okay, she thought, stay positive. Let's at least try to make a good impression for our execution.

The laziness of her day vanished in a blaze of frenetic activity. Rachel brushed her unruly hair, containing it in a neat bun at the base of her neck. She was known for her casual dress as an instructor—another pet peeve of Cohn's—so she changed into the most conservative outfit in her closet, a pair of navy blue slacks (thankfully they were pressed), a cream-colored blouse, and high heels. For good measure, she dug a silver Star of David necklace from her meager jewelry box and added that to the ensemble. Rachel even applied some light makeup, something she hadn't done in months.

She surveyed her appearance in the mirror. Not bad, she thought. She returned to her closet for a blue blazer, but when she found the jacket had not been pressed, she discarded the idea.

Looking presentable was one thing, she thought. Kissing ass was another.

As Rachel left, she took a long look at her apartment, fixing the place in her memory. It was possible that Cohn would have her escorted out of the facility as soon as she was fired. She fought back another wave of nostalgia. These two rooms had been home for the last five years. It was a place she loved, yet hated at the same time. Most of all, this was a place where she felt safe.

And one stupid moment in the gym had screwed all that up.

To get to the base commander's office in the administrative wing, Rachel needed to transit through the dormitory area.

For most of the people at the Mossad base, Rachel being a notable exception, evening hours were for study and socializing. Most people, students and instructors like, left their doors open and welcomed visitors. The secret base was in the middle of the desert. During the week, there was literally nowhere to go at night. Once the studying was done, anything went. Game nights, impromptu dance parties, or just conversation circles. More than a few romantic relationships had started at Scorpions Ascent, not to mention babies conceived.

Rachel, who normally walked in the desert in the evening, had forgotten about the level of nighttime activity. But she was immediately reminded when she stepped into the hallway. Eyes turned as her high heels clicked on the polished linoleum floor.

"Good luck, Jaeger," someone called.

"Thanks," she muttered, her cheeks aflame with embarrassment.

The transit through the student dormitory area was even worse. Here, students lived two or three to a room, making the population of people watching her denser. Conversations faltered as she passed, the volume of music lowered, and she heard whispers in her wake.

Rachel forced herself to walk at a steady pace, chin set, eyes straight ahead.

She sighed when she passed through the double doors into the administrative wing. At this time of night, the area was mostly deserted. She tried to relax as she made her way to the base commander's office. Next to the heavy wooden door, a metal strip held a black plastic name tag with white lettering. *Eliot Cohn*. There was no mention of his rank or role at the secret facility, just a name tag on an unassuming door.

Rachel squared her shoulders, drew in a deep breath, and rapped on the door three times.

"Come." She heard Cohn's voice clearly through the door.

Rachel twisted the handle and stepped inside.

Eliot Cohn, Brigadier General, Israeli Defense Forces, retired, was a tall, spare man with a bald pate and aquiline facial features. He sat behind a government-issue desk, hands folded on the empty desk blotter. When Rachel saw the look on his face, her heart sank. It was all over, she could tell.

His eyes followed her as she shut the door. She turned back to face him, came to attention, and said, "Reporting as ordered, sir."

His gaze pinned her in place. One second passed, then two, three. Rachel stared back at him. Get it over with, she thought.

He jerked his head to the right. "In the conference room," he said in a curt voice.

Rachel did a letter-perfect ninety-degree turn and marched to the door.

Of course, he has a board assembled to fire me, she thought. That's why he waited all day.

Anger surged in her gut. She'd fight it. If they believed she would just accept a dismissal, they had another thing coming at them. Rachel opened the door with more force than she'd intended. The handle slipped from her grasp and banged against the wall.

"You break it, you buy it," said a gravelly voice.

Rachel looked up in surprise.

Noam Glantz sat alone at the conference room table. His beefy forearms were planted on the dark wood, and he hunched forward in his chair. His pursed lips looked like he'd just sucked on a lemon.

"Shut the door, Jaeger," he snapped.

Rachel did as she was told, and when she turned back around, Noam had gotten to his feet.

Noam Glantz was the polar opposite of the base commander. A heavyset man, he'd long ago given up on physical fitness. His belly strained against his belt, his thick neck melted into round shoulders. Noam glared at Rachel, and for the first time, she was sorry for what had happened.

Her own father had died when Rachel was just a child. This man had filled that void in her life. Although her late husband was the one who'd broached the subject of Mossad with Rachel, it was Noam who had recruited her. Noam who had been her Kidon leader for every one of her field assignments, and Noam who had held her when her husband was killed in the line of duty. Noam made a place for her at Scorpions Ascent as an instructor when she was no longer fit for field duty. He continued the arrangement even after he was transferred to Tel Aviv to take over operations for all of Mossad.

Rachel hung her head. And now, she'd screwed that up. All day, Rachel had thought about herself when she should have been thinking about the man who had supported her every step of the way.

"Noam," she began. "I...I'm—"

"Rachel."

Noam held his arms open, and she launched her body into him.

He was like hugging a bear—and she loved it. Noam wrapped his massive arms around her. Rachel pressed her face into the heavy flesh of his neck.

"I have missed you," he rumbled.

Tears came. Rachel felt her shoulders shake, felt Noam's hug tighten. When she could talk without her voice breaking, Rachel said, "I'm sorry. Really."

"Eliot says he's an American."

"It was an accident, Noam. I swear."

Rachel felt Noam's body quake. She pushed back. "Are you laughing?"

"Eliot also says the guy's an asshole. He's sending him back to the United States."

"It's not funny," Rachel said.

"No." Noam wiped his eyes, still smiling. "It's not funny. Did you have to break his arm, Rachel?"

"I already told you," Rachel insisted. "It was an accident."

"With your skills, I don't consider that likely." Noam heaved a sigh and waved her to a chair.

Rachel sat. "You're smoking again. I can smell it on your clothes."

Noam reached for his ever-present thermos of coffee and poured two cups. "Don't change the subject. You're the one in trouble, not me." He pushed a cup across the table. "Tell me what happened."

Rachel started slowly at first, then the words came faster, and she found herself telling him about how the rainstorm made her go to the gym instead of walking. How she'd seen the bigger instructor beat up on one of her former students.

"You decided to teach him a lesson, is that it?" Noam hunched over in his chair, the coffee cup looking tiny in his massive hands.

"Not exactly," Rachel replied. "He wouldn't tap out."

Noam's lips twisted into a faint smile.

"What?" Rachel asked.

"Do you remember when you killed that guy in Mozambique with the heel of your shoe? And you told the review board?"

Rachel giggled. How long had it been since she'd actually laughed?

"Those were good times, Rachel," Noam said, a tone of finality in his voice. "But those days are gone. You need to let go."

"I'm fine," Rachel replied.

Noam turned the coffee cup in his hand. "You are not fine, my dear." He looked up, meeting her eye. "And you can't hide here anymore."

"I'm not hiding," Rachel snapped back, but even she recognized the lie. "I'm not."

Noam reached across the table and covered both her hands with one of his. "You are. And it's time to leave."

Rachel sucked in a breath, tried to hold it, and failed. She balled her hands into fists to stop the trembling. This was her home. She swallowed as if the action might hold back the fears that welled up inside her.

I don't have anywhere else to go, she thought. Out loud, Rachel said, "You're firing me?"

Noam drank off his coffee and hoisted his body out of the chair.

"That would be too easy," he said. "I'm giving you a new job."

The panic melted away. A new job...

Rachel felt a smile spreading across her face. She did feel ready to get back into the field. This was exactly the change she needed.

Then she looked at Noam.

"A *desk* job," Noam said. "Working for the Americans."

9

Dongtou District, People's Republic of China

This is a waste of time, Gao thought.

The gray hull of the thirty-foot launch smashed into another wave. A wall of cold spray lifted in the air and rained down on the occupants of the boat. Next to him, Mei Lin huddled inside the bulk of a borrowed rain slicker the color of a moldy lemon. Behind her, two enlisted Chinese Coast Guard sailors hung onto the railing with one hand and cigarettes with the other.

Gao wiped the spray off his face and pulled down the hood of his own foul-weather gear. The move surrounded his head with the smell of vomit and dirty gym socks. Gagging, he threw back the hood just in time to get another faceful of icy seawater.

Gao lurched to his feet, grabbed the railing, and hauled himself forward to the cockpit, where a young Haijing lieutenant steered the craft.

"How much longer?" Gao yelled.

Through the rain-spattered windshield, the coast guard officer indicated a point in the distance where a rocky island loomed out of the East China Sea.

"We don't come to Nanpeng Island much, sir," the pilot replied. "There's no military installations there."

"Is that unusual?" Goa asked.

The pilot pointed east. "Okinawa is four hundred kilometers that way." He swung his arm southeast. "And Taiwan is less than two hundred kilometers in that direction. As far as I know, that's the only island in these waters without at least a radar station on it."

The Dongtou District was a collection of nearly two hundred rocky islands situated where the Oujiang River ran into the East China Sea. Nanpeng Island, thirty kilometers to the southeast of the port city of Wenzhou, was part of a screen of islands that separated mainland China from the rogue province of Taiwan. To Gao, it seemed like an obvious place for a listening post. Minister Fei must have had other ideas.

Still clutching the railing, he lurched back and slammed into the seat next to Mei Lin just as their boat assaulted another wave.

"I feel sick, dear," she muttered, her face lost in the smelly rain gear.

Gao wanted to put his arm around her and hug her close to him, but he didn't dare with the Haijing officer close by. Besides, he was barely keeping his own lunch down as it was. He gripped the edge of the seat to stay in place and stared at the horizon.

Steady breaths, he thought. In and out...

In the three weeks since he'd been assigned to look into ex-Minister Fei's background, he'd uncovered exactly nothing new. The existing records were sparse, and everyone he talked to told Gao the same thing: for important decisions, the Minister always held face-to-face meetings. No recordings, no notes. The only exception to this rule was a small black travel diary, which he carried with him everywhere.

Unfortunately, no one had been able to locate the Minister's diary.

Meanwhile, in South America, the manhunt for the elusive Diego Montalban/Ian Thomas continued with a similar lack of success.

How many other cover names did that bastard have at his disposal? That was another mystery that Minister Fei had taken to his grave.

With each passing hour, Gao felt his opportunity to find something new about the ex-Minister slipping away—and with it, his chance for promotion to general.

The idea that he might be on a wild goose chase infuriated him. To find nothing would comfort the very powerful men who had given him this assignment, but that also meant the General Secretary and the current Minister would not be in his debt.

This was his opportunity to be truly useful to these powerful men. Somehow, he needed to find—and solve—a problem for them. When they got what they wanted, Gao would get what he wanted.

He poured his anger into his work. With Mei Lin by his side, he had practically dismantled Fei's residence in Beijing and found nothing. He'd pored over every scrap of paper and every email touched by the Minister in the year before his death. He examined every personal item taken from the man's office and interviewed every person the Minister interacted with regularly.

Nothing.

The only item that remained on Gao's list was a family home in the Dongtou District. Gao had discovered the deed during a search of the Minister's financial records and had set it aside for future consideration.

And now, more out of desperation than anything else, Gao was making the trek to the ancestral home of Minister Fei Zhen.

The boat lurched again, salty spray rained down, and Gao's stomach curdled. He judged the distance from his seat to the railing and wondered how embarrassing it would be if he just hung his head over the side and vomited into the churning ocean.

Suddenly, the sea calmed. Gao looked up to find they had entered the lee of the island. He got shakily to his feet and gripped the railing, dragging in great lungfuls of damp sea air. Only a hundred meters ahead, he could see a stone dock pushing out into the water. It might have been five hundred years old. On one side of the small dock, a wooden boat with an outboard motor was tied off.

The lieutenant slowed the small craft. He craned his neck, studying the water ahead of him. Then he guided the boat to the edge of the pier and nodded to his two enlisted crew to tie them off. With practiced grace, he killed the engine and leaped up to the dock.

He held out his hand to Gao. "Welcome to Nanpeng Island, Senior Colonel."

Standing on the dock, his feet on solid ground and the rancid foul-weather gear left in the boat, Gao felt his stomach settle.

"Wait here, Lieutenant," Gao ordered. "I don't know how long this will take."

The officer saluted. "Aye-aye, sir."

Gao followed a wide path into the forest, his footfalls silent on a bed of pine needles. That was the other difference with this island, he realized. In addition to hosting military installations, all of the other islands Gao had seen on their trip out here had been mostly denuded of trees and covered in small homes. He breathed in the heavy pine scent, which eased his churning stomach even more. Fifty years ago, all of the islands would have looked like this. The inhabitants would have made their living from the sea and managed the scarce trees with care. Now, they probably lived off military stipends and tourism.

Apart from the soft shush of the ocean and the tang of salt in the air, they might have been hiking in the thick forests of central China.

"This is beautiful," Mei Lin said.

"This is a waste of time," Gao replied.

"It's still beautiful," Mei Lin insisted.

The path took a turn, and a clearing came into view. A few paces more and Gao sighted the house. Sunlight broke through the cloud cover as the path transitioned from pine needles to a swept stone walk.

The structure was laid out in the traditional style of four buildings around a central courtyard. Architecture was not Gao's strength, but the structure looked old, maybe hundreds of years old. The grounds around the main house were immaculate. Neatly trimmed fruit trees, sculpted shrubbery, clipped grass. He advanced to the front door of heavy wood and knocked.

There was no answer.

Gao tried the latch. The ancient door swung inward silently on well-oiled hinges. To his surprise, Gao saw that the door didn't even have a lock.

"Can I help you?" said a voice from behind them.

The old man was well into his seventies, with stooped shoulders and a thin frame. He was dressed roughly in loose trousers, a matching tunic, and sandals. Reading glasses were pushed up into a thicket of gray hair.

"Who are you?" Gao asked.

The man studied Gao's uniform and nodded to Mei Lin. "Who are you?" the man replied. His tone wasn't exactly dismissive, but it certainly wasn't respectful. Gao felt a prickle of annoyance.

"I'm here on business from the Minister of State Security," Gao said. Normally, even a mention of the MSS made people change their demeanor, but the man's bemused smile never faltered. It was almost as if he hadn't heard Gao. "Are you familiar with this property?"

The man gave a low chuckle. "I should hope so. I've lived here my entire life. I'm the caretaker. I grew up with Zhen."

It took a moment for Gao to realize that the man was talking about Minister Fei.

"When was the last time the Minister was here?"

The old man frowned and stared off into trees. "Zhen?" he said. "A few weeks before he died, I think."

Gao tried not to hope too much, but it was better than nothing. "I have authority to search the premises," he announced.

The old man shrugged and turned away.

The interior of the Fei family home was plain. Plaster walls, tiled floors, timbered ceilings. Some rooms were sparsely furnished, but most of them were empty. Gao was searching the kitchen when he heard Mei Lin call him from the courtyard.

"Yichen," she said. "Come and look at this."

The open area in the center of the house was a garden. Gao passed trellises of vines and neatly trimmed shrubbery. Raked pea gravel crunched under his shoes.

"Where are you?" he called.

"Over here."

Gao followed the sound of her voice to an open space in the center of the garden. Mei Lin was seated on a stone bench facing a golden statue of a seated man.

A Buddhist shrine in Minister Fei's house? Gao thought. He'd seen nothing in any files about the Minister having a religious preference.

At one hand of the Buddha, a spring bubbled, filling the air with the soothing sound of running water. On the other side was a low platform on which sat an orange and a carved jade block holding three smoldering incense sticks. Gao smelled the scent of jasmine. Offerings for the dead, Gao realized.

"It's beautiful, isn't it?" said a voice from behind him.

Gao started. Somehow, the old man had crept up on them without Gao hearing him.

"I didn't know the Minister was Buddhist," Gao said.

The old man shrugged. "Beautiful, right?"

"Yes," Mei Lin agreed.

This was a waste of time. "Back to work," Gao ordered.

For the next three hours, Gao and Mei Lin went through every room again, looking for anything that seemed out of the ordinary.

"There's nothing here, Yichen," Mei Lin said when they had arrived back at the place where they had started.

Gao tried to fight back the feeling of defeat, but his shoulders slumped. "It has to be here," he insisted.

"We've looked everywhere," Mei Lin said. "There's nothing."

"I need to think," Gao replied. He left the house at a fast walk as if trying to outrun his despair. In the clearing, he found a trail that led into the woods. The ground rose steeply, but Gao kept moving.

This island visit had been his last hope. There was nothing left on his list. To make matters worse, his teams in South America had not located Diego Montalban. Unless his luck changed quickly, Gao was staring into the face of a double failure.

He broke out of the trees and stood on a ridge, the highest point on the island. The sun was strong now, and Gao shielded his eyes as he gazed out to sea. How many times had Minister Fei stood in this exact spot? He wondered if he might be able to see the lights of Taipei on a clear night.

Gao bellowed into the wind to vent his frustration, but it didn't make him feel any better. Slowly, he turned and walked back down the hill to the house.

Mei Lin was sitting by the shrine. Gao took the seat next to her and put his elbows on his knees.

"I don't know what to do, Mei Lin." Gao closed his eyes and tried to think. He was missing something. He had to be missing *something*. When he opened his eyes, the jade gaze of the golden Buddha stared back at him, taunting him with placid regard.

Why is this statue here? he wondered. It was the one thing in the entire house that felt out of place to him.

Gao got to his feet and approached the shrine. He rapped his knuckles on the side of the figure. It was hollow, and the golden Buddha sat on a thick base of granite.

"Help me," he said. "I want to see what's underneath the statue."

"What are you doing?" The old man was back, but his tone had lost the bemused quality from before.

"When was this shrine installed?" Gao asked.

"Years ago." The man's eyes shifted. He's lying, Gao realized.

"How many years ago?"

"This is a sacred place," the old man replied.

"Most men won't disturb a shrine," Gao shot back. "It's sacrilegious. Minister Fei was not a religious man, so why does he have a Buddhist artifact in his home?"

"You need to leave," the old man said.

Gao drew his weapon. "Mei Lin," he said, "use a rock and smash the statue."

"But, Yichen—"

"Do it!" Gao said. He heard her feet on the gravel, heard her pick up one of the stones on the perimeter of the clearing. Gao watched the old man's eyes. His forehead wrinkled as he looked past Gao at Mei Lin.

"Wait," the old man whispered.

The old man crossed to the shrine. He slipped his finger under the offerings table and flipped a catch, then he slid the statue aside, revealing a shallow pocket carved into the granite base.

Inside the hollow were two items. Gao picked up the first, a laptop the size and shape of a paperback book. He turned it on, but it was password protected. He snapped the lid shut.

The other item was a small black book. Leatherbound, about the size of Gao's open palm. Inside, Gao leafed through page after page of cramped, spidery handwriting.

10

Tel Aviv, Israel

Rachel forced a smile at the video screen. The tag on the collar of the new dress shirt she'd bought a few days ago was itchy. All she wanted to do was take the damn thing off, stand under a hot shower for thirty minutes, and forget about this day.

This very long, mind-numbing day. Her gaze strayed to the clock in the lower right-hand corner of the screen. It was nearly one a.m. in Tel Aviv. If she were still in Scorpions Ascent, she'd just be getting back from her nightly hike through the desert, relaxed and ready for bed.

"We need more data." Don Riley's voice came out of the speakers on her computer.

Rachel choked down a slug of cold, bitter coffee and made a noise that indicated she agreed with Don.

Rachel recalled Don Riley and his two companions from the bioweapons job in Sudan. The tall Black man who didn't say much and smiled less was named Michael. The woman, wiry physique, intense and dark-haired, was Andrea, who went by Dre. After hearing what Dre had gone through as a captive in Iran, Rachel had a lot of respect for the woman.

It was a stretch to say that she remembered meeting them. Don's team had found her unconscious in the secret bioweapons bunker in the desert. A gunshot wound in her belly and beaten half to death by a Janjaweed soldier, she'd been left for dead. Thanks to Don Riley, Rachel had woken up in Camp Lemonnier in Djibouti a day later. If she considered their relationship in that light, Rachel owed Don her life.

"We've exhausted all our facial recognition sources for the moment," Don continued. "I was hoping you had some other ideas that we hadn't thought of."

Rachel had never thought of Don as healthy looking, but he truly looked worse for wear now. Hair more gray than red, bags under his eyes. It was barely after dinnertime in the US, and Don looked like he'd been awake for a week.

"What'd you have in mind, Don?" she asked.

When Noam brought her to Tel Aviv a week ago and read her into the operation to find the Naval War College bomber, Rachel was excited. A manhunt was field work, she thought.

But Noam had other ideas. "I want you here," he'd told her, "in Tel Aviv, coordinating our field resources on the ground in South America and keeping the Americans up to date. It's more efficient."

He doesn't trust me anymore, Rachel realized. Noam was worried about his poor broken toy soldier. The idea of being the object of his pity turned her stomach.

"Well," Don's voice interrupted the running dialogue in her head. "Do you think that our target is still in the TBR? What are your local sources telling you?"

"Not much," Rachel replied. Actually, less than that. It turned out, Rachel was not very good at managing people remotely, and the reports from her field assets had been sparse at best. "But I have an idea," she added.

"We could use a fresh perspective," Don said. "What have you got?"

Rachel tried another sip of the stale coffee and spit it back in the cup. "I'm trying to put myself in the place of this guy. He's injured, but he's mobile. If I were him, I'd get out of the area. He knows we'll be looking for him."

"He's a Chinese guy in South America, and he's covered in bruises," Dre said. "He has to assume that we have his identity."

"No public transport," Rachel agreed. "No airlines, no buses, no trains."

"He probably assumes that we know his car," Dre went on.

"He'll need to find new wheels," Michael said.

"That's what I'm thinking," Rachel said. "Do you have the computer resources to find out all the cars that were stolen in the past month anywhere in that region?"

"I have more computing power than I know what to do with," Don said. "I can have that for you in the morning."

"We're talking about three different countries and who knows how many local police departments, Don. That's a big task for any agency."

Don smiled at her. "Like I said, computing power is the one asset I have in abundance. What else do you need?"

The Tri-Border Region where Argentina, Brazil, and Paraguay met had a reputation as a lawless area favored by the likes of drug dealers and people who did not want to be found. But this guy would also know there were drawbacks to staying in the area. If this guy was as good as Don said he was, he would realize that staying in the TBR more than a few days was a mistake. There was a sizeable bounty on his head. It was only a matter of time before someone turned him in.

What would I do? Rachel mused. He's been there for three years, and he has assets. He'd have places to hide. Investments in legitimate front businesses that offered him a way to make a living and make an escape.

No, this Diego guy, or whatever the hell his real name was, would be in the wind by now. Rachel was sure of that, but he'd be smart about it.

"Since you're asking," Rachel continued. She was used to people in management telling her what she couldn't have, not inviting her to ask for more. "Search for any used car sales—private sales if you can get the data. And stolen license plates."

Rachel paused, thinking. "Also, do a search on any stolen passports for Chinese nationals in the same period. If he doesn't have another identity, he's going to need to find one fast."

Don was typing on his laptop as she spoke. "Done," he said. "We'll limit the geography at first, then expand as the data starts to come in."

"I'll let you know if I get any hits from my local network," Rachel said.

Don nodded. "Same time tomorrow?" he asked.

Rachel agreed and killed the connection. She blew out a breath and sank back into her chair. This was ridiculous. She was a hunter, not a manager. You didn't hunt a terrorist from behind a desk. You immersed yourself in his environment. You forced him to make a move, make a mistake.

If Noam had told her she'd be spending her days on conference calls with Washington providing status reports about what people were doing in South America, Rachel might have quit the agency altogether.

And do what? the voice inside her head challenged her. You have no job, no friends, and no life outside of your place in Mossad.

Rachel reached behind her neck and ripped the annoying tag off the shirt. The action felt oddly satisfying.

The cold coffee quivered in the cup as a jet took off from the nearby Ben Gurion Airport. Although the room was soundproof, when the jets passed directly over the office park, the whole building trembled.

Rather than place her at the headquarters building downtown, Noam had set her up in one of the many satellite offices spread around the country. This one was a small front business that did some sort of clerical support work for the airlines. It was a good cover. Supporting an airline was a twenty-four-seven operation, so it was not unusual for people to come and go at all hours. If they needed to leave the country, the airport was only a few minutes away.

So close and yet so far, she thought. What this investigation really needed was operational leadership in the field. Trying to run assets half a world away was ineffective, in her opinion. The only way to catch a killer was to be in his element, not sitting in some business park office pretending to have the "Big Picture."

Rachel was an operator, not a manager. Noam knew that. She did her best work in the field. All her successes—including the ones that had helped him to become Director of Operations for all of Mossad—had been in the field, far from the safety and comforts of Tel Aviv.

Why, she thought, is Noam keeping me cooped up like a wild animal in a cage?

Rachel snatched up her phone, intending to call her boss, but then remembered he was in Europe all week for meetings. They were supposed to have lunch when he returned in a few days. Noam promised her they would talk about next steps.

Next steps meant a field assignment, Rachel reasoned. This whole job with Don Riley was just an interim step, a way to observe her, make sure she hadn't gone off the deep end. Then he'd put her back into field rotation. What else could it mean?

Rachel started to drink the rest of the cold coffee and stopped herself. She threw the cup in the garbage.

This was crazy. In the past, Noam had always prized her willingness to seize the initiative. Perhaps that's what he was waiting for. This whole assignment was a test. He was waiting for Rachel to make a bold move. To show him she was back to her old self.

On impulse, she checked the schedule for El Al flights from Tel Aviv to Buenos Aires. There was one leaving at five a.m. She checked her watch. Plenty of time to go back to her temporary apartment, pack, and make the flight.

Rachel considered the mobile phone in her hand. Should she call Noam?

She tapped her credit card details into the El Al website and booked the ticket to Buenos Aires. The flight had a short layover in Madrid before they continued on to Argentina.

"I'll call Noam from Madrid," Rachel muttered. "He'll understand."

Then she grabbed her car keys and phone and left the building. Overhead, a cargo jet roared into the sky. She slid behind the wheel and started the car.

It was good to be on the move again.

11

Yellow Sea

Gao ordered the helicopter pilot to approach the radar installation from the ocean.

It was nearly noon, and brilliant sunshine poured down on the rocky coast. That was unusual for this time of year, Gao knew. He'd been warned to expect low clouds and high winds, perhaps even snow.

The installation was perched on the edge of a fifty-meter-high cliff. On the shore below, breakers smashed against the rocks. Through the window, Gao studied the surf, looking for any sign of the submerged entrance he knew was hiding under the waves.

His search for Minister Fei's secrets had led him to this place.

Gao tapped the pilot on the shoulder and rotated his finger in the air to indicate he wanted the helo to circle the station before landing.

The radar station looked unassuming, a long, low-slung cinder block building dwarfed by a two-story-high geodesic radome. On the other side of the structure, a cluster of parabolic communications dishes were anchored to concrete pads. There were three military-green vehicles in the parking lot that had been carved out of the treed landscape. The place looked exactly like what the government records said it was: an early warning radar and SIGINT station.

Except it wasn't.

After discovering Minister Fei's personal diary in his family home, Gao and Mei Lin had spent a sleepless twenty-four hours comparing the little black book with the former Minister's official records. On one occasion, the Minister had traveled north to Dalian to visit the naval academy of the People's Liberation Army. Yet when Mei Lin cross-checked the Minister's visit with records at the school, she found the Minister had taken only a single thirty-minute meeting, then departed in a government vehicle.

Bureaucracy had its uses. A government vehicle needed to be signed out of a motor pool, whose keepers invariably recorded daily mileage on every vehicle and the identity of the driver. They burned another day finding the man who was on duty that day and questioning him.

Which led them to this remote installation.

Gao signaled the pilot to land. As the helicopter descended, a man dressed in a PLA Navy working uniform exited the building.

Minister Fei had come to visit a secret underground submarine base. During the early 2000s, China had constructed a number of such bases in remote locations to hide the Chinese submarine fleet from the prying eyes of the Americans.

But this base was different. Once construction was complete, the base was removed from the national registry. The man behind this bureaucratic disappearing act was Admiral Chen, a confidant of the Minister. Initially, Gao was excited, until he learned that following the failed invasion of Taiwan, Admiral Chen was removed from active duty. The PLA Navy department informed Gao that Admiral Chen was unavailable for questioning. He didn't push the issue for the simple reason that Chen was obviously dead.

He and Mei Lin put the pieces together on their own. They already knew the Minister had used an *Xi*-class unmanned submarine to attack both the United States and Russian navies in the North Pacific. It made sense to Gao that the covert submarine had been based out of this site.

He would have let his investigation rest there, but one detail drove him forward. In the margin of the Minister's diary, next to the entry about the visit to the secret base, Fei had carefully penned a single ideogram in his spidery hand.

Huichen, it read. *Dust.*

What did it mean? Gao wondered. He had immersed himself in the Minister's life for long enough to know that everything the man did had a purpose. Yet, nowhere in any of his records could Gao find the same note. Could it be a code word for a secret project?

There was only one way to find out, he reasoned. Go to the source.

Next to him, Mei Lin bounced from window to window, her lips parted in a look of wondrous delight. It was the first time she'd ever been in a helicopter, and she was clearly enjoying the experience.

She's like a child, Gao thought. A beautiful, innocent child. She looked at him and smiled. Gao smiled back.

His hand fell to the small satchel that he carried with him. Inside it was the Minister's travel diary and the small, ruggedized laptop they had taken from the Buddhist shrine in Fei's family home.

The laptop was encrypted. When they were in Beijing, he'd allowed technicians to work on the device, but only in his presence. Whatever was on Fei's laptop, Gao needed to be the one who saw it first. He knew that the current Minister of State Security and the General Secretary had people watching him, and Gao was determined that no information would pass to either man unless he cleared it first. He was the one taking the risk, and he would be the one to reap the reward.

The helo touched down. Stooping, the navy man rushed forward to open the door for them. He escorted Gao and Mei Lin under the whirling rotors to the entrance of the building. Behind them, the whine of the helicopter's engine subsided as the pilot shut down the aircraft.

"Welcome, Senior Colonel Gao." The man saluted. "You honor us with your presence. We don't get many visitors, sir."

Gao took his time returning the salute. The man was short and paunchy with strands of thinning gray hair plastered to his scalp. Even the rotor blast of the helo had not dislodged his hair. The man was far too old to be a commander. This was probably a retirement tour meant to extend his service time for additional pension money.

"I wish to see the submarine pen, Commander," Gao ordered. "And inspect your records."

"Of course, sir," the commander said. "Follow me."

Inside the building, Gao found himself in a room filled with radar workstations and a wall of SIGINT consoles. Three personnel were on duty. An enlisted man called the room to attention.

Gao waved his hand. "As you were," he called out.

A tour of the building was not necessary. In addition to the operations center, Gao could see a small galley and eating area and a hallway that led to offices, berthing, and storage.

"The radar station has a contingent of ten, including myself," the commander said. "The SIGINT collection is automated. It sends all data immediately back to Beijing. The sub base is completely independent." He paused at the steel doors of a large elevator and pushed the button.

"How long have you been in command here?" Gao asked.

The elevator door opened, and the commander indicated they should enter. "Three years, sir."

"Who did you replace?"

The commander shrugged. "There was no turnover, sir. The station was deserted when my team arrived."

Gao exchanged a glance with Mei Lin. "When was that?"

"Just after the Taiwan conflict, Colonel."

Minister Fei covering his tracks, Gao mused.

"And the submarine base?"

"Also empty."

The elevator door opened. Gao smelled seawater and diesel fuel. The ceiling of the underground submarine base was lost in shadows behind the harsh glare of arc lights.

"Divers discovered there was a natural cavern here." The commander's boots echoed on the concrete pier. "Engineers enlarged it, expanded the channel to the sea, and added supports." He pointed to steel trusses that hugged the rocky wall. "The construction was completely covert. There are only two entrances. The elevator"—he pointed at the dark water of the submarine pen—"and the ocean. It's the only way that we can be sure that the American satellites don't see one of these."

The commander nodded at a PLA Navy submarine tied to the pier on the far side of the cavern, a *Kilo*-class diesel electric fast attack submarine. The sleek hull seemed to melt into the still, dark waters of the underground lagoon. A working party of four sailors were painting the conning tower of the vessel. The sound of their voices drifted across the water.

"How large a submarine can you accommodate here?" Gao asked.

The commander shook his head. "One hundred meters is the maximum for us. That's why the site was abandoned during construction."

"I'm sorry," Gao interrupted, "what did you say?"

"According to the records, construction on this site was halted after a year because the local geology limited the size of the structure. One hundred meters is too small to accommodate most modern submarines."

That's how the Minister got the site off the national registry, Gao thought.

"But you can accommodate smaller submarines," Gao said, pointing across the lagoon.

"Of course, sir."

"What about unmanned submarines, Commander?"

Unexpectedly, the commander grinned at Gao. "I thought you might be interested in the *Xi*, Colonel. I have something to show you."

He led them to a large office carved out of the rock. Gao blinked in the bright fluorescent lights. The commander strode to a rack of large drawings stored on vertical hangers and selected one. The stack of engineering blueprints made a slapping sound when he laid them on the table. The meter-wide drawings were crammed with engineering details and dimensions. The commander leafed through the pages.

"Here it is, sir." He tapped a pudgy finger on table.

Gao squinted at the drawing. He was looking at the outline of a submarine hull, but it was different than the one moored outside. This submarine had no conning tower, just a bump where the vertical structure of the submarine sail should have been.

"No need for a conning tower on an unmanned ship, Colonel," the navy man said. "The only reason we have them is to allow the crew to pilot the submarine on the surface. No crew, no conning tower." His finger slid down the page. "But that's not what I wanted you to see."

Gao looked where the man was pointing. "Explain, please, Commander."

"We found these drawings at the bottom of a locker. They're the only ones we have of the *Xi* prototype, but these notes show that someone modified the submarine. Here, in the cargo bay."

Gao leaned closer. There was a hand-drawn sketch inside the empty outline of the cargo bay. To his eye, it looked like a hook of some kind.

"What is it?" Gao asked.

The commander shrugged. "No way to know. It was big—I can tell from the dimensions—but there's no description."

Gao studied the sketch. Maybe a sling of some sort to hold another submarine? Or maybe mines? Then he noticed the faint outline of a hand-written character off to the side. The ideogram had been drawn in pencil and partially erased, but Gao could still make it out.

He felt his breath catch. "What does this mean?" He pointed at the symbol.

The commander's brow furrowed. "Dust? I have no idea, sir."

"I want to speak with someone who worked on this project, Commander," Gao demanded.

The man's eyes shifted away from Gao. "I can't do that, sir."

"I have the highest authorization—"

"I understand. That's not the issue, sir. There isn't anyone, Colonel," the commander said. "It should be easy, but..." His voice trailed off.

"But what?" Gao demanded.

"They're all dead, sir," the commander said. "Anyone who had anything to do with the *Xi* is gone. Dead."

"You're sure?" Gao said.

"There's no one left, sir," the commander said.

This is it, Gao thought. This is what the Minister was trying to hide, but what was it?

Gao's mind churned. Whatever had taken place here, it was a secret worth killing for, which meant it was big. It was also a secret that neither the General Secretary nor the current Minister of State Security was aware of, which meant the information was valuable in the right hands.

In his hands.

He tried to push aside what this meant to his career and failed. This was what he'd been searching for.

Stop! he chided himself. Focus on the work, and the rewards will follow.

"Commander," Gao said carefully, nodding to Mei Lin to take notes, "tell me everything you know about the *X1*. Then tell me everything you suspect."

There wasn't much more to tell. The cargo bay was big enough to hold at least a dozen mines or two submersibles. The commander had done some basic searches in the PLA Navy inventory, but his security clearance had not allowed for in-depth research.

"I would start with Admiral Chen," the commander said. "The handwriting on this drawing is his."

Mei Lin nodded, still writing furiously.

An hour later, they were in the elevator. Mei Lin held the engineering drawings in a bundle under her arm. A thought struck Gao as the elevator door closed.

"Commander, how was the *X1* controlled?"

"I would assume the same way as the unmanned submarines we have in operation now. The unit has a preloaded mission," the navy man replied. "The onboard AI allows autonomous submerged operations."

"But what if you needed to alter the mission parameters?" Gao pressed.

The elevator door opened, and the three walked outside. The bright sunshine felt good after the chill dampness of the subterranean chamber. Mei Lin, still juggling the drawings, got out her mobile phone and walked away to check Gao's messages.

"The only way to contact the sub after the initial mission is by satellite, sir," the commander said. "The ship is programmed to travel to periscope depth at scheduled intervals to establish a satellite link. As long as you had the ship operating system loaded on a transmitter, you could log in from anywhere."

Mei Lin hurried back into the building. A few seconds later, the helicopter pilot exited at a run and began preflight checks on his aircraft.

"Thank you, Commander. You've been very helpful. I'll make certain I put that in my report." The commander bowed to Gao, turned, and headed back inside the facility.

Gao drew Mei Lin aside. The expression on her face told him she had important news to share. "What is it?"

"Yichen," she said in an excited whisper. "They found him. The spy in South America. They have a lead on him."

Gao pumped a fist. It was all coming together now. First, capture the spy. Next, solve the mystery of the modifications to the unmanned submarine. Then...

Mei Lin gripped his arm. "You will be a general, my love," she whispered.

Gao settled the strap of the satchel firmly on his shoulder. The rotors on the helo began to turn.

"Get me on a plane to South America," he said.

12

Sterling, Virginia

Manson Skelly looked out the window in David Landersmann's office. He liked taking his daily updates in his chief of staff's office. Landie had a window. His own office—Abby's former office—had none. It was a security risk, she'd said. To Skelly, it made the room feel like a tomb.

Two days before Christmas, he thought, and not a snowflake in sight. When he went out for a run at midday, the temperature had been a balmy 63 degrees F. Hardly winter weather.

Across the desk, Landersmann, head bowed over his tablet, droned on. All of these updates were in a daily written briefing, but Landersmann knew that his boss wouldn't read the report. To make sure he covered his ass, Landersmann scheduled twenty minutes of executive time every afternoon where he tried to bring Skelly up to speed on the daily activities of his company.

Skelly let out a bored sigh. This was all stuff that Landersmann could handle on his own. His chief of staff was droning through a list of past-due accounts when Skelly interrupted him.

"Do kids still get snow days?" he asked.

Landersmann stopped talking, looked up. "What?"

"Snow days," Skelly said. "You know, when it snows hard and you get a day off from school. Does that still happen?"

The man followed his boss's gaze out the window to the bright Virginia afternoon. Landersmann cocked an eyebrow at Skelly. "What do I look like, Father of the Year?"

"I used to love snow days," Skelly said. "Like a little unexpected vacation, you know?"

Landersmann turned off his tablet and leaned back in his chair. "Maybe you should take a few days off, boss," he said. "It's Christmas. Things are slow around here."

The words rattled around in Skelly's head. Maybe I *should* take a few days off for Christmas, he thought. The problem was he had nowhere to go. For years, he spent the holidays with Joe and Abby. After Joe passed, Abby still invited him to celebrate with her family. Even when he suspected she was just doing it out of obligation, he still went. Every year.

Now, Abby was gone, too. Now, he had nothing.

He felt his jaw tighten and that itchy feeling that made him want to move. He sat up in his chair, gripped the armrests. "I don't need a vacation."

He turned his attention back to the window. He'd been calm just a few seconds ago, and he tried to force his mind to return to the same place.

I need a window in my office, Skelly decided. His office reeked of her, reeked of Abby Cromwell and her self-righteous bullshit attitude. She was long gone, but every time he walked in the door of the CEO's office at Sentinel, he still thought of her.

"I want a new office," Skelly announced.

"You're the boss, boss," Landersmann answered. "You can have whatever you want." His lips spread into his lopsided grin. "But before we start talking about fabric swatches, I think I have something that will interest you more. I saved the best for last."

It irritated Skelly when Landersmann did this kind of stuff. Always trying to make drama out of ordinary news. "Get on with it, Landie," he snapped.

Landersmann ignored the tone. He passed his tablet across the table. The photograph was of a Chinese man with long, unkempt hair and a ratty beard. Skelly automatically stroked his own thick beard as if comparing himself to the man in the photo. "What am I looking at, Landie?"

"That's who Don Riley's been trying to find in South America," Landersmann said, an air of satisfaction in his tone.

Skelly sighed. More drama. "Skip the big buildup. Just get to the punch line."

"Remember the security job at the nickel mine in Brazil? Rio São Salvador?"

Skelly tried to recall the details. They'd been hired to provide security for a board of directors' visit to a mine. A simple enough task, except six of his team managed to get into a bar fight the night before the visit. With a reduced security presence, the Green World people staged a massive demonstration the next day. Exactly the outcome the client was trying to prevent.

To avoid a lawsuit, Sentinel had been forced to refund the deposit on the job.

"That's the guy from the bar fight," Landersmann said. "He put four of our guys down before they took him out."

Skelly studied the photo with more intensity. "This guy?"

"That guy," Landersmann agreed. His grin grew more lopsided.

"What does the CIA want with him?" Skelly asked.

"They think he's the Naval War College bomber," Landersmann answered.

Skelly's gaze snapped back to the photo. "This guy? You're shitting me."

"Nope." Landersmann laced his fingers across his belly. "And that's not even the best part: Thanks to Riley, we've got a hit on his location."

Skelly slammed the tablet down on the desk. "Enough with the drama, Landie! Just tell me what the fuck is going on."

Landersmann's smile evaporated like rain on a hot sidewalk. "Fine, just trying to have a little fun." He placed his palms flat on his desk and continued.

"I've been putting all of Riley's intel on a delay so I can review it before it goes over to ETG. I figured out the Naval War College connection when I saw that Riley was shipping some of the search results off to Mossad." The lopsided grin made a brief appearance. "I know a guy, and he told me the rumor which I confirmed through my own people. I didn't bother you with it because Riley's searches turned up nothing.

"Then, a week ago, Riley started running all kinds of new searches. Used car sales, stolen cars, stolen license plates, that kind of thing. This morning, Mama got a hit."

He turned the tablet back on and swiped through the screens to a grainy photo. "Mama says that's our guy." He paused.

More drama, Skelly thought.

"Where is he?" Skelly said.

"That's an ATM camera in Calafate, Argentina."

Skelly sighed. "Where the fuck is Calafate?"

"Patagonia." Landersmann got out of his chair and walked to the world map on the wall. Red pushpins marked locations where Sentinel had current operations. Green pushpins indicated prior operations. Skelly noted with some satisfaction the coverage on the wall hanging.

"Here." Landersmann tapped a stumpy index finger on the bottom of South America. El Calafate looked to be midsized town located on a glacial lake at the foot of the snow-capped Andes.

"What's he doing there?" Skelly asked.

"I've been thinking about that," Landersmann said. "It's three thousand kilometers from where we last had him. Riley figured out that this guy was traveling by car and staying on the move, but he has to have a reason to go there, right?"

Skelly joined him at the map, and Landersmann continued. "This guy's a pro, and he's been in South America for a few years. He must have assets in place down there. Probably a legit business as a front."

Landersmann moved his finger to the left, stopping at the Andes mountain range. "If things get too hot, he can always disappear into the mountains. He'll just be another hiker, and we'd never find him. From there, he could cross the border into Chile. That would force the CIA to involve yet another country in their search."

"How much time do we have?" Skelly asked.

Landersmann shrugged. "Twenty-four hours? Maybe two days? The guy is making deliberate moves, but we know he's back in civilization, which means he wants something that he can't get on the road."

"Such as?"

"My guess? He's outfitting for a trip into the mountains." Landersmann sighed. "The guy's a planner, and he's smart—smart enough to stay one step ahead of Riley. That takes some brains."

Skelly snorted. Although he didn't like to admit it, Riley was a good analyst.

"Whaddaya want me to do, boss?" Landersmann asked.

Skelly pinched his lip. It didn't add up. The United States government was after the most wanted man in the world, and yet they had not employed Sentinel in the manhunt. Instead, they had done everything possible to exclude his company from the operation. He suspected the only reason they were even using Sentinel's AI was because of Riley, which would explain the man's insistence on secrecy. He'd even brought an authorization letter on White House letterhead.

Why? he wondered. *What am I missing?*

He knew one way to find out.

"Let me make a call," Skelly said. "I'll get back to you in a few minutes."

Skelly strode through the empty hallways to his office. Most of the staff had asked for the holidays off, and after the pace of the last few years, Skelly had been glad to meet their requests. Still, it felt weird not to have people all around him.

The feeling deepened when he entered his office. The ghost of Abby Cromwell seemed to be everywhere in this room. From the modern furniture to the glass table to the booze in the bar. None of it was his. It all reeked of Abby Cromwell.

Too jacked up to sit still, Skelly paced. He pulled his mobile phone from his hip pocket and dialed a number from memory. After two rings, a man picked up.

"Why are you calling me?" the man said. "I told you we were done."

"Merry Christmas, Irv," Skelly replied, mocking cheer in his voice. "I thought maybe we should get together for a drink. You know, celebrate the new year."

"I'm hanging up now, Skelly," Irving Wilkerson said.

"No, you're not," Skelly replied. "I know about the Naval War College bomber."

Skelly thought he could hear Wilkerson swearing under his breath on the other end.

"Cat got your tongue, Irv?" Skelly asked.

Silence.

"Did you think you could keep that from me?" Skelly put some heat in his tone now. "Really?"

"You defied a direct presidential order, Skelly. That search by Riley is supposed to be secret."

Skelly laughed. "Okay, you got me. I've been a bad boy. I think you should call up President Rick and tattle on me." He paused. "Then I'll fill him in on what I know, and we can all have nice chat."

Wilkerson sighed. "What do you want, Skelly?"

"I want in," Skelly said.

"Not possible." Wilkerson's voice was flat. "You're a contractor for the United States government and ineligible to collect the bounty."

"I don't want your money, Irv."

Wilkerson barked a laugh in the receiver. "You're all about the money, Skelly."

"If I bring him in," Skelly said, "what's it worth to you, Irv? I'll turn him over to Uncle Sam. No muss, no fuss. Serrano claims the win. What's that worth to your boss?"

"What's the catch?" Wilkerson's tone softened. "You don't do pro bono work."

"Don't be like that, Irv," Skelly said. "I served my country with honor. All I want is a little consideration."

Wilkerson sighed again. "Why do I suddenly have the urge to vomit?"

Skelly ignored him, pressing on. "At the end of the president's first term, it's customary for his cabinet to tender their resignations, right?"

Wilkerson's tone was guarded. "Where are you going with this, Skelly?"

"If I do my part and give Serrano the big win he's looking for, I want him to accept Kathleen Howard's resignation."

"Secretary of Defense?" Wilkerson blurted out. "You? Are you out of your fucking mind?"

"Think about it, Irv—"

Wilkerson interrupted him. "Even if he did—over my objections, mind you—there is no way you would get approved by the Senate. Not in a million years."

"Money talks, Irv," Skelly replied. "I know how to hire the best lobbyists, and I know how to write checks. Big checks."

"Not gonna happen, Skelly."

"Let's not be hasty," Skelly countered. "I'll catch your terrorist, then we can talk. How's that?"

"Goodbye, Skelly." Wilkerson hung up.

"I'll take that as a qualified yes," Skelly said into the dead phone.

He looked around the office that he hated so much. Maybe the answer wasn't to redecorate. Instead, why not just get a whole new office in a whole new building...like the Pentagon.

He thumbed down to his chief of staff's number.

"Boss," Landersmann said on the first ring.

"Call in the QRF, Landie. I want to be wheels up in four hours. We're going to bag us a terrorist."

"Roger that, boss," Landersmann replied. "What should I do about Riley?"

Skelly stroked his beard. "Feed him trash. I don't want him messing up my operation."

13

El Chaltén, Argentina

The setting sun made silhouettes of the mountain peaks to the west. The rocky fingers of Mount Fitz Roy and Cerro Torre thrust out of the earth, grasping at the darkening sky. The driver followed Rachel's gaze.

"You're lucky." Javier was late twenties, with a mop of curly dark hair and a quick smile. "Most of the time Fitz Roy is hidden behind the clouds. Some people visit the park and never even see the most famous mountain in Argentina."

They had passed a sign a half hour ago declaring that they had entered Los Glaciares National Park. Javier had been trying to draw her into a conversation ever since they'd left the town of El Calafate three hours ago, but Rachel resisted. She alternated between pretending to read the briefing material on her phone and staring out the window at the scenery.

They drove west, toward the Andes that loomed out of the ground like an ancient wall. The land outside was dry and desolate, not unlike her beloved Negev Desert. Sandy, rocky soil with scrubby brush and tufted grasses. Rachel was surprised to see a bird that looked like an ostrich stalking among the low shrubs. Javier, acting as unofficial tour guide, explained. "It's a rhea," he said, "and the small deer that look like llamas are called guanacos."

Rachel nodded her thanks, but did not break her silence.

Her driver's Spanish was flawless. While she had no doubt he could blend in with the locals, his level of field experience was wanting. If she was going to take down an international terrorist, she needed to rely on her team.

Team, she laughed to herself. She had Javier and his girlfriend, Angela, whom she knew even less about. Angela was already in the town of El Chaltén, casing the area and surveilling for any signs of their quarry.

This is what happens when you go off-book, Rachel, she chided herself.

After a possible ID of Diego Montalban in the city of El Calafate twenty-four hours ago, the tactical situation changed rapidly. For starters, Don Riley went silent. As in, no communications of any kind. She had worked with the CIA before and knew how politically sensitive operations generally went. Not all the decisions in the field were left to field operatives. Riley's silence meant that the Agency had gotten what they wanted from her, and Rachel's assistance was no longer needed or wanted.

Still, Rachel worked the problem—and came up with a lead. Actually, Javier was the one who came up with the lead. Working his local contacts, he found that a Chinese guy, speaking excellent Argentine Spanish, had bought a used car. The man's cousin recognized the car buyer as the owner of an outfitter in El Chaltén.

It was the barest thread of a lead, but it was all they had. Rachel dispatched Angela to the hiking town to check it out while she and Javier kept up the search in Calafate.

Three hours ago, Angela called with an update. There was a team of four men in town, which she classified as "professionals," and they were led by a Chinese man who looked and acted like People's Liberation Army.

Rachel was torn. She didn't know Angela, but had no reason to doubt her. Still, if she made the road trip to the remote hiking town and the lead didn't pan out, she'd have wasted an entire day.

A call to Don Riley went unanswered. She ended the call with a violent stab at the phone. She'd be damned if she'd leave a voicemail to a guy who was cutting her out of an operation—even if she owed her life to him.

They passed a road sign that read Capital Nacional del Trekking. Finally, as the setting sun lit up the famous Andean peaks, the vehicle topped a rise and the town of El Chaltén came into view.

It wasn't much of a town, a triangular-shaped settlement on the banks of the Río de las Vueltas, a wide, glacier-fed river that ran through the valley. On a bluff overlooking the town was a grand hotel, the largest building in sight by at least a factor of three. As Javier steered the car down the slope to where the highway turned into the main street, Rachel studied the layout of the town. Restaurants, mostly pubs and pizza joints, a small grocery store, and a few homes with signs advertising rooms for rent crowded the main thoroughfare. The streets running perpendicular to the main street were lined with smaller houses, then shacks, then camper trailers, and finally, tents.

Rachel had seen online that the permanent winter population of El Chaltén was only 350 people. But this was December, the height of the South American summer, and the town was packed for the Christmas holidays. Tour buses idled on side streets, camper trailers dotted the hillside, and the sidewalks were thick with pedestrians.

It's a perfect hiding place, Rachel thought. A large, multinational transient population to hide his ethnicity, easy access to wilderness where he could lose himself and slip across the border into neighboring Chile. If their intel was correct, Diego Montalban—or whatever his name was now—owned an outfitters store, which gave him ready access to everything he needed to make a run for it.

Everything made sense, and Rachel's assessment of her target rose another notch. She tried Riley again. No answer.

"What's the status of the Chinese team?" she asked Javier.

The driver read a text off his phone. "Angela says they seem to be searching the town on foot in pairs. They're not anywhere close to the target."

But they'll find him, Rachel thought. It might take them a few hours, but this was a small town, and there couldn't be that many men of Chinese ethnicity in the vicinity. She wondered if her quarry knew about the Chinese hit team after him.

She felt the pressure of the situation weighing down on her. Time was not her friend right now. Why isn't Riley answering his phone? she wondered with a flash of annoyance.

"Let's do a drive-by of the store," she said.

Javier nodded as he slowly navigated the crowded street. "Feliz Navidad," he muttered.

Rachel watched a young couple with a little boy, maybe six years old, holding his parents' hands as they trudged along the side of the street. He wore a miniature backpack, an exact replica of the ones his parents wore, and the expression on his face told everyone what he was thinking: *Look at me. I'm a big boy.* She watched him in the side mirror after they passed.

"What are we going to do?" Javier asked.

"Improvise," Rachel replied. She didn't bother to elaborate because she didn't know the answer. Yet.

Think, she ordered herself. Put yourself in his shoes. Even if the target didn't know about her or the Chinese team, he wouldn't stay here long. Mobility was his best weapon, no matter who was hunting him.

Rachel had to crane her neck to see the darkening peaks of the adjoining national park. The Andean wilderness was salvation for Diego Montalban. She couldn't let him get into the mountains; they might never find him again.

"It's the white building on the left," Javier said in a low voice. He slowed the car even more.

The structure had probably been a barn at some time in its history. The entrance was a half-dozen steps above the sidewalk. A wide porch led to a pair of wooden double doors. Through the front windows that flanked the doorway, Rachel could see walls lined with camping gear, backpacks, and racks of clothing.

A hundred meters past the store, the space between buildings lengthened and foot traffic thinned. Javier pulled the car under a tree on the side of the road. The back door opened, and a young woman got in.

"I'm pretty sure it's him," Angela said in a breathless tone. "I was able to get a few brief glimpses of him through field glasses."

"What about a picture?" Rachel asked.

In the dim interior of the vehicle, Rachel saw Angela shake her head.

"He lives in the back of the store and hasn't come outside all day. He has one employee. She left fifteen minutes ago."

"It has to be him," Javier said.

Rachel grimaced. Mossad files were full of incidents where operatives were sure of their targets—and they were wrong. Sometimes the cost of hubris was in lives lost.

"We have to be sure," Rachel said.

And then what? she thought. Her two team members were junior field agents at best. Well intentioned, but inexperienced. If she wanted to take him alive, she needed backup, a full tactical team.

But she was out of time. There was a Chinese team already in town, and they would find their man. It was inevitable.

Her mobile phone buzzed with an incoming text from a blocked number.

Your Uncle Habibi is ill. Pls call home ASAP.

Rachel felt a tug at her lips. Uncle Habibi was a code they'd used in field operations a long time ago. Noam's way of telling her that if she came in now, he would protect her. She tucked her phone into her hip pocket.

There was another way. If it was him, she could catch him off guard. With the element of surprise on her side, she could take him. It was a risky move, but a calculated one.

"I'm going in," she said.

Javier and Angela exchanged glances. "Is that a good idea?" Javier asked.

"No," Rachel replied, "but it's the best idea I've got right now. I want you to stay here. Be prepared to get out of here fast."

"What if something happens to you?" said Angela.

"If I don't come out, get out of here and report back to Mossad. They'll have guidance for you."

It was almost full dark as she climbed the steps of the store with the simple sign that read, *Casa de Equipo de Montaña*, with an English translation underneath, *Mountain Outfitter*. Light spilled out of the windows onto the planks of the porch. Cool night air made the skin on Rachel's forearms prickle into gooseflesh. When she pulled open the heavy wooden door, a bell tinkled overhead announcing her arrival. She scanned the interior. No other customers. No sign of her target.

Rough-hewn timbers served as supports for high ceilings. As she pretended to browse the merchandise that covered the walls, she picked out cameras looking down on the shop floor. Rachel made her way slowly toward the rear of the store.

Still no sign of Diego Montalban.

Ten meters into the store, a set of steps led down to a lower level. Along the back wall hung a selection of hatchets and hunting knives. In the center of the floor, a forest of fishing poles and reels stood erect. Racks of clothes filled the rest of the level.

Rachel hesitated. "Hello?" she called in Spanish.

"*Cerrado.*" The voice came from behind a curtain in the back wall that separated the hunting knives from the hatchets. *Closed.*

"I'm sorry," she replied in the same language. "I'm just looking for a..." Rachel's eyes fastened on the display of fishing tackle. "A fishing rod." She went down the steps, approached the drawn curtain. "Please."

"*Vale,*" the voice said. "*Momento, por favor.*"

The curtain parted, and Rachel was face-to-face with the most wanted man in the world.

Or not. She wasn't sure.

The man was of Chinese descent, but his hair was razor-cut and stylish. He was clean-shaven and wore modern horn-rimmed glasses. The whole effect made him look ten years younger than the picture she'd seen of Diego Montalban.

Rachel and the man were exactly the same height and standing barely a meter apart. His eyes were dark and alert, and he looked like he was about to smile.

"What are you after?" he asked in Spanish.

Rachel felt her body tense. She resisted the urge to look at the display of knives. She needed to be sure it was him. She needed more time. In English she responded, "What?"

He answered her in English. "What kind of fish are you trying to catch?"

He brushed past her, leaving a pleasant piney scent in his wake.

"Oh...I'm not sure."

Look at his ear, you idiot, Rachel screamed to herself.

The man paused but did not turn around. "You don't know what kind of fish you're after?"

Rachel flashed on the image of the little boy with the miniature backpack. "It's for my son," she said in a rush. "He's six. It's a surprise."

The man seemed to relax. Rachel got a good look at one ear and saw that it was normal. She tried to edge her way to the other side.

"Six years old? Let's keep it simple." He selected a rod and reel combo. "Spin casting is impossible to screw up." His head was still angled away from her, hiding his ear. He smiled. "How does that sound?"

Rachel forced herself to smile back, but she wanted to scream with frustration. It could be him, but she had to be sure. She pointed to the wall. "What kind of rod is that?"

The man swiveled his head, and his ear came into view.

The tip of his earlobe was missing.

Rachel didn't hesitate. She launched a strike at the side of his unprotected neck. A direct hit would put him down.

Maybe he saw a shadow or a reflection—Rachel would never know for sure. All she knew was that her body was committed to the strike and his neck was no longer there.

The man twisted away from her and down. Her fist clipped the side of his head, but he was still spinning. Using his momentum, he launched a kick into her midsection.

Breath blasted out of her lungs. Rachel crashed back into the display of hatchets. Her fingers scrabbled at the wall, searching for a weapon. She latched onto a handle, pulled.

The hatchet blade caught on the display hook. It was only a split second, but it left her wide open for a punishing punch to the jaw. The store whipped by in a burst of color as her head snapped around.

The hatchet came free, and she slammed the flat of the blade against the side of his skull. His hold on her arm loosened. Gripping the hatchet handle, Rachel pushed herself off the wall.

But as soon as she was upright, she felt her legs sweep out from under her.

Rachel fell backward. Her back hit the floor, and whatever air was still left in her lungs went away.

His knee trapped the hand with the hatchet. Fingers clamped around her neck, and Rachel knew she was done.

Everything went black.

14

Comandante Armando Tola International Airport
El Calafate, Argentina

Coffee cup in hand, Manson Skelly paced the floor of the aircraft hangar. Through the open doors, past the parabolic comms dish his team had set up, the setting sun showed as a sawtooth pattern against the distant Andes. The surface of the nearby glacial lake looked like rippling gold.

He'd never been this far south before. The land here was dry and stark, reminding Skelly of Afghanistan—except that people weren't shooting at him here.

At least, not yet.

He took a swig of the truly terrible coffee and smiled to himself. This was what real power felt like. Power that had the potential to change history.

A mere eighteen hours ago, he'd been sitting on his ass in Sterling-freaking-Virginia, and now he was at the bottom of the world preparing to take down an international terrorist.

After that, he thought, the sky's the limit. Once I have that rat bastard in my mitts, Wilkerson will offer me a blow job on Pennsylvania Avenue at high noon for a chance to tell the world that his precious president had captured the Naval War College bomber.

God, how I love my job.

He approached a folding table where three techs were hunched over laptops.

"Anything yet?" he asked.

Peter Quinn was Sentinel's twentysomething head geek who seemed to think that ponytails were still cool. He had thin shoulders, a milky-white neck, and an attitude that rubbed Skelly the wrong way.

Without looking up, Peter replied, "I told you before, Skelly. When I have a solid satellite link with Mama, you'll be the first to know."

Skelly clamped a meaty hand on the back of Peter Ponytail's neck. He wrenched the kid's head backward so he could look him in the eye.

"When I ask you a question, I expect you to look at me, Peter. It's a sign of respect." He gave him a shake as he released his nape.

Peter blinked rapidly, rubbed the back of his neck. The other techs didn't look up from their screens.

Skelly pointed at his laptop. "Get back to work."

He stalked to the other side of the hangar where the assault team was assembling. The quick reaction force that Sentinel kept on standby in the Washington, DC, area was normally five people. He'd managed to scrape up Pavel Kozlov and one other operator who happened to be in the area. That gave him two fire teams of four. One led by Skelly and the other by Kozlov.

The teams were all-male, which Skelly preferred, and they knew each other well. A running banter flowed between the men as they checked their gear.

Skelly watched them run through comms checks with their throat mics, verify functionality of their IR strobes, and double-check the batteries on their night vision gear—a lesson learned the hard way by US Special Operations Forces in Mogadishu in October of 1993.

Each man carried an assault rifle, sidearm, and combat knife of their own choosing, all paid for by the company.

Each team had a demolitions man, and they inventoried their explosives load in an area separate from the main force. They spread the tools of their trade on a tarp. Prefabricated breaching charges with attached wire spools would work on concrete up to six inches thick. They also carried spare blocks of C-4 and other sundries, such as electrical tape and wire cutters. Detonators and det cord were kept segregated from all the other supplies.

Two men prepped the Gremlins, small unmanned aerial drones used for short-duration ISR missions and electromagnetic jamming. Finally, two more men verified functionality on the infrared detectors. The handheld devices were capable of picking out heat signatures through walls at a hundred meters.

Skelly finished his impromptu tour next to Kozlov, who was also watching the preparations. Kozlov looked up. "Do we have a location yet?"

Skelly grunted. "There's a hippie town about a hundred and twenty miles north of here. Unfortunately, no airport, so we have to drive."

"We're sure he's there?"

Skelly looked over his shoulder. "As soon as Peter Ponytail gets his shit together, we'll get some hard intel and we can go mobile."

Skelly kept his tone light, but Kozlov had voiced his greatest fear. The intel placing him at the hiking town was low confidence.

Popular tourist town in the middle of nowhere, only accessible by car, at the peak of the holiday season and filled with people from all over the world. If this guy wanted to send his pursuers off on a wild goose chase, this was the perfect place to do it.

For all Skelly knew, the guy was sipping a cocktail in the airport lounge across the tarmac. If he committed his men to the long drive to El Chaltén, he would lose the ability to react to new information.

To cover his bases, as soon as the Sentinel jet touched down in Argentina, Skelly put two men on the road to El Chaltén. They carried a four-pack of Gremlin drones to survey the town. With Mama's facial recognition program, they'd find their target the minute he showed his face in public.

Of course, that plan depended on a satellite link with Mama, which Peter *still* had not delivered.

Kozlov looked around the hangar. Skelly could see him adding up the cost of the private jet flight to South America, the three technicians, the satellite dish, and the eight operators getting hazard pay and holiday rates. This operation was costing a small fortune.

"It's a lot of cheddar for one guy, Skelly."

Skelly laughed at him. "Cheddar?"

Kozlov reddened. "Cheddar means money, no? I'm trying to learn American slang."

"Yeah, Pavel. Cheddar means money."

"Well?" Kozlov asked.

"Well, what?" Skelly snapped.

"Is this guy worth all the money?" Kozlov asked. "How much are we getting paid for this?"

Skelly's jaw locked. Technically, Kozlov was a partner in Sentinel, but he was supposed to be a silent partner. And Skelly did not appreciate having his decisions questioned.

Besides, Skelly was getting paid in currency much more valuable than money. He had all the money he needed. What he needed now was something that couldn't be bought.

"It's above your pay grade, Pavel," Skelly answered. "Do your job. Let me worry about the details."

He could tell by the look on the other man's face that was the wrong answer, but they were interrupted by a shout from the opposite side of the hangar. When Skelly turned, he saw Peter standing over his laptop, fists raised in triumph.

"The link with Mama is active," he announced. "We have full bandwidth, too."

Skelly stood behind him, peering over his shoulder. "How long before we get an intel update?"

Peter didn't look up. "Mama's chewing on the first tranche of data from the Gremlins now. She'll need a minute."

Skelly felt the tablet in the pocket of his cargo pants buzz. When he answered the video call, Landersmann's lopsided grin appeared on Skelly's screen.

"Riley took the bait, boss," his chief of staff announced. "Hook, line, and sinker. The CIA is on a plane to nowhere."

"Good work, Landie," Skelly answered. "I always knew you were a lying son of a bitch."

Landersmann's face grew serious. "Boss, when Riley figures this out, he's gonna be pissed. You got a plan for that?"

Skelly laughed. "Landie, the day I worry about Don Riley being angry at me is the day I die."

"Okay, your funeral, bossman. Don't say I didn't warn you."

"Fuck you, Landie."

"Fuck you back, boss." Landersmann ended the call.

Skelly continued smiling at the blank screen. Don Riley, he thought. What a clown.

"Manson?" Peter's voice rose above the din of activity in the hangar. "You need to see this."

Skelly resumed his post behind the ponytailed technician. "What am I looking at?"

Peter's screen showed a picture of a Chinese man with a crew cut standing on a crowded street talking into a mobile phone.

"This guy," Peter said. "Mama's tagged him as Chinese special forces."

Skelly swore under his breath. Somehow, the Chinese had beat him to the prize.

"Saddle up, people," he roared across the hangar. "We're on the road in five minutes."

He turned back to where Peter was still working the laptop. "The guy's packing." Peter pointed to a bulge under the man's left shoulder. "But that's not what I'm worried about."

The sound of boots on the ground filled the hangar as the operators double-timed toward the waiting SUVs.

"I don't have a lot of time, Peter," Skelly said in a growl. "Spell it out for me."

"Who's he talking to?" Peter replied.

"Can you get close enough with a Gremlin to listen in?" Skelly asked.

Peter shook his head. "He might notice, and then we're really screwed."

"I got another one," the technician across from Peter said in an excited voice. "Sending it to you now, Pete."

Peter split his screen. A new image showed up of another man of Chinese descent. This one had longer hair and a wispy beard.

"Is that him?" Skelly asked, a note of anxiety in his voice.

"Analyzing with facial rec." Peter's fingers flew over the keyboard. "Mama says no, but this guy is packing too." He looked up at Skelly. "We've got at least two competitors on the ground, probably three, if number one is talking to someone."

Skelly threw his empty coffee cup. It hit the steel wall of the hangar and shattered.

He tried to marshal his racing thoughts. The drive to El Chaltén was three hours, two and a half if they made good time. The Chinese had been on site for who knew how long. That meant two things to Skelly. One, the man they were both after was probably in that town. Two, unless he changed the rules of the game in a major way—and fast—he was going to lose this contest.

There had to be a better way. His gaze slid past the hangar doors, past the parabolic dish, to where an Argentine Air Force helicopter was parked on the twilit tarmac.

Skelly barked out, "Max!"

A burly man in his early thirties with a blond crew cut trotted up. His bulging biceps strained against the sleeves of his T-shirt.

"Yeah, boss."

Skelly pointed out the open hangar door. "Can you fly that?"

Max shrugged. "Sikorsky S-76. It's an early version of the UH-60. As long as I had someone in the copilot seat who was a good navigator and talked me through the Spanish labels and shit, I could fly the hell out of it. Sure."

Kozlov joined them. "What's the plan, Skelly?"

Skelly grinned. "Max is going to get a bonus." He pointed to the helicopter. "And I'm going to requisition a better form of transportation."

"How are you going to do that?" Kozlov asked.

"You know what the first rule of being a rich fuck is?" Skelly asked.

"No, what?"

"Everybody has a price," Skelly called over his shoulder as he trotted out the door. "Everybody."

15

El Chaltén, Argentina

Diego leaned back against the wall and studied the woman tied to the chair in the middle of his kitchen. She was his height, and he judged her to be roughly his age as well. The smooth, dark skin of her left cheek was swollen, and the right side of her head was matted with blood. That was the blow that had finally knocked her out.

He rubbed his hand against the growing bruise on the side of his own head. The woman was lightning fast and a strong fighter. She'd nearly gotten the drop on him. A reflection in a glass display case had given her away at the last second. Diego reacted out of sheer instinct—and that had made all the difference in the outcome.

But that still didn't answer the question of the moment: *Who is she?*

He turned to the kitchen table. She carried a mobile phone, obviously a burner, and no ID. The tags in her clothes had all been removed, and most of them were brands common all over the world. Her shoes were Adidas, relatively new and labeled for sale in the European Union.

What she didn't carry was a weapon of any kind. No gun, no knife, nothing.

Diego rubbed his head again. Not that she needed a weapon.

He wondered if she had backup still outside. She obviously knew who he was, and yet she'd come into his store, alone and unarmed. None of it made sense.

He made a quick circuit of his apartment, checking that doors and windows were secure. Besides the kitchen, there was his bedroom, a bath, and a small study. A trapdoor leading to a root cellar was hidden under the rug in the study.

This had been the original structure built almost a hundred years ago. The thick whitewashed stone walls and shuttered windows were designed for shelter from the harsh Patagonian winters. Today they made a strong defensible position if he needed to buy time for an escape.

There were two entrances to the house. A stout wooden door at the back of the kitchen and an entrance to his store through what had once been the front door of the dwelling. He reentered the dark store, making his way to the front windows where he stood for a few minutes, watching the street. The outfitters store was located on the edge of the hiking town. The bar across the street was doing a brisk holiday business as evidenced by the party that had spilled onto the sidewalk. He could just barely make out the sounds of voices speaking in many languages. Indeed, one of the primary reasons why he'd chosen this location was for the large transient population, including a regular influx of foreigners.

The Minister had taught him well. Hide in plain sight, become an invisible part of the community. As an elite operative for the Ministry of State Security, he'd set up dozens of front companies. He'd learned how to hide business registrations behind shell corporations, move funds in and out of business accounts, and blend in with his surroundings. He checked that the alarm system in the store was armed and padded back into his house.

The woman's head was still lolled to one side, exactly as he'd left her. Diego checked the security cameras he had surrounding his property. The night vision cameras penetrated the dark of the Argentinian night. The ghostly green images on his laptop screen all looked still.

All was quiet. Too quiet, he reflected. Who was this woman, and why had she come after him alone?

He armed the perimeter alarms set at the rear of his property. If anyone approached, he would have a few minutes' warning.

Run, he thought. Kill her and go. Get as far away from this place as possible.

And then what?

Start over. Again. A new face, a new place, a new life.

First, I need some answers. True, he'd made a mistake helping the woman in Brazil, but how had they found him so fast?

Diego crossed to the kitchen sink and soaked a washcloth in cold water, his mind still running through his options. He was tired of running, but this life was all he had left...

He pressed the wet washcloth against the woman's bruised cheek. Her head twisted, and she sank her teeth into the meat of his palm.

Diego yelped in surprise, then reached behind his back and pulled out his Beretta APX compact 9mm. He pressed the muzzle of the weapon against her forehead, jacking her head back.

"Let go," he hissed, "or I will kill you."

She relaxed her jaws, and he snatched his hand away. The bite was deep, and he let the blood flow to clean the wound. Diego heard drips spatter to the floor at his side.

The woman bared her bloodstained teeth at him like a wild animal.

"Is that what they taught you at Mossad?" Diego said. The bite was deep, and it hurt like hell. Dammit, she was fast.

Her face changed, just for an instant, but enough for him to realize his guess had landed. It all fell into place now. The shoes, the fighting style.

"Ex-Mossad, now a bounty hunter," Diego said in disgust. He saw the flare of anger in her eyes and realized he'd missed the mark. Not a bounty hunter? He covered his surprise by getting a fresh towel out of the drawer and binding his hand.

"What's your name?" he said.

Silence.

Diego pushed the gun back into his waistband, trying to process what he knew. Active-duty Mossad, but why were the Israelis looking for him?

When the answer came to him, he turned to the sink and ran the water to cover his shock.

The Americans, he realized. Mossad had no desire to capture him, but they would help the United States...which means the Americans knew who and where he was. Diego felt his heart rate tick up.

But why was she alone? It made no sense. When the Americans came after a target, they came in force.

"I'm not a bounty hunter," the woman said. Diego turned to face her. "And I have backup coming."

Diego raised his eyebrows, threw his arms wide. "Where are they?"

The woman's eyes roved around the room. He knew what she was doing because it was exactly what he would do. She was looking for opportunities, anything that she could turn to her advantage if and when she had the chance.

Maybe the best approach is the truth, he thought.

"You're working for the Americans," Diego said.

The woman raised her chin. That was a yes, Diego decided.

"Why are you alone?" he pressed. "Do you have any idea how dangerous I am?"

The woman's eyes dropped to his bandaged hand, and she laughed.

"They're wrong about me," Diego said. "I was just following orders."

"I'm Jewish." She made no attempt to hide the contempt in her voice. "Do you realize how lame that sounds?"

Diego looked away. Of course, she was right, but things weren't always what they seemed.

"I was nine years old when he recruited me," Diego said. "The Minister raised me like his own son. Trained me to kill like I was his pet lion."

"I think you mean snake," the woman said.

Diego shrugged. "You're right," he said. "I did those things, but I was just—"

"Following orders?" He heard the acid in her voice, and it burned. "You didn't know what would happen when you drove a tug full of diesel oil and fertilizer onto the beach in front of the Naval War College? You thought you were going to have a picnic?"

Diego felt his skin crawl. How many nights he had replayed that moment in his own head? He hadn't known for sure what was on the tug, but he should have guessed. What was it the Minister told him over and over again: *Do not question orders, act. Always, act.*

Maybe this is my time, he thought. I'm tired of running. Another face, another place, another day looking over my shoulder.

The phone on the kitchen table buzzed with an incoming text.

"That would be my backup." The woman's tone was smug.

Diego looked at the phone. The text was in Hebrew. He held the screen so she could see it.

"What does it say?" he asked.

He saw her swallow; her skin paled. "The Chinese are here."

Diego turned to his laptop, began searching through the video screens. "If you want to live, you better start talking," he said.

"My name is Rachel Jaeger," she said in a low voice. "I work for Mossad, but I'm on loan to the CIA."

"Why are you alone?"

"I—I was following a lead," she said. "It was a hunch mostly, but—"

"Where is your backup?" he demanded.

"There's two outside. I told them to stay back, that I'd handle you—"

"How many are coming?"

"Four, we think," Rachel said, her tone urgent. "It's a hit team. They'll kill us both. You have to let me go."

Diego made the decision. He turned and sliced through the bonds holding the Mossad agent's hands.

"There's another Beretta under the sink. You can shoot me and die or help me and live. Your choice, Rachel Jaeger."

16

El Chaltén, Argentina

Out of the corner of her eye, Rachel saw a silver flash, and the bindings on her wrists fell away.

"You can shoot me and die or help me and live. Your choice, Rachel Jaeger."

The sound of her name electrified Rachel into action. The knife caught the light as he tossed it to her. She bent down, cut her legs free, and stood. Her hands and feet tingled as new blood flowed into her extremities.

Rachel looked at the blade in her hand. Diego's back was to her as he studied the laptop screen.

Why is he trusting me? Rachel thought. I tried to kill him an hour ago and now...he's trusting me. Why?

Rachel snatched her phone off the table and dialed Javier's number from memory.

"Don't be a fool, Rachel," Diego said. "I know these men. Your friends are dead already. And if you don't listen to me, you'll be dead as well."

Beep-beep-beep.

"Perimeter alarm." Diego tapped the laptop to silence the noise. "There you are," he muttered.

Rachel saw movement on one of the windows on the laptop screen. A Chinese man, face set with deadly intent, advanced toward the kitchen door at a steady pace, weapon up.

"I'll take the two in the store." Diego punched another button on his laptop, and the room plunged into darkness. "You've got the guy out back. Don't screw it up."

He disappeared down the hall, leaving her standing in the middle of the dark kitchen.

She reached under the sink, her hand closing on the butt of a Beretta APX. The .45-caliber handgun was a reassuring weight in her grip.

Part of her wanted to go after Diego and take him out, but there would be time enough for that later. The immediate threat was the man coming for the kitchen door.

She turned the laptop so the screen faced the door. Then she unlocked the deadbolt and stepped into the space behind the door.

Rachel closed her eyes to block out the glare of the laptop. She focused on her breath and the sounds on the other side of the door. She pressed the barrel of the handgun against her thigh until she felt the metal dig into her flesh.

Seconds passed. She heard nothing. Rachel clenched her eyes together, took shallow breaths, and focused on the sounds of the night.

The tick of the kitchen clock, the gentle whirr of the laptop, the scuff of a shoe against grass...

He was outside the kitchen door, their faces only centimeters away from each other but separated by wood and stone.

Rachel tried to put herself in his shoes. He was alone. He probably believed Diego was alone as well. If he was in contact with the others who had entered the store adjoining the house, he would know Diego was not in the kitchen.

Would he breach the door or try the lock? He would opt for stealth. He would try to enter the kitchen and take Diego from the rear.

She opened her eyes. In the glare of the laptop, she saw the knob on the door, worn smooth by countless hands, begin to turn slowly. There was a tiny rubbing sound as the door separated from the jamb, then the heavy door eased open.

The muzzle of a gun poked into the room, a suppressor fitted onto the weapon. The person holding the weapon had two hands on the grip. The door opened wider. She saw two wrists, then two black-clad forearms.

Rachel threw her weight against the door, trapping the pair of hands against the jamb. She put her weapon against the back of the man's collapsed hands and pulled the trigger.

The sound of the gunshot in the tiny, stone-walled kitchen was deafening. The door exploded open, throwing her backward. Rachel bounced off the wall and rolled away. She came up on one knee, weapon up, but her Chinese attacker was faster. He advanced into the room and kicked out. Her second shot went into the ceiling, and the gun flew out of her hands.

The glare of the laptop screen reduced the room to black and white, shadow and light. The man rushed at her, his extended hands streaming black blood. Rachel seized the hands and drove her fingers into the bloody mess, twisting and tearing. She heard him grunt with pain, and she dug her fingernails into his mangled flesh.

She allowed his forward momentum to carry her backward. Kicking out with her feet, still gripping his injured hands, she pushed off his midsection and threw him over her head. With one final vicious twist of broken bone and sinew, she released his slick, bloody hands.

Where was her gun? She scanned the floor for her weapon, but it was lost in the shadows. Rachel scrambled to her knees, lunging forward.

A huge weight landed on her back. Rachel's body smashed against the floor as her attacker drove both knees into her kidneys. His arm wrapped around her neck, her chin tucked into the V formed by the crook of his elbow. Her windpipe slammed closed. He cranked her head backward, and Rachel felt the vertebrae in her neck pop like an opening zipper. She felt the blood from his injured hands run down her back. Her vision started to waver.

But the height also gave her a new perspective on the shadowy kitchen floor.

There, less than a meter away, lay her attacker's gun. Right where he'd dropped it when she put a bullet through both his hands.

Her breath was no more than a wheeze as she threw her arm out. Her fingertips slipped on the blood-slick butt of the weapon. Her vision closing in, Rachel summoned every bit of strength in her body and bucked her torso forward. She gained a scant centimeter, but it was just enough.

Her fingernails scrabbled at the grip, nudging the handgun into reach. Her index finger snaked around the trigger. She angled the muzzle behind her, laid the smooth bulk of the silencer against her skull, and pulled the trigger.

She felt the heat of the muzzle flash against her skin.

Rachel pulled the trigger again and again and again. The pressure around her neck eased, and she lowered her face to the stone floor.

When Rachel opened her eyes, she was on her back, the glare of the kitchen lights burning into her retinas.

"I should tie you up again, but I'm afraid your chair is occupied," Diego said. His voice sounded very far away.

When Rachel lifted her head, she felt her cheek peel off the floor. Blood, she realized, but she wasn't sure if it belonged to her or her attacker.

Rachel got to her hands and knees, trying not to throw up. Her back felt like she'd been placed on some medieval torture device, and her pulse banged in her ears like a snare drum. She closed her eyes, carefully twisted her body until her back was against the wall, and relaxed.

"Nice job, by the way." Diego pointed across the room.

The man who had attacked her was unrecognizable, his face a pulpy mess of bloody tissue. Rachel felt her stomach lurch.

"Remind me never to piss you off," Diego continued.

Rachel scanned the room, looking for a weapon. Nothing.

"I have the guns over here." Diego pointed to the kitchen table, next to his laptop, which by some minor miracle was still untouched. "Don't get any ideas. I don't want to tie you up again."

He went to the sink, filled a cup with water, and squatted down next to her.

"Your friends are dead." His dark eyes searched her face. "Man and woman, mid-twenties, driving a black Fiat Cronos, right?"

Rachel nodded. What was the point in lying?

"I'm sorry." He handed her the water. "The police don't get a lot of murders here. They'll be chasing their tails for a while."

Rachel sipped the water. The cool liquid felt like fire on her raw throat.

"I have a proposal," Diego said.

Rachel didn't know if she could talk yet, so she nodded.

"I'll share whatever I get from this guy"—he jerked a thumb over his shoulder—"then we go our separate ways. If we meet again, you're welcome to kill me."

Tied up in the same chair she had occupied only a few minutes before was a Chinese man. He looked vaguely familiar, especially the scar on the side of his face, but her bruised brain couldn't place him.

Diego stepped close to the man and pulled down his gag.

"Rachel Jaeger, meet Major Gao Yichen, the Hero of Taiwan."

"*Nánhái*," the man said in a voice that oozed contempt. "*Pantu*."

Traitor. Rachel knew enough Mandarin to recognize that word, but she'd never heard the term *nánhái* before.

Diego backhanded the prisoner. "Speak English, Major. We have a guest."

"Senior colonel." Gao spat blood on the floor.

"Multiple promotions?" Diego replied. "Wonderful. It's good to know that sucking cock can still get you promoted in the PLA. Let's see what you've brought along with you."

Rachel got to her feet, holding the wall for support. "What did you do to my people?" she demanded.

Her tangled thoughts came in a rush. She'd dragged Javier and Angela into this slapdash operation. Her actions had gotten them killed. This whole thing had been a huge, horrible mistake. Noam was right all along: she had no business being back in the field.

She felt her stomach flip, and Rachel wondered if she was going to be sick.

Diego unzipped a small leather satchel and dumped the contents onto the kitchen table. Rachel noted a handful of protein bars, a bottle of water, a black leather notebook the size of her open palm, and a small laptop.

"Do you recognize them?" Gao asked. He was watching Diego as if gauging his reaction. "They belong to your master. Minister Fei."

Diego picked up the notebook and opened it, running his fingers down the page. "He's dead, isn't he?"

"Very," Gao agreed, still watching Diego intently.

"Why do you have it?" Diego asked quietly.

"I'm looking for *huichen*," came the reply.

The effect was instantaneous. Diego's head snapped around, and he gripped Gao by the throat. "What did you say?" he whispered.

"*Huichen*," Gao rasped.

"What do you know about it?" Diego demanded.

Rachel cleared her ears. Her hearing was coming back slowly and muddled. She heard a steady pulsing sound in the distance. That was a new sensation, but then again, she'd never fired off six suppressed rounds right next to her ear before.

Rachel ignored the conversation. She had no idea what the word *huichen* meant and didn't care. The rhythmic whapping sound became more insistent, and Rachel cleared her ears again.

She retrieved her phone from the table. The police would have Javier's mobile by now. She needed to destroy the burner. She looked at the screen.

No signal.

Odd, she'd had five bars earlier.

Whup-whup-whup-whup.

Her body was playing tricks on her. She could actually *feel* the noise now.

But Diego had let go of Gao's chin, and he was looking up. He could hear it, too. It wasn't her imagination.

It was a helicopter.

The ceiling exploded in shards of plaster, wood, and tile. The lights burst in a flash of incandescence.

Rachel opened her mouth to scream, but the sound of the heavy-caliber slugs ripping into the house drowned out all other noises.

She felt someone grip her hand, jerk her off her feet. She hit the floor, and he dragged her body from the room. In flashes of light, she saw Diego like a stop-motion movie. He ripped a rug off the floor, lifted a trapdoor, and threw her into the opening.

As Rachel tumbled down a set of rough wooden stairs, the trapdoor slammed down behind them. The sound dampened. Lights flashed on.

Rachel blinked. They were in a root cellar. Rough stone walls, earthen floor, wooden steps digging into her back. Diego latched the trapdoor shut and flipped a switch by the top step.

"That'll slow them down." He dropped down the steps and hauled Rachel to her feet. Every muscle in her body screamed in protest. "We need to go."

The cellar extended twenty feet, ending in a heavy wooden shelf lined with dust-covered jars. We're trapped, Rachel thought.

Careful not to disturb the patina of dust, Diego reached around the edge of the shelf and felt along the wall.

Chonk. The shelf opened on a hinge, and Rachel felt a cool breeze on her bruised cheek. A rucksack hung from a peg on the wall next to a flashlight on a loop.

The shooting ceased. Diego raised his head as the sound of the helo got closer.

"They're landing." He turned on the flashlight, and the strong beam probed deep into the tunnel. "I hope you're not claustrophobic."

He slung the rucksack on his shoulder and stepped into the opening. He turned, held out his hand. "Are you coming?" he asked.

Rachel took his hand and stepped inside the tunnel.

17

El Chaltén, Argentina

Through what was left of the roof, a spotlight pinned Gao in place. He dropped his head to his chest, clenched his eyes shut against the cyclone of dust and debris that whirled around his body, cut into the skin of his face. His brain told him he was screaming, but he couldn't hear anything over the roar of the helicopter rotors.

Whump-whump-whump. The downdraft created by the aircraft compressed his body down into the chair. He couldn't breathe. He felt his spine buckle, his head slip to one side until his ear was smashed against his shoulder.

Then the light was gone, the column of air collapsed, the suspended debris from the shattered room rained to the floor.

Gao opened his eyes. The kitchen door, somehow still in one piece, opened and a stack of four men entered. They wore night vision goggles and their rifles had laser sights. The red beams, visible in the dust, quartered the room.

Three men fanned out from the kitchen; one stayed by Gao's side. They moved with the calm, unhurried precision of professionals.

Then Gao heard their voices. "Clear!" Then another, with the same word.

More English words, and he recognized American accents.

Gao felt a tremor taking over his thigh muscles. What would an American black-ops team do to a Chinese national on foreign soil illegally? Gao knew what he would do—what he had done in the past, in fact. His mind flashed back to a fight on a Taiwanese mountainside with an American Marine. He'd killed the Marine that night and left his body to rot. These men were comrades in arms to the man he'd killed.

There's no way they could know about that, he told himself. No way.

But his heart raced all the same.

He thought of Mei Lin and the life they'd started together. Gao strained at his bonds. He had to get out of here.

The man standing next to him pressed the muzzle of his rifle against the side of Gao's neck.

"Don't move," he said.

Gao froze. Who were these people?

"Papa Bear, Bravo leader," said the man next to him. "Building is secure. One hostile in custody—"

"Not hostile," Gao began. "I am—"

The rifle muzzle dug into the flesh of his neck. "I don't care." The man had a thick Russian accent.

Gao heard the helo drop to the ground, then ascend again.

"All units," said the Russian man into a microphone, "be advised Papa Bear is on the ground."

The kitchen door swung back against the wall and another man entered, talking into his microphone.

"Put the pilot on the radio with local police, and tell them this is a military operation." He paused, listening. "Fine. Tell him there's another ten grand in it for him, but it better be an Oscar-worthy performance."

"House is clear, Skelly," the Russian man said. "Perimeter's secure. No sign of the others."

The man called Skelly switched on a wide-beam flashlight, illuminating the shredded kitchen. His footsteps crunched through the debris of roof tiles, wood, linoleum, and stone littering the floor. Clouds of dust rose in his wake.

"Doesn't matter, Pavel," Skelly said. He pulled down his balaclava, and Gao could see a full beard, dark hair shot with gray. His eyes were hidden behind the glare of the flashlight on his glasses, but his smile was wide and mocking.

He patted Gao on the cheek. "Doesn't matter because we have ourselves the Naval War College bomber right here!"

It took Gao a full second to translate the words in his head, then another full second to realize the importance of what they meant.

"No!" he shouted. "Not me!"

Skelly crouched down so he was eye level with Gao, then he pulled off his glasses. His smile widened, and he assumed a look of mock sympathy. "Don't tell me"—he pressed an index finger to his lips—"you're innocent, right?"

Gao's breaths came fast and hard. He felt himself hyperventilating, and he wanted to throw up.

"My name..." He paused for breath.

Calm down, you fool, he thought. Tell them everything. It's your only chance.

"My name is Senior Colonel Gao Yichen," he said in as even a tone as he could muster. "I am a member of the People's Liberation Army." His mind raced forward. "I have diplomatic immunity," he lied.

Skelly sat back on his heels and shone the flashlight full in Gao's face.

"Pavel."

"Yeah?"

"Gimme a picture of the guy we're after."

The light went away, and Gao blinked through the purple afterimages. The man called Pavel pulled a tablet from his pocket and turned it on. He swiped through screens, then handed it to Skelly.

Skelly put his fingers under Gao's chin and cranked his head back until Gao was looking straight up. Skelly held the glowing tablet next to Gao's face.

Through the collapsed roof, Gao saw the night sky. Thousands of stars looked down on him, and he wondered if he would live to see another night.

"These people all look alike to me," Skelly said. "Let's take him with us."

"It's not him, Skelly," Pavel said. "Look at the notes on the picture."

"What?"

"The note says that he's missing the tip of his earlobe," Pavel continued. He gripped Gao's face and turned his head until his cheek was pressed against his shoulder. "Look...his earlobe is intact."

"Fuck me," Skelly raged. He drew his sidearm and pressed the muzzle into the center of Gao's forehead. "Start talking, asshole, or I will paint this room with your brains."

"I...am...Senior Colonel Gao—"

"Yeah, we got that part," Skelly interrupted. "PLA, diplomatic immunity, blah, blah. Tell me about the terrorist. Was he here?"

"Y-yes," Gao stammered.

"Where the fuck is he?" Skelly straightened up, removing the gun from Gao's head.

"There's a trapdoor in here," a new voice called out. "It's—"

Bang!

The sharp explosion froze the room into silence.

"Booby trap!" a man shouted. "Timmins is down." A pause. "He's dead."

"Jesus Christ!" Skelly thundered. "This is like a fucking daycare."

"Skelly," the man called Pavel said. "The cops are getting insistent. The pilot says he's done everything he can."

Gao watched two men carry a limp body out of the kitchen. Skelly stomped around the room, his heavy footfalls making clouds of dust that swirled in the light of the flashlight. He stopped suddenly.

"What do we have for intel?" he asked.

"We found a knapsack, a laptop, a small notebook with Chinese writing, another little laptop," Pavel said. "That's it."

"Those are mine," Gao said quickly.

Skelly whirled on him. To Gao, his eyes looked wild, hunted. His bared teeth gleamed white in the light. Dust sparkled in his beard.

"Finders keepers," Skelly said. He looked at Pavel. "Call our ride and take care of this asshole." He stalked out of the room.

Gao's thighs spasmed in fear. He heard Pavel speaking into his mic.

"All units fall back to the exfil point. We are airborne in five mikes."

Pavel waved the three men in the kitchen out of the room. They left at a run.

When Pavel drew his sidearm, Gao felt his bladder let go. Warmth flowed down his trembling thighs. Acrid steam rose in the air, and despite his situation, Gao felt a rush of shame.

"Happens to everyone," Pavel said, as if reading his mind. "Are you really PLA?"

Gao wanted to beg for his life, but his voice had deserted him. He nodded.

Pavel pointed his weapon down the empty hallway and pulled the trigger twice. Gao startled so hard, he nearly toppled his chair over.

Pavel leaned down so he could speak in Gao's ear.

"My boss is a dick," he said. "Have a nice life, Colonel Gao."

Then he was gone.

A few seconds later, Gao heard the helicopter descend, then the engines roared and he watched the navigation lights rise into the air again. The lights grew smaller, then disappeared from his field of view through the collapsed roof. The sound of the rotors faded.

Gao stared up at the stars, pinpricks of cold white light in the dark.

The piss on his thighs cooled and chilled his skin. The fear passed from his body, leaving him limp with fatigue. Hot tears of frustration welled up.

They had taken his belongings, his freedom, and his pride. But he had his life—and maybe that was enough—for now.

Gao reared back his head and screamed into the night.

"Help! Somebody, help me!"

18

White House
Washington, DC

When Don followed the Director into the Oval Office, there was a smell of Christmas in the air.

A few feet from the Resolute desk stood a perfectly conical, nine-foot Douglas fir, a little brother to the monster Christmas tree that had been erected on the Mall. Tasteful decorations hung at exact intervals on the exterior branches, and merry white lights dotted the circumference of the tree all the way up to the golden star at the apex. Brightly colored packages stacked on the navy blue carpet finished the tableau of the holiday season.

Unfortunately, the Christmas spirit had deserted the premises. President Serrano, seated behind his desk, peered over the rim of his reading glasses with all the warmth of the newly fallen snow blanketing the Rose Garden outside his window. His gaze rested on the Director, ignoring Don.

"Have a seat, Sam," was all he said.

The President's executive assistant stood in the doorway. "Shall I bring coffee, Mr. President?"

"No, thank you," Serrano said. "These gentlemen will not be staying long. Please call Irv and let him know they're here."

Don and the Director took seats side by side on the pale yellow sofa, saying nothing. The door opened again, and Chief of Staff Irving Wilkerson entered. Serrano nodded at the sofas and continued reading. Wilkerson took his seat without acknowledging the visitors.

Minutes passed. The regular ticking of the mantel clock rang like a distant hammer in Don's ears.

Finally, the President ripped off his reading glasses and tossed them onto his desk. He spun in his chair to face the snowy scene outside his window. After another long moment of silence, he got to his feet and stalked to where the three men waited for him. Before he sat in his armchair, Serrano dropped the papers he'd been reading on the coffee table.

Don saw it was the report he'd written about their attempt to capture the Naval War College bomber.

Their *failed* attempt.

"Not our finest hour, gentlemen," Serrano announced. "Not by a long shot."

"No, sir," the Director agreed.

"So, what happened?" Serrano asked.

Don cleared his throat. "We had contact on the target in Patagonia," he began. "He must've realized we were on to him, because he did a runner. Using an assumed identity, he took a plane to Córdoba—that's in Argentina —where he boarded a second flight to Bolivia. We scrambled a team to intercept him in La Paz, but we missed him."

"What do you mean, you missed him?" Serrano pressed.

"He wasn't there, sir." Don shot a look at the Director. "It's possible that he never got on the plane."

"Just disappeared into thin air?" Serrano's tone had an edge.

"This is not an exact science, Mr. President," the Director began.

"Don't lecture me about the nature of inexact situations," Serrano snapped. "I'm a fucking politician, remember?"

"Sir," Wilkerson interjected. "We always knew this was a long shot. I think Riley's team did the best they could with what they had to work with."

Don could scarcely believe his ears. Wilkerson was defending his poor performance?

The operation had turned into a cock-up of epic proportions. After using the search inputs from Rachel Jaeger at Mossad, they'd managed to catch a whiff of their quarry in the last place they'd expected to find him: Patagonia, literally, the end of the Earth.

But Diego Montalban had been there. Don knew that for certain. The intel from Mama was rock solid. The Sentinel AI had been his ace in the hole for this manhunt, and she'd performed beyond his expectations.

When Diego went on the run, Don wasn't surprised. What he'd not expected was for their target to use a commercial airline. That was risky for him. But once again, Mama came through with flying colors, providing facial recognition data in the Córdoba airport that confirmed Diego had boarded a last-minute flight to La Paz under another assumed name.

Don knew they had him. He scrambled a CIA intercept team into La Paz and met the incoming flight on the airfield. The Director had even called in a favor with the Bolivian Foreign Minister to allow the American team to mix with the deplaning passengers and take him before he cleared customs.

Their man was not on the plane. Somewhere between boarding the flight in Córdoba and the plane landing in Bolivia, Diego Montalban vanished.

"Our working theory is that he had help at the airport." Don thought the excuse sounded lame, even to his own ears.

The President agreed with Don's self-assessment. "It sounds to me like you're relying on a whole lot of computers and automated searches and not enough on good old-fashioned detective work. What about our allies, Riley?"

Don shook his head. The British had drawn a blank, and Rachel Jaeger at Mossad had gone silent, despite several phone calls to her. "Our best leads have all come from the Sentinel AI, Mr. President."

Serrano cast a sour look at Wilkerson. Don braced for a verbal dressing down by the Chief of Staff. Wilkerson had been reluctant about the operation from the beginning, and now Don would feel his wrath. Instead, Wilkerson shrugged and said nothing.

The Director spoke up. "Mr. President, perhaps this is the time for us to go public with this information. If we—"

Serrano cut him off. "I don't think you understand what I'm trying to do here, Sam. My entire first term was consumed with one conflict after another. We're not talking about pissant little regional conflicts where we can throw a few special forces operators at the problem and make it go away. No, we were one second to midnight on the Doomsday Clock. More than once."

The Director took advantage of the pause to backpedal. "I understand the gravity of the situation, sir, I just think that—"

"I don't think you do," the President snapped. "This is our chance to put all that war nonsense in the rearview mirror. Imagine the powerful image it sends to the world if I announce in my inauguration speech that we have captured the Naval War College bomber. The message is clear: you mess with America and you pay the price. No matter how long it takes, no matter the cost, you will pay the ultimate price."

"Sir," the Director said. "I can appreciate the optics of the moment, but that's not how manhunts work."

"Get it done, Sam," Serrano said. "I've given you everything you asked for. You need to deliver." His gaze shifted to include Don. "You *both* need to deliver."

"Yes, sir," the Director said, his voice tight.

"Good." The President stood. "Then this meeting is over."

Wilkerson walked them out of the Oval Office. The three of them paused outside Wilkerson's own office.

"Irv," the Director said, "you need to make him understand what we can and cannot control."

Wilkerson offered a tired smile. "He didn't get to be president by setting low expectations, Sam. You'll get it done."

The Director rolled his eyes and walked away. Don made to follow him, but Wilkerson held him back. "How are you holding up, Don?"

"Sir?" It had been years since the Chief of Staff had treated Don as anything but someone who existed to complicate his life.

"Simple question," Wilkerson replied with a smile. "How're you handling all of this?"

"It's…frustrating," Don said. "I really thought we had him in La Paz. The intel was solid."

"You're dealing with a slippery character."

Don nodded. He still wondered at the speed with which the plan had unraveled, but he'd gone back through the data from Mama multiple times, and it was rock solid.

Wilkerson clapped a hand on Don's shoulder. "Keep me posted, son," he said. "I mean it."

"Will do, sir."

Don rode the Metro Silver Line back to ETG in Tysons Corner. He liked the train. Maybe it was the stop and start of the cars, the constant movement of people around him, or the way the conductor announced each stop, but he found he could let his thoughts wander in this environment.

Maybe the President had a point, he mused. Everything they had accomplished to date was through the computing power of Mama, and how had that worked out? Maybe it was time to come at the problem from another angle, using human resources.

He walked the three blocks from the Metro station to the office, still deep in thought. The snow still looked clean and fresh in the waning afternoon sunlight. The tires of passing cars hissed on the wet roads. By tomorrow, the clean white snow would be dirty slush.

If he needed human assets in the region, Mossad had the best network by far. That reminded Don that he still had not heard back from Rachel. He pulled out his phone and dialed her number.

"Don Riley," said a man's voice.

He stopped walking. "I must have dialed the wrong number. I'm—"

"It's Noam," the voice said. "I had her calls forwarded to me."

"Okay," Don replied. "Can I ask why? Is something wrong?"

"Unknown." The head of Mossad operations let the word hang. "She has a message for you."

"Why doesn't she just call me?"

"It's complicated, Don. Do you want to know her message?"

"Sure."

"You need to take a vacation. In Colombia. I hear Medellín is beautiful this time of year."

"Noam," Don said. "Am I going to regret this?"

He could hear the smile in the other man's voice. "Unknown."

19

Sterling, Virginia

It was not quite noon when Skelly pulled into the parking lot of the Sentinel headquarters building. He spied David Landersmann waiting for him on the steps and groaned to himself.

I shoulda just gone home, he thought. It's Christmas Eve, and I'm in no mood for Landersmann's bullshit.

Skelly felt tired down to his bones, and the way the whole Argentina operation had unraveled left him with an unresolved anger that simmered under his skin. They were so close, but that little Chinese bastard managed to get away. Hell, after the stunt he pulled bribing the Argentine helicopter flight crew, he'd left town one step ahead of the law himself. Skelly chuckled as he walked toward his waiting chief of staff.

"Will Clarke is in your office," Landersmann announced.

The smile slipped from Skelly's lips. He stopped on the steps, looking up at Landersmann. "Who?"

His chief of staff rolled his eyes. "Will. Clarke," he said in a mockingly loud voice. "CEO of Falchion? The guy that you insulted a few weeks ago?"

"What does he want?"

Landersmann held up his hands. "I guess he wants to see you. What do I look like, your secretary?"

Then Skelly remembered the encounter. He tried to buy Clarke's company, and the man got all pissy with him. Now, he was coming back on his hands and knees to negotiate a deal. The itching sense of anger eased. He grinned at Landersmann.

"Everybody has a price, Landie." Skelly passed him the leather satchel containing the two laptops and the notebook he'd taken from the Chinese spy in Argentina. "Do your voodoo on this stuff. Tell me if there's any useful intel in there."

"It's Christmas Eve, Skelly," Landersmann replied. "I have plans."

"Then work fast." Skelly clapped him on the shoulder hard enough to make the other man wince. "Tell you what, take tomorrow off."

Skelly's footsteps rang in the empty halls of the Sterling headquarters. He saw the light was on in his office and the door was ajar. Skelly pushed the door so that it banged into the wall.

"Honey, I'm home," he said.

The CEO of Falchion was dressed in a tan cashmere blazer and white shirt open at the neck. He stood to face Skelly, his face serious, lips pressed into a firm line.

"Thank you for seeing me, Manson," he said, his voice low and cool.

Skelly strode to the bar and grabbed the closest bottle. He sloshed some of the amber liquid in a tumbler and turned. "Drink?" he asked.

"I prefer to wait until afternoon," Clarke replied.

"Suit yourself." Skelly took a slug and swallowed without bothering to taste it. It burned all the way down to his stomach.

Something was wrong, Skelly realized. Clarke did not have the face of a man who'd come to make a deal. The itching feeling returned, and he felt his muscles twitch.

"I haven't been to bed yet," Skelly said. "We had an op in South America. I like to ride along when I can."

Clarke said nothing. Skelly drank again to cover his discomfort. Finally, he said, "Like I told you before: name your price."

"You really don't know how to read a room, do you?" Clarke said in a flat tone.

"What's that supposed to mean?" Skelly snapped.

"I'm out," Clarke said. "Not only do I not want to sell you my company, I want nothing to do with you or Sentinel. I came last time out of respect for Abby and what she built, but after we talked..." He paused as if wondering if he should go on. "I did some digging on my own, and I don't like what I found out."

Skelly gripped the tumbler to prevent his hand from twitching.

"After Luchnik imploded," Clarke continued, "you picked up Wagner. I found out you're running them as a side business. I found out about Chad and Yemen—"

"Why are you here?" Skelly interrupted.

Clarke's lips bent into a smile, but the emotion never reached his eyes. "I'm here to make it one hundred percent clear to you that I want nothing to do with you or your operation. I'm withdrawing my bid for support in Southeast Asia, effective immediately."

Skelly drained his glass. The burning in his throat helped to quell the overwhelming desire to beat the shit out of this sanctimonious asshole.

"We have a contract," Skelly said.

"We had a contract," Clarke shot back. "It's done. Sue me, if you want. I'd love for my lawyers to depose you under oath."

"Are you finished?" Skelly stepped into the other man's personal space.

It would be so easy, he thought, to take a swing at him. The muscles in his shoulders danced with energy.

Clarke met his gaze without flinching. That made Skelly even angrier.

"I'm finished," Clarke said.

Skelly felt his breath getting uneven. A vein in Clarke's forehead pulsed, and he watched the tiny motion, mesmerized. The itching sensation threatened to overwhelm his senses.

"Get the fuck out of my office," Skelly hissed. He broke eye contact, turned his back on Clarke.

As he gulped in deep breaths of air, Skelly heard the door close. He tried to take another drink and realized the glass was empty.

Skelly paced to the bar, poured the last of the bottle into his glass, and drank deeply. He closed his eyes, welcoming the burn in his throat.

He focused on the label of the bottle still in his hand and realized he'd just drunk the last of Joe's scotch.

Suddenly, he pictured his best friend in this very room, sipping the same drink from a tumbler just like this one. He remembered the way Joe worked his jaw as he rolled the liquid across his palate. Joe would close his eyes and wrinkle his nose as he tasted.

Skelly tried it for himself. He tipped the last of the amber liquid into mouth and tried to really taste it the way Joe used to do. The alcohol tasted bitter and smoky on his tongue, like ashes.

Another part of the memory invaded his mind. A laugh, a woman with a throaty chuckle.

Abby.

Skelly swallowed and opened his eyes. The office—Abby's office—was cold and empty. He held the bottle by the neck, feeling the weight of the glass.

Then, he threw it against the wall. It shattered, the sound loud in the quiet of the space.

But it wasn't enough for Skelly. He needed more.

He threw the tumbler against the wall, and it shattered.

More.

Skelly turned to the glass coffee table that he hated so much. It wasn't his coffee table, it was Abby's. He raised his boot and stamped down on the table. The thick glass flexed but did not break.

This enraged him even more. Skelly felt the warmth of the scotch in his belly, heard the rasping of his own breath, felt the trembling tension of his muscles.

He seized one of the black leather armchairs and slammed it down on the coffee table.

The glass quivered but did not break.

Skelly grunted in renewed frustration. He lifted the chair high over his head and smashed it down with all his might.

Crack. The coffee table surrendered to his will.

Skelly staggered back, breathing ragged, head reeling. His muscles spasmed, and he felt a sheen of hot sweat sweep up his torso. Skelly laughed out loud.

"How was your meeting?" Landersmann said from behind him.

Skelly whirled around. His chief of staff had that stupid lopsided grin on his face. He tapped his chin with his index finger in a pose of mock concentration as he surveyed the trashed room. "I'm gonna go out on a limb and say it didn't go well."

"Get the fuck out," Skelly said.

"No." Landersmann crossed his arms.

"What do you mean, no?" Skelly felt another flare of itching anger.

"Santa came early, boss," Landersmann said. "Come with me. You gotta see this."

Skelly followed his chief of staff to the security office, where there was a direct interface to the company AI.

"Give us the room, guys," Landersmann said to the two techs who manned workstations.

When they were gone, Landersmann held up the smaller laptop that Skelly had taken from the Chinese PLA colonel. "Do you know what this is?" he asked.

Skelly studied the device. It was black, about the size of a paperback novel, and opened like a clamshell. "Looks like an ultralight laptop."

"Nope. It's a controller."

"You mean like for a video game?"

Landersmann chuckled. "Mama, show the man what you found."

The screen at the front of the room displayed an animated drawing populated with data labels.

Landersmann slapped the device in his palm. "Took Mama a half hour to crack this thing open. That's like years for a normal computer."

"Landie, don't be an asshole. What the hell am I looking at?" Skelly said.

"Are you drunk?" Landersmann pointed at the screen. "It's a fucking Chinese submarine. Well, it was a Chinese submarine. It sunk. But that's not the important part."

"Okay," Skelly said.

"You still don't see it?" Landersmann had that stupid lopsided grin going full throttle.

"See *what*?" Skelly let his irritation show in his tone.

Landersmann sighed. "Fine." He raised his voice. "Mama, give us a close-up of the cargo bay, please."

The image of the cargo bay of the submarine filled the screen.

Skelly saw what had so excited his chief of staff.

"Is that what I think it is?" he asked.

The grin widened. "Yup."

"Merry fucking Christmas to me," Skelly whispered.

20

Medellín, Colombia

From the window of the Gulfstream V, the city of Medellín looked like a sea of lights trapped in the trough of a wave. Like Denver, Medellín was a mile-high city. But this metropolis was four times the size of Denver and crammed into the narrow Aburrá Valley, along the Porce River. High-rise apartments rose along the edges of the city, climbing the steep slopes of the Cordillera Central mountains.

And somewhere in the sea of lights, Don mused, was Rachel Jaeger.

Noam Glantz, Rachel's boss, had been characteristically blunt. "I don't know what she's up to, but you can trust her, Don," he'd said. "She's my best."

She *was* your best, Don thought. Although he and Rachel had a strong working relationship from the Pandora operation in Sudan, that had been more than a few years ago.

Was she still Noam's best? Don did some checking on Rachel and did not like what he found.

As far as he could tell, she hadn't been in the field since Sudan. Although he did not have full access to Mossad's files, he did have a contact at Scorpions Ascent. Not only had Rachel retired from field work, she rarely even left the remote Mossad training center.

And then there was the recent incident when she broke a visiting CIA officer's arm in an after-hours sparring session...

Now, suddenly, she was back in the field and all but demanding Don meet her in Colombia.

Alone, no questions asked.

Despite his misgivings, Don made the trip.

I owe her that much, Don thought. Without her work in Sudan, the world would be a very different place today. Besides, the last time Don worked with her, she *had* been the best.

Maybe she still was, but the sense of unease lingered like a bad taste in his mouth. He'd been on enough operations to trust his gut. Right now, his gut told him this was very wrong.

As the plane banked to line up for landing, the cityscape disappeared.

"Fasten your seat belt, please, sir," the pilot said over the intercom. "We'll be landing in five."

Don gave a thumbs-up to the camera through which he knew the pilot was watching him and tugged at his seat belt. The CIA flight was just a pilot and copilot. There had not even been a flight attendant for the ten-hour trip to Medellín.

The jet landed smoothly and taxied to the private hangar area. As the engines wound down, the copilot emerged from the cockpit and released the stairs. He nodded to Don when it was safe for him to deplane and returned to the cockpit without a word.

Don descended to the dark tarmac. It was a pleasant night, mid-sixties and no humidity. At least, he'd get a nice break from snowy, damp Washington, DC.

The distant whine of an approaching engine came to Don's ear, and he spied the single headlamp of a motorcycle turning onto the tarmac. He squinted against the glare as the light aimed straight for him. He thought about climbing back up the steps. At the last minute, the motorcycle angled away, then pulled alongside Don.

A slim figure dismounted and removed her helmet. Don recognized Rachel Jaeger. Her auburn hair was pulled back, and in the light spilling from the airplane doorway, Don could see her face was bruised. Her eyes met his, and she smiled. She didn't look crazy; that was a start, at least.

"Don," she said, "thank you for coming." Her grip was firm. The woman was a few inches shorter than Don, and he had at least fifty pounds on her, but he'd seen firsthand how deadly this unassuming woman could be.

"Noam said I should trust you," he replied.

Her eyebrow ticked up as if surprised by his reply. "I'm going to need your phone and any weapons you might have with you."

Don hesitated. Giving up his phone was like giving up his right arm. Rachel noticed his discomfort.

"I wouldn't ask if it wasn't necessary, Don."

When he handed her the phone, she quickly removed the case, battery, and SIM card and put everything into an EM-safe bag that she stowed in the pocket of her leather jacket.

"Ready to go for a ride?" she asked, handing him a helmet.

Don eyed the motorcycle with skepticism. It had been decades since he'd been on a motorcycle, and that had been a roomy Harley-Davidson. This was a Haojue, a Chinese-made Suzuki, that looked more like a dirt bike than a real motorcycle. Rachel donned her helmet, straddled the bike, and kick-started it to life. "Hop on."

"Where are we going?" Don asked.

"For a ride in the country," she said. "There's someone I want you to meet."

Don fitted the helmet over his head, blocking out the noise of the engine. He slipped onto the seat behind Rachel.

She looked over her shoulder. "You're gonna want to hang on," she called back. "Don't worry. I don't bite. Much." Don caught a snatch of laughter as she snapped her visor down.

He put his arms around Rachel's waist. Even through the heavy jacket he could feel the solid muscles of her core.

"Hang on." She gunned the engine, and they raced across the darkened tarmac.

Rachel merged onto the highway heading toward the city. She drove fast, weaving her way through traffic. At the last possible moment, she took an exit into a small town and wound her way through side streets before striking north. The secondary road was paved but badly in need of repair. Traffic thinned considerably to a car or two every five minutes or so.

Finally, she turned onto a dirt road that led into a densely wooded area. The road narrowed to a single track hemmed in by trees on both sides. The headlight bored a hole into the darkness ahead. Don wondered what sort of wild animals might be living in the thick trees and decided he'd rather not think about it.

Rachel slowed the bike, then carefully steered onto a narrow path. Low-hanging tree branches scratched at Don's helmet.

The bike emerged into a clearing. Don caught a glimpse of a tiny white-painted bungalow before Rachel doused the headlight. He heard the *snick* of her visor snapping up.

"You can let go now, Don," she said.

"Sure." He released his arms from her waist, thankful for the blanket of darkness as he felt his cheeks grow warm with embarrassment. He swung himself off the bike and removed his helmet. The still night settled around him.

If Don had his phone, he would have turned on the flashlight, but Rachel made no effort to illuminate their surroundings. "This way," she said, leading him across the clearing toward the ghostly white shape of the bungalow.

Don followed, the sound of his footsteps muffled by the damp earth. Rachel paused at the doorway. The flare of a match burst into Don's vision as she lit a lantern. She adjusted the flame down to a soft yellow glow and handed it to him.

"I want you to keep an open mind, Don," she said. "Not everything is what it seems at first glance." She held the screen door open with the other hand.

"Spare me the fortune cookie wisdom." After a ten-hour plane trip, a harrowing ride on the back of a motorcycle, and a walk in the dark jungle, Don felt his frustration bubbling over.

He stepped into the house. It smelled of dust and mold, and the floor-boards creaked under his weight. The dim light of the lantern did little to dispel the gloom.

"In here," a voice called from straight ahead. Don stepped through a short hallway that dead-ended into a small kitchen. He caught a glimpse of an old-fashioned water pump and woodstove. Don smelled the faint remnants of a cooked meal.

On his first pass of the room, Don missed the figure blending into the shadows around the back door of the house. A movement caught his eye, and Don saw a man leaning against the doorjamb, arms crossed.

Don raised the lantern, stepped forward.

The man did not move.

It took a full second for Don's brain to process the image. Dark hair, Chinese facial features, a slight smile on his lips...

The Naval War College bomber.

"Rachel," he whispered, "what have you done?"

He started to back away, but Rachel was close behind him. She clamped her hand on his shoulder. "It's not what it looks like, Don."

He twisted away, backing up against the stove. The cast iron was warm against the back of his leg.

"It's exactly what it looks like." Don could hear the anger cracking in his voice. "You're helping a terrorist, Rachel."

He needed to get his phone away from her. He needed to call this in. *Jesus, what have I gotten myself into?*

"You need to hear what he has to say, Don."

This is all wrong, Don thought. All the rumors he'd uncovered about Rachel were true. She'd gone off the deep end.

Neither Rachel nor the man made a move toward him, but they were also covering both doors. He was trapped.

"Does Noam know about this?" Don demanded.

The words hit home. Rachel looked away.

"No," she said finally.

"What have you done?" Don said. "Why is he still alive?"

Rachel seemed to shrink before his eyes. Her shoulders slumped, and she would not meet his eyes. "It's complicated."

"It's *not* complicated," Don shot back, his voice rising. He stabbed a finger at the man standing in the doorway. "This man killed and maimed hundreds of people. He is responsible for—"

"It's for the greater good." The man hardly raised his voice, but he stopped Don's words cold.

Don felt like he'd entered an alternate reality, like the shadows in the room were talking to him. He was face-to-face with the most wanted man in the world being protected by one of Israel's most celebrated covert operatives. He wasn't sure if he should fear for his life or laugh out loud.

"What do you know about the greater good?" Don said. "Who are you, anyway? Ian Thomas? Diego Montalban? I don't even know what to call you!"

"My name was Nánhái." The man's voice was soft, matter-of-fact.

The word sounded familiar. Don knew some basic Mandarin, but he struggled to remember this one.

"It means No Name," Rachel said.

"No Name, great," Don said, acid in his tone.

"The Minister trained me to be the man without a name. I was whoever he wanted me to be."

There was emotion behind his words, but Don didn't have a clue what it was. Pride? Regret? Sadness?

"I did the things you accuse me of," he continued. "And more. Much more."

"Great," Don said. "You confessed. That makes it easy. Now all you have to do is turn yourself in."

The man's smile was a slash of white teeth in the darkness. "I won't do that, Don."

"Then why am I here?" he shouted.

"There's something you need to know, Don," Rachel said. "Something only he can tell you."

Is she serious? Don wondered. Did she actually think this was a negotiation?

"Let me guess," Don said. "You tell me a deep, dark secret, and in return, I let you go free. I don't tell anyone about this meeting and the fact that you have completely lost your fucking mind and thrown in with a terrorist." He held the light up so that it illuminated Rachel's face. "Do I have it right?"

She shrugged, but her face was defiant. "Yes, that's right."

"You don't know me as well as you think you do, Rachel." Don let the sarcasm ooze through his words.

"Enough," the man said. "I will tell you what I know, Mr. Riley, and you can decide its worth. All I ask is that you keep Rachel out of it."

"I won't do that," Don said.

"You haven't heard what I have to say."

"It won't matter."

The man smiled again. "Do you know the word *huichen*?"

Don blew out a breath of frustration. "No."

"It's the Mandarin word for dust."

"Fascinating," Don replied.

"It has another meaning to a small group of operatives trained by the Minister," the man continued. "It was a code word."

Despite his anger at the situation, Don felt the gravity in the man's tone.

Why was he here? Why risk a meeting with a CIA officer? He knew the United States was sparing no expense to hunt him down. He had to know that Don would turn him in as soon as Rachel gave him back his phone.

"What did the code word mean?" Don asked.

"I need you to listen carefully." As the man began to speak, Don felt the room go very still. He felt his anger drain away. In its place were new feelings. Urgency. Dread.

When the Chinese spy finished, Don stayed silent.

"Do you see now why I asked you to come here?" the man asked.

Don nodded. "You need to take me back to the airfield," he said to Rachel. "Right now."

"What are you going to do, Don?" she demanded.

Don sought out the eyes of the world's most wanted man, then he came back to Rachel's searching gaze.

"Honestly, I don't know."

21

Gao jolted awake as the vehicle he was riding in hit another pothole. The sky, visible through the horizontal slit windows at the top of the metal box, told him it was still night outside.

His third day—no, this morning would be the fourth day—since he was captured.

The interior of the van reeked of vomit and shit, but Gao scarcely noticed anymore. He shifted on the metal seat, trying in vain to find a more comfortable position. Go back to sleep, he told himself. He peered into the swaying dimness at his four traveling companions. They seemed to have no trouble sleeping.

He tried to rub his face, but the shackles would not allow his hands to rise above his waist. He bent down to complete the task. Every part of his body ached. He was hungry, thirsty, and almost delirious with lack of sleep.

But most of all, Senior Colonel Gao of the People's Liberation Army was scared.

When the crazy American named Skelly had taken his satchel, he had not only taken Gao's only way of communicating with Beijing, he had taken everything Gao had learned about Minister Fei's treasonous plot. There were no copies of the travel diary, and he had not gotten around to decrypting the small laptop.

You fool, he thought. By keeping them on your person, you thought you were keeping them safe. Instead, you served them up on a silver platter.

But to whom? he wondered. The man they called Skelly was obviously American and had military training, but what had happened in El Chaltén was not a US military raid—of that, Gao was sure.

The next obvious guess was the CIA, but then, how to account for the man with the Russian accent, the one they called Pavel? It was possible such a man worked for the CIA, but something about the interaction bothered Gao. It felt too...unconventional to be an official operation. The American term "cowboy" came to mind. Was that just his anti-American bias, or was there something there?

The transport made three stops a day to refuel and let the prisoners out. They were led to the side of the road and allowed to go to the bathroom. Then they were given water and something to eat, usually stale bread or some kind of meat, before they were locked back into their seats in the van. Prisoners who failed to follow orders received swift justice at the end of a *batuta*, under the watchful eye of a second guard armed with an *escopeta*, or shotgun. Gao was picking up Spanish vocabulary at a rapid rate.

When he considered the last four days, a gap in communications was what had landed him in this smelly metal box.

After Skelly and his companions departed the traitor's house in El Chaltén, local police flooded the area. They found Gao tied to a chair in what remained of the kitchen. Torrents of Spanish flew back and forth across the room as the local policemen tried to figure out what they were dealing with.

They spoke no Mandarin and he spoke no Spanish, but he did pick one word out of the rapid-fire exchanges that seemed to come up again and again.

Drogas.

It took Gao a few minutes to realize the word probably meant drugs. They think this is a drug deal gone bad, he thought. They think I'm a drug dealer.

Not that he blamed them. He had no identification, not even a mobile phone. Somewhere in the wreckage of this house were the bodies of his hit team, who were all armed and also had no identification on them. The operation was covert. Mei Lin was the only person who knew where he was, and his last reported location had been El Calafate, two hundred kilometers away by car.

"No drugs," he tried in English. The reply—a slap—was delivered by a burly officer who was clearly assigned to guard him.

His situation went from bad to worse when they untied him and immediately put him in handcuffs. As the officer walked him to a waiting police car, Gao protested loudly. He received a swift shot in the ribs as the officer stuffed him into the back of the vehicle.

The journey to the police station was only ten minutes. The single-story brick structure looked more like a park ranger's office than a police station. While he waited in the back of the car, his guard consulted with another policeman in the parking lot. This man had more gold on his uniform, so Gao guessed he was the local authority.

At last, he thought, I'll be able to get some help.

The police chief was a big-bellied man with an enormous mustache that he liked to stroke as he talked. He walked to the car and peered into the back seat at Gao.

"Telephone," Gao shouted at the window.

The man stroked his mustache. His mouth formed the word *drogas*.

"No drugs," Gao shouted, but the man was walking away from the car.

The burly officer got behind the wheel of the car and drove away.

"Where are you taking me?"

No answer from the driver, but when the sun came up, Gao saw that they were on the outskirts of El Calafate.

Finally, he thought. Someone here will find a translator. I'll be able to make a phone call.

This police station was modern, two-stories and faced with natural stone. The officer parked in the back and left Gao in the car. By the time he returned a half hour later, the rising sun had begun to warm the interior of the vehicle. He had another uniformed officer with him. He was older, clean-shaven, and he wore a different uniform than the driver. Gao caught the word *federal* on his gold badge.

That's when it occurred to Gao that normal police procedure would have been to book him and take a statement, possibly even give him a phone call.

None of that had happened yet—and he knew why. He'd seen the same bureaucratic dance in his own country. Gao's presence was a political liability. He was being passed from one jurisdiction to another until someone either agreed to accept him or was unlucky enough to be saddled with the problem.

And the clock was ticking.

"Telephone," he said through the glass with renewed urgency.

The federal police officer just looked at him. Slowly, he nodded his head. He turned and spoke to the officer who had driven Gao through the night.

Gao's spirits rose as the car door opened. Fresh air flooded into the cabin. The officer gripped Gao's elbow and hauled him out of the back seat. Gao's legs trembled as he stood, and his arms had gone numb. But he breathed deeply of the clean morning air.

"I need a telephone," he said. He jerked his head toward the police station.

The police officer led him away from the door of the station.

"Telephone!" Gao tried to pull away, but the man's grip was like a steel clamp on his arm.

Gao twisted, trying to catch the eye of the federal police officer, but the man was opening the door to the station, his back to Gao.

"Telephone," Gao screamed.

The door closed, and the federal officer was gone.

They rounded the corner of the building where a black van was parked. The diesel engine rumbled in the quiet morning as Gao's guide spoke to two more uniformed police officers.

They looked at each other and shrugged. Gao's companion used a key to unlock the handcuffs pinning his arms behind his back. Then he walked back the way they had come.

Gao's fingers tingled as blood rushed to his extremities. "Telephone," he said to one of the new guards.

The man laughed as the second officer retrieved new shackles from the back of the van. Gao tried to run, but his legs were weak. At the first sign of movement, both guards leaped into action. They seized his arms and slammed him flat against the side of the van. While one held a baton across Gao's throat, the second expertly shackled his feet, then secured his hands to a chain around his waist. They marched him to the rear of the van and chained him to a metal seat.

The van door slammed shut with a heavy boom.

Gao jerked awake as the vehicle hit another pothole in the road. Against all odds, he'd managed to drift back to sleep.

The sun was visible through the slit windows at the top of the van walls, and the vehicle seemed to be slowing and speeding up. A car horn blared outside. They were in a city, Gao realized, but which one?

A new sound reached his ears. The wail of a police siren. The van surged forward, then slowed. The cabin swayed as the vehicle made a turn and came to a stop. The siren came close to the van, then cut off abruptly.

Gao's dry tongue rasped against the top of his mouth. He closed his eyes and let his chin fall to his chest.

The door of the van opened. Bright sunlight streamed in, and Gao clenched his closed eyes even more tightly. Hands fumbled at his shackles, unlocked the chain from the ring welded into the floor at his feet. Two men hoisted him up. When his feet touched pavement, Gao's knees buckled, but the hands supported him.

"Senior Colonel Gao," said a voice. "Gao Yichen?"

Gao's mind drifted. It sounded like the voice was speaking in Mandarin.

"Colonel Gao," said the voice, more insistent and definitely in Mandarin. Gao opened his eyes.

The voice belonged to a young man, mid-thirties, with carefully parted dark hair and rimless glasses.

"My name is Minister-Counselor Li. I am from the Political Section at the embassy. Are you Senior Colonel Gao Yichen?" He held a mobile phone in his hand, and he compared Gao's face to the screen.

"I...am Gao," he managed.

Minister-Counselor Li went into action. He roared at the guards in Spanish. Gao's shackles disappeared. The two guards escorted him gently to a waiting car. One held his arm while the second opened the door of the black sedan. Gao slipped inside, his aching body melting into the soft leather cushions. Li slid in from the other side.

"Drive," he said to the driver in Mandarin. "To the nearest hospital."

The car pulled away from the curb smoothly, and Gao saw they had a police escort through heavy morning traffic.

"Water," he whispered.

"Of course," Li said, "how inconsiderate of me." He twisted the cap off a plastic water bottle and handed it to Gao.

Gao struggled to get the first sip down, then he drank greedily, chugging the water. He sat back in the seat, his stomach rebelling at the sudden influx of sustenance.

"Where am I?" he asked.

"Buenos Aires," Li said. "We've had teams out looking for you for five days. It seems the Argentinians thought you were a drug dealer." Li eyed him. "Beijing wants to talk to you, Senior Colonel. Urgently."

"Take me to the airport." Gao sat up in his seat.

"Sir, you need to see a doctor."

"Then send the doctor to the airport," Gao snapped. "And find me some clothes."

* * *

Eighteen hours later, as Gao stared at the blank wall of an interrogation room in the Beijing Airport, he wondered if perhaps he had been too hasty in his return to China. After all, not only had he lost the traitor, he'd lost all possible clues to finding him and discovering whatever else Minister Fei might have planned.

The new Minister of State Security would not be pleased, but Gao was more worried about the General Secretary. Gao's performance had turned his mere existence into a political liability.

The leader of the People's Republic of China was a man who liked to emphasize his strengths...and dispose of his weaknesses. Unless Gao did something to prove his worth to the Party in very short order, he was a weakness that needed to be purged.

He checked the clock on the wall. He'd been in the interview room for nearly ninety minutes, which told him they were waiting for someone to interview him. Someone very important. The fact that they had not moved him yet meant they wanted to limit his exposure outside the controlled confines of the airport.

Neither thought was comforting to Gao.

He heard voices on the other side of the door. An argument between a man and a woman. The timbre of the angry woman's voice sounded familiar to Gao.

Mei Lin.

The breath caught in his throat, and he felt tears prick his eyes.

Her shouting escalated. "I have authority from the General Secretary himself to talk to this man immediately. Do you hear me? This is an urgent matter of state security."

The male voice sounded less certain now.

Suddenly, the door swung open and Mei Lin stumbled in. She slammed the door closed behind her and flattened her back against it. Her delicate features were flushed red, and her chin trembled. She clutched a file folder to her chest.

"Yichen," she said, "I thought you were dead."

"What are you doing here?" Gao hissed at her. "There's nothing you can do for me now. You need to get away."

In that moment, Gao realized that he really did love her, that he was worried about her safety. It was an odd feeling for him, to care about another person more than himself.

"No!" she replied. "I found something." She rushed forward and slapped the file folder on the table. "You can use this...I think."

Gao opened the folder. The first page was the line drawing of the *Xi* unmanned submarine with pencil marks and notations around the cargo bay. He flipped the page to find another drawing of a JL-2 missile; the notes said the Julong-2 was a submarine-launched ballistic missile variant. There were more pencil marks with measurements. Gao realized Mei Lin was speaking, but the words seemed to flow over him without entering his brain.

"What?" he said.

"Admiral Chen had access to the nuclear inventory," Mei Lin said, pulling a third sheet out from under the two drawings. "I tracked every transaction the admiral made. This one"—she stabbed her finger at a red-circled line item on the page—"this missile was decommissioned, Yichen. But when I went to the facility where it was supposed to be destroyed, there was no record of it."

"I don't understand," Gao said. His mind swam with the emotion of seeing Mei Lin again as well as all the information she was throwing at him. "Where is it?" he asked.

Mei Lin rested her finger on the drawing of the submarine. Gao's eyes fixed on the empty cargo bay.

Gao collapsed back in his chair as the full impact of what Mei Lin was telling him hit home.

Minister Fei had put a nuclear weapon inside the belly of the *X1*. The unmanned submarine had been sunk in the North Pacific.

China had lost a nuclear weapon—and no one knew about it. Yet.

This was his chance at redemption. If he could recover the lost nuke, he'd be a hero. Again.

Gao seized Mei Lin's face between his hands and kissed her hard. He pressed his forehead to hers.

"We're back in business," he whispered.

22

White House Situation Room
Washington, DC

Standing behind the lectern, Don bounced on the balls of his feet. It was the only thing he could think of to dissipate the nervous energy that coursed through his body. He shook his hands as if he could fling away the tingling feeling like drops of water.

It's just another briefing, he told himself. You've briefed the President a hundred times. It's just another day at the office.

Except it wasn't, because today he was going to lie to the most powerful man on the planet.

Well, not exactly lie, he reasoned. More like withhold certain information about his source. For example, the fact that his primary source was also the Naval War College bomber was not likely to go over well with this audience.

He could have—no, scratch that, *should have*—reported the meeting with the Chinese spy and thrown Rachel Jaeger under the bus. She deserved it, after all. But this man, Diego Montalban, Ian Thomas, or whatever his name was, Rachel had seen something in him. When Don thought back on the encounter, he'd felt it, too.

The man was telling the truth.

At least a dozen times since he'd returned, Don had picked up the phone to call the Director and lay out the whole situation. And the same number of times, he'd not gone through with it. This delay lengthened from minutes to hours to days to a whole week, and still Don kept the secret of the source's identity hidden from his chain of command.

Instead, he focused on trying to verify the theory of the lost nuke and the unmanned submarine. It was the slimmest of threads, but Don's team went to work trying to connect the theory with any supporting historical intel.

And they came up with nothing. Michael Goodwin, who'd led the investigation at ETG, summed it up as: "Either the information is wrong, or the Chinese don't know they're missing a nuke."

The record showed that the *Enterprise* strike force sank an unknown submarine contact in the North Pacific during the standoff with the Russian Navy. The Russians claimed it was not one of theirs. At the time, the working theory in the intelligence community was that the submarine was probably Chinese.

But with the Battle of Taiwan and the possibility of World War Three looming before them, the analysis had gone no further. Now, as Don looked back into the historical records, he saw that the Chinese had made no attempt to search for the submarine.

The former Chinese spy filled in the gaps for Don. The submarine that had attacked the *Enterprise* was indeed Chinese, but it was unmanned and carrying a nuclear weapon. More importantly, the Chinese military didn't know it existed.

The Chinese had lost a nuclear weapon, and they didn't even know it.

Don bounced on the balls of his feet again. There were so many elements in the narrative that he could not confirm, it was foolish to present this analysis as actionable.

On the other hand, the potential threat was too great to ignore.

The door to the Situation Room opened, and President Serrano entered with Chief of Staff Wilkerson in tow. The room rose as one. Normally, this was a noisy affair in a packed room, but the Director had requested this meeting be restricted to principals only.

Serrano still wore his overcoat, and his cheeks were flushed from a Rose Garden walking interview with one of the major news networks about his plans for his second term, part of his pre-inauguration media blitz.

"Seats, everyone, please." He shucked his coat and tossed it onto an empty chair. When he spied Don at the lectern, a shadow flitted across his features. "Riley, when I see you up there, that's never a good sign."

"Good morning, Mr. President," Don replied evenly.

"Well, let's have it," Serrano said. "I'm sure we'd all like to enjoy our Sunday afternoon."

"Yes, sir," Don continued. "In the course of our manhunt for the Naval War College bomber, we came into some new intel about the Chinese." Don hesitated. "There's no easy way to say this. We believe the Chinese may have lost a nuclear weapon."

To his credit, the President did not flinch, but he was in the minority. Serrano cleared his throat. "Perhaps you should start at the beginning, Riley."

Don felt his throat tighten. Here comes the lie, he thought.

"Approximately a week ago, our contact in Mossad, who'd been assigned to assist with the manhunt, turned up new intel about the Chinese. We treated it as a rumor at first."

National Security Advisor Valentina Flores asked, "Specifically, what was this rumor?"

"We'd suspected that the Chinese were using a submarine to instigate attacks on Russian and US naval forces during the run-up to the invasion of Taiwan," Don said. "The available intel has confirmed that. What's changed is that our contact added new information to the mix. The submarine was unmanned, and it was outfitted with a nuclear weapon."

"And you've verified this?" Flores asked. Don could tell by her tone that she was annoyed. Don didn't blame her. He'd been under orders from the Director to keep this new intelligence closely held until this meeting.

"Not at first," Don admitted. "Although the idea was plausible, there was nothing in the historical intel to support it."

"What changed?" Serrano asked.

"Forty-eight hours ago, the Chinese launched a massive internal investigation focused on their nuclear weapons facilities. They have completely locked down the Yulin Naval Base facility on Hainan Island where all PLA Navy nuclear weapons are built and maintained. We have reason to believe they are conducting a physical count of every nuclear weapon in their naval inventory. We've also seen evidence that they are disrupting their submarine deployment schedules to conduct this count."

Don let that tidbit settle. Fleet ballistic missile submarines, commonly known as "boomers," were part of the nuclear triad. The Chinese Type 094 *Jin*-class ships and the newly built Type 096 each carried a dozen missiles. The submarines operated on rigid annual schedules designed to ensure continuous nuclear protection. The authority needed to alter that schedule could only come from the highest levels of the political structure.

"What kind of weapon are we talking about here, Riley?" the President asked.

Don showed his first slide of the briefing, a picture of a plain white cylinder with a conical top breaching the surface of the ocean in a cloud of spray and smoke.

"The JL-2 is the most likely candidate, sir," Don replied. "The Julong, or Giant Wave, missile is capable of carrying a single one-megaton-yield nuclear warhead. More likely, it is configured with three to eight lower-yield multiple independently targeted reentry vehicles."

Don showed an image of a nuclear warhead configured with MIRVs. It looked like a disc with six conical witches' hats arranged in a circle. Except that each one of those cones had the ability to travel thousands of miles, strike a target with an accuracy of one hundred meters, and packed enough power to destroy a midsized American city.

"I don't understand," said the President. "You just said that the Chinese were searching their nuclear inventories. How does this fit with the unmanned submarine?"

The Director answered the question. "It's always been our opinion that the setup for the Taiwan invasion was a closely held operation inside the power structure of the Chinese Communist Party. We're now thinking it is possible that Taiwan was a rogue operation, at least in the beginning, meaning that the late Minister Fei was behind the whole thing."

"You expect me to believe," Serrano said, "that this unmanned submarine was part of an operation so covert even General Secretary Yi didn't know about it?"

"It's a working theory, sir," the Director admitted. "But the pieces fit."

"Assume you're right," Serrano said. "How long before the Chinese figure it out?"

The Director shrugged. "Impossible to say, but Riley has a plan."

The President crossed his arms and leaned back in his chair. "Of course he does. Let's hear it, Don."

"Our last known contact with the Chinese submarine was here." Don showed a chart of the North Pacific with a red-boxed area 325 nautical miles east of the Russian Naval Base at Petropavlovsk. "It was in this area that the *Enterprise* strike force was attacked by a submerged contact. We assumed it was the Russians, of course, but we know from subsequent communications intercepts that was incorrect." Don paused. "Which leaves the Chinese as the culprits."

"The sub was sunk?" Serrano directed his question to the CNO.

Admiral Tanaka frowned. "We've gone back and reconstructed the naval engagement as best we can, sir. Recall that the *Enterprise* strike force was pretty beat up after the war for Taiwan."

"I seem to remember something about that," the President responded drily. "Do we have a datum to search from or not, Admiral?"

"We have an area of interest, Mr. President, but there are complications."

Don interrupted. "Sir, this is a challenging operation. We're talking about fifty square miles of ocean in water depths up to sixteen thousand feet. In addition, we want to keep this operation clandestine, if at all possible."

"But you have a plan?" Serrano asked.

"Yes, sir," Don answered. "The USS *Rickover* is outfitted with a pair of experimental remote-operated vehicles that are equipped with the kind of sonar and video cameras we would need for this kind of search."

"She's currently on patrol near the Kuril Islands," the CNO added. "We can have her inside the search area in less than twenty-four hours."

"What happens when you find it?" Flores asked. "Can an ROV recover a nuclear warhead?"

"No, ma'am," the CNO replied. "Show them Phase Two, Don."

Don showed a picture of what looked like a grappling hook attached to a giant spool.

"This is the Flyaway Deep Ocean Salvage System," the CNO continued. "We developed it after we lost an F-35 in the South China Sea. As the name implies, we can fly this rig anywhere in the world and mount it to a ship. It's capable of lifting as much as sixty thousand pounds from depths of up to twenty-five thousand feet. Our recommendation is that we mount the FADOSS to the USS *William P. Lawrence*, which is currently in Yokosuka, Japan, and send the *Lawrence* to rendezvous with the *Rickover* for the recovery operation."

Serrano studied the viewscreen. "How long?"

"If you give the order now, sir," the CNO said. "I can have the *Lawrence* on station in a week, maybe six days if all goes well."

Serrano cast a glance over his shoulder at Wilkerson. "Can you have the operation completed before the twentieth, Admiral?"

"The twentieth of January, sir? I don't follow."

But Don followed. The twentieth of January was Inauguration Day. If Serrano didn't have the Naval War College bomber in custody, he wanted a different trophy to kick off his new term.

Serrano's gaze connected with Don. He did not look away as the President's lips bent into a smile.

"Never mind, Admiral," the President said. "You have my permission to begin the operation to recover the lost Chinese nuke."

23

USS *Hyman G. Rickover* (SSN-795)
North Pacific Ocean, 50 miles east of Urup Island, Kuril Island Chain

To Lieutenant Commander Janet Everett, executive officer of the USS *Hyman G. Rickover*, it seemed as if her head had barely touched her pillow. She'd been asleep for what seemed only a few seconds when she heard a sharp rapping at her stateroom door.

Her hand fumbled for the switch to turn on the reading lamp in her bunk. The ultra-bright white LED light scorched her retinas, forcing her to slam her eyelids shut again.

Knock-knock-knock.

Janet sat up in her bunk, rested her feet on the chill of the linoleum floor. Colorful afterimages from the bright light floated in her vision. She did a quick check to make sure she was sufficiently clothed to answer the door and found she was still wearing her uniform. She'd been so tired after the last drill session that she'd just collapsed on her bunk fully clothed.

She rubbed her hand across her face. "Come," she called out in a voice harsh with sleep.

The door snapped open, and a young petty officer radioman dressed in dark blue underway coveralls handed her a tablet. "Flash message traffic from SUBPAC and a P4 for you, ma'am."

Janet unlocked the tablet screen and tried to focus.

"Thank you, Petty Officer Dixon," she said. "I'll take it from here."

"Yes, ma'am. Captain wants to see you in his stateroom as soon as you've had a chance to read the message traffic."

"Very well, Dixon. That'll be all."

"Aye, ma'am." The door closed with a snap of the lock.

The message from SUBPAC was characteristically terse.

USS Rickover (SSN-795) proceed to coordinates—the message listed a latitude and longitude—*at best possible speed. Conduct clandestine search for downed Chinese submarine. Waterspace tasking and further details to follow.*

Janet looked up, not believing what she'd just read.

The Chinese had lost a submarine? Surely, they would have already seen message traffic on an incident of that scale. What kind of submarine, nuclear or diesel? Were there survivors?

She looked at the coordinates again. Water in that part of the North Pacific was deep, far beneath the crush depth of any operational submarine that she knew of. A salvage operation, then.

Janet turned her attention to the second message. A P4, or Personal For, was a private message intended only for the recipient. When she saw the sender was Don Riley, she felt an involuntary smile tug at her lips.

Of course Don was involved. It seemed that no matter where she went in the Navy, her old boss at ETG managed to find her. She opened the message.

Janet –

By now, you've received tasking from official Navy channels. I'm sure the wording will be vague, so I'll try to fill in the gaps here. The submarine you're looking for is an experimental unmanned platform sunk by the *Enterprise* strike force three years ago. We suspect the submarine carried a

Chinese JL-2 missile. Your mission is to find the submarine, rendezvous with USS *Lawrence*, and retrieve the nuclear warhead.

Good luck –
     Don

Janet sat back on her bunk, trying to process everything she'd just learned. The exploits of the *Enterprise* strike force in the run-up to and during the Battle of Taiwan was required reading for every officer in the Navy regardless of service selection. But she'd never seen a mention of an unmanned Chinese submarine from the conflict.

The coordinates pointed her to the engagement with the Russian Navy out of Petropavlovsk prior to the Chinese invasion of Taiwan. There had been a subsurface engagement in that battle. She recalled the strike force reported a subsurface kill, identified as a Russian boat. The Russians denied it, of course. Was that what Don was talking about?

Her brain finally kicked in. *Get your ass in gear, woman. You're not going to solve this mystery sitting on your bunk.*

Janet entered the head adjoining her stateroom. The size of a small closet, the Navy bathroom was a study in stainless steel. Stainless steel walls and shower, stainless steel sink, toilet, and washbasin underneath a shatter-proof mirror. The floor was poured epoxy. The milspec washroom was designed to withstand the rigors of both everyday use and the possibility of a violent explosion from a torpedo, depth charge, or mine.

Janet splashed water on her face and took a quick look in the mirror. Her skin was breaking out again from the moist, oily atmosphere of an underway submarine. She'd taken to keeping her hair in a short bob to avoid having to spend valuable waking time on haircare.

She poked at dark circles under her eyes. The ship had been splitting time between monitoring Russian naval activity around the Kuril Islands during the daylight hours and running shipwide engineering drills in the evening.

"This'll have to do," she said to her reflection as she finger-combed her hair into a stubby ponytail. She sniffed her underarm. A fresh uniform could wait for another watch rotation.

With the message tablet under her arm, Janet passed the CO's cabin and entered the control room. She made her way to the Nav Command Table and called up the coordinates in the message on the electronic chart display. The *Rickover* was only about 250 miles from the datum, a distance the submarine could easily cover in a half day or less given the necessary waterspace arrangements from SUBPAC.

Armed with these details, Janet stepped out of the control room and walked two paces down the passageway to the commanding officer's stateroom door. She knocked, waited for a response, and entered.

Commander Akihiko Nakamura was a wiry man with intense dark eyes who went by the nickname Andy—not that he'd ever asked Janet to call him by his nickname. He was only an inch or so taller than Janet, and only a few years older, but his thick hair was always neatly combed and fitted his head like an iron-gray helmet.

"XO," he said in his neutral tone.

The truth was she barely knew her commanding officer. Janet had arrived on the *Rickover* about three months ago after the previous XO had been placed shoreside for an undisclosed medical condition. Within a month, while the *Rickover* was still in a pierside refit, the previous commanding officer was relieved and Nakamura arrived on the scene.

The two months since had been a blur of activity as they sought to put the submarine to sea again after an extended maintenance period. Never an easy task, the sea trials had gone better than Janet expected. The *Rickover* was blessed with an experienced chief engineer, Derek Lawson, who had taken the load from the newly installed senior leaders.

Nakamura was single and had a reserved nature. Unlike previous COs Janet had served with, in his short time aboard, he made no effort to develop a personal relationship with either Janet or the rest of the wardroom.

"You wanted to see me, sir?"

Nakamura gestured to the only other chair in the room. The commanding officer's stateroom on a *Virginia*-class submarine was not luxury accommodations. The CO's room was slightly larger than Janet's with a single bed instead of the second bunk in her stateroom, but it had the same fold-down desk, the same LED reading light, and the same cold linoleum floor. The door to the CO's head stood latched open, showing a stainless steel bathroom identical to hers.

As Janet sat on the edge of the chair, Nakamura surveyed her. "What do you make of the new mission, XO?"

"The directions from SUBPAC are sparse, but I received a P4 from a friend at the CIA with a few more details." Janet quickly filled him in on the message from Don Riley. She held nothing back. Don had not asked her to keep any confidences, and she was obligated to do everything she could to help her CO make the best possible decisions.

"I've seen your file, XO," Nakamura continued. "At least the parts I'm allowed to see."

Janet looked away, her cheeks warm from embarrassment. The number of redactions in her service record from classified CIA operations was not something that endeared her to the detail-hungry nature of submarine commanding officers.

"Yes, sir," she replied even though he hadn't asked a question.

"Do you trust this Don Riley character?"

Janet tried to stop her smile and failed. "With my life, sir."

It was not an exaggeration. Don had been there for her in every way. As a boss, as a mentor, as a friend, as a savior. He'd given her first aid when she'd been gravely wounded in a North Korean bunker on one of those redacted missions that obviously annoyed her CO.

Nakamura nodded. "Good. I'm putting you in charge of the Narwhals."

"Aye, sir."

One of the major alterations done to the *Rickover* during the recent refit was a modification to her vertical launch system. Three VLS tubes and the associated armament had been removed to make room for two unmanned robotic vehicles.

Rather than use some arcane acronym, the US Navy called the new addition to the *Rickover* sensor suite by what it looked like: a whale with a tusk.

The Navy version of the "unicorn of the sea" had the same form factor as a Tomahawk missile, roughly twenty-one feet long and twenty-one inches in diameter, with a four-foot-long probe on the front of the submersible. Unlike a missile, the unit was stored upside down in the vertical tube, with the propeller facing up. The extended probe at the front of the robotic unit connected to the submarine, serving as both a data link and a charging point for the batteries. In theory, this meant that the Narwhals could be launched and recovered multiple times while the mother submarine was submerged.

That was the theory, anyway, thought Janet. In reality, the *Rickover* had deployed the Narwhals exactly one time before they departed for their mission in the Kuril Islands.

"Next question," Nakamura continued. "What about prep for ORSE?"

The Operational Reactor Safeguards Exam was an annual event for every United States Navy nuclear-powered submarine. The ship boarded a special team of investigators who examined all the nuclear records on the ship and ran a series of engineering drills to test the crew's readiness to deal with a nuclear incident.

When the prior CO had been relieved early, Janet expected the ORSE to be delayed, but that hadn't happened. When the *Rickover* was assigned to replace the USS *Tucson* for the Kuril Islands surveillance mission, Janet again expected a delay.

Nothing.

Janet chose her response carefully. It was the premier engineering examination for the ship, and by extension, her captain. A marginal score on an ORSE was a black mark against the commanding officer. A failing score was grounds for dismissal.

"Our progress on ORSE drills has been slow but steady, sir," she said. "The engineer's on it."

"Hmm." Nakamura focused his dark eyes on her.

Janet sensed he wanted to ask her something, but for the life of her she could not divine what he might want to know that she hadn't already told him.

"Is there something else, sir?"

"I don't want to ask for a delay in the ORSE schedule, XO," Nakamura said, his eyes still watching her intently. "It would look bad."

"I agree, sir. Maybe the commodore can help?"

Nakamura shook his head. "I don't want that kind of chatter anywhere in my chain of command. The *Navy* chain of command."

Finally, Janet saw what he was driving at. A request to delay the exam from inside the Navy network would make her CO look weak, but if the request came from an outside source, such as the CIA, then Nakamura was just following orders.

That, Janet thought, is not going to happen.

"I'm sure we'll manage, sir," she said, trying to keep the sarcasm out of her voice. What Nakamura was suggesting wasn't unethical, it was actually pretty clever, but it rubbed her the wrong way. Why not just come out and ask for her help?

She got to her feet. "Request permission to take the ship to periscope depth and collect our message traffic, sir. I'm sure SUBPAC will have our new waterspace allocated by now."

Nakamura regarded her coolly, his expression unreadable.

"Permission granted, XO."

24

Emerging Threats Group
Tysons Corner, Virginia

The large conference room at ETG smelled of stale coffee and overheated electronics. The gentle whirr of a computer fan provided a sleepy, white noise background. An open box of donuts perched on top of the sleek speakerphone in the center of the conference room table, the crusty glaze like ice on the few remaining pastries.

Don had just come into the building from outside. The atmosphere of the room felt stifling after the clean freshness of the predawn winter morning. On the whiteboard, someone had used dry-erase markers to write in elaborate, multicolored letters:

Welcome to Operation Needle in a Haystack.

Below the artwork was a second line in different handwriting: *Abandon hope all ye who enter here. If the coffee doesn't kill you, the boredom will.*

In a perfect world, Don would have moved the command center for the operation to find the lost Chinese nuclear weapon to the Planetarium, the nickname for the Sentinel operations center in Sterling, Virginia.

But this was far from a perfect world. Any ideas he'd had to involve Sentinel had been summarily shot down by the White House. Although the directive came from the President, it was Chief of Staff Wilkerson who delivered the news—and he had been unequivocal.

"Under no circumstances are you to involve Sentinel in this search in any way," Wilkerson told Don. "And that includes the use of the AI."

Dre Ramirez yawned as she got to her feet. "I am so glad to see you, Don," she said. "This is like watching paint dry."

"Tell me what you've got and you can head home, Dre," Don replied.

She indicated the topographical chart on the wall screen. The point in the ocean where they believed the Chinese sub had sunk was their starting point for the search. Grids, each one a square kilometer, radiated out from the center, twenty kilometers to a side. Four hundred square kilometers of ocean.

And that search grid assumed their initial datum was correct. A big assumption, Don knew. They'd used information gleaned from the naval tactical data link at the time of the attack to locate the enemy sub's likely last position, but there were so many variables that could come into play. How fast was the sub moving? Did it sink immediately, or did it limp along for a few kilometers before it sank? Did it break apart as a result of the attack? Did the sinking sub drift in the underwater currents?

Hell, Don thought, we're not even sure the sub actually sank.

"Don," Dre interrupted, "I'd really like to go home sometime this morning."

"Sure," Don replied.

Dre walked to the wall screen where the center cluster of the gridded chart was colored green. "The green squares are searched," she said. "Janet sends us updates every six hours or so. You should expect one soon."

Don studied the chart. Considering they'd been at this for almost four days, the green section on the chart was depressingly tiny.

"I take back what I said before," Dre continued. "Watching paint dry is *more* exciting than this."

"What about the *Lawrence*?" Don asked.

Dre's face brightened. She plucked a piece of paper from the table and handed it to Don. "There we have some good news. The installation of the deep-sea recovery system went off like clockwork, and the *Lawrence* is en route to Janet. They're hauling ass. ETA forty-eight hours."

"Good. Now all we have to do is find this damn thing."

"Yeah, about that," Dre said. "It's not going well. At this rate, it'll take us about a month to search the whole area."

"If it's there," Don said, "Janet will find it."

Dre yawned and stretched her arms over her head. "Good for her. Right now, the only thing I'm going to find is my bunk."

When Dre departed, the room fell silent. Don made his way to the break room and fixed his first coffee of the day. The halls were empty. It was still too early for most people to be in the office, and the few early birds had their office doors closed. Don respected their privacy.

Back in the conference room, he reviewed the message traffic for the last day. Janet's reports were concise, but the news was not heartening. She was using a pair of prototype, remotely operated search vehicles. While she was able to optimize the width of the side-scan sonar search area, she was only able to get about six hours of search time before the units needed to return to the *Rickover* to recharge their batteries. Once redocked with the mother sub, Janet downloaded the search data. Invariably, there were areas that needed to be searched again—another hindrance to forward progress —either because there was a gap in the data or an anomaly that needed to be investigated. He didn't even want to think about what would happen if one or both of the Narwhals was lost or damaged.

"Don?" Harrison Kohl stood in the doorway of the conference room.

"Morning, Harrison. What's up?" Don could tell by the scowl on the man's face that the news was not good.

"May I?" Harrison advanced to the keyboard on the conference room table.

Don nodded. Harrison changed the image on the screen to the east coast of China. He zoomed in to the Chinese coastline along the Yellow Sea, the body of water between the Korean Peninsula and mainland China.

"This is just in from NGA," he said.

Don could see from the date-time stamp that the electro-optic image from the National Geospatial-Intelligence Agency was less than an hour old. He studied a row of PLA Navy piers with docked warships. "What am I looking at?"

"Qingdao. Home of the Chinese North Sea Fleet. Lots of ships in port, right? Makes sense. It's the holidays, and Chinese New Year is only a few weeks away." His scowl deepened. "Now look at this."

Harrison touched the keypad, changing to a thermal image. Don saw bright spots of color bloom across the screen.

"In the last two hours, every single ship in that port has lit off their engines, Don," Harrison said. "PLA message traffic has gone bonkers. They're recalling personnel from leave and loading stores like crazy people."

Don cleared his throat. "What's your assessment?"

Harrison barked a laugh. "My assessment? They're on to you, my friend. Janet's going to have company."

"How much time?"

Harrison shrugged. "They'll have air assets on station within twenty-four hours, maybe less than that." He gestured at the brightly colored thermal display of the PLA Navy piers in Qingdao. "From the looks of this, they're assembling a task group, and it's a long haul up to where Janet is— three thousand nautical miles at least. She's got a week, maybe ten days at the outside."

"What about enemy subs?" Don asked.

Harrison switched back to the visual image of the Chinese Navy piers. He pointed to an empty spot at the pier. "There was a *Han*-class fast attack here yesterday. She's gone."

25

USS *Hyman G. Rickover* (SSN-795)
North Pacific Ocean

"Depth five-zero meters and holding, speed zero," the pilot said. "Ship is hovering, ma'am."

"Very well, Pilot," Janet replied.

Although they had all performed this evolution at least three times a day for the last nine days, Janet felt her stomach churn with anxiety. There were too many variables, too many things to go wrong. True, the Narwhal ROVs had exceeded everyone's expectations, but they were just prototypes, not ruggedized milspec equipment. The tiniest mistake could end the *Rickover*'s mission in an instant.

Take it slow and easy, Janet told herself. You've been lucky. Let's not blow it now.

"Sonar," she said. "Report all contacts." Janet studied the broadband waterfall display as the sonar supervisor gave his report. The only surface contact on the screen was the USS *Lawrence*, fifteen thousand yards to the east, which showed up as a steady bright line on the display. The guided missile destroyer had arrived days ago and now carved lines in the ocean, waiting for the *Rickover* to find the downed Chinese submarine.

Janet picked up the handset and buzzed the CO in the wardroom.

"Captain," Nakamura answered.

"Officer of the Deck, sir," Janet replied crisply. "Request permission to recover the Narwhals, take ship to periscope depth, and transmit the data package. The ship is hovering. We hold one sonar contact, identified as the USS *Lawrence*, bearing two-eight-zero at one-five thousand yards."

"Permission granted, XO."

Janet hung up the phone. "Fire Control, open VLS tubes ten and twelve."

"Open VLS tubes ten and twelve, aye, ma'am," replied Petty Officer Prescott, the on-watch fire controlman. He touched his display. A second later, Janet gave an involuntary wince as she heard a *thump* forward of their position and above them.

"Tubes ten and twelve indicate intermediate," the pilot announced. Janet saw two green circles on the VLS status board disappear. A few seconds later, the display showed a red dot. "VLS tubes ten and twelve indicate fully open, OOD."

"Very well." Janet blew out a breath. "Petty Officer Prescott, initiate recovery procedure on Narwhal One."

Prescott was a blond-haired, blue-eyed kid from somewhere in the Midwest who did not have to shave yet. "Recovering Narwhal One, aye, ma'am," he said, tapping his display.

For the next few nerve-racking minutes, there was literally nothing for her to do. The Narwhal recovery procedure was automated. The ROV approached the submarine from the rear, using a series of transponders fixed on the top surface of the sub hull to line up its approach.

"Narwhal One is in place over VLS tube ten, ma'am," Prescott announced. "Beginning inversion."

Janet watched the display over the fire control technician's shoulder. The graphic showed the cigar-shaped Narwhal parallel to the deck of the *Rickover*. The thin point of the Narwhal probe made the unit look like a hypodermic needle. She tried to imagine a twenty-one-foot hypodermic needle floating in the water above them.

As she watched, the needle point began to dip, and the unit rotated until the Narwhal was pointed straight down at the host submarine. The laser sensor on the end of the Narwhal horn found its target at the bottom of the vertical launch tube.

"Narwhal One is in position," Prescott reported. "Five meters and closing."

The display showed the needle slowly dropping toward the *Rickover*.

"Four meters and closing."

Janet tried to relax her clenched jaw. The probe was the most delicate, and the most critical, part of the Narwhal. It was how the unit connected to the *Rickover* to download the sonar data and to recharge her batteries. She could think of at least ten ways the probe could be damaged during the recovery. If that happened, it was game over. The only way to repair the Narwhal was in port.

"Two meters."

Another minute that felt like an hour passed.

"Probe contact," Prescott announced.

"Very well, Fire Control," Janet muttered. She held her breath.

"I have a good connection," Prescott announced.

Janet exhaled. The last four times they'd recovered a Narwhal, they'd needed to unseat and reseat the probe to establish a connection between the ROV and the host ship.

"Close VLS tube ten," Janet ordered.

"Closing tube ten, ma'am," Prescott said.

Janet waited for the indicator light on the VLS tube to change from red to green, which was reported by the pilot.

"Start the data download on One, Fire Control," Janet said.

"Aye, ma'am," Prescott said. He tapped his display. "Data is incoming, and Narwhal One is recharging."

"Okay," Janet said. "Now, let's do it all again. Nice and easy. Begin recovery of Narwhal Two to VLS tube twelve."

Although it seemed longer, each recovery took between ten and fifteen minutes, depending on whether or not they needed to reseat the probe multiple times.

A half hour was a long time for a submarine to sit still and shallow in enemy waters. Janet had no doubt that the PLA Navy had submarines in the area. It was possible they were being watched right now by an ultraquiet diesel-electric enemy sub. The very thought made Janet's skin crawl.

"Narwhal Two is in position over tube twelve," Prescott announced. "Starting inversion."

Keeping one eye on the fire control display, Janet paced to relieve some of her nervous energy.

"Four meters and closing," Prescott announced.

The sonar supervisor sat bolt upright in his seat. "High-speed aerial contact approaching from the east at low altitude. Designate Sierra two-six."

Janet's eyes snapped to the broadband sonar display. A bright diagonal stripe cut across the screen. The line showed regular tick marks indicating a turboprop plane moving at high speed.

"Give me a classification," Janet said.

"Probably Chinese Yankee-Eight maritime patrol craft," the sonar supervisor said. "They're close. They're gonna overfly us, ma'am."

"Narwhal Two is two meters and closing," Prescott said.

Janet snatched the IMC from the cradle in the overhead. "Captain to Control," she announced over the shipwide intercom.

"One meter," Prescott said.

"He's turning!" the sonar supervisor said. "He's picked us up."

Captain Nakamura entered control.

Janet gave him an update. "We're still recovering Narwhal Two, sir. We've just had a flyover by a Chinese maritime patrol craft, and they're doubling back." She turned to Prescott. "Status of recovery?"

"We do not have a connection, ma'am," Prescott reported.

There was no way to know if the Narwhal was fully in the VLS tube or was hung up partway. If they shut the tube door, it would permanently damage the Narwhal.

"Sonobouys!" sonar reported. "They're dropping sonobouys."

Janet's gaze clocked back to the sonar display. White dots trailed across the screen.

"Pilot, flood into forward and aft trim," Janet ordered.

"What are you doing, XO?" Nakamura demanded.

The pilot hesitated, and Janet snapped at him. "Flood, Pilot. Now!" She turned to the CO. "We have a layer at one hundred meters, sir. We'll get below the layer, reseat the Narwhal, and get the hell out of here."

"Eight-zero meters and dropping fast," the pilot reported. "Fifteen K in forward and aft trim."

"Secure flooding at one hundred meters and start pumping, Pilot," Janet ordered. "Pump, not blow."

The pilot repeated the order. The chief petty officer was ramrod straight in his chair, and a sheen of sweat glistened on his forehead. Janet had just turned their perfectly trimmed submarine into a stone, and they were descending fast.

"Sonobuoys going active," the sonar supe reported.

"Passing one hundred meters," the pilot said. "Pumping from forward and aft trim." A few seconds later, he spoke again. "Passing one-ten meters. Request permission to blow trim tanks, OOD."

Janet could feel the eyes of the captain on her. "Negative, Pilot. Keep pumping."

Using high-pressure air to force large volumes of water from the trim tanks was much more efficient, but it was also noisy. If there was a Chinese submarine in the area, the last thing she wanted to do was advertise their position.

At least they'd made it below the thermal layer before the sonobuoys triangulated their location. The change in water temperature would block sound energy from above and would hide them for the time being. Eventually, the Chinese aircraft would realize their mistake and use a different type of sensor to come after the *Rickover*.

"Holding at one-eight-zero meters, OOD," the pilot said, relief evident in his voice.

"Very well." Janet released the back of the vinyl-covered chair that she had been holding in a death grip for the last few minutes. "Fire Control, proceed with recovery of Narwhal Two."

"Aye, ma'am."

The designers of the Narwhal ROV had anticipated the challenge of seating the unit's probe into the host submarine. The crew of the *Rickover* called the process "burping the baby," and they had used it multiple times already.

Prescott called up the subroutine on his computer. "Commencing recovery."

Two seconds of reverse thrust on the Narwhal's motor was supposed to back the unit partially out of the tube. Forward thrust would reseat the probe.

"I have probe contact!" Prescott announced.

Janet breathed a sigh of relief, then her shoulders sagged when she saw the display. The connection light flickered and went out.

"Data connection?" she asked. Hoping against hope that it was a faulty sensor.

Prescott shook his head. "No data link, no power link."

"Run it again," Janet ordered.

Three minutes later, they had the same result. Janet cursed to herself. Had the sudden change in depth flooded the connection and caused the failure?

"Run it—" she began.

"XO," the captain interrupted. "Close VLS tube number twelve and clear datum for an hour."

She knew Nakamura was right. Narwhal Two was gone. Thanks to her, they'd just lost half of their assets in the search for the Chinese nuclear weapon.

"Aye-aye, sir."

26

White House
Washington, DC

When Don and the Director walked into the Oval Office for the third time in as many weeks, President Serrano and Chief of Staff Wilkerson were already seated in their normal places. There was coffee on the table between them, and each was holding a full cup.

Serrano got up to greet them, all smiles. "I understand congratulations are in order." He took Don's hand. "Well done."

"We're not out of the woods yet, sir," Don replied.

Serrano increased the wattage on his smile. "I know you, Don, and you wouldn't be here unless you had a way to close this deal."

Don cut a look at the Director. Be careful what you wish for, he thought.

Serrano ushered his guests to the waiting sofa and reached for the coffeepot. "Coffee, gentlemen?"

Don and the Director both said yes. While the President poured coffee, Don felt Wilkerson's eyes on him. When he met the older man's gaze, Wilkerson nodded and—Don could scarcely believe it—the Chief of Staff smiled at him. Granted, it wasn't much of a smile, but coming from Wilkerson, it felt huge.

But why? Don wondered, then he thought: he won't be smiling when I tell him why I'm here.

Serrano sat back in his chair and crossed his legs. He balanced the white china cup and saucer on the point of his knee. "We have a meeting with the full National Security Council in a few hours, but you gentlemen asked to see me in advance. I smell a rat." The President turned his Serrano Stare onto Don full blast. "Let's have it, Don. The good, the bad, and the ugly."

Don extracted a picture from a manila envelope and placed it on the table. It showed a grainy multicolor image of three geometric lumps on a rocky surface.

"This was taken with side-scan sonar. It's likely that we have found the lost Chinese submarine. That's the good news," he added.

Serrano studied the photo, then passed it to Wilkerson. "What's the bad news?"

Don placed a large-scale chart of the ocean floor on the table between them. There was a red circle on the chart. "It's in nine thousand feet of water, so it's possible for the recovery system on the *Lawrence* to retrieve the Chinese weapon."

"I'm not following," Serrano said, a line of frustration creasing his forehead. "You know where it is, and you just said the *Lawrence* can retrieve it. That's the bad news?"

"We know *about* where it is, Mr. President," Don replied. "For us to locate the wreck with enough accuracy for a retrieval, the *Rickover* has to keep searching. Once they find the exact location, they'll do a video survey of the wreck and place a locator beacon for the *Lawrence*."

"Ah," Serrano said. "I see. This is about the damaged equipment on the *Rickover*, right?"

"Sort of, sir," Don said. "That slows us down, but even if we had both of the underwater vehicles working, we still can't beat the clock."

"What Riley is trying to say, sir," interrupted the Director, "is that we're out of time. The Chinese task force is only a few days out. Once they reach the search site, there's no way the *Rickover* will be able to stay on station."

Serrano's face twisted as he digested this news. He set down his cup and saucer with a *clack* on the table.

"We can bring in more air assets," the President said, "from Alaska and the West Coast."

The Director shook his head. "The PLA task force is more than a dozen ships and who knows how many submarines. They'll blanket the area, and *Rickover* will be trapped."

"No." Serrano leaped to his feet and began pacing. "We've come this far. There has to be a way—"

"Mr. President," Wilkerson said, "if we try to challenge the Chinese, we'd be risking an international incident on the eve of your inauguration."

"There is a way, sir," Don said. Wilkerson shot a visual dagger across the lacquered surface of the coffee table.

Serrano paused. "Tell me."

"Mr. President," the Director said, "I should warn you. This is the ugly part. We're here because we wanted you to know all of your options, but..." The Director seemed to search for the right words. "We wanted you to have the chance to consider this idea privately first."

Don would have liked to break the tension by sipping his coffee, but he was afraid his hand might shake if he tried to pick up the cup.

"Out with it, Riley," the President said.

"Mr. Wilkerson is right, sir," Don began. "There's no way we could scramble a task force of equal size to the Chinese and get them there in time to help the recovery effort. Even if we could, the timing is terrible." Don's tongue was dry. "But what if someone did it for us?"

"What does that mean?" Serrano said.

"We could ask the Russians for help," Don replied. "*You* could ask the Russians for help."

For a moment, the room was still. Don heard the Director breathing next to him, heard the gentle whoosh of the forced air heating system.

Then Wilkerson cursed out loud. "That is the stupidest fucking idea that—"

Serrano cut him off with a hand gesture. "Let him speak, Irv."

Don went back to the chart on the table. He tapped the left edge of the image, where the brown and green represented land. "This is Petropavlovsk Naval Base on the Kamchatka Peninsula. It's a day's sail from the search area. They could be on station a full day before the Chinese arrive." Don paused. "If they left in the next twelve hours."

"What would I tell them?" Serrano asked, pursing his lips.

"Sir, you can't seriously be—"

The President cut Wilkerson off with a chop of his hand.

Don felt the heat of Wilkerson's anger shift to him.

"Tell them the truth," Don said. "Tell them we found the wreck of a Chinese submarine and we're trying to recover it. The Chinese want to stop us, and it'd be better if they didn't."

"They'll want us to share what we find," Wilkerson said.

"A small price to pay," Don replied, "as long as they buy us the time to finish the job."

"What if it goes sideways?" Wilkerson countered.

"What if it does?" Serrano said. "It's between the Chinese and the Russians, we're not involved."

"Mr. President," Wilkerson said. "You can't—"

"It's the only way, Irv," Serrano snapped. "We get this nuke and we've got the Chinese over a barrel. General Secretary Yi? This information could destroy him if it ever came out. We would own him."

Wilkerson changed his line of attack. "The Russians will find out about the nuclear weapon, Mr. President. When they do, they'll be pissed you didn't tell them up front."

Serrano walked away. He crossed to the windows looking out over the Rose Garden. Sunlight spilled over his shoulders, turning the highlights in his hair into flame.

"Set up the call, Irv. Person-to-person between Nikolay and me, no interpreters, no recordings. As soon as possible."

Don and the Director stood along with Wilkerson. Don felt unsteady on his feet, as if he'd just unleashed something over which he had no control.

"Don?" the President called over his shoulder.

"Yes, sir?"

"Good job."

"Thank you, Mr. President."

Wilkerson brushed past him. "This is on your head, Riley," he hissed.

27

USS *Hyman G. Rickover* (SSN-795)
North Pacific Ocean

As the *Rickover* made the trip to periscope depth, Janet sat behind one of the control room displays set to monitor the feed from the photonics mast. The Officer of the Deck, the most senior lieutenant in the wardroom, had control of the optical mast, and he slowly rotated the view in low power as the submarine climbed. As they neared the surface, Janet felt the ship rock gently.

The monitor went from black to gray to light gray, then broke free of the ocean.

"Scope is clear!" the OOD announced. He swept a full 360 degrees in low power. "No close contacts."

The low sky was the color of slate. Meter-high swells from the west, wind creaming the tops of the waves.

"I hold a contact on bearing three-zero-two." The OOD shifted the image to higher-power magnification, and Janet saw the superstructure of a warship poking above the horizon.

"Sierra seven-nine, sir," the sonar supervisor reported. "Classified as Russian *Slava*-class cruiser. Range nine thousand yards."

That would be the *Varyag*, Janet thought. Flagship of Rear Admiral Piotr Morozov.

"Give me the bearings for the other Russkies, Sonar," the OOD ordered.

He searched the sonar contact bearings in vain for the more distant and smaller vessels. In addition to the *Varyag*, there were two *Udaloy*-class destroyers and a pair of *Steregushchiy*-class corvettes.

Add the USS *Lawrence* to the mix, and that gave them a grand total of six ships against the incoming Chinese task force.

"I don't understand the world, XO," the OOD said. "Twenty-four hours ago, the Russians were our enemies. Now, they're protecting us."

"The enemy of my enemy is my friend," Janet said.

"If you say so, XO," the OOD replied. "Permission to transmit?"

"Granted," Janet replied, lost in her own thoughts on the subject.

Two days ago, when the first message arrived about the Russian assistance in their search, Janet was dumbfounded. Her confusion deepened when a fake story was leaked to the press to cover the sudden naval movements.

Unnamed sources confirmed that the Russian Navy had lost a Gen 5 fighter jet in the North Pacific and had requested assistance from the United States in recovering the asset. The USS *Lawrence*, equipped with the FADOSS deep sea winch, was the designated vessel. There was, of course, no mention of the *Rickover*.

In this version of the story, the Chinese were the villains, sailing north to harass the peaceful Russian-American joint operation. Naturally, Beijing was not about to acknowledge they'd lost a submarine, much less a state-of-the-art unmanned asset carrying a nuclear weapon, so they limited their public utterances to bombastic diplo-speak.

But actions spoke louder than words, and their response to the sham joint operation was a task force of fifteen warships and support vessels closing on the *Rickover*'s location at a steady fifteen knots.

"Conn, Radio, we have an updated intel package in the queue," the duty radioman reported over the intercom.

The tactical situation was changing rapidly, so the *Rickover* had been making trips to periscope depth every four hours to keep as up to date as possible.

"Radio, XO, acknowledged," Janet replied. She displayed the new information on her screen.

"What do we have, XO?" Captain Nakamura said from over her shoulder.

Janet pinched her lip as she absorbed the new tactical picture. "Not good, sir. Since the last update, the PLA task force has increased speed to twenty-five knots and split into two groups."

"They're going to surround us," the captain said.

"I agree, sir."

"How much time do we have?"

Janet flipped to a new screen showing projected tracks of the incoming task force. "At that speed of advance?" Janet quickly ran the numbers. "Eight hours, sir. Give or take."

Nakamura had a habit of cracking his knuckles when thinking. Right now, it sounded like a xylophone quartet was playing next to Janet's ear.

"If we don't get out of here soon," the captain said, "we won't make it out."

That was an optimistic assessment, in Janet's view. PLA maritime patrol aircraft had been dropping hundreds of sonobuoys to the north and east of their position. She could only imagine the tension in the skies above them. Since the involvement of the Russian Navy, the PLA had redoubled their efforts to find the *Rickover*. The PLA aircraft carriers were launching fighter combat air patrols to escort the Y-8 maritime patrol craft. Already, there had been two close calls between US and Chinese aircraft. At this point, it was more about who was going to fire the first shot than if it was going to happen.

Still, they were close to finding the downed Chinese submarine, she could feel it. All they needed was a little more time. And a second Narwhal would be nice, Janet thought ruefully.

The Narwhals had never been designed for this kind of open ocean search. The units tracked their course and speed after they departed from the mother ship, with offsets calculated by onboard accelerometers. But as the Narwhals changed depth and came into contact with different undersea current patterns, the resulting location data became more and more unreliable. As a result, the *Rickover* had spent the last two days trying to pinpoint the site of the submarine wreck.

To minimize the risk, Janet programmed the remaining Narwhal to video mode. The unit dove to the ocean floor and slowly recorded the images from a height of ten meters. The result was hours of underwater rock formations followed by a few seconds of hope, quickly dashed. Twice they'd come across undersea wrecks, but they turned out to be merchant ships.

"Conn, Radio." The blare of the intercom interrupted Janet's train of thought. "We have incoming flash traffic."

"Radio, Captain, bring it to Control," Nakamura replied.

A few seconds later, the duty radioman handed the captain a top-secret message tablet. Janet watched the CO's face as he unlocked the tablet and read the message. The man gave nothing away. He passed her the tablet, and Janet scanned the screen.

USS Hyman G. Rickover to abort current mission. All prior orders canceled. Depart current search area by best available route under current tactical situation. RTB Hawaii.

Janet cursed to herself. They were giving up. All the work they'd done to get so close to finding the missing Chinese wreck was all for nothing. Their mission was a failure.

"Sir," Janet began, "what if we—"

Nakamura held up a hand to silence her. He raised his voice. "Attention in Control, we have new orders. The ship will recover the Narwhal, send the final data upload to Washington, and clear the area."

"We're going home." Janet heard the whisper in the room. She'd served on submarines long enough to know the news would pass through the ship like a brushfire in a gale-force wind. Within a minute, everyone on the ship would know they were headed back to Pearl.

We are so close, Janet thought. I know it.

"XO," the captain said.

"Sir," she said, aware of the sharpness in her voice. There was nothing to do. They'd taken their shot and missed the mark.

"Recover the Narwhal and transfer the data into the buffer," the captain said. "We'll make one more trip to PD to transmit the package, then I want to beat feet out of here. Get the Nav working on our best route home."

Janet repeated the order back to her captain and watched him depart the control room. She raised her voice, "Attention in Control, this is the XO. I have the deck and the conn." She waited for acknowledgments of the change in command before she continued. "Pilot, make your depth five-zero meters. Fire Control, best course to intercept the Narwhal."

As the deck of the *Rickover* angled downward, Janet threw herself into her work. She split her time between preparations to recover the ROV and determining the safest path away from the search site. She knew that work was the best antidote against her disappointment.

We went looking for a needle in a haystack, and the haystack won, she thought glumly.

She paused behind the sonar supervisor's chair. He nodded at the waterfall screen where a bright band of yellow had formed to the southeast.

"Check this out, ma'am." He handed her a set of headphones. When Janet put them on, it sounded like hammers on metal, hundreds of them. It drowned out all the normal noises of the ocean.

The sonar supervisor was a gray-haired senior chief. He shook his head. "I've never seen so much active sonar in my life, ma'am. They're putting so much energy into the water, you'd think they were trying to boil the ocean."

"Can they actually get a return?" she asked.

"Not a chance." He snorted. "It's like a heavy metal rock concert out there. Besides, they're going so fast they'd run over something before they got a return."

"So it's a scare tactic, senior?" Janet asked.

"Hey," the older man replied. "They sure as hell got my attention. I'm glad we're putting this place in our rearview mirror."

"I have the Narwhal in trail position, ma'am," Prescott reported.

"Very well," Janet replied. "Pilot, all stop. Hover the ship and stand by to recover the Narwhal."

The one benefit to having completed dozens of launch-and-recovery evolutions on the Narwhals over the past two weeks was that the crew knew exactly what to do. The recovery went off textbook perfect, a fitting conclusion to the operation.

"VLS tube twelve indicates closed," the pilot reported.

"Very well, Pilot," Janet replied. "All ahead one-third."

"Downloading the video data now, ma'am," Prescott reported.

"Very well, Fire Control. Verify integrity of the file and upload it to the transmission buffer."

"Do you want me to review it, ma'am?"

"Review what you can with the time allowed, Prescott," Janet said, turning her attention to the navigation plot where the Navigator had laid out three options to make their way through the fields of Chinese sonobuoys.

Janet focused on the task at hand. She tapped her finger on the northernmost route out of the search area. "This path is more out of the way, but these sonobuoys have been in the water for the longest amount of time. A lot of them might be dead by now—"

"Officer of the Deck?" It was Petty Officer Prescott. "You need to see this, ma'am."

Janet stood behind the fire control tech's chair. "Show me."

"Watch." Prescott rewound the video a few seconds, then hit play. Janet saw a slow crawl of rocks and mud, then a black shape came into view. Geometric, man-made. He paused the video. "That's a propeller, a submarine propeller." His voice had a lilt of energy, as if he was trying not to shout.

Janet felt the navigator peering over her shoulder. "Holy shit," he said. "We found it."

Cheers erupted in control. Two sonar techs high-fived each other.

Prescott started the video again. The camera angle moved across the sunken wreck. The dark skin of the submarine was torn where an explosion had happened. More ocean floor showed.

"There's another piece up ahead...," Prescott said. "Right here." He stabbed his finger at the screen.

Janet saw the new section of the sub. The skin of the ship was cleaved in two. The cut steel showed as a line of reflected light on the video.

A pillar of white came into view. A missile.

"That's it!" Prescott shouted. He pumped a fist in the air. "We found it!"

Janet felt her mouth go slack. She clamped a hand on Prescott's shoulder. "Stop." She was having a hard time forming words. "Go back. Show me that again."

This was not happening, Janet told herself. There was no way what she was seeing was true. The excited buzz of conversation threatened to overwhelm her senses.

"Quiet!" she roared.

Silence.

Janet reached into the overhead and found the IMC handset by touch.

"Captain to Control."

28

USS *Hyman G. Rickover* (SSN-795)
North Pacific Ocean

Captain Nakamura watched the video twice. Janet sat across from him in his stateroom, studying his face and not getting any reaction. He set the tablet down on his desk.

"Did you see it?" she asked.

The details of the video were etched in her mind. The Chinese submarine had broken into three pieces. The largest chunk, the midsection containing the cargo hold, had settled on its port side.

There was some sediment in the water showing up as white flashes, making it seem as if the submarine was in a snowstorm. Despite the image quality, there was no mistaking what she'd seen. The flank of the Chinese submarine had been opened up with a laser torch. Clean, bright lines of freshly cut metal. A series of square sections of the steel hull lay scattered in the sand a few meters away.

The opening exposed a long white cylinder. It was difficult to appreciate the scale of the object, but judging by the height of the submarine, the cylinder was the size of an old-growth tree. In fact, Janet had looked up the dimensions. A Chinese JL-2 submarine-launched ballistic missile was nearly two meters in diameter and over ten meters long.

She closed her eyes. What she'd seen was unthinkable, unbelievable.

They'd discovered a complete Chinese ballistic missile on the bottom of the ocean—except for one problem.

The nuclear warhead was missing.

Nakamura broke the silence with a single word. "How?"

"All due respect, sir," Janet replied, "I don't think that's the question we should be asking."

Nakamura's expression softened. "What question should we be asking, Janet?"

Although it was the first time the captain had ever used her given name, Janet barely gave the event a passing thought.

"The question isn't how," she said. "It's who."

Nakamura picked up the tablet and restarted the video.

"It can't be the Chinese," she continued. "Why would they send a dozen warships up to stop us if they'd already recovered the weapon? Besides, they'd never let us near this place if they knew where it was."

"The Russians?" the captain said.

"I doubt they have the technology to pull it off," Janet replied. "If it was them, then they are the best actors I've ever seen."

Janet pointed to the screen. "Those cuts are fresh. There's no marine growth on them. This is recent."

"Maybe the Taiwanese?" Nakamura continued.

Janet shook her head. "This is the kind of operation that we barely have the ability to pull off. The tech alone is hundreds of millions of dollars and years of development." She sighed. "I guess it doesn't matter. Let Washington figure it out. We've done our part, sir."

"Agreed." The captain sat up in his chair and pulled the JA handset from the cradle next to his bunk. He tapped the buzzer to alert the control room.

"Officer of the Deck," he said, "make preparations to come to periscope depth." He hung up the phone.

From the display on the captain's wall, Janet could see the *Rickover* cruised due north at six knots, still at fifty meters depth. The same conditions as when she turned the OOD duties over to her relief so she could consult with the captain in his cabin.

Nakamura had the intercom feed set to a low volume, the sound of the control room activities providing a gentle background to their discussions.

Faintly, she heard the OOD order a two-thirds bell. The change in speed pushed her gently back in her chair as the engine room responded to the order.

"Right ten degrees rudder," she heard the OOD say. The ship banked slightly as they began a slow turn to clear baffles, the area behind the propeller where sonar was unable to hear clearly.

"Metal transient!" The shout pierced the low murmur of the control noise. "Submerged contact, bearing one-eight-six!"

Nakamura was out of his chair before Janet even processed the words. The door of his stateroom slammed against the wall, and he launched into the passageway. Janet followed.

The OOD had a deer-in-the-headlights look. "Contact was in the baffles, Captain. Came out of nowhere."

"Sonar," Nakamura said, "give me a range."

The sonar supervisor had his hands clamped on the shoulders of both of his sonar technicians and leaned between them, studying their screen. "He's close, sir, probably inside of three thousand yards."

"Helm," the captain said, "right full rudder—"

"Captain!" the sonar supe shouted. "Underwater telephone transmission."

"Steady as she goes, Helm," the captain snapped. "Sonar, put it on speaker."

A hissing sound filled the control room, punctuated by the clicks and snaps of the marine life in the ocean around the submarine.

A flat, distorted voice reverberated out of the speakers. "American submarine, this is PLA Navy submarine. Acknowledge."

The sound of the ocean blanketed the silent control room.

Captain Nakamura licked his lips. He walked to the rack of equipment and removed the handset for the UQC underwater telephone. He threw a switch, and Janet saw a red light on the panel illuminate.

"Sonar," the captain said. "Transmitting."

"Aye, sir," the sonar chief replied in a whisper.

The CO held the microphone close to his lips and pressed the transmit button. He spoke slowly and clearly. "Submerged contact, identify yourself. Over."

Seconds passed.

"Do not change course or speed. We have fire control solution...torpedo loaded. Do not attempt to open torpedo doors. Do you understand? Over."

Janet looked at the weapons status board. The *Rickover* had a torpedo loaded in tube one, but the tube was not flooded and the outer doors were closed. Both of those were noisy evolutions, which would be immediately apparent to the enemy submarine. At this distance, there was no way they could outrun an enemy weapon.

The *Rickover* was a sitting duck.

The captain cut a look at the sonar supervisor. "Chief?"

"The transient we heard was probably doors being opened, sir," the chief said. "I have a better estimate on range. Two thousand six hundred yards."

Nakamura's face was gray stone.

"American submarine." The underwater transmission warbled as if they were on a weak analog telephone connection. "Do you understand last transmission? Over."

Nakamura swallowed, then raised the handset to his lips.

"We are in international waters," he said in a measured voice. "What do you want? Over."

"Maintain course and speed. Break. Surface your ship. Break. Do not transmit. Break. We will contact you by VHF. If you fail to comply, we will attack. Acknowledge."

Nakamura drew in a sharp breath. The Chinese had him in a box, and everyone knew it. He motioned for Janet to come closer.

"Get down to the torpedo room, XO," he said. "Get all the tubes loaded and pressure equalized. Quietly. I'll buy you as much time as I can."

"Aye, sir," Janet said. "You're going to surface?"

"Do I have a choice?" Nakamura's mouth tightened in a smile. "This will be the slowest surfacing evolution in the history of the submarine service."

He held the microphone to his lips and pressed the transmit button. "Copy all."

29

Emerging Threats Group
Tysons Corner, Virginia

Don's restless gaze scanned the news headlines on his computer screen. The *New York Times* caught his eye.

As Inauguration Day Nears, Tensions Rise in Pacific.

He clicked on the article and ran his eye down the screen. The Russian and Chinese navies were facing off in the North Pacific over the search site of the lost Russian aircraft. There was predictable editorial opining about the presence of the USS *William P. Lawrence* in the potential conflict, but unnamed sources assured the paper that the United States was a neutral party in the situation.

The story was holding so far, Don thought, wondering again what President Serrano might have promised to his Russian counterpart to make him play along with this farce. Whatever it was, Don would bet his wallet there would be a future price to pay, a hefty one.

"Doesn't matter," Don muttered. "The search is over."

Well, almost over. He consulted his watch. He'd been expecting the final data upload from the USS *Rickover* for over an hour. Don secretly hoped that the delay was a sign that they'd found the lost submarine.

The idea soured as soon as it passed through his mind. What good would it do them now? With the PLA task force bearing down on the search area, even if they found the lost sub, there was no way the Chinese would allow the *Lawrence* to deploy their recovery system. For the People's Republic of China, what was at stake was nothing less than the global nuclear balance of power. They would attack before they let the *Lawrence* recover one of their nuclear weapons.

Don closed the news story. The whole thing was an unmitigated mess, and they should consider themselves lucky if it stayed a secret.

His desk phone trilled. Don punched the intercom button. "Riley." His curt voice matched his mood.

"Hey, Don." Dre's voice. "I got something you should see."

Don sighed. "That doesn't sound good."

"Maybe, maybe not," was her reply.

"Don't be so mysterious, Dre."

"Just get down here." She hung up.

Nerves were on edge with everyone, Don reflected, as he made his way toward the conference room. Between the hunt for the Naval War College bomber and the search for the Chinese sub, the team at ETG had been going nonstop for over two months. A lot of people had sacrificed nights, weekends, and holidays and had nothing to show for their extraordinary efforts.

After inauguration, he decided, I'll set up a vacation schedule and make sure people get some time off. Including myself, he added as a mental note. I need to go somewhere with no mobile phone service and drink a few margaritas to the ones that got away.

He wondered where Rachel and the Chinese terrorist were right now and then pushed the thought from his head. That was a problem he would settle in his own time and on his own terms.

When he entered the conference room, Dre had a video feed up on the wall screen. She and Michael stood in front of the image in quiet conversation.

"What do we have?" Don asked, joining them at the screen.

It was top-down view of a seething ocean. A streak of white foam trailed across the screen.

"Video feed from an overwatch drone," Dre said. She tapped the white line running across the screen like smoke. "That's a submarine surfacing in the search area."

Don rocked back and forth on his heels. The *Rickover* did not need to surface to transmit the last data package. In fact, based on the little he knew about submarines, the only time they ever surfaced was to go in and out of port.

Or if there was an emergency. A serious emergency like a fire or a nuclear accident. He controlled the tone of his voice as he said, "Is it Janet?"

"Dunno." Dre chewed on her thumbnail, a habit that only manifested when she was deeply worried about something. "I've been on the phone with SUBPAC, and they don't know for sure from this angle—or they won't say. What they did tell me is that whoever they are, they are taking their sweet old time. My contact says they should have been on the surface with the bridge manned an hour ago."

"What does that mean?" Don asked. "There's been an accident?"

"They don't know."

"What about radio contact?" Don pressed.

Dre shook her head, went back to gnawing her thumbnail. "That's the other thing. *Rickover* hasn't missed a single transmission window in this entire operation. Now, they're an hour overdue for check-in, and there's a mystery submarine surfacing in the search area."

Dre's secure desk phone rang, and she stepped away to take the call. Less than a minute later, she was back.

"That's my guy at SUBPAC," she said. "It's the *Rickover* surfacing, but they still haven't been able to make contact. They don't know what's going on. The sub obviously has power, so that rules out a problem with the reactor. If they had a fire, he says we'd be seeing them venting smoke. The working theory is they had a flooding accident and the ship's too heavy to surface."

"But that doesn't explain why there's no radio transmissions." Don rubbed his neck, trying to think. "Where's the *Lawrence*?" he asked.

Dre expanded the image. She pointed at a rough semicircle of ships. At this scale, the plume of the surfacing submarine was lost in the sea clutter.

"*Lawrence* is on picket duty with the Russians about forty miles away from where the submarine is surfacing," she said. "They set up a picket line between the *Rickover* and the whole damn Chinese Navy that's headed their way."

"They should send the *Lawrence* to intercept the sub," Don said. "Maybe they can communicate with her."

"Listen to you," Dre said, smiling. "All Navy and stuff." Her expression sobered. "Subs have backup systems on their backup systems for satellite communications. There's at least six ways they could send a message before they have to fall back on VHF line-of-sight comms, Don." Dre looked at Michael.

"She's right," Michael said. "Let SUBPAC handle it."

"Something's wrong," Don replied. "How well do you know this guy at SUBPAC? At least make the suggestion."

"You win." Dre held up her hands. "He owes me. I'll make the call."

Dre was back in less than a minute. "Well, Admiral Riley, they liked your idea. The *Lawrence* has orders to intercept the *Rickover* and report back."

"Now what?" Don asked.

Dre folded her arms and faced the screen. "Now we wait. Welcome to the Navy, Admiral."

30

USS *Hyman G. Rickover* (SSN-795)
North Pacific Ocean

As the ship rolled, Janet caught the edge of the doorjamb leading into the control room.

Her stomach lurched, but whether the queasiness was from the North Pacific swells outside the submarine or their terrible tactical situation, she couldn't tell. Probably both.

She was covered in sweat, and her hands were slick with the grease used in the torpedo room. Moving twenty-foot-long Mark 48 torpedoes that weighed the better part of two tons was a delicate task when the ship was stable. Performing the same evolution in heavy seas was downright dangerous. The team in the torpedo room had just loaded the remaining three tubes in record time.

Nakamura looked up as she entered. "Captain," she reported, "all four torpedo tubes loaded, pressures equalized, and tubes flooded."

Their Chinese captors had given them a small win. By forcing the *Rickover* to surface, the job of equalizing pressure between the torpedo tube and the external ocean was made easier. Shallower depth meant less sea pressure to deal with. But the torpedo tube doors were still closed, so they still could not fire a weapon yet.

"Do you plan to open outer doors, sir?" Janet cast a look at the fire control display. With the ship manned for general quarters, every seat except one in the double row of monitors was manned. The empty chair was for her.

The ship took another roll. Past the captain, Janet could see a video image of the outside world. Swells surged at them from the northwest, and a brisk wind whipped spray from the wave crests. The eastern sky was getting lighter. It would be dawn in another hour.

"We can't risk it," the CO replied in a grim tone. "Not yet. If they hear the transient, we're toast."

Janet took her seat and configured the display to show the fire control system. Nakamura was right. The Chinese submarine captain knew what he was doing. He kept his ship at a range of less than two thousand yards from the *Rickover* and behind them.

"If we make one wrong move," the captain said from behind Janet, "they'll put a pair of torpedoes in us before we can react."

It was worse than that, Janet saw. In addition to the precious seconds it would take the *Rickover* to open torpedo tube doors and launch their own weapons, the Mark 48 torpedo was equipped with an anti-circular run safety protocol, designed to prevent a torpedo from circling back and destroying their own ship. By staying close to the *Rickover* and behind them, the Chinese captain was using the safety protocols of the Mark 48 torpedo against them. By the time the *Rickover* changed course and got far enough away from the PLA sub to fire her own torpedoes, they'd be dead.

Well played, she thought. Despite the circumstances, the daring elegance of the Chinese captain's plan was impressive.

She scanned the rest of the tactical situation. A Chinese Y-8 maritime patrol craft circled overhead their position to ensure the US submarine maintained radio silence.

The USS *Rickover* was alone.

"Underwater telephone transmission, Captain," the sonar supervisor reported.

The CO reached above his head and turned the dial to raise the volume on the UQC. The surface action of the ocean made the transmission trashy with static, but at this distance it was impossible not to hear the other submarine.

"American submarine." The voice came across distorted, warbled. "Come...all stop...man bridge...prepare...boarded...Over."

The staticky sounds of the ocean washed over the control room. Janet saw the muscles on Nakamura's jawline dance with anger.

A report from the Electronic Support station broke the tension. "New radar contact bearing one-six-nine, designated SPS-67 surface search radar. Contact is USS *Lawrence*, Captain."

"What's the range, ESM?" the captain asked.

"It's faint, sir. Gotta be at least thirty miles out, probably more."

"American submarine...acknowledge...transmission." Even through the static and distortion, Janet could detect the insistence of the Chinese captain's voice.

Nakamura crossed his arms. Janet could read his thoughts. The aircraft above them was monitoring their transmissions. They'd know in an instant if the *Rickover* tried to contact the *Lawrence*.

The captain reached into the overhead and turned down the volume on the UQC. "Radio, Captain, when is our next satellite window?"

"Captain, radio, three minutes, sir."

Nakamura acknowledged the information. He paced between the double row of monitors, his body swaying with the movement of the rolling deck.

"Attention in Control," he announced. "On the next satellite pass, I intend to transmit. We will provide Washington with the location of the Chinese submarine wreck and what we've found out about the nuclear weapon. As soon as the transmission is acknowledged, we will open all torpedo tube doors. If we are fired on by the Chinese sub, we will return fire with tubes one and three and then go deep. Are there any questions?"

In the harsh light of the control room, the faces turned to the CO looked waxen.

This is suicide, Janet thought. Of course, they needed to get the message to Washington about the missing Chinese nuclear warhead, but unless they complied with the Chinese demands they were—

Janet shot out of her chair. She stepped close to Nakamura. "Captain, I have an idea."

Nakamura's face was gray, his eyes fierce. Determined, Janet thought, but also afraid. Her gaze swept around the control room. They were all afraid, herself included. Nobody wanted to die.

"Captain," she repeated.

"Radio, captain, time to satellite window."

"One minute twenty seconds, sir."

Nakamura looked at her. "You have fifteen seconds, XO."

"What if we give them what they want, sir?" Janet said. Her voice sounded urgent and desperate.

The captain jerked back as if she'd slapped him. "You want to let the PLA board a US submarine? Are you out of your fucking mind, XO?"

Janet slammed her eyes shut, then opened them again. She was having trouble finding the right words.

"That's not what I meant, sir," Janet said. "The Chinese are after the lost nuke. We know where it is, and we know the warhead is missing. We have pictures! That's gotta be worth something, right?"

Nakamura stared at her as precious seconds drained away.

"Forty-five seconds to satellite window, Captain," the radio operator announced.

"How?" Nakamura said. "I'm not letting them on this ship."

Janet blinked. That was a problem. There was no way either captain would allow the other on his ship.

"The *Lawrence*," Janet said. "We'll ask them to come to the *Lawrence*."

Nakamura's eyes lost focus as he thought through the idea. Then they hardened again. His gaze raked across Janet's features, and she knew he had come to a decision.

The captain stepped away and turned his back on her.

"Attention in Control," he said. "We have a new plan. Pilot, all stop."

"Engineroom answers all stop, sir."

Nakamura plucked the underwater telephone handset from the overhead cradle. He looked at Janet.

"XO, man the bridge."

USS *Hyman G. Rickover* (SSN-795)
North Pacific Ocean

"This is a bad idea, ma'am." The torpedoman chief didn't use his headset. Instead, he leaned down and shouted into Janet's ear.

She kept her back to the stinging rain and the biting north wind. She pointed across the heaving gray sea to where the USS *Lawrence* plowed through the swells three thousand yards away.

"I'm getting on that ship, Chief," she shouted back.

The only people on the slick deck of the *Rickover* were Janet, Chief Tobin, and a young petty officer named Hastings who probably wished he'd never volunteered for Navy Dive School. While he shivered in a form-fitting rescue swimmer dry suit, Janet and the chief wore blaze-orange dry exposure suits and matching Kapok life preservers. All three of them wore safety harnesses that were clipped to the deck of the submarine.

The ship moved slowly though the water, steering a course that minimized the wash over the curved hull. For this dangerous evolution, the captain had decided that only the chief, the ship's diver, and Janet would be allowed topside. The captain would supervise from the conning tower, along with two lookouts.

"Well, if that's your plan, then I think you're gonna have to jump, XO." Tobin was a bear of a man, easily six-five and built like a redwood. While Janet's thick, oversized dry suit felt like she was wearing a clown costume, Tobin filled his out pretty well.

Janet looked up at Tobin, icy rain needling her exposed cheek. "Let's do it, Chief."

Tobin grinned at her. *He's enjoying this,* Janet thought. The man raised the VHF handset to his lips and shouted, "Bring your boat along the lee side. She's gonna jump for it."

A rigid-hulled inflatable boat, or RHIB, lined up fifty yards to the stern of the *Rickover*. It topped a swell and slammed down into the following trough.

Janet swallowed, trying not to think about all the things that could go wrong. She could slip and get crushed between the RHIB and the sub, she could go under and—

Stop, she ordered herself. *Focus.*

Janet cut a look up to the top of the conning tower. Captain Nakamura looked down at her with an expression that might have been concern or might have been *I'm glad I'm not doing that.* She forced a smile and gave him a mock salute.

The RHIB was parallel the *Rickover* now, moving slowly along the hull. Even though the bulk of the submarine shielded them from the worst of the wave action, the small craft still bucked and heaved.

This is all about timing, she thought.

Behind her, Tobin unclipped her safety harness from the deck and attached a line to the carabiner. His heavy hand clamped onto her shoulder. "I've got you on a line, XO. If you go in the drink, I'll haul you out." He twisted toward the diver. "Stand by, Hastings."

If the diver answered, Janet didn't hear it. The high, deep-V hull of the RHIB drew closer. There were three *Lawrence* sailors in the boat. The pilot stood in the rear cockpit while the other two held on in the open forward section of the craft. That was her target.

The boat pitched in an irregular rhythm. Tobin shouted in her ear. "Wait...wait..."

Janet felt the pressure of his hand on her shoulder. Her earpiece crackled. "XO, Captain, it's too dangerous—"

The boat was a few yards aft of their position. Under Tobin's guiding hand, Janet felt her body matching the movement of the waves.

"*Now!*" Tobin roared. Janet took a running leap to clear the distance between the curving slope of the submarine hull and the high side of the smaller craft. The hull of the inflatable caught her in the midsection. Her hands scrabbled for purchase on anything. She felt her body slipping, but the two sailors seized her arms and dragged her aboard. The wet line attached to her safety harness arced across the gray sky and landed on her heaving chest like a dead snake.

She felt the boat peel away from the *Rickover* and enter rougher seas. The hull slammed down, forcing more breath from her lungs. Janet sat up. The forward hatch on the *Rickover* was already open. Tobin paused, waved, then disappeared into the submarine. The hatch closed after him, leaving a sleek dark line in the turbulent gray waters.

* * *

The commanding officer met her on the fantail of the guided missile destroyer. Janet got her first look at the FADOSS. The salvage system reels of steel cable took up a good chunk of the fantail, leaving only minimal space for flight operations.

The CO shook her hand and shouted over the howling wind, "Welcome to the *William P. Lawrence*. Hal Wilcox."

"Thank you, sir. Lieutenant Commander Janet Everett, XO of the *Rickover*."

Wilcox's gaze tracked past her to where the *Nanchang*, a PLA Navy Type 055 destroyer that served as the flagship for the Chinese task force, plowed through the heavy seas. Beyond the Chinese ship, almost lost in the hazy horizon, was the Russian flagship. "I have many questions for you, XO. I'd like some answers before our guests arrive."

Janet was quickly lost as she followed Wilcox through the ship. Sailors called ahead of him. "Make a hole, cap'n's coming through." Ship's crew flattened against the painted steel walls of the narrow passageways.

They ended their journey in what looked like a large hotel room. A neatly made queen bed and adjoining bathroom occupied one end of the room. At the other end was a large desk and a table that seated six. The room was easily three times the size of her own commanding officer's stateroom.

"This place is huge," Janet said.

Wilcox laughed. "It's my in-port cabin. I have a smaller cabin up next to the bridge. We'll receive our visitors here. There's less for them to see on my ship that way."

Wilcox doffed his foul-weather gear, revealing the standard underway khaki uniform, commonly called a 2POC.

"Coffee?"

"Please." Janet stepped out of her foul-weather gear and slid a small waterproof backpack off her shoulders.

Wilcox hit a buzzer under the edge of the table. Seconds later a young man entered dressed in a red culinary specialist shirt pulled on over his uniform. Wilcox pointed at the foul-weather gear.

"Hershel, can you clear away this stuff and bring us some coffee, please?"

When the young man departed, Wilcox invited Janet to sit. He had piercing blue eyes and a square jaw. She got the impression he was a guy who liked to laugh, but he was not smiling now.

"Can I call you Janet?" he asked.

"Of course, sir."

"Good, I'm Hal," he replied. "Now, Janet, I want you to tell me what the ever-loving fuck is going on."

Janet took a deep breath. She and Nakamura had agreed it was best to share everything with the CO of the *Lawrence*, so she recounted the search for the lost Chinese submarine and nuclear weapon as concisely as she could. The only interruption in her monologue was the arrival of the coffee service. Wilcox let her speak without asking any questions. When she was done, he sat back in his chair.

"Ho-lee shit," he said.

"That's about the size of it," Janet replied. The coffee was outstanding, and she filled her cup for a third time.

"So why are you here?" he asked. "Why not your captain?"

"In case this goes sideways, he'll be ready to fight the boat," Janet replied. "Also, I'm the technical expert on the recovery effort."

"I think there's another reason, Janet," Wilcox said with a sly smile.

"What does that mean?"

"Your captain didn't want to do that at-sea transfer." He belly-laughed. "I'll show you the video. That big guy with you just threw your ass across the gap. You looked like a big ol' orange starfish trying to hold onto the side of the boat." He wiped his eyes. "That was priceless."

Janet laughed along, even as she felt the bruises on her lower rib cage. A sharp buzzing noise interrupted the captain's laughter. His face went still as he pulled a handset from beneath the table.

"Captain." He listened, then hung up. "Your friends are inbound."

A few minutes later, wearing a borrowed jacket, Janet watched a Chinese Z-20F helicopter make a landing on the fantail of the *Lawrence*. The captain explained that normally helos approached the landing zone from behind the ship, but this was made tricky by the addition of the FADOSS to the fantail of the ship where large spools of steel cable lined the edge of the deck.

The PLA Navy helo, looking like a clone of a US Navy SH-60 Seahawk, made an approach, then backed off and tried again. It looked like a tricky landing to Janet, but the pilot succeeded on the third try. Three men disembarked under the whirling rotors and made a stooped run for the helo shelter. When they were clear, the helo pilot increased power and took off again.

Captain Wilcox advanced on the group of three. Since one of the men was an admiral, he and Janet saluted the entire party. "If you gentlemen will follow me, we'll get this show on the road."

Wilcox led the way to the meeting room with Janet bringing up the rear. Wilcox led the party outside the superstructure of the ship, then entered a watertight door as close as possible to his in-port cabin.

Janet got her first look at their guests when they removed their foul-weather gear.

PLA Navy Vice Admiral Shi was a short, barrel-shaped man with a unibrow that hooded close-set eyes that devoured the details of the US

Navy ship. Janet felt like he was making a mental comparison between this ship and his own. His pursed lips offered no clue as to his final decision. The translator spoke English with a New Jersey accent. "I went to Rutgers," he explained shyly. "Six-year plan. Call me Benny."

The third man was unexpected, a PLA officer with a wicked scar on his jawline that had turned white in the cold weather outside. He introduced himself as Senior Colonel Gao, but offered no explanation for his presence. Even more interesting to Janet, the admiral seemed deferential to the junior army officer. Whoever this man was, she decided her audience for this presentation was Senior Colonel Gao.

"Lieutenant Commander Everett will handle the technical briefing," Wilcox announced from the head of the table. Janet sat alone on one side of the table with the three Chinese men facing her. She opened her laptop to the video from the Narwhal and spun the screen around to face her audience.

"This is video footage from an underwater drone taken less than twenty-four hours ago." She ran the video at half-speed so that they would not miss any of the details.

When the JL-2 missile came into view, the eyes of all three men widened. When they realized the warhead was missing, their mouths gaped. Gao said nothing, but the admiral unleashed a torrent of Mandarin at his translator.

"He wants to know what you have done with the warhead," Benny said.

"It wasn't there," Janet replied. "It was missing."

"You are lying," Gao declared in English.

"Hold on, now," Wilcox said. "Those big spools your pilot had to fly over to land on my ship? That's the deep-sea recovery system. You've been watching us for two weeks. Have we deployed the winch?"

Benny translated, and minutes passed as the two senior officers conferred in Mandarin. Gao turned to Janet. "Show me again," he demanded.

"Say please," Janet muttered as she hit play. The PLA team watched the video three more times, asking Janet to stop at certain times.

Gao produced a thumb drive. "Copy, please," he said.

Janet shook her head. "I can make you a copy, but we need to discuss terms first."

Janet noted Wilcox's eyes widen a bit, but he quickly recovered.

When Benny translated, a stony silence settled over the room. Gao barked at Benny in Mandarin.

"He says this is People's Republic of China property," Benny said. "You have no right to withhold it from us."

Wilcox leaned forward on his elbows. "Tell him that international salvage law applies here. The Law of Finds says that we have full rights to the contents of that wreck, Benny."

The explanation had the desired effect. Gao's face went white with anger, and the admiral looked like he was going to storm out of the room.

Janet let it go on for a few seconds, then said to Benny, "Tell him we don't want the submarine or the missile. Tell him we are willing to give him a copy of the video and the exact location of the wreck."

The translation calmed them.

"Now, Benny," Janet said, "let's build some trust. Tell them I want all of the PLA aircraft in the area to clear out before we have any more discussions."

After a long conversation, Gao made a call on a satellite phone. Fifteen minutes later, the captain's phone buzzed. He nodded at Janet.

"Tell them thank you," she said to Benny. "Next, we need assurances of safe passage for the *Lawrence* and my submarine."

Gao balked at this request. "He says they need to search your submarine for the warhead," Benny explained.

Janet shook her head. "No deal. We've already covered this. The submarine has no recovery capability."

"How do we know that?" Benny translated.

"You don't," Janet said to Gao. "You just have to trust me."

"No," Gao said.

Wilcox pulled the phone from beneath the table and said into the handset, "OOD, contact the Russians on VHF and tell them to converge on our location. We're going to escort the *Rickover* out of the area." He waited for a repeat back, then said, "Last thing, set general quarters."

The general quarters alarm pulsed throughout the ship. The sounds of running feet and slamming hatches passed through the closed door of the cabin. The captain's phone buzzed again, and he received the OOD's report.

"Very well, OOD. Let me know when the Russians are in position."

Benny took a gulp of his coffee before he translated. Gao stared daggers at Janet as he listened.

"You are not coming aboard my submarine, sir," Janet said to him. Benny started to translate, but Gao cut him off with a hand motion.

Janet busied herself downloading a copy of the video onto her own thumb drive. She placed it on the table between them. "This is for you," she said. Gao picked it up and said something to Benny.

"He wants to know the location of the wreck."

"We'll send it to you in twelve hours, via the US ambassador to China," Janet replied.

"No," Gao said.

Janet stood. "Those are our terms, Senior Colonel. If you cannot agree to those terms, please return the thumb drive." She held out her hand.

The scar on Gao's chin writhed under the pressure of his jaw muscles. He clenched the thumb drive in his fist and nodded curtly. When he stood, his chair slammed back against the wall.

Thirty minutes later, Janet let out a sigh as the Chinese helo lifted off from the fantail of the USS *William P. Lawrence*. Her ribs ached, and she felt drained of energy. She closed her eyes and sighed.

"Thank God that's over," she said.

"Remind me never to play poker with you, Everett," Wilcox said.

She grinned at him. "Taking the ship to general quarters was a bit much, sir."

"I do have a flair for the dramatic," he replied. "I set that up in advance so that they'd see how fast we set GQ. The Chi-Comm admiral is going to go back and kill his crew to beat that time. Poor bastards." His laugh echoed in the helicopter hangar.

"How about some chow, Janet? You look destroyed."

Janet shook her head, already dreading the return trip to the *Rickover*. If anything, the sea conditions had gotten worse. "I need to get back, sir."

"Tell you what." Wilcox jerked his head at the SH-60 Seahawk helo parked in the hangar behind them. "How about I give you a lift home?"

32

Emerging Threats Group
Tysons Corner, Virginia

The mystery surrounding the radio silence from the USS *Hyman G. Rickover* was solved at midnight on Saturday with a message from Janet, sent from the USS *Lawrence*.

Earlier that night, Don had sent everyone home except for the security team and the skeleton crew they kept on staff during nights and weekends. Don printed out Janet's message and put the accompanying video on the wall screen. The halls of the ETG building were silent as he read. Then he watched the video.

He'd feared for the safety of the *Rickover* and her crew, but this was almost worse.

Don texted Michael and Dre to return to the office immediately. He switched off his phone, posted his chin on his fist, and watched the video again. He stopped on the image of the JL-2 missile sans warhead. When he zoomed in, he could even make out a few of the bolts that had secured the warhead lying on the rocky bottom of the North Pacific.

What he was seeing was impossible. Inconceivable. Just finding the downed Chinese submarine was a minor miracle, but to discover that someone else had been there first and removed the nuclear warhead was…

His brain searched for the right word and came up blank.

Michael and Dre arrived together to find Don rewatching the video for the umpteenth time. He handed them the printed message. "Read this first," he said.

Dre read first, passing pages to Michael. When they finished, all three watched the video in silence.

"It's just gone?" Dre asked.

"It's just gone," Don agreed.

"How?" Michael asked. "Who?"

Don grimaced. "That is what we need to find out." He looked at his watch. It was just past three in the morning. "People are going to want some answers, and they'll be expecting us to provide them."

"The *Rickover* and the *Lawrence* have cleared the area?" Michael asked.

Don called up a separate radio message on his tablet. "The PLA has control of the search area. Janet's already transmitted the location of the wreck to the State Department so they can deliver it to the Chinese at noon today."

"Janet seems convinced it's not the Chinese playing us," Dre said.

"We should trust her instincts." Don picked up the loose pages of the message. "She thinks this PLA guy Gao is the one responsible for recovering the nuke, and he about had a kitten when she told him the news. We can't dismiss the possibility, but our working assumption has to be that someone else has the warhead."

Michael said, "I'll look at satellite coverage for the last month and see if I can find any surface ships lingering in the area."

"There can't be that many ships in the world capable of recovering something in nine thousand feet of water, right?" Dre asked. "I'll start a list."

Don held up his deactivated phone. "I'm going to make some calls."

He paced through the empty hallways toward his office, rehearsing the conversation in his head. Finally, he powered up his mobile phone and dialed the Director.

"This is Blank," answered a voice hoarse with sleep.

"It's Don, sir. There's been a development."

The Director's voice sharpened, and it sounded like he was getting out of bed. Don heard a door open, then close again.

"Tell me, Riley."

Don explained the little they knew in concise terms and described their plan of action.

When he finished, the Director grunted. "Do we still have control of the intel?"

"The CNO and the Chairman are both copied on the intel, but as far as I know, the operation is still contained. Do we need to brief the White House, sir?"

"I'll update the DNI myself, and he can make the call about briefing the President," the Director answered. "My guess is no. Everyone is focused on the inauguration. No one wants to piss in the pool during the big party."

"Of course, sir," Don replied.

"Call me as soon as you find something, Don." The Director hung up.

By dawn, Dre had compiled a list of two dozen deep-sea salvage ships that had the capability to retrieve an object in nine thousand feet of water. The list was a mix of military vessels, research ships, and oil industry support vessels for deep-sea drilling. Dre set to work finding out where each of these ships was currently located.

At seven in the morning, Michael uncovered their first real clue.

Satellite coverage in that area of the North Pacific Ocean was not continuous, but rather a patchwork of satellite passes over that section of ocean. The weather was another factor. The default condition for the North Pacific in the winter was cloudy, which interfered with some satellite imagery techniques.

Michael scanned through the electro-optic images from the National Geospatial-Intelligence Agency, uncovering only two usable images during the search window. He moved on to radar images, which indicated the presence of dozens of ships transiting the area of interest.

Using the initial data, Michael and Don began the painstaking work of correlating the ships with AIS transponder signals to determine the ship's identity. The Automated Identification System was a requirement for all

international transits. The publicly available information allowed them to
rule out certain types of vessels from his search.

While Michael used satellite imagery to further investigate the behavior
of potential targets, Don reviewed Dre's progress. He was deep in the details
of ship registries when Michael called out, "Don, I have something."

When he and Dre turned, Michael had broadcast an image on the wall
screen. The picture, taken from an oblique angle, showed a ship about two
hundred feet long with a heavy crane on the fantail.

"Satellite coverage is spotty," Michael said, "but it's possible this ship
stopped inside the search area in the last month."

"What about AIS?" Don asked.

Michael shook his head. "Nothing."

"That doesn't look like any ship I have on my list," Dre said.

"Can we get a ship name off the image?" Don pressed.

"That's the other thing," Michael replied. He expanded the image until
they could make out the side of the hull. The ship's name was painted out.

"I think lawyers call that 'consciousness of guilt,'" Dre said.

The knot in Don's shoulders eased slightly. This was their first real
evidence of who might have taken the nuclear warhead. "The ship had to
come from somewhere," he said. "Let's find it."

The next two hours flew by as they slowly expanded their search area
from the datum of the sighting of the mysterious ship backward in time.
Where weather degraded electro-optic satellite coverage, they sought out
alternatives, such as synthetic aperture radars, that could "see" through
clouds.

Again, it was Michael who made the find. He threw the new image to
the wall screen. The information was just over three weeks old, but the
picture was much clearer.

"According to their AIS, the ship is the SS *Wisteria*. She's listed as a
breakbulk freighter registered to BBC Chartering out of Los Angeles."

"If that ship is a break-bulk freighter," Dre said, "then I'm Jennifer
Lopez."

Michael chuckled as he split the screen and put a new image next to an
updated satellite picture of the mystery ship. "According to the internet,
that's the *Wisteria*."

The photograph showed a high-sided vessel with three deck cranes and a high superstructure near the aft end of the ship. Michael had found a better image of the mystery ship, so he put up that one as well.

"Wait a minute." Dre walked to the screen, studying the updated picture of the target vessel. "I've seen this ship before." She rubbed the back of her neck. "It was..." Seconds passed as she frowned at the screen. Then her face cleared. "It was in a documentary about finding the wreck of the USS *Indianapolis*."

She raced to her own laptop and hammered at the keyboard even more aggressively than usual. "Yes!" she whispered as she threw a new image to the wall screen. "It's the research vessel *Kestrel*."

To Don, the new photograph certainly looked like the ship they were after.

"It's homeported out of Maui," Michael said.

"And there's a reason why it didn't show up on any of my searches before," Dre added. "It's privately owned by Phillip Edgar."

"He'd have enough money to alter the AIS transponder, that's for sure. Assuming he wanted to hide his ship." Michael frowned as he realized what he was saying. "Do you think...?" His voice trailed off.

This does not make sense, Don thought. Why would a software billionaire hunt for a nuclear weapon?

"Get me everything you can about Edgar," Don ordered. "We need to figure out how he's involved in this."

Dre stood up and pulled her car keys out of her pocket. "Let's go, boss."

"What are you talking about?" Don said. "He lives in Seattle."

"Sure," Dre answered, "but he's in DC along with every other billionaire in the country. The inauguration is in two days, remember?"

* * *

The Kalorama neighborhood of Washington, DC, was only a short drive north of Dupont Circle but a world away from the lives of regular people. The area was home to previous presidents as well as upwards of seventy embassies and diplomatic residences. On the drive in, they passed more than a few black SUVs with tinted windows and government license plates.

And then there were the billionaires. Communications magnates, online retail giants, and software moguls, they were all represented in the quiet neighborhood of Kalorama.

The residence of Phillip Edgar was a stately brick mansion on a tree-lined street. The sidewalks were brick and cleared of snow. A security man waited for them at an open parking spot on the curb.

"What?" Dre muttered as she put the car into park. "No valet?"

The security man gave them a tight smile. "I'm going to have to ask you to leave all weapons and electronics in the vehicle, please."

Don was annoyed, but he'd also anticipated this. He placed his phone in the glovebox and tucked a manila folder under his arm.

"The young lady can wait here, please," the man said to Don.

Dre made a hiss of annoyance but did not put up a fuss.

The foyer of Edgar's home was expensively furnished but understated in the same way a celebrity might wear a pair of jeans to a movie premier. Sure, they were just blue jeans, but they probably cost $800. As the security man led him deeper into the house, Don guessed the artwork on the walls was probably worth more than his annual salary.

They ended their walk in the kitchen, where Don found the Director sharing a mug of coffee with one of the richest men in the world. They appeared to be two ordinary guys knocking back a cup of joe on a lazy Saturday. Don had been unaware that the Director had a relationship with the tech billionaire. Nor had he known the Director would be in the meeting.

Edgar got to his feet and held out his hand. "Phillip Edgar."

"Don Riley, sir."

Edgar was medium height and slim with thinning hair that had a tendency to fly away from his scalp, giving him an absent-minded professor look. He took Don's hand in both of his. "Call me Philly," he told Don. "Sam here says you're one of his best and brightest."

The Director laughed. "I told you that in confidence, Philly." The Director met Don's eyes. His look said, *Be careful, Riley*.

Edgar waved Don to a chair and poured him a cup of coffee. "This is from my estate in Maui," he said. "Shade-grown, hand-harvested. Wherever I am in the world, I make sure this coffee gets to me."

Don took a sip, and the flavors exploded on his tongue. He tasted dark chocolate and butter with some fruity notes and not a hint of acidity.

Edgar eyed him keenly. "Sam says that there's something I can help you with, Don. Something about national security, all hush-hush. This old bastard wouldn't say anything until you got here."

Don extracted a picture of the mystery ship from the manila folder and placed it in front of Edgar. "Do you recognize this ship, sir?"

"Of course I do. It's the *Kestrel*. She was the star of the show for that documentary about finding the wreck of the *Indy*. She's been modified a bit, but that's definitely her."

"Do you know where the ship is now?"

Edgar's brow wrinkled. "No idea, why?"

"We urgently need to find this ship, Mr. Edgar," Don insisted. "It's a matter of national security."

"Sorry." Edgar picked up his coffee cup. "I can't help you. I sold her last month. Ridiculous cash offer. I didn't need her anymore, so I figured, why not?"

Don's mouth went dry. "You sold the ship? To whom?"

Edgar sipped his coffee. "Sentinel Holdings."

33

Lagonoy Gulf, Philippines

From the bridge of the ship formerly known as the *Kestrel*, Skelly watched the sun set over the Philippine Sea in a blaze of red and gold. The sun turned the blue ocean into a trembling sea of molten lava.

Manson Skelly hadn't grown up poor, but his family hadn't been rich either. His old man worked in the oil fields in Texas. When those jobs all but disappeared, he retrained to be a solar panel installer. Skelly recalled how his father would come home every night and tell them about the houses he'd seen that day. Early in the solar boom, it was all rich people, but then everybody was getting solar panels, and the stories got less interesting. After a while, the stories all blended together, and Skelly stopped listening.

He smiled to himself. He'd never told President Serrano that his old man, Jack Skelly himself, had worked for Serrano's solar company. Technically, it was a franchise, he supposed, but Jack's uniform polo shirt still said *Serrano Solar* on it.

Actually, Skelly had never met Serrano in person. Although Abby Cromwell had been to the White House multiple times and even gone to

Camp David with Serrano, Wilkerson had not managed to get him invited to the White House even once. The Chief of Staff had blown him off about the tickets to the Inaugural Ball, too. Skelly couldn't even remember the exact amounts on the checks he'd written to Serrano's many PACs, but he seemed to recall they all had a lot of zeroes.

And it had meant nothing.

The sun dropped behind the horizon, and he could see his reflection in the darkening glass. The whine of the helo engine cut through the dusk, followed by a slow *whump* as the rotors began to turn.

That would be number four, he thought, baring his teeth at his own reflection. He called that one the Moscow Mule.

The thing that people did not understand about being rich—not just rich, but filthy, Scrooge McDuck rich—was that it was *awesome*. No matter the cost, you could buy literally anything. You just did it.

He rapped his knuckles on the teak dashboard of the bridge. Like a boat that could retrieve a nuclear warhead from the bottom of the ocean. Like a couple of unscrupulous Pakistani scientists who were capable of breaking down that warhead into component parts and repurposing them into suitcase nukes.

Money was a goddamn miracle. Anything he wanted was his, as long as he added enough zeroes to the price tag.

Money can't buy love. Skelly could hear his mother saying that. What his mother failed to realize was that even if money couldn't buy love, you could rent the hell out of it for as long as you liked.

The Chinese nuke came apart like a Lego set. The whole thing weighed about a ton, but half of that disappeared after they removed the cap covering the MIRVs. The individual reentry vehicles were cones about a meter long, but less than half of that bulk was the actual warhead. The tip of the cone was a contact fuse and the base an array of nozzles to steer the weapon when the device reentered the atmosphere. Those were both removed.

The warhead itself was an eighteen-inch center section of the cone, but even that was mostly just a stainless steel case. The actual nuclear device was a dull metal sphere about the size of a volleyball with a radiation warning sign emblazoned on the side. It was connected to a series of armor-plated wires and a cylindrical base. The scientists explained to him that all the stuff you saw in movies about using a pair of wire cutters to snip the red wire was all horseshit. If you were planning on cutting anything in that device, you better be packing a blowtorch.

As they worked, the discarded pieces went over the side into the ocean. By the time the ship reached the Philippines, his team had five stripped-down nuclear devices sitting on the bench in their workshop on the second deck of the *Kestrel*. In the calm waters of Lagonoy Gulf, they attached new arming mechanisms to the weapons and loaded them into black plastic Pelican cases.

The finished weapons weighed about fifty kilograms each. Although it was physically possible for one man to lift a Pelican case with a nuke inside, the package hardly deserved to be called a suitcase nuke.

Skelly walked out on the catwalk surrounding the bridge and watched the helo take off. As the aircraft disappeared in the gathering gloom, he leaned on the railing. The January night on the tropical waters was perfect. Maybe he should buy an island and just stay here.

And do what? he wondered. Sit on my ass and drink beer all day?

The door opened, and Pavel Kozlov's figure was outlined in the dim light of the bridge behind him.

"You wanted to see me." Not a question, but a statement ripe with anger.

Skelly glanced through the glass. Since the *Kestrel* was mostly auto-mated, there was only one watchstander on the bridge, but this conversation needed to be kept absolutely private. He motioned to Kozlov to follow him. Skelly took the steps down a deck and through a watertight door into a narrow hallway. He entered the room marked Founder's Suite.

Phillip Edgar had purchased the *Kestrel* from an oil company that had used the ship to service deepwater rigs. Using his billions, he gutted the vessel and rebuilt her into a state-of-the-art deep-sea salvage ship that he used to find underwater wrecks, including the *Titanic* and the USS *Indianapolis*. The old man had spared no expense on the tech. If a piece of technology couldn't be purchased, Edgar had it built. He also decided that life at sea did not need to be a life of deprivation. His cabin, the Founder's

Suite, might have been lifted from a current issue of *Architectural Digest*. The floor was mahogany planks, decorated with plush rugs that felt great on Skelly's bare feet. The furniture was leather. Not the black leather modern shit that Abby had in the Sentinel CEO's office, but Old World, classy stuff. The sitting area faced an entire wall of windows, looking out on the dark sea. Skelly punched the controls to draw the drapes across the view.

"I'm going to miss this place." Skelly poured a drink for himself at the wet bar and offered one to his guest.

"Vodka," Kozlov said.

Such a cliché, Skelly thought. This guy really was dumb as a rock. If he was the best and the brightest from Wagner, it was no wonder Skelly's crew had annihilated them in Ukraine.

He removed the Beluga vodka bottle from the freezer and sloshed an inch into a crystal tumbler. He brought both drinks back to the sitting area and handed the vodka to Kozlov.

The Russian was watching him in a way that Skelly found vaguely irritating. He raised his glass in a toast.

"I'm leaving on the next helo," Skelly said.

Kozlov looked around the well-appointed room. He leaned over so he could get a glimpse through the open bedroom door. "Can I move in here?" he asked.

Skelly drank. "That's not going to be possible."

"Why not?"

"Because you are going to sink the ship," Skelly replied.

Kozlov said nothing, but his chin jutted out the way it did when they were about to have an argument. They seemed to be doing that more and more these days.

Based on Kozlov's stony silence, Skelly concluded he was going to have to carry the conversation. "We need to disappear," he said. "Eventually, someone will figure out what happened—my money is on the Chinese, but you never know—and they'll find Edgar. Edgar will talk even though we paid him twice what this boat is worth. They'll come looking for this ship." He finished the rest of his drink in one gulp. "She needs to disappear."

"And the people?" Kozlov asked, his voice rising. "The crew? The Pakistani guys? They need to disappear too?"

"It's ten people," Skelly said, unable to keep the mocking note out of his tone. "I've seen you kill that many before you've had your morning coffee."

The comment seemed to irritate Kozlov even more. "Why me? Why don't you do it?"

"Because you work for me, Pavel." Skelly knew he shouldn't have said it, but why did every conversation with this Russian prick need to be an argument. Sure, they were technically *partners*, but Sentinel was his company, and he called the shots.

Kozlov came off the couch. For a second Skelly thought he was coming over the coffee table. He wrapped his fingers around the crystal glass and mentally counted the steps between his position in the armchair and the Glock behind the bar. The Russian's face was flushed red, and thick veins corded his neck.

"I didn't mean that," Skelly said. "We're partners."

Kozlov sat back down, but he did not relax. "What are you doing, Skelly?"

"I saw an opportunity, and I took it."

"These are nukes, Skelly. It's different."

"You don't understand my strategy."

Kozlov's head snapped up. "What's that supposed to mean?"

"They're just weapons, Pavel. More powerful weapons, but all that means is that people will pay more. Having a nuke in your back pocket is like bringing a bazooka to a knife fight."

"I don't like it." Kozlov's lips curled as he drank his vodka.

This guy has the IQ of a toilet brush, Skelly thought. "Don't worry, I have it all planned out. It's simple game theory."

"You used your AI," Kozlov said.

Skelly shrugged. Despite the soundproofing in the suite, he could feel the vibrations of an incoming helo landing on the deck above him. His ride had arrived. Skelly stood.

"This ship needs to be gone by sunrise," he said. "The crew, too. You need to get it done."

Kozlov stayed seated. "Then what?"

"Then you go home, and you wait."

"Moscow?" Kozlov looked up. "What are you going to do?"

"Don't call me, Pavel," Skelly said. "I'll let you know when I need you. Enjoy Moscow. You deserve a vacation."

"What are you going to do?" Kozlov repeated.

Skelly grinned. "I have it all under control."

34

Sterling, Virginia

Dawn pinkened the eastern horizon as the black government SUV made the right turn into the driveway of the Sentinel Holdings headquarters. Seated in the back seat, next to Liz Soroush, Don leaned into the turn.

The familiar sign shot past his window, the S of the word *Sentinel* captured in a shield that always reminded him of the Superman logo. He could remember the first time he'd driven this road, the day he'd met Abby Cromwell.

How times have changed, he thought. Back then, they were a team fighting the national security threat of the Chinese invasion of Taiwan, and they were fighting together. He glanced over his shoulder at the five identical black cars following the lead vehicle.

Today, he was returning to Sentinel headquarters with a federal search warrant and the full force of the Federal Bureau of Investigation.

Not that any of that had been easy—politics was never easy. In fact, the very idea that Don wanted to raid the offices of a prominent political donor on the eve of the inauguration seemed to be downright offensive to some people. While Don tried to convince his chain of command that this was necessary to contain a national security threat, Liz fought the same battle at the Department of Justice.

To Don, a nuclear weapon in the hands of a non-state actor, even a US-based private military contractor, seemed like a no-brainer security threat.

Apparently, brains were required. A lot of them, in fact. It took twenty-four precious hours for the search warrant to make its way to the Attorney General. Don imagined each layer of bureaucracy considering the impact of an approval, deciding that this was too sensitive to risk their own signature, and moving it up the chain.

When the approval finally came through at five in the morning of Inauguration Day, Liz Soroush did not waste a single second. She'd had a team on standby for the last eighteen hours.

Liz stirred on the seat next to him, her face a mask of concentration in the dawn light. For the last two years, Liz had led the National Security Branch at the FBI.

Don guessed it had probably taken every ounce of Liz's considerable sway in the Bureau to keep her team in place during the long wait of the approval. With the eyes of the world on Washington, DC, to witness the swearing in of Ricardo Serrano, the forty-eighth President of the United States, for a second term in office, it was understandably a busy day for the FBI.

Just getting out of DC was a logistical nightmare. The heightened security turned the city into a warren of blocked streets, one-way roads, and checkpoints. On the other hand, once out of the city limits, it was clear sailing. Today, everyone who was anyone was going into the District, not away from the metropolis.

The vehicle swayed as it followed the road inside the Sentinel property. Don glimpsed the headquarters building through the bare trees. Pockets of snow gathered in shady spots along the wooded road.

There was no visible security, but Don was familiar with Sentinel's security measures. The people inside the headquarters building had known the FBI was en route since they'd passed through the last town ten minutes ago. Using Mama, the resident AI, a combination of air- and land-based sensors had tracked and catalogued the incoming convoy. They knew exactly how many people were in the cars, had tracked any EM transmissions from the vehicles, had run faces and voices through recognition programs, and analyzed the weapons loadout of the team.

Despite the fact that he hadn't had a decent night's sleep in the last week, Don did not feel the least bit tired. As they came up on the last turn, he fingered the latch on his seat belt, his mood a strange mix of exhilaration and dread. It was about time he got some answers to the many questions that plagued his every waking moment.

How had Sentinel found the Chinese wreck so quickly? Where was the salvage ship? What was Skelly planning to do with a nuclear warhead?

When they cleared the last turn, Don blinked. The Sentinel parking lot had one car in it. He'd been here at all hours of the day or night and had never seen the lot this empty before.

The SUV ground to a crunching halt on the gravel. Don unlatched his seat belt and pushed open his door at the same time. A blast of chill morning air washed across his face, elevating his senses even more. He followed the phalanx of FBI agents up the steps and through the automatic doors into the vestibule of the building.

A man greeted them with a lopsided smile. Don recognized David Landersmann, Skelly's chief of staff. As FBI agents fanned out into the building, Liz approached Landersmann.

"I'm Special Agent—"

"I know who you are." Landersmann yawned. "And I know why you're here. Took you long enough. I've been waiting for two days for you to show up."

"I have a warrant to search the premises for evidence of—"

"Search away," Landersmann interrupted again, waving his hands in the air. "We've shut down this facility as of last week. Nobody works here anymore. This is no longer our headquarters building." He winked at Liz. "We're digital nomads now."

"What about Mama?" Don asked.

Landersmann's grin widened. "Don Riley. Good to see you back. Mama's in lockdown. Skelly said you would know what that meant."

Don did know. It meant that Mama would respond only to inputs from admin-level users, and there was only one of them left: Manson Skelly.

"Where is your boss?" Liz demanded.

Landersmann shrugged. "I wish I knew, Agent Soroush. He doesn't call anymore, he doesn't write. Like I said, he's a digital nomad now."

Liz turned away from Landersmann and spoke to her lead agent. "Seize everything. Laptops, phones, you know the drill. Let's get a team on powering down and disassembling the AI system."

Don stepped close and lowered his voice. "Don't do that, Liz. If you power Mama down, we might lose everything."

"He's a smart guy, Agent Soroush," Landersmann added. "Best listen to him."

"Don, are you sure?" she whispered.

Don nodded. "Secure the facility, and I'll get my people here to analyze the system."

"Okay, I'll trust you on this." Liz left to deal with the logistics of the search.

"That's a bold move, Riley," Landersmann said, "but Skelly said you'd figure out that it was safer to leave Mama online."

"Safer?" Don said. "What does that mean?"

Landersmann gave a palms-up gesture. "That's what he said. Just passing along a message."

"Look," Don said, "Skelly's off the rails on this one. We're talking about a nuclear weapon. If you know something, Landersmann, you need to tell me."

"I can neither confirm nor deny..." Landersmann winked as he recited the line that servicemembers were required to use when discussing the presence of nuclear weapons in their command. He started to walk away, then turned back to Don.

"By the way, I'm sorry about South America. Wasn't my idea, man." He grinned out the right side of his mouth. "No hard feelings, okay?"

Don watched Landersmann's back retreat down the hallway, feeling the heat of embarrassment climb up his neck. He'd gone to Skelly for help, and Skelly had played him. Don had lost to Skelly in the hunt for the Chinese terrorist and the missing Chinese nuclear weapon.

In a final screw-you gesture, he left Mama in lockdown, knowing that Don would put a team together to break into the system and confident Don would fail. Again.

Skelly had been two steps ahead of him at every turn. He'd embarrassed Don professionally just for the sport of it and even left his chief of staff to rub salt in Don's wounded ego.

Don pulled out his mobile phone and dialed ETG. Dre answered the call. "I need you and Michael out at Sentinel ASAP. Come prepared to stay for as long as it takes."

The fatigue that he'd held at bay settled like a heavy blanket on his shoulders.

Keep your cool, Don told himself. Do your job. Slow and steady wins the race.

Not for the first time in his career, Don wondered if he was up to the task.

35

White House
Washington, DC

The night before the inauguration, Chief of Staff Irving Wilkerson slept on a cot in his office. There were bunks downstairs that could be used by White House staff during emergencies, but when he had to stay over, he preferred the solitude of his office.

The cot was from his Army days, his first brush with success in the public service arena. As a junior captain, he'd parlayed an aide-de-camp assignment into a civilian staff position with a senator on the Foreign Relations Committee. That was forty-five years ago. Less than a decade after staffing for that senator, Wilkerson won that same senator's seat in a special election.

His rapid rise to power and his generosity in sharing the spotlight made him a favorite on both sides of the aisle. What's more, Wilkerson was never perceived as a threat to those around him who had grander ambitions. He'd realized early in his career that he was more comfortable behind the scenes than at the podium. Presidential aspirants from both parties sought his advice and counsel, and he always did his best to deliver his honest assessment.

Irv Wilkerson, the Obi-Wan of the Potomac, was sometimes called the last honest man in Washington, DC. A man who used his access to power for the good of his country.

Wilkerson stared at the ceiling. *That isn't exactly true anymore, is it?* he mused.

Even though he'd barely slept three hours, he woke at four a.m. After a few more minutes of tossing and turning, he gave up on getting back to sleep. Clad in boxer shorts and a white T-shirt, he threw off the covers and placed his bare feet on the carpeted floor.

He allowed himself a yawning sigh. Yesterday had been brutal. A million details about the inauguration and all the celebrations surrounding the ceremony had crossed his desk. It seemed like his staff concluded that every decision, no matter how tiny, needed his personal attention.

This dignitary wanted to be invited to that event. This donor wanted to meet with the President. This member of Congress was not happy with his seat on the dais. From dawn until well into the wee hours, he'd soothed and cajoled, made deals and returned phone calls until the last decision was put to rest. And all with hardly a raised voice.

It was his job, and he was good at it.

Then he broke out the Army cot, had one finger of the single malt he kept in his bottom desk drawer, and went to sleep.

"I think I'm finally too old for this shit," he said to the empty room.

He got to his feet and took a moment to get his bearings. The dark office was lit only by a seam of light under the door and the gap in the drawn curtains. Without his glasses on, the furniture was shadowy blobs and the wall of pictures just black squares. He fumbled on the edge of the desk for his spectacles and put them on. The details sharpened into the familiar contours of his office.

Every part of this place told a story from his long career in politics. The desk was from his old Senate office, the coffee table from his father's law office in Oregon. The photographs depicted his rise to power in the Senate, Wilkerson shaking hands with heads of state from all over the world. Him and Irma with their three grandchildren last Christmas.

When it came time to leave this place, he would retire with honor after decades of public service.

But that time was not now. As was custom, he submitted his letter of resignation to President Serrano along with all the other cabinet members. He'd even said to Serrano that it was time for him to retire. He wanted to enjoy his grandchildren, write his memoirs, and take Irma on that round-the-world trip he'd been promising her for the last thirty years.

"I'm ready, sir," Wilkerson said to the President. "It's time."

Serrano plucked Wilkerson's letter from the pile and tore it in half. He came around his desk, gripped Wilkerson's shoulders, and fixed his Chief of Staff with that famous stare.

"I need you, Irv," the President said. "I can't do this without you. You know that."

Wilkerson nodded. They both knew it.

Irving Wilkerson first met Rick Serrano more than twenty years ago. At that time, Serrano was a junior member of the legislature in the Great State of Texas. A self-made billionaire, the son of Mexican immigrants had turned sunshine into gold through a series of solar company franchises. One out of ten people in the state of Texas either worked for Rick Serrano or for a company that had some sort of business connection to the man.

But it was more than just money. Even then, there'd been something different about him. He had a presence that defied political gravity, an appeal that crossed lines of color, creed, and most importantly, political tribe.

All politicians had massive egos; everyone knew that. It was a necessary part of the job requirement. The question was what you did with that gift of self-confidence. Did you use your position as a leader to gratify yourself by basking in the limelight, or did you direct that energy in a way that helped others?

Serrano was a unicorn, the rare politician who managed to do both. Just his mere presence seemed to influence people to act. His sincerity about the causes he really cared about elevated his own brand above the rest.

Which is what made the international conflicts of his first term so disheartening to Serrano—and by extension, his Chief of Staff. Through no fault of the President, his first four years in office would go down as some of the bloodiest years in the nation's history.

All the things they'd planned for—revitalizing the American Midwest as a manufacturing powerhouse, converting the American energy infrastructure to 100 percent renewables, rebuilding the secondary education system—they'd barely scratched the surface.

"We have so much work to do, Irv," Serrano told him. "I need you by my side."

"I understand, sir," Wilkerson replied.

Wilkerson did understand. He'd stood by Serrano through thick and thin. Even tough calls, like the decision to deploy killer drones in Taiwan. The use of the Sentinel Cicada assassin drones broke the Chinese will. Taiwan was free today because of Serrano's gutsy call.

The President of the United States used a weapon of mass destruction to end an unlawful invasion. Some people saw evil in that decision, but Wilkerson had no time for armchair generals.

He lowered his bulk into the chair behind his desk and switched on the desk lamp. The sudden illumination made him clench his eyes shut.

There were other tough calls. Calls so difficult that Wilkerson could not even say the words to the President for fear he might implicate him. For those decisions, he relied on the unspoken bond between them, the trust they'd built up over the years. In those rare instances, it was his job to act, to address the issue without the President's knowledge. He was the firewall between the great man and what needed to be done.

Those decisions were secrets he would take to his grave.

Wilkerson smiled to himself. If he really was Obi-Wan, that made Serrano his Jedi apprentice. It was an apt metaphor. Obi-Wan made sacrifices that his young Jedi could not even contemplate.

Those sacrifices were the legacy of Irving Wilkerson.

He pulled a small electric kettle out of the bottom desk drawer, along with a mug and a jar of instant coffee. He filled the kettle from a carafe of water he kept on the sideboard and plugged the device into a wall socket.

As the shadowy room filled with the hiss of the kettle starting to boil, he sat down on the couch, resting his head back against the leather cushions.

On mornings like this, when he was so damn tired, Wilkerson wasn't sure if he had the energy for another four years.

The buzz of a mobile phone cut short his reprieve. Wilkerson raised his head to look at the clock over the door. It was barely past four in the morning. Who the hell was calling at this hour?

He heaved himself to his feet, his spindly legs carrying his body across the room. He ferreted through the papers on the desk until he found his mobile.

Wilkerson focused on the blank screen.

Bzzt. The sound came from the top drawer of his desk, from his other phone.

Only a few people had that number. His wife, his daughter, the President... a call on his personal phone at this hour was surely a disaster of some kind.

Wilkerson jerked open the desk drawer. Caller ID gave him no idea who was calling. He slid his finger across the screen to answer the call.

"Hello?"

"I hope your boy's ready for his big day, Irv." The voice was male and mocking.

"Skelly." Wilkerson sat down heavily in his desk chair. "How did you get this number?"

"Did you really think it was a good idea to raid my company?" Skelly asked. "The FB-fucking-I was in *my* headquarters building." The mocking was gone, replaced by an edge of steel.

"That's DOJ. We—I—had nothing to do with that. DOJ operates completely independently from the White House. You know that. You brought this on yourself."

Silence.

"What do you want, Skelly?" Wilkerson asked.

"I think my invitation to the Inaugural Ball must've got lost in the mail," Skelly said. "But that's okay, because it turns out I'm going to be out of town for a while."

"Riley says you have the Chinese nuke. Is that true?"

"I don't understand why we couldn't just come to terms on this thing, Irv," Skelly said, his voice full of mock earnestness. "All I wanted was to be Secretary of Defense, and you couldn't even do that. After all, Irv, what are friends for?"

"You and I were never friends, Skelly."

"Irv, that's hurtful." Skelly sighed. "Now that I'm a nuclear power, do you think Serrano will want to meet with me?"

Wilkerson let the silence hang, not because he was being coy but because he needed time to think. "What are you going to do?" he asked finally.

"I haven't decided yet," Skelly replied, and for once, Wilkerson actually believed him.

"Turn the weapon in, Skelly. You'll be a hero."

"Iiiiiirv." Skelly drew out the word like some schoolyard taunt. "I think we have a trust deficit, you and me."

Wilkerson closed his eyes. "I don't even know what that means, but I do know that you can still fix this thing."

"What if I don't want it fixed?" Skelly shot back. "What if I think it's time to shake things up? You love to use me for your dirty work, but you never seem to want to share the credit when the job's done."

"That's enough, Skelly. As soon as I tell the President about this call, he'll use every asset he has to hunt you down. Don't be a fool."

Skelly's voice hardened. "I'm the fool? I don't think so. In fact, you're not going to tell Serrano we even had this call. I expect you to be my man on the inside, my fly on the wall..."

Wilkerson detected a slur in the other man's words. For God's sake, this idiot had a nuclear weapon and he was drunk-dialing the White House.

"...they'll never find me," Skelly concluded.

"I will not help you, Skelly."

The silence went on so long that Wilkerson feared they'd lost the connection.

"It was a closed casket. Did you know that, Irv? All they found were pieces. Not even the good parts...just pieces. That's on you, Irv, and if you want me to keep your little secret, then I suggest you play ball."

The line went dead.

The electric kettle went *click*.

Wilkerson lowered his face into his hands.

36

Don peered out the window into the darkness as Air Force One rolled to a stop on the icy tarmac. The aircraft was a US Navy C-40A Clipper, not the highly customized Boeing 747 that was usually associated with the name. The livery on the aircraft was also not the standard blue and white associated with POTUS. Still, this aircraft carried the temporary call sign of Air Force One because it carried the President of the United States.

While Don had not slept a wink on the flight, the newly inaugurated President Serrano closed his eyes when the plane took off and opened them as soon as they touched down.

Serrano stretched and yawned. "You get any sleep, Riley?"

"No, sir."

"Gotta learn to sleep under all circumstances, Don. It's an occupational hazard."

"Yes, sir."

Serrano stood, rolled his shoulders. He nodded to the other passengers —two Secret Service agents who Don thought looked very unhappy and two translators, one for Russian and one for Mandarin.

"Let's get this show on the road," the President said.

The last time anyone had seen the actual President of the United States was shortly after eleven p.m. the prior evening when he left the Inaugural Ball for the return trip to the White House. The press corps saw him enter the residence a half hour later—about the same time as the real President reached the gates of Andrews Air Force Base.

Even Don hadn't known about the secret mission to Iceland to meet with the presidents of Russia and China. He'd received a call at eight p.m. telling him to prepare a brief for the Director on the status of the search for Manson Skelly and the missing Chinese nuclear warhead.

A car picked him up at nine p.m. The Director was waiting for him in the back seat. He put up the divider between the driver and the rear of the vehicle.

"We're going to Andrews," the Director said without preamble. "At midnight, you're going to catch a flight to Iceland."

"Iceland?" Don asked.

"You're going with the President to brief Yi Qin-lao and Nikolay Sokolov," he replied. "Alone."

"Alone?" Don tried to wrap his head around what he was hearing. "What am I supposed to tell them?"

"Everything. That's what the President wants, anyway." He eyed Don. "I suggest you use your judgment."

"You won't be there?"

"Which part of *alone* is not clear, Riley?" The Director was slow to anger, but he had a temper when things were not proceeding the way he wanted. He looked out the window, blew out a breath. "The President wants this tight. Each head of state can bring one expert and a pair of translators into the meeting. That's it. Too many cooks and all that happy horseshit."

In his head, Don started reviewing what was undoubtedly going to be the most important briefing of his entire life.

"The briefing will be done on paper," the Director continued. "No electronics of any kind allowed in the room. Any questions?"

Don hadn't had any questions at the time, but he had plenty now. An icy wind sliced through his suit jacket as he hurried down the steps of the jet and into a waiting SUV.

He peered into the darkness, aware that there were multiple layers of security on the ground, at sea, and overhead, but seeing none of it.

The drive took all of one minute. The car stopped at a single-story building next to an enormous pile of dirty snow. A Secret Service agent disembarked and entered the building. He returned a minute later and held the door of the car open. "They're ready for you, sir."

Don had a brief glimpse of an office area, then they passed into what appeared to be a large training room. Drapes were drawn across the windows that looked out on the airfield. The opposite wall showed photographs of different kinds of jets.

The small tables in the room had been arranged into a three-sided conference table. The eight people already in the room had taken opposite sides of the seating arrangement, facing each other.

President Nikolay Sokolov headed the Russian contingent. He'd aged since Don had last seen him in Helsinki, but with his swept-back blond hair and noble features, he was still a handsome man. At his side was Vladimir Federov, the head of the FSB and Sokolov's right-hand man, as he had once been to Sokolov's deposed uncle.

Chinese President Yi Qin-lao was a large man with bland, doughy features. When he shook Serrano's hand, his expression did not vary. The man next to the General Secretary was a surprise to Don. He'd expected the Minister of State Security, but instead he found a wiry man with a scar on his chin. The same man who had met Janet aboard the USS *Lawrence*, an army colonel named Gao.

The principals took their seats. Their advisers sat to their right; the pairs of translators flanked their heads of state but with their chairs pushed back away from the table.

"Mr. Riley?" It was the Secret Service agent. "I need your phone, sir. No electronics."

Don flushed. He'd meant to leave it on the plane. He handed the device to the agent, who left the room, closing the door behind him.

President Serrano cleared his throat. "Thank you all for coming on such short notice, but I think we can all agree that the situation warrants these special circumstances."

The low voices of the translators provided a backdrop to Serrano's words.

"The threat is clear," the President continued. "We have a lost nuclear weapon. That's a concern for all of us."

"What I want to know," Sokolov said in English, "is why you chose not to tell me what we were dealing with when you asked for my help in the North Pacific."

Sokolov's face was flushed, his words hot.

This is not the beginning the President wanted, Don thought.

"I take responsibility for that mistake, Nikolay," Serrano said. "I apologize. I had hoped to recover the weapon and return it to the PRC, but events overtook us."

President Yi's thick lips twisted in disdain. That was clearly a lie, and the room knew it. He whispered to his translator.

"The General Secretary wishes to know where is the warhead now?" the young woman asked.

Serrano turned to Don. "Let's get everyone on the same page, Riley."

Don stood, opening a manila folder as he walked to the front of the room. He passed a photograph to each table. "This is the ship that was used to recover the nuclear warhead from the Chinese submarine. It's the research vessel *Kestrel*. A company called Sentinel Holdings purchased it from the previous owner and sailed it from Hawaii."

"An American private military contractor," Yi said. "A mercenary, sponsored by the United States."

"That's a distortion of the facts," Serrano said, "but let's not quibble over details. We have a problem, and we need to deal with it. Together."

"How did you find out about the nuclear weapon in the first place?" The translator's question came from the PLA senior colonel.

Don cut a look at Serrano. "Our source is classified, I'm afraid." He felt his armpits dampen. Even the President didn't know that his source was the Naval War College bomber. "I can't say more than that." Don could feel waves of anger radiating from the PLA officer.

Out of the corner of his eye, he saw Federov lean close to the Russian President. Sokolov nodded and directed his question to the Chinese. "How did the research vessel know where to look?"

Senior Colonel Gao looked as if he'd been slapped. He muttered a reply to the translator.

"We do not know the answer to this question," the translator said.

Bullshit, you don't, Don thought. According to Ian Thomas, Skelly had gotten the exact location of the wreck from Gao himself. *I guess we all have our secrets.*

"Where is the ship now?" Sokolov asked. "Have you been able to track it?"

Don shook his head. "Using historical data, we tracked it heading toward the South China Sea, but it's disappeared. We have assets looking all over the region, but it could be anywhere in Southeast Asia by now."

"If you had told us sooner," the Chinese President said in an acid tone, "we could have helped you."

"There is still a way you can help us, Mr. President," Don said to Yi. The man's eyes raked over Don. He gave an imperceptible nod for Don to continue.

"It would help if we knew the configuration of the warhead, sir."

The Chinese leader frowned, and the senior colonel leaned in to explain what Don was asking.

"Why do you want to know?" the translator asked Don.

"We believe that Manson Skelly's first move will be to dismantle the warhead into component parts. If the weapon had multiple reentry vehicles, we could be searching for more than one weapon."

The Chinese President said to Gao, "Tell them."

"The stolen warhead had five independent reentry vehicles," Gao said.

Five. Don forced himself to take a deep breath and let it out slowly. Skelly had been ahead of them at every turn. He surely would have lined up the technicians needed to repackage the individual units into separate bombs. He'd just as surely have assets standing by to scatter them across the globe.

Their problem just got five times more complex.

They couldn't even find an entire ship. How in the hell were they going to find five different weapons small enough to fit inside the trunk of a car?

"We need to talk about cooperation here—" Serrano began.

Tap-tap-tap. A knock at the door interrupted the President.

"What?" roared Serrano.

One of the Secret Service agents poked his head inside. "Pardon, sir, but there's a phone call."

The agent looked at Don, and he recognized his blue phone case in the agent's hand. He felt the heat of the President's glare. Don opened his mouth to respond, but the agent preempted him. "He said to tell you it's Skelly."

Don traded a look with Serrano as he accepted the phone.

"Hello?"

"Oh, Donny-boy." Skelly sang the old tune off-key. "Do me a favor and put me on speaker, buddy."

Serrano motioned for Don to give him the phone. He touched the button to put the caller on speaker. "This is President Serrano speaking."

"Mr. President, this is your favorite military contractor. How's Iceland, by the way? Are your buddies from China and Russia there, too?"

The Chinese and Russian contingents exchanged worried glances. The secret meeting location had been selected and security guaranteed by the United States.

But Don's attention was less on Skelly's words and more on his delivery. The man always maintained an air of irreverence, but this seemed amped up even for him. Was he just trying to impress his audience, or was there more at play?

"Don't worry, everybody," Skelly continued. "I'm not going to tell the world about your secret meeting. In fact, you're doing me a favor by getting together in one place. I think it's time we talked about the future."

Serrano leaned over the mobile phone on the table in front of him. "I think we can talk about many things, Mr. Skelly, *after* we've secured the nuclear weapon."

"Weapons," Skelly replied, drawing out the plural in a hiss. "I've broken the warhead down into five suitcase nukes. They've already been dispersed to undisclosed locations."

Don watched the full scope of their predicament register on the faces of the three world leaders. Yi's fleshy lips thinned, Sokolov's Nordic features turned a shade paler, and Serrano gnawed the inside of his cheek.

"I'm disappointed to hear that, Mr. Skelly," Serrano said in a careful tone.

"Yeah, well, Mr. President, I work in the private sector. Time is money."

"So, you're looking for a ransom, then?" Serrano ventured.

"I told you already." Skelly's voice turned insistent. "I want to talk about the future."

Serrano scanned the room. "I'm afraid you're going to have to be more specific, Mr. Skelly."

There was a long pause before Skelly spoke again.

"The face of war has changed. You all know that. It used to be the countries with the biggest armed forces set the rules—that's you guys. But there's a hundred and ninety-two other countries in the world. That's where I come in. Many of those countries are my clients, and you know what? They don't like your rules."

Skelly paused as if for dramatic effect.

"Imagine what the world order would look like if someone had a seat at the table to represent the little guys out there," Skelly continued. "That's what I want: a seat at the big boy's table."

"Mr. Skelly," Serrano said, "may I remind you that you run a US-based company—"

"May I remind you, Mr. President, that I'm the guy with five nuclear weapons? One tweet from me and you guys will be balls-deep in crashing stock markets and panic-buying of toilet paper."

"Mr. Skelly, that sounds like a terroristic threat, and you of all people know how the United States deals with terrorists."

Silence.

Sokolov and Yi both looked at Serrano. Serrano looked at Don.

"Mr. Skelly?" Serrano said. "Did you hear me?"

"I heard you." Skelly sighed. "I don't think you're taking me seriously, Mr. President."

Skelly hung up.

37

The Philippines

The C-130 transport plane took off from the Subic Bay Freeport Zone at dusk. The flight plan listed Osaka, Japan, as the plane's destination, and the aircraft set a northeasterly heading.

Two hours into the flight, the pilot turned due east. After another hour, he reduced altitude to four thousand feet and keyed his microphone.

"Stand by to deploy the package," he announced.

"Standing by," came the response from the crew chief. Although both men had done hundreds of cargo airdrops in the military as well as in their subsequent careers with the world's largest private military contractor, this cargo drop felt special.

It wasn't so much what their orders said, it was what their orders *didn't* say that bothered them both.

They were to fly to a designated point in the Philippine Sea and deploy a Sentinel Raptor drone.

"Lowering the aft loading ramp," the pilot said.

"Copy."

He watched his panel until the indicator showed the ramp was fully deployed. His crew chief reported the ramp was down.

The pilot eyed his copilot. "You got it. I'm going to watch the drop from in the back."

In the military, he'd probably be court-martialed if he left the pilot's chair during a sensitive in-flight evolution, but he wasn't flying for Uncle Sam anymore, and he could do as he pleased. His copilot shrugged her shoulders as if she couldn't care less.

The first thing he did when he got to the cargo bay was put on a safety harness. Though he had a lot of disdain for military rules, he wanted to stay alive.

Clipped into a safety line and wearing a set of headphones connected to the internal communications system, he walked to the back of the cargo bay where the crew chief stood by the ramp. He could feel the windy vortex trying to suck him out of the plane.

The darkness was absolute. They were hundreds of kilometers from any inhabited land. Thanks to heavy cloud cover at ten thousand feet, there were no stars tonight. According to the latest weather report, a tropical depression that had the makings of a monsoon was brewing in the east.

The crew chief looked at him. "You ready?" he mouthed.

The pilot nodded.

The two men moved back up the mostly empty bay to their sole piece of cargo. The Raptor rested on the deployment sled in a custom cradle designed to handle the barrel-shaped object bolted to the belly of the drone. The object was made of steel and looked sort of like a metal trash can. It was far from aerodynamic.

The crew chief switched to a private channel on their headset. "I've worked with these drones for years. I have no idea what that is." He looked at the blackness beyond the lowered ramp. "Or why we're deploying it out here."

The pilot shrugged. He'd learned long ago not to ask questions if you didn't want to know the answer. Cash your paycheck and keep your trap shut, that was his motto.

"Another day, another dollar. You ready?"

"Ready as I'll ever be."

The pilot switched channels to put the copilot back on the network. "Jane, we're deploying the package."

"Roger that."

The act of deploying the drone was anticlimactic. The crew chief put the Raptor turboprop engine on standby and released the loading skid. The cradled drone rolled slowly down a track, angled down the ramp, and disappeared into the darkness.

The pilot high-fived his crew chief. He returned to the cockpit and dropped into his chair.

"Take us to eight thousand feet and put us in a holding pattern," he said. "Make it so, Number One."

The copilot rolled her eyes, but she complied.

When they were steady on course and altitude, the copilot cocked an eyebrow at him. "What're we waiting for?"

The pilot checked his watch, doing the mental math on their ETA into Osaka. "We're supposed to wait for an hour and recapture the drone before we head out."

"What's the drone doing?"

"Beats me. I just work here." The pilot yawned.

* * *

The drag chute on the deployed Raptor kept the drone level long enough for the turboprop engine to take over.

The unmanned aircraft leveled off at the default parameters of 2,500 feet and 200 mph. While the craft automatically adjusted trim to accommodate for the unusual cargo, the flight computer immediately sought a GPS satellite fix to ascertain its position relative to the mission plan.

The airdrop from the C-130 had been good. The Raptor was less than a kilometer from mission datum. The drone entered a holding pattern and transmitted a readiness message back to the Sentinel artificial intelligence system.

The execution order came through at midnight local.

The Raptor sent an arming signal to the metal canister strapped to its belly. Then, the drone slowly reduced altitude until it was flying a few meters above the wavetops at stall speed.

The Raptor released its payload. The steel canister clipped the top of a swell, tumbled end over end, then came to rest in the trough of a wave and sank.

As the steel cylinder dropped through the dark ocean, a metal plate, glued in place using seawater-soluble adhesive, dislodged to reveal a pair of pressure sensors. The pair, a primary sensor and a backup, both measured sea pressure and compared their readings to ensure accuracy.

As the steel canister dropped, the pressure of the seawater around it increased. It took nearly twenty minutes for the primary sensor to reach the set point. The secondary sensor took another full minute to reach 2,247 psi, which equated to five thousand feet deep.

In an instant, the nuclear blast that rent the depths of the Philippine Sea created a void in the water hundreds of meters across. The bubble distended the surface of the ocean like a boil.

When the void collapsed, a column of seawater erupted thousands of meters into the dark sky. Positive ions generated by the explosion interacted with the atmosphere, creating thousands of local lightning strikes as the column rose through the cloud cover.

The resulting shock wave broke windows in buildings hundreds of kilometers away and lit up the seismographs of volcanologists all over the world. Scientists later calculated that the shock wave raced around the Earth four times before it dissipated.

All over the Pacific, tsunami warnings sounded as coastal communities prepared for possible monster waves and volcanic aftershocks.

The Philippines Eruption, as the event was quickly dubbed, was nearly as large as the Tonga Eruption in early 2022. The probability of two such powerful volcanic events occurring within the same decade was vanishingly small and a rare opportunity for quantitative comparison.

One prominent volcanologist, who spent more time in front of a TV camera than in the field, was quoted as saying, "This event will allow us to unlock the mysteries of Mother Nature."

He was very mistaken.

38

Moscow, Russia

Pavel Kozlov's knowledge of women was limited. Not in quantity, of course —he'd been with more women than he could count—but in quality. To him, women served a function to which he, as a man, was entitled. Usually, that function involved a little money and even less emotional involvement.

He had never been in love and never wanted to be in love. He wasn't even sure what that word even meant.

That was his view on life *before* he met Iliyana Semenova.

When the private elevator to his sixth-floor luxury apartment overlooking the Andrew's Bridge entrance to Gorky Park gave a discreet ding, Pavel felt his mouth go dry. The wood-paneled door rolled open smoothly to reveal a tall woman dressed in a high-collared sable coat. Over the glossy black fur that brushed her cheekbones, a pair of crystal-blue eyes surveyed the room.

The security man held the door for her as she stepped out of the elevator. Pavel gave the man a curt nod of dismissal. The door rolled closed, leaving him alone with this magnificent woman.

Iliyana glided toward Pavel. Although she wore high heels, they did not make a sound on the polished hardwood floor of the entryway. She touched her lips to his cheek, making him jolt with pleasure.

"Pavel," she breathed, "I'm so glad you called. I was beginning to wonder if you'd forgotten about me."

Leaving the supple fur collapsed in his arms, she breezed by him. Pavel's eyes followed her.

He'd been introduced to Iliyana less than a week ago. A call girl, she worked only by referral but came highly recommended. At first, her list of demands for a "date" had almost put him off, but he agreed as much out of boredom as anything else.

It was no exaggeration to say that one night with Iliyana had changed his life. Since then, he'd thought about almost nothing else. His worries about the fact that there were five rogue nuclear weapons—including one in Moscow—under the control of an increasingly erratic Skelly seemed to melt away when he thought of this woman.

Iliyana's black dress was cut with an open back, giving Pavel a preview of the evening to come.

"It's a beautiful view," she said from the window.

"Yes," he agreed, not talking about the winking lights amid the snowbound Gorky Park six stories below.

Pavel grazed his fingers along her bare back and was rewarded with a sigh. She leaned into him, and he slipped an arm around her waist. His fingers felt a band of lace beneath the thin material of her dress. His pulse surged, and he licked his lips in anticipation.

Iliyana moved closer, facing him. Lightly, she traced the outline of his lips with her tongue, brushed her hip against his trousers. She took his bottom lip gently between her teeth. Pavel felt his breath stutter, his vision darken.

When she released his lip, he tasted his own blood.

"Perhaps some champagne?" she whispered.

Pavel just nodded.

The evening passed in excruciating foreplay. Every morsel of food was an instrument of torture in Iliyana's capable hands. He'd spared no expense on the champagne, the caviar, the wine, the pheasant, the lavish chocolate sculptured dessert, and yet he might as well have been eating crushed ice.

The only thing on the menu that interested him was Iliyana Semenova. The way her blond hair glowed in the candlelight like burnished gold, the way her eyes teased him, the way her hand stroked his forearm.

Half of Pavel's brain wanted to sweep away the table setting and rip off her dress. The other half of his brain never wanted the torture to end.

The last dish was cleared, the candles extinguished. All that remained on the table was a bottle of vodka and two glasses. Iliyana poured two measures and placed one in front of Pavel. She drank her shot in one long swallow, then stood and shrugged out of her dress.

The black material pooled at her feet. In the dim light of the cityscape outside the window, her face was shadowed, but Pavel saw the glint of her eyes, the flash of a smile. She paused as if she could feel his gaze devouring her body. Slipping down her shoulders, taking in her breasts, her belly, the triangle of dark silk and following the taper of her long legs to the floor.

When he had finished, she turned slowly and sauntered into the bedroom. Pavel downed his shot of vodka and followed.

* * *

Pavel stared at the ceiling of his bedroom, a ghost of a smile on his face. The clock said it was three a.m., but he was not the least bit sleepy. Part of it was the glow of having made love to this incredible woman—twice—but he knew it was something else.

Manson Skelly. The name dissolved his blissful mood.

Careful not to wake the sleeping Iliyana, Pavel slid from beneath the covers. He pulled on his undershorts and padded across the room. Easing open the door to his study, he slipped inside.

At the window, he watched the frozen park below. Apart from the lone car making its way down the icy avenue, the night was still.

Pavel poured himself a drink from the bar and lounged on the leather sofa. He ran his eyes across the rows of books lining the wall, recognizing none of the titles. This place was not his style. After a few days here, Pavel realized he preferred a smaller apartment, less ostentatious, but now that he'd met Iliyana, he felt like he needed to stay here to keep up appearances.

For a woman like that, he'd live anywhere. Money wasn't an issue, not since he'd joined up with Skelly. Maybe it was time to retire.

Maybe it was time to get clear of the evil that was Manson Skelly.

The thought took him by surprise. Pavel did not consider himself a good man. He had killed people—many, many people—in cold blood for a paycheck. Men, women, children, even infants had died at his hand, and it bothered his conscience not at all. He'd never had trouble sleeping.

Until tonight...tonight he could not sleep. Tonight, he had a beautiful woman in his bed, and he was in the next room. Drinking. Alone.

Why nuclear weapons? he wondered. Why did Skelly have to cross that line? It wasn't as if they needed money. He could buy ten apartments like this one and still have money left over.

No, with Skelly it was something more. Something that Pavel did not understand.

He retrieved the bottle of vodka and refreshed his drink. Then he turned on the TV, keeping the volume low so as not to wake Iliyana. Without thinking, he flipped through the channels.

At first, he thought the image of a mushroom cloud was part of a documentary. He had already advanced three channels before his brain told him to stop. The previous image had been on Al Jazeera and had a breaking news label on it.

He reversed direction on the channels to find a news anchor sharing the screen with the mushroom cloud image.

"We are reporting what appears to be an underwater volcanic eruption in the Philippine Sea, midway between Manila and the island of Guam." The news anchor, a trim Middle Eastern man with perfectly coiffed hair, frowned at the camera. "Scientists are startled by this event, saying they had no idea there were active volcanoes in this area of the Pacific Ocean..."

Pavel muted the TV, then he dropped the remote. He reached for the neck of the vodka bottle and drank.

The picture on the silent TV changed to the photo of the mushroom cloud. It towered over the ocean, a cloud of vapor and smoke looking like an enormous jellyfish.

This was no volcanic eruption. This was Skelly.

Why? He was supposed to sell the nukes, not use them. Had one of the detonators gone off accidentally?

He looked at the chart now displayed on the TV. The detonation was represented by a star in the middle of the ocean due east of the Philippines, a few hundred miles from where he'd left Skelly.

The graphic updated with arrows representing wind speed and direction.

Pavel was just old enough to remember his parents talking in hushed tones about the Chernobyl nuclear accident in the old Soviet Union. The only thing he knew about nuclear fallout was what he'd learned—and mostly forgotten—from his time in the Army. They'd had a one-hour training on how to put on a chemical suit and were given iodine pills to take in case of exposure.

"What's happened?" Iliyana's voice startled Pavel.

She stood in the open doorway, a sheet wrapped around her body like a toga. Her blond hair was mussed with sleep, but she looked beautiful.

Pavel fumbled for the remote, dropped it, and found it again. The television screen went dark.

"A volcano erupted." Pavel thought his voice sounded unsteady. "Somewhere in the Pacific. It's nothing."

Iliyana whispered something under her breath.

"What?" Pavel asked.

She shook her head. "I need to go."

"It's the middle of the night."

But she was already back in the bedroom. By the time Pavel joined her, she had stepped into her dress and was strapping on her high heels.

"I'll drive you," Pavel said, reaching for his trousers.

Iliyana had her mobile out and was tapping the screen. "I have a car," she said. "Please call the elevator."

What was going on? Pavel wondered. It was a volcano, as far as she knew.

He buckled his belt and followed her through the apartment. At the elevator, he held her coat. She settled the mantle of glossy fur across her shoulders and bussed him on the cheek.

"Goodbye, Pavel," she said.

The discreet ding of the elevator superseded Pavel's response.

The elevator door slid open, but Pavel's security man was not there. Another man, bald with penetrating hazel eyes, wearing the uniform of a general officer in the Federal Security Service of the Russian Federation. He was flanked by a contingent of heavily armed security men.

Iliyana strode to the man and kissed him on the cheek. "He's all yours, Vladimir."

Pavel swallowed. He looked down where three red laser dots trembled in his thick hair covering his bare chest.

He did not move. Pavel knew that if Vladimir Federov had planned to kill him, he would be dead already. He also knew that Federov had a way of making men wish they were dead.

The FSB man stepped into Pavel's apartment with his security team in tow. The elevator door rolled closed, and Iliyana disappeared. Forever.

Federov sighed. "Come, Pavel, we have much to discuss."

39

Washington, DC

The man stood at the entrance to the McPherson Square Metro station, facing out toward Franklin Park across the street. He was dressed for the weather in a puffy jacket with a thick scarf around his neck, blue jeans, and work boots. If he'd been part of the crowd, Don would have assumed he was a tourist.

But he wasn't part of the crowd. He stood on a milk crate holding a cardboard sign over his head.

The end is nigh was printed in block letters on the sign.

Fitting, Don thought.

In the twenty-four hours since Manson Skelly detonated a nuclear weapon in the Philippine Sea, the world changed. But none of these people knew it yet. Skelly had been smart. He detonated the weapon deep underwater, giving rise to the possibility that the cause of the mushroom cloud was a volcanic eruption. Skelly knew his ploy wouldn't fool his target audience, the leaders of the United States, Russia, and China, but it gave them a thin façade to explain away the catastrophe. He'd gotten his message across and avoided a worldwide panic. For now.

Don paused, letting the people flow around him. It was a beautiful day in Washington. The sun bright, the air crisp. Don tried to remember the moments before 9/11. Had they been like this? All these people thinking that tomorrow was going to be a carbon copy of today?

Under the pretense of an upgraded terrorist threat, Washington, DC, transformed into a city under siege. Police were everywhere, and roadblocks had sprung up all over the city. The enhanced security perimeter around all government buildings went up overnight, and public access to the buildings was curtailed until further notice.

Not that people seemed to care. The Metro cars he'd ridden into the city had all been packed. Most of the people were headed to a protest on the Mall.

He looked around. These people had no idea they were as close to nuclear annihilation as the country had been at any point in the last fifty years.

Less than a month into his second term, President Serrano was dealing with another international crisis that threatened to destroy his country.

A gaggle of teenagers brushed past him, jarring Don back to the moment. "Sorry," a girl called back to him, her eyes hidden behind a wall of dark bangs.

Don waved his hand. He had glimpsed a future shaped by Manson Skelly, and it was a dark place.

And not one of these people knew it.

He joined the flow of foot traffic down 14th Street and took a right on New York Avenue toward the East Wing entrance to the White House. He cleared security and made his way to the Situation Room, where he took a seat against the wall, behind the Director.

I'm a back-bencher again, he thought glumly.

As soon as the news broke about the nuclear detonation, the first action by National Security Advisor Valentina Flores was to take the hunt for Manson Skelly and the lost nukes away from ETG. In truth, Don wasn't even sure why he was here. He'd been cut out of most of the top-level security briefings over the last twenty-four hours, so he had little to contribute.

Even the Director seemed surprised to see him. "What are you doing here, Riley?" he asked.

"I got a text that I was supposed to attend."

The crease in the center of the Director's forehead deepened. "From whom?"

Don checked. The ID on the number just said White House. He showed it to the Director.

The other man shrugged. "Probably an old distribution list. Well, you're here, you might as well sit in."

With that underwhelming vote of confidence from his boss, Don resumed his seat against the wall.

The room around him was chaos, and Don knew why. They had nothing, not even a sniff of a clue about how to track down Manson Skelly. Over at Sentinel HQ in Sterling, Michael and Dre's efforts to break into the AI had come to naught. The job had been officially turned over to the NSA, but Don, who once served as the Deputy J2 at US Cyber Command, had managed to keep Dre on site working in the background.

The hubbub of voices ceased as President Serrano entered the room and everyone stood. He paused before he pulled out his chair, his eyes surveying the room. His gaze passed over Don without seeming to recognize him.

"Seats," Serrano said.

Although Don could not imagine the pressure he was under, the President looked like he was holding up. His Chief of Staff, on the other hand, looked like death warmed over. Irving Wilkerson's face might have been carved of candle wax for all the life it showed. His normally bright gaze was listless and dull. He stared at the floor between his shoes. Don wondered if Wilkerson was ill.

"Status, Valentina," the President said.

Flores wore a dark blue fitted dress with matching fingernail polish, and her hair was wound into a severe bun. She looked over a pair of reading glasses toward her briefer at the lectern. The young woman was a Valentina clone right down to the accented English and the impeccable outfits.

Don listened, his bad mood deepening. Having given thousands of briefs in his career, he recognized a whole lot of nothing when he heard it.

In summary, they had no idea where Manson Skelly was, and they had no idea where the remaining four nuclear weapons were. To add to their pain, the United States' allies, especially the nuclear-capable ones, were pissed that America had withheld the issue until it blew up in their faces— literally. The United States' allies of convenience, namely Russia and China, had gone radio silent.

Then came some new bad news that Don had not heard yet. Skelly was advertising his new weapons for sale on the Dark Web.

"That's fucking wonderful," the President said when the briefer had finished. "Any tinpot dictator with a bank account can buy their own nuke."

"We're doing our best to track any transactions that might take place over the Dark Web," the DNI said.

A bold statement, Don thought, and an empty one. They called it the Dark Web for a reason. Most people had no idea the part of the internet open to the public and accessible through search engines like Google only accounted for about five percent of the activity and data that resided on the World Wide Web.

The Dark Web allowed a user to access the other 95 percent of the internet using specialized, secure protocols. Since none of the websites on the Dark Web were indexed, only people with the right access could find them.

People who would rather not expose their identity or their search history to outside eyes worked in this unregulated internet space. It made Don's head hurt to consider the complexity of tracking Skelly's activities on the Dark Web.

The meeting soon fizzled out.

It was official, Don thought. The most powerful nation in the world was reduced to hoping Skelly made a mistake that they could exploit.

An unsecure phone call or email, a physical sighting by facial recognition, a bank transaction on one of his monitored accounts. Any of these would show up on the NSA's radar, but Don knew Skelly well enough to know that none of that was going to happen.

As he made his way out of the White House, Don heard someone call his name. A young woman who Don recognized as a White House intern caught up with him. She was out of breath.

"You're wanted in the Oval Office, sir. Right away."

40

Don hustled back through the White House complex toward the Oval Office, his mind racing with what President Serrano might want from him. He thought about calling the Director to see if he needed any specific intelligence for the meeting but decided he did not have the time.

When Don reached the anteroom to the Oval Office, he was breathing heavily from the effort. The Director was not in the room, but Chief of Staff Wilkerson sat in an armchair, his shoulders hunched forward. The older man struggled to his feet and held out his hand to Don. His skin was cold and clammy.

"Thank you for coming, Don," Wilkerson said in a kind voice.

Don couldn't help himself. "Are you okay, sir?" he said. "You don't look well."

Wilkerson attempted a smile. "I'll feel much better in a few minutes. Follow me, please." He nodded at the President's executive assistant and opened the door to the Oval Office. Don wanted to ask if they should wait for the Director, but Wilkerson drew him into the room and closed the door behind them.

President Serrano had his chair swiveled toward the south-facing windows. Legs crossed, he dangled a pair of reading glasses as he stared out at the trees beyond the bay window. When he saw Don, the President's brow creased into a frown.

"We need five minutes, sir," Wilkerson said. "Riley needs to be part of this conversation."

Serrano didn't look convinced, but he rose and strode to the sitting area. Don wasn't convinced either, but he allowed Wilkerson to plant him on a sofa. The Chief of Staff took the seat opposite him.

"You look terrible, Irv," Serrano said. "Can I get you a coffee or something?"

Don perched on the edge of the sofa cushion. He wished the Director were here. Something was off about this meeting. Serrano clearly did not want him here, and yet Wilkerson insisted. To make matters worse, the Chief of Staff had the air of a child who'd been called to the principal's office. Don watched the older man tuck a trembling hand under his leg to hide the infirmity.

Why does he want me here? Don thought. He and Wilkerson had butted heads on more than one occasion, but now the Chief of Staff was inviting him into the Oval Office for a personal chat with the President.

"What's this all about, Irv?" Serrano seemed to realize that his mentor was hurting.

Wilkerson took a deep breath and let it out. "I need to tell you something. Both of you."

Serrano cut a mystified look at Don, who offered only a slight shrug.

"The reason why Riley's team was unable to track down the Naval War College bomber in South America was because of me," Wilkerson began. "I told Manson Skelly what Don was trying to do. I knew he would probably go after the target on his own, and that meant feeding Don's team bad intel. That's what happened. We missed out on capturing the most wanted man in the world because of my indiscretion."

For a split second, Don wondered if Wilkerson had somehow found out that he'd been face-to-face with the Naval War College bomber. A bolt of fear ran up his spine, and sweat broke out across his chest. His sudden discomfort went unnoticed by the other men.

"Why in the hell would you do something like that, Irv?" the President demanded. "We went to extraordinary lengths to keep Sentinel out of it. I signed a letter directing Skelly to stay away from the operation. If what you're saying is true, then this is on him. I'm disappointed, but considering what has—"

"I'm not finished yet, sir," Wilkerson interrupted.

Serrano frowned but kept his silence.

Don felt his heart skip a beat. Here it comes, he thought. Wilkerson knows about the clandestine meeting with Rachel and Ian Thomas. It's all going to come out right now.

"I've been back-channeling with Manson Skelly for some time," Wilkerson said. "He's been pressuring me to get you to nominate him as Secretary of Defense—"

Serrano barked out a sharp laugh. "You're kidding, right? I hope you told him that that was never going to happen."

Wilkerson nodded. "Of course, sir, but he was...persistent."

Serrano's face went still. "There's something you're not telling me, Irv," he said in a guarded tone. "Out with it. Right now. Whatever it is, we'll deal with it."

Don watched Wilkerson's face. Behind the owl-like glasses, he saw the older man's eyes go glassy. Tears rolled down his cheeks. He started to cough, but the cough turned into a racking sob. His shoulders hunched forward. His mouth gaped open, then closed again. Finally, he choked out, "There's no fixing this, Mr. President. Not this time."

Serrano moved to the sofa next to Wilkerson and put his arm around the older man's shoulder. When he spoke, his voice was warm with kindness. "Irv, whatever this is, we will get through—"

"I'm responsible for Abby Cromwell's death," Wilkerson blurted out.

Serrano's arm fell away. He separated himself from Wilkerson, returning to his own chair. The President looked at Don, then back to his Chief of Staff.

"Perhaps you'd better start at the beginning." Serrano's voice was chilly now. "And don't leave anything out."

Wilkerson used a handkerchief to wipe his eyes. He drew in a deep breath, held it for a second, then let it out slowly.

"During the Ukraine crisis," he began, his voice quivering, "when we were using Sentinel, the strategy was working. We had the Russians on the back foot, but Cromwell, she got wobbly, especially toward the end."

"I remember," Serrano said.

"I started a dialogue with Skelly then. He was on the ground in Ukraine. I pushed him to get Sentinel more involved."

"The autonomous weapons attack," Don said. "The K-10s. You were the one who told Skelly to do it."

"That was me," Wilkerson agreed. "And Abby Cromwell found out about it."

Serrano cleared his throat. "What exactly are you telling me, Irv?"

"I'm telling you that I ordered Skelly to use those robot dogs. When Abby found out, she was going to blow the whistle on us."

"The *Washington Post* story," Serrano said. "Abby was the source."

Wilkerson nodded. "She was going to tell everything, so I... I..."

"You told Skelly to kill Abby Cromwell," the President finished for him.

"I—I...yes, sir." The old man's pale cheeks were slick with tears. "I did it."

"Abby's jet was shot down by a Russian surface-to-air missile," Don said.

Wilkerson shook his head. "That was Skelly's doing. He cut a deal with the number two in Wagner. Pavel Kozlov is the guy's name. Skelly paid him to shoot down Abby's plane when they took off."

"Irv," the President began, but Don cut him off.

"Skelly was blackmailing you," Don said, his voice hot with anger. "Everything we were doing at ETG, you gave it to Skelly."

Don didn't pose it as a question. Wilkerson didn't object. He just nodded.

"Skelly found the Chinese agent in South America." Don felt the pieces falling into place at last. "That's how he found out about the lost Chinese nuke. That's how Sentinel found the lost submarine so much faster than us."

Wilkerson nodded again. "It was all me," he said. "I knew Skelly was getting more unstable, but I thought I could control him."

"What about the investigation into the deaths of Abby and Dylan

Mattias?" said Don, referring to the CIA agent who had been traveling with Abby Cromwell when her plane was shot down.

Wilkerson's shoulders sank lower. "I covered it up." He looked at the President, his eyes pleading. "I knew it was wrong, Mr. President, but I thought if I kept you out of it, I could manage the issue."

Serrano's face was still, lips compressed, nostrils flaring in anger. When he spoke, his voice was like flint.

"How could you do this?" He let out a sharp hiss, and Wilkerson shrank back like he'd been slapped. "How could you do this to me? I trusted you, Irv, and this is how you repay me?"

Serrano was out of his chair, looming over Wilkerson cowering on the sofa.

"You had an American citizen assassinated? You let a nuclear weapon fall into the hands of a power-hungry madman?" Serrano's features were twisted and drawn. Spittle showered Wilkerson.

"I'm sorry—" the old man began.

"Sorry?" Serrano shouted. "How could you do this to me? You have jeopardized everything."

For Don, the President's tirade faded into the background. Manson Skelly killed Abby Cromwell. At some level, he'd always known there was more to her death than a battlefield casualty, but the clarity of Wilkerson's explanation left him with an unfamiliar feeling.

Rage. Hot, seething anger that made him want to stand up and scream at the top of his lungs.

Abby Cromwell, his friend, the person who had helped him bring an end to the Russian invasion in eastern Europe, had not died in some random battlefield accident. She'd been murdered by Manson Skelly.

For what? Money, power—

"Riley!" The President's sharp tone snapped Don back to reality.

"Sir." Don got to his feet.

Serrano walked to the windows behind his desk. "You can leave us," he said over his shoulder. "I hope it goes without saying that I'm relying on your discretion regarding everything you've just heard."

"Of course, Mr. President."

As Don turned to go, Wilkerson reached across the coffee table and seized Don's hand.

"Riley," he hissed. "I want you to make this right."

Don didn't trust himself to speak, so he just nodded.

41

Emerging Threats Group
Tysons Corner, Virginia

Don shut the door to his office and turned to face Michael and Dre.

"What I am going to tell you cannot leave this room," he said.

Normally, an opener like that would be followed by the signing of a nondisclosure agreement to allow Don to read them into a special access program.

But today, there would be no signatures.

The TV, tuned to CNN, had the sound muted. The news channel was still replaying the satellite images of the subterranean "eruption" on a loop while the host interviewed an expert on underwater volcanoes. So far, Serrano's public story was holding.

Don took a seat behind his desk and sized up his two most trusted officers. He had no right to involve them in what he was about to do, and yet without their help, he had no chance of pulling it off.

"What's up, Don?" Dre's careful tone suggested she understood his inner conflict.

You're a selfish bastard, Don chided himself. Then he plunged ahead.

"I've just come from the White House," he said. "There's been a...development." Don sketched out the details of Abby Cromwell's death and the role that Skelly had played in it. He kept his tone as neutral as possible.

When he finished, Michael spoke first. "I'm sorry, Don. I know you and Abby were close."

Were we? Don wondered why he was taking this news so hard. He and Abby had been work colleagues, and friends of a sort, but nothing more. There'd been a mutual respect, but not the kind of personal connection that warranted the deep emotion he was feeling.

It was the injustice of it, he decided. The waste. Abby Cromwell was a decent human being and a patriot. She'd chosen to do the right thing and paid for that decision with her life.

And then the people who killed her covered it up.

He tried to imagine what her last moments might have been like. Had she seen the missile coming? Did she suffer? For a second, he struggled to breathe. He gripped the edge of his desk until his knuckles turned white. The sense of bottled-up rage threatened to take over. He wanted to scream and cry at the same time.

He slammed that mental door shut. There would be time enough to grieve, but he had work to do first.

"There's a worldwide manhunt on for Skelly, Don," Dre said. "Someone will find him. It's just a matter of time."

"That's not good enough," Don said. "I want to find him. I want to be the one to take Skelly down."

"Don," Michael said, "every intelligence agency in the world is hunting him and we are on the outside looking in. How do you propose to find him first?"

"I'm not going to look for him," Don said. "I'm going to make him come to us."

The look between Michael and Dre might have been skepticism or it might have been pity.

"What can we do to help, Don?" Dre asked.

"How much do you know about the Turkistan Islamic Movement?" Don asked.

Michael shrugged. It was a softball question. Part of their job was to stay current on terrorist groups around the world.

"The TIM is an Islamist militant group active in the western Xinjiang province in China. They have links with al-Qaeda and with the Taliban in Afghanistan. The Chinese government classifies it as a terrorist organization and links it to the Uyghur Muslims in western China. The US says that relationship is overblown, but China uses it as an excuse to continue their crackdown on the entire population of Uyghurs."

Don nodded. "I want you to find Manson Skelly on the Dark Web and pose as a buyer for the TIM. I want you to set up a meet. Wherever he wants, I don't care, but it has to be in person. We'll agree to his price, but it needs to be as soon as possible, and I want to take possession of the weapon at time of sale. Got it?"

"You realize there's a problem with that plan, boss," Dre commented. "We can pretend to be whoever we want on the internet, but Skelly's not an idiot. How are we going to take an in-person meeting? Our cover will get blown in a New York minute."

"You're absolutely right, Dre," Don said. "The only way we're going to get a meeting with Skelly is if we have a buyer who has real terrorist bona fides. Someone who has an ax to grind against the Chinese government."

Michael and Dre looked at each other, confused.

"You have someone in mind?" Dre asked.

"You find Skelly," Don said. "I'll find the buyer."

* * *

Chetumal, Mexico

Don burned eighteen precious hours finding Rachel Jaeger.

The only possible way to contact her was via Noam Glantz. The Mossad Director of Operations was skeptical when Don called him.

"I have no idea where to find her, Don," Noam told him. That was a lie, and they both knew it. Still, the conversation gave Noam plausible deniability in the event Don's plan went off the rails. A not unlikely possibility, Don thought.

"Well, thanks anyway, Noam," Don told him.

It took eight hours for Rachel to call him back.

"This better not be a trap," Rachel said when he answered the same burner phone he had used to call Noam.

"I need to talk to you," Don replied. "In person. As soon as possible."

There was a pause, then Rachel said, "Chetumal, Mexico. Take a walk around the Punta Estrella on Boulevard Bahía at dusk."

"How will I contact you?"

"You won't." Rachel hung up.

Now, as he strolled along the concrete seawall next to the Boulevard Bahía, Don wondered if this was a good idea. The light was fading, and the walk wound through clumps of tall bushes and trees. He imagined in the daytime lots of people walked here and enjoyed the view of the water from the benches that dotted the side of the path. This didn't look like the best part of town to be walking alone at night. Getting mugged on his way to meet with the world's most wanted man would be the ultimate irony.

Scratch that, Don thought. The world's second most wanted man. Manson Skelly now occupied the top spot.

Chetumal was perfect for Rachel's purposes. The Mexican city was on the Chetumal Bay, near the mouth of the Río Hondo, and on the border with the country of Belize. Guatemala was less than an hour away by car. In the event Don tried to trap Rachel, she could escape by sea, land, or air to three different countries.

Don slowed when he came upon a couple occupying one of the benches sheltered within a stand of trees. The two were twisted together, and the intensity of their grinding hips suggested they were going to be there for a while.

Don peered down the path. The last of the daylight had fled, and he could not see the other side. Turn around or keep going? he wondered.

The man noticed Don had stopped and broke off his engagement with the woman to glare at him. Don held up his hands in surrender and stepped down the dark path.

A few steps along, Don heard the scrape of sandals on concrete behind him. When he started to turn around, Rachel's voice said, "Keep walking."

Don walked with Rachel a few paces behind him for another hundred meters before she spoke again.

"Stop."

Don complied.

She frisked him from behind, taking his phone and wallet. He heard her place the items in a bag.

"Do you have any tracking devices on you?" she asked.

"No," Don said.

"Turn around."

A car passed, allowing Don to see Rachel. She was dressed in dirty khakis cut off mid-calf, a dark T-shirt, and worn sandals.

"Keep walking," she said, slipping the bag containing his phone and wallet into her hip pocket.

"By the way, if you're lying to me, I'll kill you," Rachel continued in a conversational tone.

Despite the warmth of the evening, Don felt a chill.

"I need to see him," he said.

"Why?" Rachel's face was lost in the shadows, but her tone left no doubt about her suspicions.

Don wondered what the relationship was between the Chinese spy and the Mossad agent. He decided he didn't care.

"I need to talk to him," he said again. "Please."

Rachel struck off at a pace that forced Don to jog in order to keep up. His breathing grew heavy, and his shirt was soon soaked with sweat. After about ten minutes, Rachel left the bayside path and cut into an older section of town. She led him through a maze of streets and alleyways, even crossing through someone's backyard, before pausing at a narrow flight of steps leading up the side of a house.

Light from an open window fell across her face. Her dark features were bunched into a scowl. "If this is a trap, you're a dead man." She took the stairs two at a time, leaving Don on the sidewalk.

Don plodded after her, tired from the exertion of following the Mossad agent. At the top of the steps, he found a small rooftop bar of four white plastic tables and mismatched plastic chairs under a tarp canopy.

In the corner farthest from the entrance, wearing a straw hat and sunglasses, was the second most wanted man in the world. Rachel leaned close to him, whispering in his ear, no doubt briefing him on their encounter so far.

The man nodded when Don collapsed into an open chair. He held up two fingers, and a pair of sweating beer bottles appeared before Don and Rachel. The green bottle read Belikin, but Don didn't care. It was cold and wet, and that was all that mattered. He drained half the bottle.

When he came up for air, the man had removed his hat and glasses, and he studied Don without comment.

Don shifted under the man's gaze. "I don't even know what to call you," Don said. "What's your name? Your real name."

The man exchanged a glance with Rachel. "I was Ian Thomas for a long time. That's as good a name as any."

Don nodded.

"I never expected to see you again, Mr. Riley," Ian said.

"The feeling was mutual," Don agreed.

"And yet, here you are." The Chinese man leaned forward on the rickety plastic table. "Why?"

Don swallowed. The moment of truth.

"I want you to work for me," he said.

The answer seemed to take the former Chinese operative by surprise. He shot a look at Rachel and sat back in his chair.

"What is that supposed to mean, Don?" Rachel said.

"I need a terrorist," Don replied. "You're the only one I know."

Rachel's expression hardened. "Is that supposed to be funny?"

"No," Don snapped back. "It's supposed to be penance. This is his chance to make up for what he did."

Ian put a hand on Rachel's arm. "Maybe you better start at the beginning, Mr. Riley."

Don nodded, angry with himself. He was antagonizing Rachel, and he needed her on his side. "Are you familiar with the Turkistan Islamic Movement?" Don asked.

Ian nodded. "Of course."

"I want you to pose as a weapons buyer for them."

"What kind of weapons am I trying to buy?"

"A two-hundred-kiloton suitcase nuke," Don said.

The answer shocked both Ian and Rachel into silence. Don heard someone in the street strum a guitar and start to sing in Spanish, a mournful ballad. Through the open window of a house a few meters away, he could make out the clatter of silverware on plates and the clinking of glasses. Muted laughter drifted on the night air.

"I'm listening," Ian said.

Don leaned across the table, pitched his voice low, and told him the story of Manson Skelly and the stolen nuclear warhead.

"The only reason why we even know the nuclear warhead existed is because of the information you gave me," he concluded. "I need someone who can get close to Manson Skelly. Your bona fides are impeccable. You're a known terrorist, and Skelly knows about you already. I can get a meeting with him, but I need you to pose as the buyer."

"It's a suicide mission," Rachel said. "The answer is no."

"Please," Don said. "You're my best chance. I need your help."

He could feel Ian Thomas's eyes assessing him, and he tried not to look away.

"This is personal for you," Ian said.

"Skelly killed my friend," Don admitted. "And he's dangerous. If you help me, we can stop him."

Ian looked away into the night. Below them, the streets were coming alive. More voices sang along with the guitar player. From the open window came a burst of raucous laughter. Strangely, the sounds of community made Don feel even more alone. This was a crazy, stupid idea.

"Will he get a pardon?" Rachel asked.

Don shook his head. "This is all off the books. If it works, no one will ever know about it. If it doesn't...well, then, it doesn't matter."

Rachel's face screwed into a scowl. She started to speak, but Ian held up a hand to stop her.

"I'll do it."

42

Moscow, Russia

It was well after eight o'clock in the morning when the rising sun touched the Odintsovsky District on the outskirts of Moscow. Pavel's vehicle passed through the urban center of Zarechye, an area of treelined streets and middle-class apartments blocks. This commuter neighborhood was built just outside the Moscow city limits, adjacent to the Moscow Ring Road. As the crow flies, Pavel guessed they were less than fifteen kilometers from Red Square.

As the car continued, traffic thinned and the scenery changed into faceless warehouses, freight companies, and storage units.

An industrial area close to the city center with easy access to major highways leading away from Moscow. It was, he supposed, a perfect place to hide a nuclear bomb.

Pavel tried to imagine the millions of people that could be killed or maimed by such a weapon, and his imagination failed him. He wasn't a peacenik or even someone who gave a shit about his fellow man, but this... this was too much, even for him.

The driver, navigating the Range Rover through the snow-choked streets, nailed a pothole, jarring Pavel back to reality. He cursed, and the driver glared at him in the rearview mirror.

Yuri, Pavel's normal driver, was dead, a victim of Federov's men. His replacement was an FSB agent. Short and muscled with a twice-broken nose and a crew cut, all he needed was a scar on his cheek to complete his disguise as an underworld thug.

Pavel tried to light one of his Prima cigarettes, but his hand was shaking so badly it took him two tries. The driver gave him another glare through the smoke. Pavel blew a blast of blue-black exhale back in his direction. The driver rolled down his window, letting in the bitterly cold Moscow morning air. Pavel took one last drag and flicked the butt out his window.

Yesterday, he'd had command of thousands of battle-hardened men within the largest private army in the world. Today, he was fighting for the right to smoke a cigarette in his own car.

His earpiece crackled to life. "Take the next left. Second building in on the right-hand side."

The FSB driver, who also had an earpiece, turned the wheel. The Rover fishtailed on the slick road, and he expertly brought it under control. The second building on the right was a two-story, metal-sided warehouse with a panel of high windows and rollup doors on either end of the building. The only other entrance that Pavel could see was a passenger door on the corner of the building. The driver pulled to the side of the road and put the vehicle in park.

"Stay here," Pavel ordered. "That's what my men would do."

The FSB driver grunted, his close-set eyes in the rearview mirror leaving no doubt as to what he thought of Pavel.

It had taken Federov's men only a few hours to figure out where Skelly had hidden the nuclear bomb in the Moscow area. It had actually taken Pavel longer to convince Federov that Skelly had not shared the location with his second-in-command than it did to figure out where the weapon was hidden. The break came when Pavel described the three men Skelly had assigned to guard the weapon.

Alexei, the man in charge, was a social media addict. Wagner Group, under the leadership of Pavel's former boss, had used the young man's skills to stage an incident in Lithuania as a pretext for a Russian invasion. Alexei had played the part of Leonardas Petraukas, a right-wing provocateur, during an invasion in a small town in Lithuania. It was inconceivable to Pavel that Alexei could be in Moscow and not at least check his social media accounts.

Within hours, they had a location, and before the sun was up, Pavel had a new job working for the FSB as a double agent.

Not exactly a promotion, but the alternative was a bullet in the brain.

A small part of Pavel even welcomed Federov's offer. He was done with Skelly. Every man had a line he would not cross, he told himself, and his line was nuclear weapons.

Pavel's first mission was to gain entrance to the location and verify the weapon was there. Oh, and not get vaporized in the process.

This will work, he thought, stepping out of the Rover. These men know you. No matter what Skelly has told them, they will trust you.

His breath steamed in the morning air. Despite the cold, he left his coat unbuttoned to allow ready access to his sidearm. His boots crunched through the snow. When he arrived at the door, Pavel looked up at the security camera and pounded on the metal surface.

"Open up," he shouted. "It's me."

The high windows suddenly blazed gold in the rising sun. Pavel wondered if that was the last beautiful thing he would see on this earth before he disappeared in a nuclear blast.

The magnetic lock clicked and the door swung open. Sander De Vries had his long blond hair pulled back into a ponytail, and he wore an apron. The smell of Sander's famous *pannenkoeken* wafted into Pavel's face. The man held a Beretta 9mm in his right hand.

"Boss," Sander said, "what are you doing here?"

"New orders," Pavel said.

Sander blocked the way. "Where's Yuri?" He gestured at the idling Rover.

"He's sick," Pavel snarled. "Get out of my way. I'm freezing my balls off out here."

A flicker of doubt crossed the Dutchman's face, then he broke into a smile, his default state. "Sure thing. You're just in time. I'm making breakfast."

"I can smell it. You're making me hungry!" Pavel stepped inside, letting the door close behind him. He heard the magnetic lock slam into place.

Why did it have to be Sander? he thought.

At the end of a narrow hallway, Pavel entered what had once been a break room for the previous inhabitants of the warehouse. Sander returned to a makeshift kitchen set up along one wall and flipped a pancake. Three cots lined the opposite wall, and a sleeping form occupied one cot. Of the other two, one was twisted bedsheets and the other neatly made. That would be Sander's bunk.

A kitchen table littered with the detritus of a never-ending poker game filled the center of the room. A large flat-screen TV surrounded by three armchairs occupied one corner. Behind the door was an overflowing trash can.

How many weeks of my life have I spent in places like this? Pavel wondered. The jokes, the tired stories, the card games, the fights, the endless waiting to be called into action...

"Breakfast?" Sander held up a plate of steaming pancakes.

"Where's Alexei?" Pavel asked.

Sander pointed to a closed door. "With the package."

Pavel jerked open the door and entered what had once been a store-room. Alexei sat in a cheap folding chair, elbows on knees, scrolling on a mobile phone. He looked up when Pavel entered. Shock crossed his face, and he hurriedly stuffed the mobile into his pocket.

"Boss, what are you—"

"Is that it?" Pavel interrupted, pointing at a black Pelican case in the center of the room.

Alexei nodded.

"I have it," Pavel said.

Alexei frowned. "You have what, boss?"

But his words were not intended for Alexei. Outside the warehouse, his words triggered a series of actions. FSB teams set up in surrounding buildings turned on jammers to block any EM transmissions into or out of the warehouse, isolating the weapon from any remote triggers. Pavel imagined a platoon of Spetsnaz commandos bearing down on the three entrances.

All because of his three little words.

"Alexei?" Pavel said.

The man blinked. He looked tired, bored. "What, boss?" he said.

"You're a dumb fuck." Pavel drew his compact SR-1 Vektor and shot the other man in the left eye. His head snapped back, and a spray of red painted the wall.

Before Alexei's body even slid to the floor, Pavel was back in the kitchen. He put two bullets into the sleeping man, then turned his weapon on Sander.

The Dutchman dropped the plate of pancakes and raised his hands.

"What's happening, boss?" he said.

Pavel heard the roar of diesel engines outside. In seconds, they'd breach the door and take them both hostage. His weapon was steady on the younger man's chest. Pavel swallowed hard.

"Trust me, Sander. It's better this way."

He pulled the trigger twice.

43

Andaman Sea

"Small world," Manson Skelly muttered to himself. He leaned back in the deck chair, staring at the laptop screen containing the message from Diego Montalban.

A month ago, he tried to kill this guy. Now, the same guy wanted to go into business together. Skelly grinned at the screen. *My enemy—with a big bank account—is now my friend.*

Welcome to twenty-first-century warfare. The best that money can buy.

He got up, stretched, and paced to the railing of the yacht, two stories above the water. The sea was calm tonight, and the humid air coated his skin with a layer of slick saltiness. Despite his training as a Navy SEAL, Skelly would have preferred to be based on land. He felt more sure of himself when he could plant his two feet in the dirt.

But for now, the best place to be was off the grid and highly mobile. Mama gave him a greater than 85 percent chance of survival if he stayed seaborne and limited his external communications to bare essentials. The secure satellite uplink gave him a data link as well as voice comms. He used both sparingly.

The *Centurion* changed heading, something he'd ordered the crew to do at least three times an hour at random intervals. At thirty meters, the *Centurion* just barely qualified as a "luxury yacht," a label generally reserved for vessels longer than eighty feet.

Skelly didn't care about the label. He wanted to blend in. Showing up in a port on a 250-foot luxury behemoth was bound to get the locals wondering who owned the ship. The last thing he needed was some asshole trying to get internet-famous by unmasking the owner of the yacht. He'd seen some very fine people, mostly Russian oligarchs, go down that way.

What Skelly needed at a time like this was understated luxury, something that was comfortable but still allowed him to blend in with his surroundings.

The smaller craft also allowed him to reduce the crew down to four, the captain and first mate, both men, the cook, also male, and a very attractive twentysomething female steward who served Skelly all his meals. The crew had not been happy with the increased workload, but their bitching and moaning faded when he doubled their salaries. There had been more complaining when he'd confiscated all their electronics, satellite TV, and internet access. The last thing he wanted was some stupid internet post to give away his location to the authorities.

Of course, he had internet because he needed to access the Dark Web. Selling a nuclear weapon was much harder than he'd expected. His little demonstration in the Philippine Sea had generated plenty of interest in the world of black market arms dealers, but it left him with two problems.

The first issue was price. Very few buyers were going to be able to pay what he was demanding for the weapons. And then there was the headache of trying to separate real buyers from fakes. It was a given that the United States intelligence community would flood the zone with phony offers, hoping to get him to slip up and divulge a clue about his location.

Which was why this buyer who'd just popped up was perfect. He scanned the dossier he'd downloaded from Mama about the Chinese spy. Right now, Skelly thanked his lucky stars that he hadn't killed this guy in Argentina.

Diego Montalban, formerly known as Ian Thomas, as well as a whole list of other aliases, was the real deal. A Chinese agent operating under a non-official cover as a maritime insurance agent in Singapore, he'd racked up an impressive string of operations against the United States, culminating in the Naval War College bombing. When the Chinese tried to tie up loose ends by sending a wet team to take him off the board, Diego eliminated the team, then went rogue. Skelly recalled the Chinese colonel he'd told Kozlov to kill in the Argentine hiking town. That guy was proof that China was still trying to take out their former agent.

And now, old Diego, or whatever he called himself these days, was going to get back at his former masters in spectacular fashion.

Turns out, Diego was a Muslim with ties to the Turkistan Islamic Movement in western China. Since the Chi-Commies refused to let Diego live out his retirement in peace, he was going to rejoin the cause and make them pay. Big time.

And Skelly was going to sell him the means to do it.

A suitcase nuke was the perfect weapon for Diego's needs, Skelly reflected. It would be easy to smuggle across one of the many borders into China. Myanmar, Laos, Vietnam, India, take your pick. Pick a city in China and press a button. Mission accomplished.

Even more important, the guy had the coin to make the buy. Skelly had seen a screenshot of a Dubai bank account that would make him even richer than he already was.

Skelly returned to his laptop and changed screens.

The familiar itching sensation prickled across the back of his neck. According to Mama, the Moscow unit was still offline. They'd lost satellite contact earlier in the day and had yet to regain it.

Skelly cursed, jumped out of his chair, paced again. He returned to his seat and checked the units on boats in the Mediterranean.

One weapon was off the coast of North Africa. Skelly had penciled in Saudi Arabia as the buyer for that weapon. Politically, it was a tough sell, but his vetted contacts assured him the deal would go through, they just needed more time for internal discussions. If that opportunity didn't pan out, he could always sell to some tinpot dictator on the African continent, although he might have to negotiate on the price. That was the other good thing about the deal with Diego Montalban: the buyer was willing to sacrifice price for speed. He wanted the deal done as soon as possible and was willing to pay a premium.

The second weapon was off the coast of Turkey. Tentative buyers: Syria or Iran. Both were interested, but neither wanted to pay his price. Yet. They'd get there eventually.

Skelly swiveled in his chair and propped his feet up on a black Pelican case. The final nuclear weapon was right by his side.

He narrowed his eyes as he thought through the problem of what to do about the Moscow unit. Even if the weapon was lost, there was no way to trace it back to his location on the high seas. Every storage site was independent of the others. The only possible link was through Mama, and it would take the NSA years to crack the encryption on the Sentinel AI system.

No, Skelly thought, I'm safe for now, but I can't live on this damn boat forever. Eventually, we're going to need to put into a port for food and fuel, and that means risk.

I'll deal with that problem later, he thought as he patted the black Pelican case. But first, I need to sell this baby.

He turned back to his laptop and reopened the secure chat window.

We have a deal, he typed. *Phuket, Thailand. 24 hours.*

44

Phuket, Thailand

It's all happening so fast, Don thought. Too fast.

A gentle breeze blew through the open sliding glass door that led to the terrace overlooking the bay. Don stood in the doorway, taking in the view. The lights from hundreds of ships, large and small, dotted the night horizon. The air smelled of salt and smoke from the charcoal braziers used by the street food vendors who lined the boulevard along the water. Voices and laughter rose above the shushing sound of the gentle waves breaking on the white sand beach only a few meters away.

A day ago, the weather outside Don's window in Washington, DC, was light snowfall. Now, in this tropical paradise, he felt a trickle of cold sweat run between his shoulder blades.

Back in the safety of ETG, the concept of running a sting operation on Manson Skelly had seemed like a good idea. When they'd actually managed to make contact with the rogue arms dealer and broker a deal, the idea went from good to brilliant. But now, when he was on the verge of executing his bold plan, Don's confidence ebbed.

He was running an unauthorized shoestring operation against a man with a nuclear weapon. A man with no compunction about killing innocent people by any means necessary. And the linchpin of his brilliant strategy was a Chinese intelligence officer responsible for a brazen attack on the United States.

I have truly lost my fucking mind, Don thought.

Don shifted his gaze from the harbor to Ian Thomas. The man stood on the terrace, watching the ocean. Even though he was the one most exposed in this operation, he seemed at ease. In contrast, Rachel Jaeger, who rarely left his side, exhibited signs of extreme discomfort. Her body shifted constantly as if it pained her to stay in one place for too long.

Ian reached out and took her hand. Rachel brushed him off.

Don had seen some complicated relationships, but this one—whatever was going on between the Chinese spy and the Mossad agent—had disaster written all over it.

Behind him, Will Clarke entered the room. When Skelly had given the location of the meet, Don immediately called the CEO of Falchion for logistics support. He knew of no better operator in this part of the world, and he also knew that Clarke was no fan of Manson Skelly either.

Dressed in what one might call business paramilitary, Clarke moved toward Don with purpose. His features showed the strain of trying to meet Don's long list of demands in the space of a single workday.

"Sea transport is set," he said to Don, "and we have two cars with drivers out front. Drones are in the air. We're ready."

Don nodded. His chest felt tight, making it hard to breathe. If you call it off now, he told himself, you can still walk away.

"Look, Will." Don lowered his voice. "I need to come clean with you. This operation is...well, it's off the books. If it goes sideways, it's on me. I want your guys to disappear. You have my word that—"

"Don, relax," Clarke interrupted. "This is not my first rodeo. I know who you're going after, and I'm in. If it goes off the rails...well, we'll burn that bridge when we get there." He nodded at Michael, who was hunched over his workstation, deep in concentration. "How about your people? They good with this?"

Don followed his gaze to rest on Michael's broad back. When he'd laid out his plan to use the Naval War College bomber to take down Manson Skelly, Michael and Dre had voiced concerns.

More than concerns. Fear that their boss and friend had lost perspective on the problem. Patiently, Don kept at them, because he had no other choice: he could not pull this off without them. He needed them.

They trust me, Don thought. I hope to God that I don't betray that confidence.

He dismissed the thought. He was in too deep to let it go. Thanks to Wilkerson's tearful confession in the Oval Office, putting down Manson Skelly had crossed from the professional to the personal.

Don had seen the President's reaction to Wilkerson's confession, and he knew the truth. He felt it in his bones. Unless he acted, there would be no justice for Abby Cromwell. To admit her death had been murder was to admit the truth about Sentinel's involvement in Ukraine, a truth that implicated the President.

Don knew that would never happen. There was too much at stake for Serrano.

Even if Skelly were captured, justice for Abby—real justice—was a fantasy. There would be deals and money and pardons. Her murder would be one more detail bargained away in the name of the greater good.

Don could not let that stand.

"Bring it in," he called out.

The low chatter in the room ceased, and the team—the very small team —gathered around their leader.

In addition to Rachel, Ian, and Michael, Don had brought two more members of ETG into his confidence. Tom Sellner and Andy Myers were field operators with decades of experience fighting all over the world, first for the US Army 5th Special Forces Group, then for the CIA Special Activities Division. The pair, who went by the joint nickname of S&M, only worked as a team.

Fearing their reactions, Don had kept Ian's true identity a secret from the pair.

Another lie, Don thought. Add it to the bill.

"Logistics," Don said to Clarke.

"It's high season down here," the CEO of Falchion began, "and this is a resort town. Traffic is ferocious, and there's mobs of people everywhere.

Don't be surprised if it gets loud out there. Fireworks as a form of celebration are not uncommon.

"We're driving Toyota Land Cruisers, which will blend in with the local traffic," Clarke continued. "Ian will be in vehicle one with a Thai driver who knows the area. I'll be in vehicle two, along with S&M. Don, Michael, and Rachel are here at home base directing traffic."

Rachel glowered at Clarke. The private military contractor had drawn a line at letting Rachel be part of the operation. Don had agreed with Clarke.

"If we need access to the water," Clarke pointed out the sliding door, "we've got transport standing by on the beach with a boat driver who knows the harbor."

He motioned at the ceiling. "We've got an overwatch drone upstairs that can track both cars as well as the buyer. Michael has that feed on his screens. He also has access to our secure channel comms. All the mobile units will be on comms, except for the buyer. Too risky if he's searched."

Don took over the briefing. "We're operating on the assumption that Skelly will have a small security footprint. It attracts less attention, makes him more mobile, and it makes for fewer potential leaks." He held up a palm-sized tablet. "The buyer will carry this tablet. Even if it's shut off, the GPS chip is active. For financial security reasons, Ian will refuse to make the bank transfer on any device except for this one."

Saying out loud his assumptions about Skelly and how he would react made Don squirm. *God, I hope I'm right,* he thought.

The sound of distant fireworks and the roar of a crowd drifted through the open slider. Michael's computer chimed, and he stepped away to check the screen.

"New message," he called out.

They all crowded around the laptop screen to see a string of GPS coordinates and the words: *One hour*.

Michael copied the coordinates and switched screens to a map view.

"It's a night market," he announced, "about ten kilometers from here."

"I know the place," Clarke replied.

There was a bustle of activity as Ian departed in one of the Land Cruisers and the two ETG operators left in the second vehicle with Clarke.

Don pulled up a chair next to Michael. Together, they watched two red dots representing the Land Cruisers crawl across the map.

Fifteen excruciating minutes passed in silence as Don reviewed in his mind every lingering detail of the operation.

Michael interrupted his thoughts. "Where's Rachel?"

Don stepped out onto the terrace and checked the kitchen, then both bedrooms and the bathroom.

He returned to his place next to Michael, cursing to himself.

Rachel was gone.

45

Phuket, Thailand

Rachel watched Ian exit the Land Cruiser on Dibuk Road and walk into the haphazard rows of the Phuket Indy Night Market.

The outdoor market ran every weeknight, offering anything from noodles to knock-off Nikes, secondhand electronics to live eels. It was a sea of colorful humanity, a setting where another Asian face would blend in with the multicultural crowd. The smell of roasting meats and nuts hung heavy in the air, and the sounds of traffic and holiday partying rang out.

Rachel left her helmet on as she steered her idling Honda Click scooter into the flow of people navigating the periphery of the market stalls. The battered silver motorbike was a twist-and-go scooter, so-called because there were no gears or clutch, just a throttle and a brake. The 125-cc engine was more than enough power to motor on traffic-choked city streets, and the slim design gave her the ability to slip to the head of the queue at stoplights. Indeed, she'd arrived at the night market ten minutes ahead of Ian's Land Cruiser. Even better, the ubiquitous ride let Rachel blend in. With her helmet on and visor down, dressed in jeans, T-shirt, and a light jacket, she was just another brown-skinned woman in a beach city at the height of tourist season.

She watched Ian stop at a stall selling shoes and pretend to inspect the wares. He smiled at the woman proprietor and moved on at a slow pace.

In the months she'd known Ian, his hair had grown out. She'd cut it before they left Mexico so it would better match his new passport photo. He parted it on the left and swept the hair back from his forehead using thick hair gel. He wore a loose-fitting linen jacket and matching pants, looking every inch the confident Chinese tourist out to explore the nightlife of Phuket.

Rachel scanned the crowd around Ian, looking for anyone paying special attention to Ian's presence in the market.

Don's decision not to use her skills on this mission was a bitter pill to swallow for Rachel, but she didn't blame him. She had her own doubts about the operation. It wasn't that she didn't trust Don or his people, but she was used to working alone.

Instead, Rachel and Ian hatched a plan for her to act as his backup. It was risky, but Rachel knew herself well enough to know that she was not cut out to sit in a command center listening to someone she cared about put his life at risk.

What am I doing? Rachel thought. She'd asked herself that question since she'd come face-to-face with Ian in the tiny Argentine hiking town. He'd bested her in their first encounter. By all accounts, she should have died that night by Ian's hand.

Rachel replayed the scene in her head. Her tied to a chair. Ian, with new enemies approaching, could have killed her—should have killed her—and...he didn't. Instead, the man whom she had come to kill did something she did not expect.

He freed her. He asked for her help. He gave her a choice.

In that moment, Rachel decided to risk everything.

Even today, she did not completely understand her own actions. Without even knowing her, when faced with the decision to kill his captive or set her free, Ian decided to trust Rachel.

Maybe that's it, Rachel decided. For so long, she hadn't felt worthy of anyone's trust, even her own.

But it was more than that. There was something different about Ian.

Like her, he was damaged. Like her, he was lethal. Like her, he'd been trained to trust no one except himself.

Both of them had learned these unbreakable rules the hard way. It was how they had survived this long.

And yet, they were both so tired of being alone.

Together, they broke the rules that had governed their lives for as long as either of them could remember.

Together, they'd started to build a life. It wasn't much. They lived on the run, a Spartan existence of constant vigilance, but it was enough for her. Still, it was too good to last. Eventually, she knew, their past would catch up with them.

It was Ian who insisted that she contact Don Riley to warn him about the nuclear threat. Reluctantly, she agreed. But when Riley asked for Ian's help to take down Manson Skelly, Rachel said no.

Here I am, she thought. Still astride the bike, Rachel nudged forward to keep visual contact with Ian. He paused at another stall, said something to the proprietor.

She and Ian had decided the flaw in Don's plan was transportation. Land Cruisers were an effective cover and a great way to move people and weapons, but they were slow in traffic.

In the early afternoon, Rachel had departed the safe house and walked down to the café on the corner. It was simple enough to find a teenager with his own motorbike who spoke English. He said his name was Teddy.

"Okay, Teddy," Rachel said with a knowing smile. "I want to rent your bike tonight."

Teddy looked at her slyly. "Why? You can rent a new one over there." He pointed across the street at the rental shop.

"I want to go see a man tonight." Rachel winked. "No one can know."

Teddy liked that answer. He liked the fifty American dollars she offered him even more, so an agreement was reached. Teddy would remain at the café with his bike all night if necessary. Rachel gave him ten dollars and assured him that even if she never used the bike, he would still receive full payment.

Assuming I live that long, she thought.

Rachel stiffened as a young Thai boy approached Ian. He looked no more than eight years old, with a red, too-large Chicago Bulls tank top hanging from his thin brown shoulders. He handed Ian a mobile phone, which Ian held to his ear. His eyes looked up, found a landmark to the west, and he started walking.

Rachel started her bike and snaked her way along the fringes of the night market, trying to keep Ian in sight. He was walking quickly, as if whoever was on the phone was urging him on. He cut through an open-air coffee stall and ran across four lanes of traffic. Rachel cursed to herself. He was not making this easy.

Just as Ian reached the other side of the road, a black Mercedes with tinted windows pulled to the curb. Ian got in, and the car made an immediate right into a complex of steep-sided Buddhist temples.

Rachel turned into the flow of traffic and gunned the engine of the little motor scooter.

46

Phuket, Thailand

The interior of the Mercedes S-class sedan was ice-cold. Ian felt the sweat on his face start to evaporate as soon as he slid across the rear bench seat. One of the men who'd stopped him on the sidewalk got in. The second came in from the opposite side, leaving Ian sandwiched between the two.

Doors slammed. The car accelerated from the curb. The whole encounter, door open to door closed, had lasted less than ten seconds.

As the car made an immediate right into what looked like a temple complex, the man to his right searched Ian. He plucked the tablet from his jacket pocket and powered it down. He did not return it to Ian.

Steep-sided buildings with elaborately styled roof carvings flashed by the window as the driver picked up speed. Through the windshield Ian glimpsed stylized spires and what looked like a giant painted snake, but the garishly bright colors were muted by the heavily tinted windows.

When they'd traveled the equivalent of a city block, the Thai driver, who wore dark glasses and a hard expression, took a sudden right into traffic and changed lanes immediately. Car horns blared behind them.

The men on either side of Ian were White, heavily muscled, and armed.

The one to Ian's left had hair; the other was bald. Both wore dark blue jackets to conceal their sidearms, and despite the chill of the car, they both sweated heavily.

Hairy and Baldy stared straight ahead and said nothing. The driver made a lefthand turn at the light. The car surged across two lanes of traffic.

"I came alone," Ian said. "You don't have to do this."

Silence. They were professionals. They had a plan, and they were going to stick to the plan.

The driver made a right into a narrow alley and punched the accelerator. Ian felt Baldy tense up as they cleared the edge of a dumpster with centimeters to spare.

The Mercedes emerged into traffic and changed lanes again.

Ian assessed his situation. He was in the hands of professionals with a local driver who had clearly been ordered to lose anyone attempting to trail them. There was no way the Land Cruisers would be able to follow this driver. If Rachel was behind them on a more maneuverable motorbike, she had a better shot, but this driver was a man on a mission.

No need to worry, Ian thought as the driver made another wheel-screeching turn. At least the GPS is still working. He had backup.

It was an odd feeling to be working with a team. Ian had spent his entire adult life as a deep cover agent hiding in plain sight. By definition, he was always alone.

But the time he'd spent with Rachel had changed him. He'd never had a partner before, but as unlikely as the pairing between a Chinese deep cover operative and a Mossad field agent sounded, that's what they'd become. Partners.

He'd argued with Rachel when she came up with the plan to trail him tonight, but he'd known from the start his objections were useless. Rachel would do exactly what she wanted to do, no matter what he said. In fact, Ian was touched by her concern for his safety. He never had a partner before and the feeling was...

Ian searched for the right word to describe his emotions. *Satisfying* was the only thing that seemed to fit.

They entered a residential neighborhood, and the driver slowed. He turned onto a street with massive trees and wide sidewalks. Ahead of them, Ian saw an overhead garage door rolling up, spilling light into the darkness. The driver hit the gas, made a hard left into the opening, and came to a stop next to a second vehicle. Ian heard the garage door close behind them.

When the rattle of the overhead door ceased, the men on either side of him exited the vehicle. Baldy motioned for him to follow, and Ian complied. The driver stayed in the car. The slamming doors were loud in the open garage.

Ian studied his surroundings. Banks of fluorescent lights buzzed overhead. The space was bright and clean with rows of neatly arranged tools on the wall and shelves laden with car parts. Ian searched for any container close to the dimensions of the nuclear weapon Don had described.

Nothing.

The second car, identical to the first, also had a driver who wore earphones, stayed behind the wheel, and seemed to be making a show of not watching what was going on outside his windshield. Maybe the weapon was in the trunk of the other car?

More importantly, there was no sign of Manson Skelly.

"Over here," said the hairy guard. He had a mobile phone out, which he pointed at Ian. "Say cheese." He took a picture, then said, "Show me your ear."

Ian complied, and he took a picture of that too.

Hairy opened a slim laptop and typed. Minutes passed as he stared at the screen. Baldy hung back a few paces, always just out of Ian's peripheral vision.

The laptop chimed. Hairy spun the laptop to face Ian. "Boss says to transfer half the money."

"No," Ian said mildly.

The skin on Hairy's forehead creased. "No?"

Ian forced himself to concentrate on the man in front of him, not the one behind him. He kept his voice calm. "I want to see what I'm buying first."

As Hairy went back to work on his laptop, Ian considered his tactical situation. Two professionals on alert with positional advantage. His chances of taking both of them out were small. Plus, if he made a move, he would not get to Skelly.

Hairy looked up again. "Boss says no money, no deal."

"Fair enough." Ian offered a tight smile. "Maybe you can drop me off at the Four Seasons?"

Hairy rolled his eyes. He shot a look at his bald companion, who was still lurking behind Ian. "Okay, strip."

"Excuse me?" Ian shifted his feet subtly to give himself a better fighting stance.

"Clothes off, man," Hairy said. "If you're going to see the boss, you need to strip."

A few seconds later, Ian stood in his boxers, his clothes heaped on the table between him and Hairy. The other man pulled a face when he saw the knife-wound scars on Ian's chest and abdomen.

"Jealous girlfriend," Ian said. "I had to break it off."

Hairy laughed, then he said, "Bend over and spread 'em."

Ian cocked an eyebrow. "You're not serious."

Hairy grinned. "It's the little things that matter."

After the body cavity search, while Hairy held a gun on Ian, Baldy ran his fingers through Ian's hair, looking for any kind of device.

"What is in your hair?" he asked. "It's gross."

"Are you jealous?" Ian shot back.

Hairy laughed and tossed Ian a pair of drawstring pants and a T-shirt. The man threw Ian's tablet onto the pile of clothes, screen side up. "This stuff stays here," he said.

"You're gonna want to bring that with you," Ian said, pointing at the tablet. "It has a digital token that I need to transfer the money."

Hairy's eyes shifted to his partner, then back to Ian. He put the tablet into his jacket pocket.

He heard Baldy moving behind him, and when Ian turned, he was holding open the door to the second car. "Get in."

* * *

Seated next to Michael in the safe house, Don let his face fall into his sweaty hands.

Moments earlier, the video feed on the overwatch drone showed Ian depart the night market, cross four lanes of traffic on foot, and get into a black Mercedes.

Then, with the trail vehicles still blocks away from the scene of the pickup, the GPS tracking signal disappeared. The overwatch drone managed to keep track of the Mercedes sedan for a few more blocks, but it lost visual contact as well.

Now, while Michael desperately searched traffic camera feeds for any sign of their quarry, it dawned on Don that he was leading the greatest unauthorized fuck-up in the history of clandestine operations.

Ian Thomas was gone. The tablet that gave him access to the bank accounts with hundreds of millions of dollars was gone. Rachel was God knew where.

He considered the possibility that he'd been scammed by Rachel and Ian, but dismissed it. After all, he'd come to them, and this op was as risky for them as it was for him.

But maybe, he thought, doubts seeping into his consciousness. It was possible.

"Don?" Michael said.

"What?" Don raised his head, focused on the computer screen.

"Do you want me to kill access to the bank accounts?"

If he was being played, this was his ace in the hole, his fail-safe. Don had the ability to isolate the bank accounts linked to the tablet Ian was carrying. But if Ian was still on Don's team, then that was a death sentence.

Don tried to weigh the decision with logic.

Killing access to the money meant no deal, no recovered nuclear weapon, and most of all, no Skelly. If he stopped now, he might, just maybe, be able to salvage his career *and* not go to jail.

"Don," Michael said again.

On the other hand, did he trust a Chinese deep cover operative and a rogue Mossad agent enough to risk a few hundred million dollars of Uncle Sam's money?

A freshening sea breeze blew through the window curtains into the room. Don sat up straight in his chair and sucked in a deep breath of fresh salty air.

What does your gut tell you, Riley?

"No." Don wiped his sweaty hands on his thighs. "Let it ride."

47

Phuket, Thailand

When Rachel saw the car carrying Ian make a right turn at the temple complex, she gunned her motorbike and plunged into traffic. At the light, she made a left turn and buzzed down the street.

Rachel caught a glimpse of a black Mercedes with tinted windows crossing the next intersection, and she veered into a hard right turn that earned her an angry horn blast from a Toyota sedan.

She weaved through the moving traffic, trying to keep visual contact with the right black Mercedes. This was a popular vehicle in the more affluent sections of the Thai tourist town.

She stopped for a light, fretting as her target disappeared in a sea of red taillights. When the light changed, she powered across the intersection and buzzed up the next block.

It was no use. The car was gone. Sometime in the precious seconds she'd lost contact, the Mercedes sedan must have turned.

Right or left? she wondered.

She chose left, a side street with less traffic. She raced ahead for three blocks, then slowed for another light. Walking her motorbike as far as she dared into the intersection, she looked up and down the street.

A squeal of tires caught her attention, and two blocks ahead she saw a black car taking a sharp turn at speed.

The light changed. Rachel twisted the throttle, and the little bike leaped forward. She leaned over the handlebars, hoping to coax a little more speed out of the machine.

There was no sign of the car at the next cross street. The area was residential, so she slowed down. After two more blocks, she stopped at the side of the road.

If that was Ian's car, she'd lost it again. All she could hope for was that Don's team still had GPS contact. Rachel ground her teeth in frustration.

Tree canopies shielded the night sky. Widely spaced streetlamps left pools of light on the quiet street. A block to her right, a sliver of golden light appeared as a garage door started to open. From the other direction, a car approached, turned, and quickly passed into the open doorway. The garage door started to shut.

Rachel blinked. It had been a sedan, a dark color, possibly a Mercedes, but she'd only gotten a glimpse, and from a distance.

She stepped off the bike and removed her helmet. Her right hand touched the Glock 9mm in the belly band holster at the small of her back.

Rachel walked past the garage at a stroll. A mechanics shop, specializing in imported cars. There was a security camera out front and another on the side of the building.

Pausing at the corner, out of sight of the cameras, Rachel sucked in a breath, then took out her phone and dialed Don.

"Where are you?" he demanded.

She ignored him. "Is Ian safe?"

"We lost the tracker signal," Don said.

Rachel closed her eyes. "Listen, I need you to check out Royal Motors." She read the English translation off the street corner signs.

"Stand by." She heard him talking to Michael, then he came back on the line. "It's a legit business. Did you find the target?"

"Maybe." She *wanted* it to be the target, that was true. But all she'd seen was a dark car driving into an auto repair shop well outside of business hours. On the other hand, what else was she going to do?

Rachel squatted down. "I'm going to wait."

"Copy that," Don said. "The chase cars are coming to you."

Ten minutes later, she spied one of the Land Cruisers park two blocks down from her position. Almost as if on cue, the garage door of Royal Motors opened. A black Mercedes S-class sedan with tinted windows rolled smoothly onto the street. The garage door closed behind the car. She shrank back as the vehicle passed by her location.

Rachel wanted to pump her fist in the air. It was the car she was after. She watched the Mercedes pass the Land Cruiser. A few seconds later, the trail vehicle followed. She redialed Don.

"It's them," she said. "I recognized the driver and the license plate."

Don's reply sounded like he was gasping for air. "Great job, Rachel. The GPS tracker is still out, but Will Clarke's team has good trail on the target." He paused. "Thank you. I mean it."

Rachel felt like she was walking on air as she returned to her bike. She swung her leg over the seat and pulled on her helmet. The bike kicked on immediately, and she pulled away from the curb. Just as she passed the auto shop, the door started to open again.

It took everything she had not to stop in the center of the street. She let her speed ebb and came to a complete stop at the end of the block.

In her rearview mirror, she saw a second Mercedes S-class with tinted windows exit the garage and turn away from her. The red taillights winked as the driver applied the brakes at the other end of the street.

Rachel felt her stomach drop. She fumbled for her phone and called Don back.

"We have a problem."

* * *

Ian sat between the two guards in the back seat of the second Mercedes, shoeless and dressed in borrowed clothes. His only consolation was that he had managed to convince Hairy to retain his tablet, which was rigged with the GPS tracker.

He breathed in. It had been a long time since he'd allowed himself to remember his training. A long time since he'd allowed the Minister's voice in his head. The mantra came back to him unbidden:

My mind is my sword.
My body is my shield.
My existence is not my own.
I am a weapon of the State.

Ian let out a deep breath and with it all his fears for this night. Don Riley had given him the opportunity to atone for his sins, and Ian seized it.

If he survived this night, so be it. If not, he was ready.

In the cold light of hindsight, Ian realized now that he'd been groomed. The monks who had cared for him as a baby never loved him—they weren't supposed to. They were raising a future weapon for the State, not a child.

Their regimen was simple but effective. They called him *Nánhái*, No Name. Young Ian was told that he had to earn the right to a unique identity. He was smart, physically gifted, and he used all his skills to excel in every aspect of his training. But still, the monks did not give him a name of his own.

And then the Minister entered his life.

A young boy, intelligent, talented, and hungry for a father figure meets a man with an agenda. It didn't matter what was asked of him, Ian performed.

The child with no name never stood a chance.

The Minister might have asked his young charge to tear down the Great Wall and Ian would have found a way. Instead, the Minister asked him to steal, to seduce, to kill in the name of the State.

Ian performed every task with swift precision, eager to please.

By the time he was in his twenties, he had assumed the deep cover role of Ian Thomas.

The garage door began to open again. The Thai driver put the car in gear and eased forward. He turned right and picked up speed down the empty residential street.

There were no attempts to shake surveillance this time. The driver kept the car at the speed of traffic but made no sudden movements.

The car headed south, and traffic thickened again as they neared the beach area and the associated nightlife. Ian spotted a roundabout with a clock tower in the center island. The driver expertly navigated the heavy traffic and exited on a road lined with dive shops, fishing charters, bars, and guesthouses. The party was in full swing here, spilling onto the road and forcing the driver to lay on his horn to make progress. In a vacant lot, next to a bar called the Happy Dolphin, an elephant dozed.

"Don't see that every day," muttered Baldy.

Through the windshield, Ian saw the lights of a jetty stretching out into the bay, and he knew they were headed to a boat. Hundreds of lights dotted the dark horizon.

The car drew to a stop at the end of the pier, and the two guards hustled Ian out of the vehicle. The Mercedes sped away.

Ian pretended to stumble. He ran his fingers through his hair, squeezing the digits together to get as much of the gel on his hand as possible. Then he gripped the metal post nearest the street for support.

He wiped his hand down the post.

* * *

In lighter traffic, the maneuverability advantages of Rachel's motorbike were nullified. Although she pushed the tiny engine, on a highway her speed was no match for the more powerful Mercedes engine.

Traffic slowed again. Up ahead, Rachel saw a clock tower rising above the sea of cars, trucks, tuk-tuks, and motorbikes. She weaved through slower vehicles to get closer and saw the clock tower was a roundabout.

She scanned the tops of cars for the now familiar lines of the Mercedes and didn't see it. She dialed Don.

"I've lost my target," she said. "What's the status of the other team?"

"Target is headed north," Don replied. "Away from the city."

He sounded nervous, and she didn't blame him. They'd divided their meager forces to follow multiple targets.

Rachel circled the crowded roundabout, considering her four exit options. Two of the roads leaving the roundabout ran east and west, paralleling the coast. Another curved inland, back the way they'd come. The final route, which was named Sunrise Road, ran down to the water. It was crowded with people and vehicles of every shape and size. Fifty meters down the roadway, traffic had come to a complete stop for an elephant show.

Rachel steered her bike down Sunrise Road. If the Mercedes had taken any of the other exits off the roundabout, it was long gone. On the road to the water, traffic was slow. If the Mercedes was there, it might be stuck behind slower vehicles.

"You're guessing," she muttered to herself.

Rachel navigated around the stopped cars. While drivers stood in their open doors watching the elephant show, Rachel ran her bike onto the sidewalk and pressed forward. Clear of the blockage, she sped to the end of the road and stopped.

A long pier, lighted at regular intervals, stretched out over the water to an offshore marina. White lights from anchored ships littered the horizon like jewels. To her right, a small fleet of beached boats for rent waited in the shallow water.

If they'd stopped here and moved Ian to a boat, he could be anywhere on the water by now. Her eyes tracked down the road that ran along the shore. Or maybe they kept going.

Think, she told herself. If they had stopped here to move Ian onto a boat, what would he do?

He'd leave a sign, Rachel thought.

She extracted a pair of glasses from her jacket pocket. Although they looked like sunglasses, the lenses were equipped with special filters designed to highlight a taggant.

It had been Ian's idea to use the chemical marker. Taggants were often used in specialty inks as a way to protect against counterfeiters. Invisible to the naked eye, they could only be detected using filtered light. Rachel's contribution to the problem had been to mix it with Ian's hair gel.

The special lenses turned the nighttime scene dusky blue. Couples strolled along the water. A group of very drunk, very sunburned British tourists stumbled past. No one paid any attention to the slim, dark-skinned woman wearing a motorcycle helmet and sunglasses turning in a slow circle.

A slash of pink jumped out at Rachel. She walked toward the post, touched the worn metal. It was still wet. In the field of view of her glasses, the end of her finger glowed pink.

Ian had been here.

She pulled off the glasses. The waterfront scene brightened in her unobscured vision. Her phone was already out and dialing Don.

"He's on the water," she said. "They've taken him to a boat."

Don took a long time to answer.

"Are you sure?"

Rachel removed her helmet and left it with the motorbike at the end of the pier. If someone stole it, she'd buy Teddy a new one.

"I'm sure."

48

Phuket, Thailand

Back in the safe house, Don went into damage control mode.

"Get a satellite picture of the anchorage," he ordered Michael, "and reposition the drone over the water."

While Michael worked, Don called Will Clarke on an encrypted satellite phone.

"Are you sure she's right?" Clarke was clearly annoyed that Rachel was running her own independent operation. "If we break off contact with this vehicle, it's gone for good. Are you willing to take that chance?"

Don glanced at his watch. With every passing minute, the tactical picture got more tenuous. His assets and the target were getting farther apart, but if he was wrong...

"Stay on the second car," Don said. "Michael and I will handle this end."

"You're sure?"

"I'm sure."

Don hung up.

"If Rachel's right," Michael said, "it's just us against whatever Skelly has with him."

Don didn't want to think about that now. "Where are we with the ships at anchor?"

Michael put a satellite image on the screen. The Phuket Bay covered about ten square kilometers and was shaped like a half-moon. Since the island of Ko Lon blocked most of the opening with the Andaman Sea, the anchorage waters were especially tranquil. A long concrete pier, which served as both the ferry terminal and a private marina, jutted into the bay.

Hundreds of boats dotted the anchorage, any one of which could be the hiding place for Skelly and the nuclear weapon.

Think, Don screamed in his head.

"Let's do some triage," Don said out loud. "Assume Skelly is using this ship as a base, so it has to be a seagoing vessel. Screen out anything less than fifty feet."

That still left dozens of possible candidates.

Don racked his brain. "Skelly's on the move, so screen out any ship that's been here more than a week."

Michael updated the screen. There were still at least twenty ships left dotted across several square kilometers of open water.

"Get names and registration details on all of them, Michael," Don said.

As the younger man bent over his keyboard, Don called Rachel.

"We're narrowing down the ships that he could be on," Don said when she answered.

"How long?"

"You'll know as soon as I do," Don said. "You should have told me what you were doing, Rachel."

"This is not the time, Don," she replied in a tight voice.

"The other teams," Don said. "I'm keeping them on the other car. Just in case."

"I'm right, Don. He's on the water. Ian left me a marker."

"It's too late for that, Rachel. The other teams are too far away. If you'd trusted me, maybe this would have turned out differently."

"Find that ship, Don. Find him."

Rachel hung up.

Don gripped the handset, resisting the urge to throw his phone against the wall. Whose side was she on, anyway? The woman was on some kind of suicide mission, and he was just along for the ride.

"Don?" Michael's voice brought him back to the moment.

"Yeah." He placed the phone carefully on the desk next to Michael's laptop.

"I've narrowed it down to six ships," Michael began. "They all arrived within the last forty-eight hours and are all luxury yachts between eighty and two hundred fifty feet long. I don't have visuals on all of them yet. This is just from the port database. They record the ship details when they authorize the anchorage."

"Read them out loud," Don said.

"You mean the names of the ships?"

"Yes," Don snapped. "The names of the ships."

"*My Fair Lady, Princess, Margaritaville, Centurion—*"

"Stop," Don said. "That's the one. The *Centurion.*"

Michael's frown creased his forehead. "How do you know?"

How do I know? Don wondered. I know Skelly is a vain bastard. Even if he was trying to hide, there's no way he would cruise the waters of Southeast Asia in a ship called the *My Fair Lady.*

"I just know," Don said. "Get a visual on that ship and check the registration."

He picked up his mobile and sent a text to Rachel.

* * *

Rachel stood at the end of the concrete pier that jutted out into the waters of Phuket Bay. A hundred meters down the pier she studied the brightly lit marina containing at least a hundred boats in rented slips. A security guard stood at the ramp that went from the pier to the floating marina.

She could make her way past the guard without attracting attention, but then what? Steal a boat? Try to convince someone to take her out on the water?

Too risky, she decided. Her eyes shifted to the strip of beach to the right of the pier. The space was crowded with traditional Thai long-tail boats. The wooden watercraft resembled gondolas with their long, sleek hulls and wide flat bottoms. Their signature high wooden prows pointed out toward the water as if they were ready to put to sea.

As Rachel watched, a young couple made their way onto the sand and negotiated a ride. The Thai driver handed them into the boat and pushed off. He started the engine and lowered the long shaft with a caged propeller into the water.

Rachel walked down to the sandy strip, surveying her options from the twenty or so available boats. She bypassed the largest ones closest to the pier. Riding alone, she would be too conspicuous in a boat capable of carrying two dozen people.

She took off her shoes and waded into the gentle waves. Rachel smiled, waving off the more aggressive boatmen trying to convince her to ride in their craft. At the very edge of the illumination cast by the lights of the pier, a boy of perhaps fourteen stood in the surf. His boat was smaller, capable of handling six people at most, Rachel guessed, but it had a fresh paint job and bright sashes tied around the jutting prow.

"English?" Rachel said to the boy. He was short and thin as a reed. His T-shirt and shorts hung on his frame like rags on a scarecrow.

"Yes, lady," he said. "You want ride? Private tour. Very beautiful at night."

Rachel did her best impression of a gullible tourist. "How much?"

The boy quoted her a price in Thai baht, and she pretended to think about. Her phone pulsed with a text. She looked at the face of her phone. A picture of a yacht and the words: *Centurion. Arrived at sunset.*

Meanwhile, the kid thought he was losing his fare. "Lady, I give you special price—"

"Okay." Rachel handed him a wad of bills that was probably more than he earned in a week. She stepped into the boat and sat down. "We need to go now."

"Right away!" The kid, overjoyed at having snagged a paying fare, pushed the craft off the sand and leaped into the boat. When they had drifted a few feet from shore, he expertly tugged at the cord to start what looked to Rachel like a repurposed lawn mower engine. He dropped the long-shafted propeller into the water, and the boat surged forward.

When they passed the bright lights of the marina, Rachel moved back to a seat next to the boy. She pulled out her mobile phone and showed him the picture of the *Centurion*.

"You know this boat?" she asked. "It came in tonight."

"I know it," the boy replied. "I take two people by this boat." He mimed hugging and kissing. "Very romantic."

Rachel gave him more money. "Take me there. Right now. As fast as you can."

While the boy bent to his task, Rachel moved back to the center of the boat. She trailed her hand over the side. The bay was the temperature of bathwater and slick with salt.

She stripped off her jacket and dropped it on the seat beside her. In the dark she checked her weapons. The elastic band around her midsection carried her Glock in a low-profile holster against the small of her back, a spare magazine, a suppressor, and a foldable tactical combat knife.

When she considered what she was up against, her meager armaments didn't seem like much.

You have the element of surprise, she told herself. It will be enough. It *has* to be enough. Ian is depending on you.

The moorings in the bay seemed stratified by the size of the vessel. The boy passed through a band of smaller craft, mostly speedboats, then into a grouping of larger boats, mostly sailboats and larger powerboats up to about fifty feet long. Often, the cabins and aft decks were alive with light and laughter. She caught snatches of different languages—French, English, Thai, Russian, German—as they passed by and the smell of charcoal grills. A few groups waved at them, and Rachel waved back and smiled.

As they left the last sailboat behind, the boy slowed their progress and changed direction. Before them, half a kilometer away, a grouping of luxury yachts glittered like waterborne palaces in the darkness.

Rachel slid back toward the boy. "Why are you slowing down?" she asked.

"Don't get too close," the boy said. "Security." He formed his thumb and forefinger into a pretend weapon and mimed shooting.

Rachel nodded. She held up her phone. "Which one is it?"

The boy pointed to the last ship in the gathering of anchored vessels. Rachel squinted, wishing she had field glasses.

The *Centurion* was not the smallest ship in the anchorage, but not the largest either. The forward part of the yacht was dark, but the upper deck at the aft of the ship was lighted, and she could see movement. There was a motorboat tied off at the aft landing and a small helicopter perched on a rooftop pad.

Rachel leaned close to the boy. "What's your name?"

"Kiet."

"Okay, Kiet, how close can you get to that ship without security seeing you?"

The boy frowned as he considered her question. "Hundred meters," he said. "No lights, I can get closer, but..." He hesitated. "No lights. Not legal."

Rachel pulled all the money she had out of her pocket. She pressed the money into the boy's hand. "Get me as close as you can. No lights. Then you go home. No more work tonight. Understand?"

Kiet looked from Rachel to the yacht ahead of them. He pocketed the money, then he reached behind him and touched a switch mounted on the gunwale. The illumination in the cockpit disappeared, plunging them into darkness. Kiet touched a second switch, and the navigation lights on the long-tail boat went out. He slowed their speed to minimize their wake.

Rachel squeezed his arm. "Thank you, Kiet. Stay on this course, nice and slow. Then go home."

"I understand, lady."

Rachel moved back to the center of the craft. The water was still, and the slight bow wave thrown up from Kiet's boat showed as a line of creamy white in the darkness. She breathed deeply, letting the act of filling her lungs with the humid air settle her nerves.

The *Centurion* drew closer, details sharpening. Behind the drawn curtains of the lighted cabin, she could make out the shapes of moving people, at least three of them. Ian was probably in there. Now that she was closer, Rachel could see there was also movement on the bridge, but the ship was still at anchor.

How many crewmembers on a yacht this size? She guessed six, maybe more.

Six or twenty-six, it mattered not. She was going to board that ship.

The long-tail boat drew abreast of the *Centurion*. This was as close as Kiet would get to the ship. The rest was up to her.

She cast a quick glance aft where the slim figure of Kiet merged with the tiller and the engine into a dark blob.

Rachel slipped over the side into the warm waters of Phuket Bay.

49

Phuket, Thailand

From the wooden landing at the stern of the yacht, the bald guard led Ian up the steps to the main deck. His colleague with hair finished securing the motorboat to the stern.

Ian swept his eyes around the space. He took in an unlighted lounge area with open sliding doors leading deeper into the ship. Inside were leather couches, a bar, and a glass dining table.

A third guard armed with a Heckler & Koch MP7A1 and a pair of night vision binoculars greeted them. He pumped his thumb in the air. "Boss is upstairs." He went back to scanning the water.

Three armed guards plus the crew, Ian thought, and he didn't have so much as a paperclip for a weapon.

The two guards escorted Ian to a lighted stairwell that ascended to the next deck. The hard rubber treads of the steps bit into the soles of his bare feet.

Like the deck below, the level was designed as an indoor-outdoor space separated by glass. The accordion-style sliding glass doors were folded flat against the bulkhead. Manson Skelly sat in a captain's chair in the center of the space. To his right, a black Pelican case lay on the deck. Skelly had placed a tumbler filled with ice and an amber liquid on top of the black case.

The weapon, Ian realized. The case was exactly what Don had described.

He felt Skelly's eyes rake over him as soon as Ian walked into the light. The man advanced on Ian, hand outstretched. Short and powerfully built, his black beard was shot with gray. He gripped Ian's hand with more pressure than was necessary.

"Diego Montalban," Skelly said. "Your reputation precedes you."

Ian looked him in the eye. "Last time our paths crossed, you tried to kill me."

Skelly roared a sudden laugh, a reaction so over the top that Ian wondered if he was drunk. "No hard feelings?" Skelly asked.

"I'll expect a discount," Ian replied drily.

Skelly returned to his seat, motioning for Ian to take a facing chair. "Tell me about your cause."

"My cause is my business," Ian said coldly. "We're not friends, Mr. Skelly, and I don't appreciate how I've been treated."

The comment seemed to sober Skelly up. "Fair enough. Let's get on with it. You have my money?"

Ian nodded. "Show me the weapon."

Skelly cleared the glass from the top of the Pelican case and unsnapped the locks on the container. He raised the lid and turned the case so Ian could see.

The sight was underwhelming. Ian had been briefed on what a disassembled warhead would look like, but Skelly had gone to the trouble to repackage it. A matte-black box the size of a small microwave was nestled into pre-cut foam. Next to the box lay a controller the size of Ian's open palm.

Skelly picked up the controller and touched the screen. The glare of the screen lighted his face.

"This device is registered to a user's DNA." He turned the screen to face Ian. "Once open, you have the option to do a time-based detonation or a remote trigger using a satellite phone connection. You can also do a combination of the two."

Skelly's eyes narrowed as he continued. "At present, all four of the weapons are registered with my AI, so I can track them. I can also detonate them, if I choose."

Ian kept his face blank. Four weapons, he thought. He's probing to see if I know he's lost the Moscow weapon.

"What if I want to buy all four of them?" Ian asked. "Do I get a discount?"

Skelly chuckled. "I have buyers for the others. If they fall through, maybe we can do another deal."

"How do I know this is the real thing?" Ian asked.

A fourth guard entered the room. He bent to whisper in Skelly's ear. A flash of bared teeth showed Skelly's irritation.

Ian braced. Was this it? Had they detected Don's assault team?

"Tell the captain to get underway," Skelly muttered, "and get the helo ready."

"Yes, sir." The guard disappeared.

"Is something wrong, Mr. Skelly?" Ian asked.

"None of your goddamn business." Skelly shifted in his chair. "Okay, Diego, or whatever you call yourself these days, we need to wrap this up. Do you want it or not?"

I need to buy some time, Ian thought.

"How do I know it's the real thing?" Ian repeated.

Skelly's discomfort increased. He got out of his chair as if he could no longer sit still. He kicked at the still open case. "Do you want it or not? I've got other buyers."

In the distance, Ian heard the clank of the anchor chain being retrieved from the sea. He was running out of time. "I don't have a way to get it back to shore."

Skelly's laugh was longer and more brash than the comment warranted. "The motorboat you arrived in is part of the purchase price. We'll even help you load it." He lifted a laptop off a nearby table. "You can use this to transfer the money."

"I'm afraid I need my own tablet for the transfer, Mr. Skelly," Ian replied smoothly. "It has a digital signature on it."

Skelly's eyes snapped to the two guards who had escorted Ian to the yacht. Baldy handed over the tablet, but when Ian energized the screen, there was no signal. He stood, walked to the edge of the room to see if he could get better reception.

"You need to take the sticker off the back," Skelly told him. "It's an EM blocker."

"Of course." It took all of Ian's composure to smile back. All this time, he'd believed that the tablet was transmitting his position back to Don and his team, but he'd been wrong.

Ian was on his own. No one was coming to save him.

He peeled the sticker off the back of the tablet, and the satellite reception icon in the upper right corner appeared.

"Hmm," Ian said.

"Is there a problem?" Skelly asked.

Without looking up, Ian tried to gauge the tone of the other man's voice. His mind automatically registered the location of the two guards and assessed their state of readiness. They were too far away and too heavily armed for him to take them both out.

He heard the deep rumble of the ship's engines and felt the vessel begin to move. The guard who had talked to Skelly a few minutes before reentered the salon and mounted the steps up to the helo pad.

Skelly cut a look at Ian, then nodded.

Ian's nerves stretched to the breaking point.

What had that man told Skelly? Was Ian's cover blown?

Every sense he possessed, every moment of experience in his life weighed into this instant. He felt balanced on the knife-edge of action.

Wait, he told himself.

Ian plastered a grin on his lips and looked up.

"No problem. It'll just take a few minutes to set up the wire transfer."

He lowered his head and began typing on the tablet.

* * *

Michael and Don paused on the veranda of the safe house. The younger man placed a round object the size of a loaf of bread on the small metal table. The matte finish of the Sentinel Gremlin drone seemed to absorb the light that spilled from the room behind them.

Michael tapped his laptop keyboard, and the carbon fiber skin of the drone unfolded like the petals of a flower. Another tap and the drone rose into the air and sped off into the night.

Michael snapped his laptop closed with one hand and slipped it into a waterproof sack. "It's on the way. Let's go."

Don led them down the steps to the beach. He wore dark cargo pants, steel-toed boots, a black T-shirt, and a bulletproof vest that was already cutting into his flesh in all the wrong places. In a hip holster, he carried a SIG Sauer P320 and two extra magazines.

Don's T-shirt was soaked with sweat. Breathing like a wounded bull, he did his best to keep up with Michael as they headed for their ride.

The Falchion driver waited for them. He'd already pushed the speedboat, a twin-engine outboard runabout, off the sand and turned the craft to face the water.

They crossed the narrow strip of sand that separated the safe house from the water and splashed into the gentle surf. Michael hopped over the gunwale in one smooth motion. Don threw his leg over the side and tumbled into the bottom of the boat.

The driver wasted no time. The dual engines rumbled to life, and the craft eased forward. He peered over the side. When he was confident they were clear of the shallow bottom, he nailed both throttles all the way to the stops.

The bow tilted upward as the powerful engines drove them forward. Don tumbled back into a seat, his fingers reaching for a handhold. He righted his body.

Wind blasted Don's sweaty face, but the air did little to cool him down. Inside, he was a raging bundle of nervous energy.

His genius operation had turned to shit. Clarke and the rest of the team were at least an hour away, and Rachel was in the wind. The harbormaster's description of the *Centurion* said the yacht had a helicopter. If Skelly was there, he wouldn't be there for much longer.

And Ian Thomas? If he wasn't dead, he was living on borrowed time. If

Skelly suspected anything, he would not hesitate to kill Ian and anyone else who got in his way.

"Don!" Michael leaned over to yell in his ear. He shoved the laptop screen at his boss.

It took a second for Don to realize what he was seeing. A bright red dot pulsed on the image of Phuket Bay.

The GPS tracker in Ian's tablet was active again.

"He's accessing the bank account," Michael yelled.

Ian was alive. The only way to access the banking system was with Ian's passcode. From the little he knew about the Chinese agent, he believed getting the passcode by force would be a long process.

"Can you jam the signal?" he asked Michael.

"You sure you want to do that?" Michael's dark features were grave with concern. "They'll know we're coming."

Don squinted out at the lights on the horizon. Which one was the *Centurion*? "Do it," he ordered.

Michael tapped the keyboard on the laptop, then changed screens. Don saw his lips move in a silent curse. Don leaned over so he could see the laptop screen.

The drone was close enough to give them a live video feed. Don followed Michael's index finger. There was a small bow wake on the yacht. The ship was underway.

Michael's finger pointed higher on the screen. "The helicopter, Don."

The helo that clung to the top deck of the *Centurion* was a Bell 505, a small four-passenger craft favored by corporate types and extreme sports enthusiasts.

A pilot was visible through the bubble of the windshield, and the single rotor was slowly spinning.

"I think they're getting ready to take off," Michael yelled.

Don took the laptop from Michael. He recalled how Abby had demonstrated the controls for the Gremlin drone on one of his visits to Sentinel headquarters.

"On a laptop, altitude is controlled by the up and down arrows," she'd said. "Use the mouse pad to drive the drone and the space bar for speed."

Don lined up the reticles of the Gremlin's camera on the helicopter and dropped the altitude of the drone until he was below the level of the rotors.

On the touchpad, he moved his finger forward. Then he mashed down the space bar as if the pressure from his finger could make the drone fly faster.

The image on the screen, a distant lighted ship, drew closer and closer. The field of view tightened rapidly until the only thing Don saw was the image of the helicopter pilot turning his head, his face a mask of surprise.

Then the screen went dark.

50

Phuket, Thailand

Rachel swam underwater as much as she could, poking her head up only when she needed a breath. If someone saw her in the water, she'd be shark bait before she even got on the ship.

Midway to the *Centurion*, she heard a rattling sound underwater, but paid it no attention. The sea was full of sounds.

She came up for a breath and adjusted her course toward the yacht.

When she emerged again for a final breath, Rachel realized the yacht was beginning to move. Her plan was to arrive amidships, under the swell of the hull, and climb on board. Now she needed to pour on the speed just to catch the vessel at all.

She dove under again, driving her body forward with strong, even strokes. She heard the spinning of the propellers crossing in front of her, then she saw the outline of the trailing boat reflected in the water above her.

Rachel pushed upward, launching out of the water to catch the gunwale on the trailing speedboat. Her fingers ached under the strain as the yacht towed the smaller powerboat—and Rachel—toward the open sea.

She risked a peek over the edge of the hull at the upper decks of the yacht, then quickly lowered herself back down.

Less than five meters above her, a man stood in profile at the railing. His eye sockets were shaded a ghostly green from the night vision binoculars he was using to scan the horizon. An H&K submachine gun hung from a chest strap.

Rachel risked another look. The powerboat was tethered to a wooden landing at water level, but with the man so close, she was pinned down here. All she could do was wait for him to move.

She counted to twenty before she risked another look.

The man was gone. She hoisted herself out of the water and slithered into the bottom of the boat, curling up under the dashboard, out of sight of the deck above.

Rachel took the chance to catch her breath. The swim had been hard, but she felt the familiar surge of adrenaline raging through her body.

Another peek told her the overwatch guard had not returned. She uncoiled her body from under the dash and made her way onto the bow of the powerboat. She pulled on the tether line to close the distance to the rear of the yacht.

A short leap to the wooden landing and she was on board. Rachel moved to the steps leading to the deck above and flattened her body against the wall.

There was only one way onto the boat: across the deck with the armed guard. She slipped the foldable knife from her belt. Pressing the release, she flicked her wrist and heard the satisfying *snick* of the six-inch blade locking open. Taking care of the armed man on the deck above her needed to be done as quietly as possible.

Rachel crept up the steps, her muscles bunching for the sudden release.

She raised her head above the level of the deck to locate her target.

He was at the stern railing, binoculars dangling from a strap around his neck. He leaned over as if studying something below him, his face creased into a frown.

With a start, Rachel realized what he was seeing. Her footprints. When she crossed the wooden deck, she'd left wet footprints on the dry wood.

His head came up, swiveled toward her hiding place on the steps.

Somewhere on the decks above them came a huge crash, the sound of metal smashing into metal. The guard's head snapped upward, toward the sound.

That was all the opening Rachel needed.

She surged out of the stairwell, using the railing to pivot her body, and launched at the man. He was larger than her, but she had superior speed and the element of surprise.

He reeled backward, his hand dropping toward the submachine gun on the sling across his chest. Instead, his grasping fingers found the field glasses.

That split second of confusion cost him his life. Rachel's blade entered his neck at his larynx, slicing up and through his carotid artery. The force of her attack drove his head backward. His taller, heavier body crashed into the waist-high railing, and she used his momentum to lever him over the edge. The big man sprawled on the landing below her, his fingers still locked on the field glasses.

Rachel switched the blade to her left hand and drew her handgun. She needed to stop the ship before they got to open water.

Moving with deliberate purpose, weapon forward, she fast-walked across the deck and onto the breezeway that followed the curve of the hull toward the bridge.

A door opened, spilling light across her path. A crewmember dressed in a white polo and shorts stepped onto the walkway. With hardly a pause, she clocked him with the butt of her gun and pushed him over the railing into the water.

The door to the bridge was open. Rachel entered, scanning the room. An older man stood at the controls, talking on a phone. Something about a helicopter.

The pilot jumped when Rachel moved into his peripheral vision. He raised his hands.

"Stop the ship," she said.

He pulled back on two levers that Rachel guessed were the throttles. The ship slowed. He turned off the engines, and she felt the deck beneath her feet go still. The noise of the wind at the door of the bridge went quiet.

"How many on board," she said. "I'm only going to ask once."

"Four crew, four guards, and Mr. Skelly," the man said without hesitation.

Rachel moved forward, forcing the captain away from the controls, backing him toward the open bridge door on the opposite side of the room.

"Where is Skelly?" she said.

The captain pointed with a hand that shook like a tree branch in a windstorm. "That door. Salon One is on this level. Please don't kill me."

He'd backed out of the bridge onto the open breezeway, his back to the water.

"Jump," Rachel said.

Under different circumstances, the captain's bobbling nod might have been comical. He went over the side without a word.

Rachel returned to the bridge and the door that the captain had directed her to. She flattened herself against the wall, threw open the door, and cleared the passageway beyond the opening with her sidearm.

The long hallway was lit by soft yellow accent lights that highlighted the polished wood and brass. The door at the other end of the hallway was closed. She stepped into the narrow passageway, her senses screaming with tension. She felt her bare feet grip the carpet. The point of her shoulder grazed the wall as she carefully moved forward.

An explosion behind the closed door at the end of the hall made her drop to her knees and take cover in one of the rooms. Her ears rang.

A concussion grenade, she realized. That could only mean one thing: Ian was still alive.

Rachel got back on her feet and reentered the hall. She advanced on the closed door. There was a polished brass plate screwed into the dark wood.

It read: *Salon One.*

* * *

Ian finished entering the final digits on the tablet that gave him access to the Dubai bank account.

He dragged a chair next to the black Pelican case, facing Skelly, and sat down. This move halved the distance between himself and the bald guard.

"I'm into the account," Ian said. "I need your banking information for the transfer."

Ian tapped the button to refresh the screen.

Nothing happened.

He tapped again with the same result. Then he saw the satellite dish icon in the upper right corner of the screen was grayed out.

"I lost the satellite link," he said.

Skelly's head snapped up. "What did you say?"

Ian turned the screen so Skelly could see it. He raised his voice over the rising whine of the helicopter engine. "No satellite connection."

Skelly cut a look over Ian's shoulder at the bald guard. He opened his mouth to speak, but the words were drowned out by a zipping noise, then a crashing sound from above them.

The helicopter.

For Ian, instinct took over. This was his moment. He spun out of the chair, holding the tablet like a discus. The fingernails of the bald guard scraped his nape and ran down his back, trying to find a grip on Ian's T-shirt and coming up empty.

The man was off-balance now, bent at the waist, weight forward, grasping for an object that was no longer there. Ian whipped his hand down, using the centrifugal force of his spin to bury the corner of the tablet in the bald guard's ear.

The big man went down, his body draped across Ian's empty chair. Blood spurted out of his ear.

Ian wrenched the 9mm from the man's holster and put two rounds into his rib cage. He spun, tracked to Skelly's last position.

The chair was empty. Skelly was gone.

The other guard dropped and rolled, firing as he moved. Ian felt a tug at his left arm as one of the incoming rounds found its mark.

He ducked and ran, taking cover behind a white leather couch inside the salon. He snapped a look around the edge of the sofa and received a three-round burst from the guard's MP7.

Where the hell was Skelly?

In the space of a breath, Ian took stock of his situation. Pinned down by the guard who had more firepower, his situation was not tenable. Around him, the salon was a fishbowl of curtain-covered windows. Skelly was probably lurking in the darkness outside now, getting into firing position.

Ian glanced behind him. The only exit from the room was a door of polished wood that led into the forward part of the ship. There was at least five meters of open space between his position and the door. The guard would cut him down before he covered half the distance.

He scanned the windows again, looking for any sign of movement.

Above the salon, the helicopter had stopped rotating, and Ian could smell the sweet stink of jet fuel.

Then he felt the ship's engines stop.

He got to his knees. Time to move.

Over his head, he saw a flash of movement and turned his head. An object passed over his position and bounced off the wall.

Ian recognized the stun grenade before it rolled to a stop. He slammed his eyelids shut and curled his body into a fetal position, covered his ears, and opened his mouth.

Even with his eyes closed and facing away, the flash was blinding. Trapped between the sofa and the wall, the shock wave blasted into his prone body.

Ian had no idea how long he was unconscious. When he opened his eyes again, the salon was a war zone. The tasteful architectural lighting was gone, replaced by the harsh glare of two emergency lights. Pulverized glass littered every surface, making it seem as if the room was covered in glittering ice. Floating afterimages from the stun grenade clouded his vision.

The remaining guard stood over Ian, his MP7 pointed at Ian's chest. His lips moved. Despite the ringing in his ears, Ian made out the words. "Get up."

He lifted his body off the bed of broken glass, feeling the slipperiness of blood on his skin.

"On your knees." Skelly's voice penetrated the wailing in his ears.

Ian turned his head. Every muscle felt like it had been beaten with a hammer. He blinked, trying to focus on Skelly.

The man looked untouched by the mayhem around him. Even his clothes were still clean. He sat on the black Pelican case, elbows on knees, leaning forward as if he was about to share some intimacy with Ian. A Walther PPS M2 dangled loosely in his grip.

A Walther. The James Bond weapon, Ian thought. What a jackass. Despite the dire circumstances, the idea seemed hilarious to Ian. If he could have sensed the muscles of his face, he might have tried to smile.

The guard prodded Ian with the muzzle of his weapon. "On your knees," he ordered.

Ian felt the bite of broken glass on his shins. He tucked his feet under his haunches and raised his eyes to meet Skelly's gaze. The clamor in his ears was dying down, and he could make out Skelly's words without reading his lips.

"Who are you?" Skelly said.

Ian felt his lips crack as he smiled. "I am exactly who I said I was."

"Who do you work for?"

"Myself."

Skelly looked like he might pistol-whip Ian, but instead he got to his feet and stepped past Ian. "Finish him," he ordered the guard. "Let's get out of here."

There is some poetic justice in this end, Ian thought. I have killed so many, and yet I will die on my knees.

Fitting. I will die the same way I started. A nobody.

He drew in a breath, taking in all the smells for the last time. Blood and shattered glass, sweet jet fuel and salty sea air, burned leather and—

Movement at the end of the salon flashed in his peripheral vision. Ian turned his head. The polished wooden door crashed open, and a slim figure in black burst into the room.

I'm hallucinating, he thought as spikes of fire darted from Rachel's hand.

One...two...three shots echoed in Ian's tortured ears. He sensed the guard behind him hit the ground.

She's a beautiful angel of death, Ian decided.

Then, her aim shifted, and Ian realized she was going to kill Skelly.

He staggered to his feet, threw out his arms.

Ian's voice sounded very far away.

"Don't kill him," he shouted.

51

Phuket, Thailand

Any lingering doubts Don might have had that he'd crashed the Gremlin drone into the wrong yacht disappeared when he saw the flash-bang go off on the second level of the ship.

The yacht was dead in the water but drifting. The anchor had not been deployed. A speedboat was tied off to the rear landing. The damaged helicopter on the top deck was skewed on the landing pad. One side of the single-bladed rotor hung limply like a broken limb. Don could make out a figure slumped in the pilot's seat.

The blast from the concussion grenade had blown out the windows and shredded the curtains of the upper-level room. Don spied movement, then flashes of gunfire.

The Falchion driver slowed the boat. The wind noise died down. "We should wait for backup," he said.

"Get us on that ship," Don replied. "Now."

The driver's lips pinched closed. He nodded grimly and pushed the throttles forward.

As they drew closer, Don and Michael scrambled to the bow of the craft, ready to board the yacht.

The gunfire on board had stopped. Except for the upper-level room, the yacht was dark. Harsh light from what looked like high-mounted spotlights spilled into the darkness.

"Emergency lights," Michael said. "I can see movement. Someone's still up there."

Don nodded, his body twitching with nervous energy. He unholstered his sidearm, then replaced it. He wanted both hands free to board the yacht.

Who is up there? he wondered. Skelly and his men? Rachel? Ian?

Every instinct in his body said that boarding that yacht was a terrible idea, but he was going to do it anyway. He'd started this whole chain of events, and he was going to see it through to the bitter end.

When the water-level landing of the *Centurion* came into view, Don felt a surge of hope. A man's body sprawled across the slatted wooden deck. His throat was cut, and thick, black blood congealed on the deck.

"Jesus," said the driver.

"No, that's Rachel," Don replied. "Put us alongside."

The driver expertly used speed and rudder to lay the hull of the power-boat next to the landing. Don and Michael boarded and drew their sidearms, making their way up the steps.

The first-level salon was dark and empty. Don made for the set of steps that would take them up to the lighted area. With Michael at his back, they mounted the stairs two at a time.

He sneaked a look, then dropped his head below the deck.

"Rachel," he shouted. "It's Don and Michael."

"Come up." Rachel's voice was cold and still.

Don climbed the steps, glass crunching under his boots. When he saw the scene, he holstered his weapon.

The harsh emergency lights created shadows everywhere. Every surface shone with shattered glass. Heavy pieces of furniture, the white leather scorched and burned in places, were tossed about like discarded children's toys. Despite the sea breeze coming through the blasted-out windows, the smell of jet fuel hung heavy in the air.

In the midst of the destruction, pinned in the floodlights, Manson Skelly knelt, his hands on his head, fingers laced together.

Next to him, glittering with glass dust, was a black Pelican case.

Don and Michael exchanged glances. Michael moved toward the case and opened it.

Rachel stood before Skelly, her weapon aimed at his head. She was bloody and wet, and her dark skin had an ashen undertone.

"Ian says I can't shoot this motherfucker," Rachel said. Don noted the tension in her grip, the gaze that never left Skelly's forehead.

Skelly swiveled his head, his dark eyes meeting Don's. "Don Riley," he said, "fancy meeting you here."

Then Skelly laughed, and Don felt the stress and the rage bubble up in his throat. He reached for his sidearm.

"You need him alive." The voice, a hoarse shout, belonged to Ian, who stepped in front of Skelly.

The look of the Chinese spy shocked Don back to reality. Ian was dressed in what looked like shredded rags, and he was barefoot. His body was covered in bleeding cuts, and someone had tied a bandage on his left bicep. Dried blood painted the skin under his nose and ran from one ear.

"Yeah, Donny-boy," Skelly added, "you need me alive."

"Give me one good reason," Don said.

Skelly lowered his hands. "I'll give you three." Ignoring Rachel's weapon, he swung his arm in a wide arc. "Somewhere out there in the world are three nuclear weapons with remote detonators."

When Skelly got to his feet, Don could see he was uninjured. In contrast to Ian and Rachel, his clothes were clean. Skelly adopted the tone of a sales pitch. He gave Don a greasy grin.

"You saw my demo, right? That 'underwater eruption'"—he mimed air quotes—"in the Philippine Sea? Can you imagine if one of these babies went off outside of London? Or Washington?" He touched his chin in mock concentration. "Or Moscow. That would be messy. Am I right?"

"We have the Moscow weapon," Don snapped.

Skelly's grin froze, but only for a second. He laughed. The sound, too long and too loud, sent a chill up Don's spine.

Don tried again. "You'll tell us where they are." He nodded at Rachel. "Or I'll let her shoot you."

Skelly's feral grin widened. "That's the beauty of this plan, Don. I don't know."

"He's using Mama to control them," Michael said.

* * *

Skelly felt another laugh escape. The way they were all looking at him. The way they all *feared* him. This was too easy.

"Bright boy," Skelly said to Michael. "It's all in Mama's hands. The location, the conditions, everything. Remember the SentiMonitor chips? Mama watches me like a hawk. If I flatline..." He snapped his fingers. "Boom, boom, out go the lights."

Another laugh...the looks on their faces really were priceless.

"Pretty cool, right?" Skelly continued. "There's one more feature—just for you, Don, because I know how you CIA assholes think. In case you're thinking about rendering me to some black site in east Bum-fuckistan, I need to check in with Mama every so often to reset the counter. Otherwise, you know..." He made an exploding motion with his fingers. "Ka-boom."

Don looked like he'd swallowed a fish hook, with the fish still attached. His face went purple, and his mouth worked like he was trying to say something and couldn't get the words out.

Then, Don Riley went still. His eyes hardened, and he looked at Skelly with a sudden intensity.

"I have a deal for you, Skelly," Don said.

Now we're talking, Skelly thought. He let out a theatrical sigh.

"It's about time, Riley. Where do we start the bidding?"

"Not that kind of deal." Don shook his head. "You give me the control codes to Mama, and I let you live."

I'm surrounded by pinheads, Skelly thought. That familiar itching sensation flashed across his skin. His breath caught in his throat, and when he spoke, his voice was clipped with anger. "You're kidding, right? Donny, I hold all the bones in this negotiation. You do what I say."

"Michael, pass me the controller for that weapon," Don said.

Don hefted the device in his hand. He activated the screen and turned it to face Skelly. "Unlock it."

Skelly's jaw tightened. "Why?"

Don laughed at him—actually laughed—as if he had not a care in the world. "Humor me, Skelly. I'm an interested buyer."

"Fine." Skelly swiped his finger across the DNA reader.

Don tapped on the screen, then showed it to Skelly. The counter was set to one minute.

Skelly frowned. "Don't fuck with that, Riley."

Don touched the device. The counter started.

"You have"—Don consulted the screen—"fifty-seven seconds to give me the access codes for Mama."

"You got the wrong idea, Riley. I don't scare."

Don pursed his lips as he watched four more seconds tick away. He seemed relaxed in a way Skelly had never seen him before.

"Do you know that this entire operation is off the books?" Don said. "Let me tell you how far off the reservation I am right now. I cut a deal with the Naval War College bomber, Skelly. When the President finds out, I'm going to jail."

Don's voice cracked. Skelly felt the others in the room start to back away. Don showed Skelly the counter.

"Thirty seconds." His skin had gone blotchy, and Skelly saw tears in his eyes. "Your call, Skelly."

This wasn't amusing anymore. This idiot was going to get them all killed. Skelly reached for the device, but Don snatched it away.

Skelly's mouth went dry, and he could hear his own breathing. "There's two more bombs out there—"

"What do I care?" Don interrupted in ranting tone. "We'll all be dead!"

Skelly's mind seized with red panic. There's no way, he thought. Riley would never—

Don's taunting voice cut through the static of Skelly's thoughts. "Fifteen seconds to live, Skelly. What's it gonna be?"

"How do I know I can trust you?" To his own ears, Skelly's shout registered an octave higher than normal.

"I'm a Boy Scout, remember?" Don's tone was quiet, final. "You can trust *me*."

Skelly opened his mouth, but nothing came out.

Don's face filled Skelly's vision. The move was strangely intimate, and not in a good way. Hot breath painted his cheek. Don's eyes were like ashes.

Skelly could not look away. *Christ, he's going to do it. We're all going to die. Right here, right now.*

"Say it," Don hissed, his gaze freezing Skelly to his core.

"I'll do it," Skelly whispered. He fell backward onto the deck. Glass scattered as he tried to scrabble away, but Don followed him.

"I'll do it," Skelly shouted. "Just turn it off."

* * *

Don touched the controller screen. The numbers stopped moving.

"Give me the access codes." He felt hollow, drained, as if he was operating outside his own body. His voice was flat, and his eyes never left Skelly's.

Skelly trembled, but he spoke a string of alphanumeric digits.

In the background, Don heard Michael on the phone. He felt Ian take the controller out of his hand, and he let go of the device.

"Dre says she's in," Michael reported. "Skelly is locked out. She's locating the other weapons now."

"Good," Don said, his response automatic.

Skelly got to his feet. Color had returned to his cheeks. He grinned weakly at Don. "Well, Boy Scout, I'll be going, then."

It might have been Skelly's tone of voice, or the condescending smile. It could have been the months of stress caused by this monster of a human being.

Or it might have been Don's own realization that he would have let the counter run to zero—even if it meant his death and the death of all those around him.

As long as Skelly was dead, it was worth it.

Don felt his brain slip into neutral. His vision went blood red. He heard someone shouting. Then he realized it was his own voice. He was shouting —screaming—at the top of his lungs, ranting like a madman.

There was something in his hand. A gun, *his* gun. Don felt the angles of the weapon cut into his flesh, felt every nub of the checkered grip against his palm. He opened his eyes and saw the muzzle was flush against Skelly's forehead.

He slipped his index finger forward.

This is for Abby. Don wasn't sure if he shouted the words or just thought them, but the words were there. They were real.

He closed his eyes and pulled the trigger.

But his trigger finger would not move. From far away, Don heard himself scream in frustration. Then in pain. His index finger was on fire.

"Don!"

He opened his eyes. Rachel had one hand on the barrel of his gun; the other was bending back his index finger.

He surrendered his weapon, staggering backward.

"Why?" he screamed at her.

Rachel had a cut on her cheek, and glass dust made her dark skin glitter. But her brown eyes were soft. "Because you're not him, Don. You're better than this."

Tears stung Don's eyes. He hissed back at her, "He killed Abby. He deserves it."

Rachel slipped her arm around his shoulders and guided him to a chair. "You gave him your word. This is not who you are, Don."

She looked past him to where Skelly was standing, pale and shaking. "All he's getting is a stay of execution. I promise you, for the rest of his short life, every single day he will look over his shoulder. Every time he closes his eyes, I will be there."

Skelly's gaze ricocheted around the room. He took a step backward, slipped on the broken glass, righted himself.

Rachel tightened her arm around him, and Don felt the rage pass through his body like a fever.

"Go," Don said. "Before I change my mind."

Skelly clattered down the steps. A few seconds later, Don heard an outboard motor start and drive away into the darkness.

Don's gaze fell to the controller sitting on the black case. The display read three seconds. He started to shake.

"What now, Don?" Michael asked.

Don nodded at the nuclear weapon. "Get that loaded on the boat." He looked around the shattered room. His nostrils filled with the stink of jet fuel.

"Then light this place on fire."

52

Don arrived at the Roosevelt Room with Dre, Michael, and Harrison Kohl. The White House staff had removed the large mahogany table from the room and arranged the chairs in two rows facing a podium. There was a bar at the back prepped for service, but no bartender yet.

Too bad, Don thought, *I could use a shot of something right now.*

The top secret classification of the ceremony meant the audience would be small. That was okay with Don. The people who meant the most to him were here. That was what mattered.

Six weeks had passed since that night in Phuket Bay. The official version of events, still classified at the highest levels, went something like this:

Don, working with a deep cover Mossad agent, tracked down one of the lost nukes on a yacht outside of Phuket, Thailand. The successful recovery of the weapon gave Don's team the necessary information to crack the encryption on the Sentinel AI system. The penetration of the Sentinel system allowed safe recovery of the remaining two nuclear weapons.

Unfortunately, Mossad agent Rachel Jaeger was killed in the assault on the yacht. During the fierce gun battle, a jet fuel leak on the yacht helicopter caught fire. The resulting blaze burned so fiercely that the Thai Navy was forced to tow the ship out of the bay and sink it to avoid an environmental disaster.

Rachel's body was not recovered.

Manson Skelly was still at large.

The thing about cover stories, Don mused, was that as long as the ending was what people wanted to hear, they tended to accept whatever details led up to the desired outcome.

A lost nuclear weapon had threatened a fragile balance of power between three global powers. The weapons had been recovered safely and with minimal public exposure.

Everyone was happy. Ask me no questions, I'll tell you no lies.

Don eyed the bar again. He could really use a drink.

Manson Skelly was a wanted man, but no one seemed to be pushing that right now. The hunt for the Naval War College bomber continued as well, but it too had lost some of the pre-inaugural intensity. The world was moving on, and that was fine with Don.

Liz Soroush entered the room. She'd chosen a navy blue sleeveless sheath dress for the occasion with a gold-threaded pashmina. She immediately came up to Don and kissed him on the cheek.

Her eyes shone with pride as she touched the lapel of his brand-new bespoke suit. "Look at you," she said. "You look amazing, Don."

He felt amazing. Don's go-to for suits had always been Men's Wearhouse, and he'd fully intended to buy a new suit for the ceremony.

Two weeks ago, when the news of Don's award was announced by the White House via secure email, the Director sent Don a note with a phone number.

My tailor is expecting your call today. It's on my tab.

Best,
   Sam Blank

. . .

To Don, the idea of a bespoke suit seemed extravagant, but he called anyway and made an appointment for a fitting. The charcoal gray suit with the faintest of crimson pinstripes that arrived by special delivery a week later was a thing of beauty.

When Don put the suit on, paired with the snow-white shirt and a blood-red tie that picked out the faint lines of color in the suit material, he felt like a different person, as if the clothing was a suit of armor.

Liz kissed him again, her jasmine perfume triggering a memory for Don. She'd worn that same scent the day of her husband's burial ceremony on the grounds of the United States Naval Academy.

"I'm so proud of you," she said, as if reading his mind. "I only wish Brendan were here."

Don clenched his eyes shut, then opened them again. "I still miss him, Liz."

Her hand made a minute adjustment to his pocket square. "So do I." Her voice softened. "Every day."

The Director entered and made straight for Don. He stopped a few paces away, surveying Don's sartorial splendor.

"The man is a genius," he said. "How does it feel, Don?"

"Amazing. I had no idea," Don replied. "But I can't accept this as a gift, sir. Let me pay you back."

The Director laughed and waved him away. "If I only give out custom suits to people who have saved the world from nuclear terrorism, I think I've set the bar pretty high." He paused, held out his hand. "Maybe I'll buy you another suit when you catch the Naval War College bomber."

"I'll do my best, sir." Don shook his hand. Part of him still wondered if his boss knew about what had really happened that night on the Phuket Bay—and how much he wanted to know.

An aide appeared in the open doorway. "The President is on his way," she announced.

Ricardo Serrano, the forty-eighth President of the United States, was at the zenith of his political power, and he looked it. He strode through the doorway, his face lit up with a beaming smile that encompassed everyone in the room. Even Don felt his lips curve in an empathetic response.

"Good evening, everyone," the President boomed. "So sorry to keep you waiting.'

Randall Tynan, the President's new Chief of Staff, stood quietly next to the closed door. He was half the age of Irving Wilkerson but carried a seriousness beyond his years. Tynan watched his boss with bright eyes.

A true believer, Don realized. Someone who would risk everything for his president. Serrano discarded Wilkerson and then immediately chose someone just like him as his replacement.

Rinse and repeat, the cycle of politics. The more time he spent on the front lines of national security, the more Don felt the fragility of his country's system of government. He cast his eyes around the room.

Serrano, Wilkerson, Liz, even Don himself, were just placeholders in a long line of Americans who tried—and sometimes failed—to keep their country on the right track.

And along the way, Don thought, we make compromises with ourselves. Or to ourselves—that happened as well.

The attendees migrated to their seats as Serrano stepped to the podium. He motioned for Don to join him at the front of the room.

The President cleared his throat. "I always feel a little guilty when I have a ceremony like this one. Today, Mr. Riley will receive the National Intelligence Cross, the highest award possible in the United States Intelligence Community. He's a national hero and should be recognized as such." He paused.

"Yet, because of the nature of the event, there will be no public citation. The people of this great country will never know how close we came to disaster.

"That fact is both the pity and the strength of our system of government. Very few people outside this room will know or even care about the amazing work done by Mr. Riley and his team. We allow the average citizen to live in ignorant peace. I would love nothing more than to publicize this man's heroism on the front page of every newspaper and website in the entire world, if only to let people know that nuclear catastrophe is not some fantasy. It is, and will continue to be, a real and present danger of our era.

"But that will not happen. Not today, not tomorrow. A great nation like ours is built on the bravery of individuals like Don Riley. It is my deepest regret that we need to hide from the world the details of that bravery."

The President's gaze settled on Noam Glantz. "It is fitting we have our allies in attendance today. Our nation is made greater because of the countries we can call 'friend,' and on whom we rely for so very much. I deeply regret the loss of one of Israel's most accomplished intelligence professionals during this operation. Our nation mourns her passing, and we recommit ourselves to our continued partnership, in the name of her sacrifice."

Noam, his face as impassive as always, nodded in acknowledgment of the President's words. For the briefest instant, his eyes connected with Don's, then cut away.

Don's mind drifted as the President continued. Everywhere he turned, he saw secrets. Noam's reaction to the mention of Rachel, the whole nature of the operation, even this award ceremony. Everything was hidden.

Don had his own secrets. Promises of silence made to people who had risked everything for him and his cause.

He would not break those promises, no matter the consequences to himself. Not today, not tomorrow, not ever.

The remainder of the ceremony passed in a blur. Director Blank assisted the President in fastening the medal around Don's neck. The award itself was a square, 24-karat gold cross. In the center of the medal, a gold star was inset atop a sub-rosa device to signify the secrecy of their profession.

Photos were taken. Handshakes between the President and Don, and with the Director, then the awards were taken away by the Director's aide.

After the ceremony, Don found himself at the bar next to Noam Glantz. Once they both had drinks in hand—Noam a white wine, Don a Jameson's in a crystal tumbler—the Mossad chief expertly navigated Don out of earshot of the rest of the group.

"I just happened to be in Washington," Noam said. "I'm honored to be here."

"Thank you for coming." Don hesitated. His tongue felt like sandpaper. The act of lying to this man seemed to suck all the moisture out of his mouth. Don took a sip, and the whiskey lit his throat on fire.

"I—I'm sorry about Rachel," Don said.

Noam held up his glass. "To absent friends," he said in his gravelly voice.

"Absent friends," Don agreed.

They touched glasses, and Noam drank, smacked his lips. He skewered Don with his sharp gaze. In that instant, Don knew he wasn't fooling anyone.

"She's in a better place," Noam said.

53

Beijing, People's Republic of China

As soon as he opened the door of their apartment, Gao could tell the cleaning woman had been there. The sharp smell of the ammonia solution she liked to use on the floors was only partially masked by her overuse of the lemon-scented furniture polish.

"I told that woman to use a different cleaning solution, and she keeps ignoring me," Gao growled. "This is the last time. I want you to get a new service."

"But I like her." Mei Lin let the door close behind her. She wrapped her arms around Gao's neck and kissed him. "She reminds me of my auntie."

He felt his resolve softening. Then a new idea entered his head. He slipped his hand down to caress her belly. "What I meant was that we should get a live-in maid and cook. You know, for the baby."

She melted into his body, and Gao felt himself responding to her. He slipped his hand lower. Somehow, the idea that his child was growing inside this beautiful woman made her even more desirable.

The doorbell rang, interrupting the romantic moment.

"You get that," Mei Lin whispered. "I'm going to change."

"Don't ever change," Gao quipped. "I love you just the way you are."

Mei Lin rolled her eyes, kissed him again, and disappeared into the bedroom.

Is this place big enough for a growing family? Gao wondered on his way to answer the door. With his new promotion, maybe they should move to a house in the Chaoyang Park neighborhood.

The doorman waited in the hall, his hand on a cart piled high with Gao's luggage. He bowed when the door to the apartment swung open.

"Congratulations on your promotion, General," the man said.

"Thank you, Mr. Lao," Gao replied, stepping aside to let him enter with the cart. It was the third time the man had offered his congratulations, and they'd only been home for fifteen minutes.

"Well deserved, sir. I am honored by your presence."

He unloaded their bags quickly. The last item on the cart was a bin. "Your mail, sir."

Gao indicated he should put the container on the dining room table. He extracted a handful of bills from his pocket, aware that he was over-tipping the man, but wanting him gone so he could get back to Mei Lin.

The doorman bowed again, his eyes on the money. Gao hustled him to the door and closed it before he received yet another congratulations. When he turned back, Mei Lin had emerged from the bedroom.

She wore a dark blue kimono with golden embroidery that she'd bought in the market in Sanya on the island of Hainan. The robe was far too short—it barely covered her bottom—and she had it only loosely knotted at her waist. She bit the end of her finger and eyed him through downcast lashes. She'd put her hair up, the way she knew he liked it, to show off the curve of her neck.

Although they'd spent their honeymoon at a beach resort, Mei Lin had been scrupulous about protecting her skin from the sun. She ran a finger along the lapel of her robe, dragging the edge of the dark material down the swell of her milk-white breast.

"General, I have urgent tasking for you," she breathed.

Gao stepped forward, swept her into his arms.

Mei Lin gasped.

"What?" Gao asked.

"It's here!" She broke from his embrace, racing to the mail bin on the table. She pulled a package from the top of the pile. She turned to her husband, eyes alight. "Our wedding pictures!" she squealed.

Gao slipped his hand under the short hem of her kimono. "Later," he said.

Mei Lin slapped his hand away, then tore into the packaging. "Now."

She pulled the lid off a heavy box embossed with the logo of the photography studio. Inside, wrapped in a velvet mantle, was a bound leather volume. Mei Lin removed it from the box and laid it on the table. She clasped her hands together.

"It's beautiful, Yichen."

It's expensive, Gao thought, and pointless. The pre-wedding photo shoot was an ordeal he'd rather forget. The daylong affair had involved costume changes, multiple venues, a small army of makeup artists and hair stylists, even wind machines. The cost, not including the expected gratuities, had come to over 100,000 yuan—and that fee hadn't even included the book that now rested on his dining room table.

"Look!' Mei Lin cooed, pointing at the two of them costumed in crimson traditional Chinese dress in a setting that was supposed to be the Forbidden City.

Somewhere in that leather-bound volume was a picture of Gao in dress uniform with his new rank of Major General and Mei Lin in a white wedding gown. As far as he was concerned, that was the only photo worth keeping, but he could tell from the look on his wife's face that they were keeping all of them.

He pulled out a chair and sat down, watching his wife dance about in her sexy kimono and clap her hands like a delighted child as she turned each page.

It had all been worth it, he told himself. He'd taken a risk and come out on top. Again. Now they would reap their just rewards.

He had Mei Lin to thank for that. Her discovery of the missing nuclear inventory had saved him from certain death at the hands of the Minister of State Security. But when Gao informed the General Secretary of the breach, he shifted the spotlight of blame to the Minister. After all, the man had years to uncover Minister Fei's treachery to the State. Had it not been for Senior Colonel Gao, the State never would have found out about the lost nuclear weapon.

He allowed a self-satisfied smile as Mei Lin let out another squeak of joy. To the victor go the spoils. He'd played the system and won. Again. Nothing could stop him now.

Seeing that Mei Lin was only a quarter of the way through the photo album, Gao realized his wife's attention was not going to include sex, at least not for a while. With a sigh, he pulled a stack of mail from the bin and began to sort through it.

There were a few bills, some fat envelopes addressed to the couple, probably wedding gifts, and junk mail. At the bottom of the pile, he found a colorful postcard.

PHUKET, THAILAND was emblazoned in bold letters. On the face of the postcard was a picture of a traditional Thai long-tail boat with a bright red sash tied to the jutting prow.

Odd, he thought. He hadn't received a postcard in years.

He flipped it over, and Gao felt the blood drain from his face.

The address was hand-lettered in English. The postmark indicated it had been mailed while he and Mei Lin were honeymooning in Sanya.

In the space reserved for a message, there was a single hand-drawn Chinese ideogram.

Huichen. Dust.

"Yichen!" Mei Lin's cry startled him. "Look!" She turned the book to face him.

Gao stood tall in his olive-green dress uniform, the oakleaf and single star of a *Shao jiang*, Major General, adorning his epaulets. Mei Lin, looking radiant in a flowing white wedding dress, clutched his arm. They both looked happy.

He stood behind his wife and wrapped her in his arms. Her body quivered with joy at the beautiful pictures of their beautiful life. He clenched his eyes shut.

There was no way that man could touch them. Not here in China. He would not dare.

Gao pressed his lips to the top of his wife's head and held her even tighter.

He would not dare.

54

Beau Vallon, Seychelles

As the orange sun slipped below the horizon, Rachel removed her sunglasses. She watched the fiery red of the western sky bruise into purple and indigo as the darkness collapsed around them.

"Beautiful," said Ian.

"Hmm." She found his hand in the gloom, laced her fingers into his.

They sat side by side, facing the water and the sunset, their backs to a wall that was painted a brilliant turquoise blue. In fact, bright color seemed to be the calling card of The Copper Pot Indian restaurant.

The business was an addition to the home of the owner, a man named Prakesh, who they'd come to know through the course of the afternoon.

A motor scooter pulled into the driveway, and a young woman claimed her takeout order. She spoke to Prakesh in Seychellois Creole, one of the three national languages of the tiny island nation, sprinkled with a smattering of English. She waved shyly to the couple as she left the establishment.

Prakesh didn't seem to mind that the two foreigners occupied a table in his restaurant for the entire afternoon and evening. His business, he explained, was almost entirely takeout since the pandemic, and he welcomed the company.

He even joined them for a cup of Masala chai in the late afternoon, during a break in the takeout trade. Prakesh liked to talk, and he regaled them with stories about life on the islands and his business.

Rachel pointed to a walled compound a hundred meters down the road. "We saw that place online, but it looks like it's rented already. Is it nice inside?"

"Englishman built it years ago." He waved a dismissive hand at the height of the walls. "He wanted his *privacy*. Big walls make bad neighbors. You don't want that place, lady."

"Is someone living there now?" Rachel asked.

"Five someones," Prakesh answered. "All men, big eaters. They order at least twice a week from me, but they refuse to come pick up. They pay me to walk down the street with their food, but they never let me inside. I have to wait in the street."

"Five men?" Rachel said. "What are they doing in there?"

"I don't know, but"—Prakesh lowered his voice to a conspiratorial whisper—"they have guns."

"Really?"

Prakesh nodded. "I saw them with my own eyes. The man at the gate had a pistol in a holster, and I saw another man with a machine gun on a strap around his neck."

"And you say there's five of them? They all have guns?"

"Well," Prakesh began, then paused. "Four of them do. The other man stays in the house all the time. I've only seen him in the window. Never outside."

"Very mysterious," Rachel said.

Another motor scooter arrived, and Prakesh excused himself.

Rachel leaned back against the wall. "It checks out. Four guards."

Ian nodded. "How's the weather report?"

Rachel consulted her phone. Evening rain showers, often short-lived but heavy, were a common event in the Seychelles. Tonight was no exception.

"Looks like two hours," she replied.

"Dinner?"

Rachel smiled. "Sure."

She watched Ian negotiate an order with Prakesh, explaining that they just wanted some light fare. The restaurateur brushed aside Ian's requests and instead filled the table with food.

As a finishing touch, he placed a silver candelabra in the sea of dishes and lit two candles. He kissed his fingers. "For the mood," he said with a wink.

They both ate sparingly, but they at least tasted every dish. Rachel watched Ian by the flickering glow of the candles.

This man made her happy. No, that wasn't quite true. He made her content. Somehow, he'd filled the hole in her heart that she had just assumed would be there forever. Rachel couldn't explain it—didn't want to know the answer. For now, it was enough.

They were two very broken people who had caused too much death for one lifetime. But they were broken together—and somehow that made all the difference.

Her mind drifted to Noam. She wondered if he knew the real story of what happened in Phuket. Noam deserved better, but he of all people would approve of her disappearance.

"A clean break," she could hear his voice in her head. "With plausible deniability."

She realized Ian was staring at her.

"What?" she said.

"Where to after this?" he said.

"Does it matter?" She almost added, *As long as I'm with you*, but stopped herself. No need to rush. They had all the time in the world.

Plonk! A single heavy raindrop rapped like a rimshot on the tin roof above them.

Ian looked up. "Right on schedule."

He got up and walked inside to pay Prakesh. She heard the two men discussing the bill, Ian insisting on a large tip. He declined the man's offer to box up the leftovers, telling him they were traveling light.

By the time Ian reappeared, the sound of the heavy rain drumming on the tin roof made conversation all but impossible.

Rachel unzipped her backpack and pulled out a formfitting black jacket. With dark pants, the jacket, and dark trainers, her slim figure all but disappeared into the shadows cast by the candlelight. She bound her hair into a ponytail and slung the backpack over her shoulder. The weapons inside made for a reassuring weight.

Prakesh appeared in the doorway. "It's pouring rain! You can't leave now."

Ian took Rachel's hand. "In this weather, we do some of our best work."

Together, they stepped into the night.

55

Beau Vallon, Seychelles

Working by the dim light of the single bulb above the bathroom mirror, Manson Skelly positioned himself so he could see the dirty bandage that ran down the edge of his right shoulder blade. Using tweezers to extend his reach, he slipped his left hand over his right shoulder, trying to reach the top edge of the bandage.

It took him two tries. Finally, he managed to work one of the corners of the medical tape free and got a decent purchase on the gauze. The bandage came off with a ripping sound. He felt the material separating from the scab that had formed over the wound on his back.

He untwisted his body and rested both hands on the edge of the sink. The bloody bandage lay in the basin, and even though the light was shit, he could see flecks of yellow pus mixed in with the scab.

The slight fever he'd felt for the last day, the warmth on his skin, and now this, all pointed to the same conclusion: the wound was infected.

He cursed to himself. If the wound was infected, there was no way any doctor in his right mind would perform plastic surgery on him. They'd give him a course of antibiotics and tell him to wait until the infection cleared up.

That meant more time. Time he didn't have.

Rain lashed the cracked bathroom window. Between the fever and the noise, he was having a hard time putting two thoughts together.

It was his own fault, really. After fleeing from the yacht in Phuket, his first order of business was to get the SentiMonitor chip removed from his back.

In those early hours after his escape, time was of the essence. Once Riley got full control of Mama, he'd have access to the SentiMonitor feeds, and by extension, Skelly's location. Skelly had wrapped his torso in aluminum foil as a first-order countermeasure, but he wasn't positive that would block the signal.

No, the only sure answer was to get that chip out of his body as fast as possible.

A hospital was out of the question, as was a licensed doctor, so Skelly found a veterinarian. At least the guy claimed he was a vet. After seeing his handiwork, Skelly wasn't so sure.

The guy had done the operation without anesthesia and at gunpoint. He'd worried the doctor might try to slit his throat, but the guy's hands shook so badly Skelly wondered if he'd cut off one of his own fingers before he finished the operation.

The SentiMonitor chip was a flat disk about the size of a fingernail on his pinky finger—and it was designed to stay in place. The flexible device was inserted rolled up, then unfolded once in place. He vaguely remembered the doctor who installed it telling Skelly that the chip was covered with a growth hormone that eventually made it fuse to the bone on the scapula.

In his career, Skelly had been shot twice and stabbed once. The pain caused by the removal of the chip without anesthesia was like all three of those traumatic events at the same time.

Normally, when operators left the company, the chips were not removed. Instead, they were deactivated by a palm-sized device that delivered a directed electromagnetic pulse to the SentiMonitor chip. The painless procedure took all of five minutes and didn't even require the patient to remove his shirt.

Unfortunately, Skelly did not possess one of the EMP devices. Even if he did, the only way to ensure the chip was dead was to verify it with Mama, and he couldn't do that either.

Skelly turned and twisted his body so he could see the wound again. The flesh was an angry red color, warm to the touch, and blood leaked down his back.

That fucker Don Riley tricked him. Skelly should have negotiated harder to keep his access to Mama. He should have rigged one of the other nukes to detonate. A real detonation this time, not an underwater explosion that allowed Serrano and the rest of those useless political pricks to explain away the event as a subsea volcanic eruption.

Even as he thought about it, he knew he'd made the best of a shit situation. How was he supposed to know that Riley would use the actual Naval War College bomber to lure Skelly into a trap? He still had no idea how that fucking Boy Scout managed to pull that one off.

His dim reflection in the mirror hardened. Still, he showed them. Riley might be a wily son of a bitch, but Skelly was smarter, had more resources, and he always came out on top. Always.

He bared his teeth at the haggard face in the mirror. Manson Skelly was a winner.

He turned to where he'd laid out the medical supplies on the closed lid of the toilet. In the yellowed lighting, with the sound of the rainstorm hammering the roof, Skelly took in the filthy cracked tile, the trickle of water that ran from the base of the toilet to the drain in the floor, and the smashed body of a too-slow cockroach. Then he grimly eyed the Glock 9mm next to the medical supplies.

This is what winning looks like, he thought.

Skelly seized the bottle of hydrogen peroxide and wrenched the cap off. With his back to the mirror, he poured half the bottle over his right shoulder. It felt like fire ants were eating the flesh down his back. He felt the cool liquid seep into the waistband of his shorts.

He clipped off a six-inch length of gauze with some dull scissors and fixed a piece of medical tape to one end. Angling his body so he could see what he was doing in the mirror, he tried to arrange the new bandage over the seeping wound.

After a full minute of wrestling with his reflection, he managed to drop the gauze onto the floor. He gripped the edge of the sink in frustration, cursing, feeling a flush of fever sweep across his bare chest.

Skelly hated to ask his bodyguards for help. It made him look weak. He sighed, deciding it was necessary.

Skelly opened the door of the bathroom, letting it bang against the wall.

"Rosco!" he yelled over the din of the thunderstorm. "C'mere."

No answer. Fresh rain slashed the bathroom window.

"Rosco!"

Skelly felt the hairs on the back of his neck come to attention. His four bodyguards had specific instructions. At all times, two were on duty outside and one inside. The inside guy was never out of earshot of Skelly. To stay alert, they rotated positions every two hours. There was only one bathroom in this shithole, and he was in it.

Skelly retrieved his weapon and snapped off the light. He allowed his eyes to adjust, listening. The thunderous rainstorm masked all sound in the house.

He moved through the door, weapon out, stepping fast, hugging the wall. God, he was burning up from the fever. A wave of chills swept over him, and he heard the pathetic rasping of his own panting breaths.

Pull yourself together, he ordered.

A clinking noise in the next room. Someone was in the kitchen. Skelly flattened against the wall, licked his lips. He would have liked to have a stack of men behind him, body armor, night vision goggles...but those days were gone.

He felt the seeping wound on his back stick to the wall. Barefoot, bare chested, wracked with fever, he could smell the desperation in his own sweat.

Skelly sensed more than saw the shadow detach from the wall. Lightning flashed. It was the woman from the yacht, the one who had stopped Riley from shooting him.

Time slowed to a crawl. Skelly felt his muscles tense, he tried to swing the muzzle of his weapon up, but it was stuck in place. His skin rippled with another wave of chills, and in his heightened state, Skelly felt the prickle of gooseflesh like insects on his skin.

Rachel, that was her name. When that woman stopped Riley from shooting him, she'd said something...what was it?

He watched, mesmerized as Rachel's weapon came to bear. Another white flash of lightning. Her face was a mask of rigid fury. Skelly saw the end of the muzzle explode with light, felt his own eyes react to the glare.

The first bullet entered his flesh on the left side of his chest, just below his collarbone. The second another centimeter below the first.

Skelly spun. He would have collapsed except for the wall. He felt the suppurating wound on his back tear open as he slid to the floor. His weapon might as well have been on Mars for all the good it did him. He could not lift his arm.

She appeared over him, kicked away his useless gun. Skelly's gaze fixed on the thin trace of smoke that wisped from the muzzle of her weapon.

Then Skelly remembered the words: *You're better than this, Don.* That's what she'd said to Riley.

Skelly offered up a broken smile. "Do it," he said.

The end of Rachel's weapon exploded in fire.

COVERT ACTION
Command and Control #5

Following their military defeat in the Battle of Taiwan, China opens a new front in the struggle for geopolitical supremacy.

As China's Belt and Road Initiative brings together the final pieces of a 1000-mile rail and road connection between China and Tehran, a series of terrorist attacks rock the fractious states of Central Asia. A declining Russia, an isolated India, and a rising Iran all have a stake in the region.

But who is behind the mysterious attacks?

President Serrano, in the midst of another election cycle, just wants the problem to disappear. He puts his trust in Don Riley, the newly appointed CIA Deputy Director of Operations, to deal with the situation.

Quietly.

As tensions escalate, Don leads a covert action to protect America's interests in the region and blunt the Chinese economic juggernaut. What he discovers threatens to drag the United States into another international conflict.

Get your copy today at
severnriverbooks.com/series/command-and-control

ABOUT THE AUTHORS

David Bruns

David Bruns earned a Bachelor of Science in Honors English from the United States Naval Academy. (That's not a typo. He's probably the only English major you'll ever meet who took multiple semesters of calculus, physics, chemistry, electrical engineering, naval architecture, and weapons systems just so he could read some Shakespeare. It was totally worth it.) Following six years as a US Navy submarine officer, David spent twenty years in the high-tech private sector. A graduate of the prestigious Clarion West Writers Workshop, he is the author of over twenty novels and dozens of short stories. Today, he co-writes contemporary national security thrillers with retired naval intelligence officer, J.R. Olson.

J.R. Olson

J.R. Olson graduated from Annapolis in May of 1990 with a BS in History. He served as a naval intelligence officer, retiring in March of 2011 at the rank of commander. His assignments during his 21-year career included duty aboard aircraft carriers and large deck amphibious ships, participation in numerous operations around the world, to include Iraq, Somalia, Bosnia, and Afghanistan, and service in the U.S. Navy in strategic-level Human Intelligence (HUMINT) collection operations as a CIA-trained case officer. J.R. earned an MA in National Security and Strategic Studies at the U.S. Naval War College in 2004, and in August of 2018 he completed a Master of Public Affairs degree at the Humphrey School at the University of Minnesota. Today, J.R. often serves as a visiting lecturer, teaching national security courses in Carleton College's Department of Political Science, and hosts his radio show, *National Security This Week*, on KYMN Radio in Northfield, Minnesota.

You can find David Bruns and J.R. Olson at
severnriverbooks.com/series/command-and-control

Printed in the United States
by Baker & Taylor Publisher Services